ALSO BY SHERWOOD SMITH:

CORONETS & STEEL
BLOOD SPIRITS

The History of Sartorias-deles
INDA
THE FOX
KING'S SHIELD
TREASON'S SHORE

BANNER OF THE DAMNED*

*Coming in Spring 2012 from DAW Books

SHERWOOD SMITH

Blood
SPIRITS

DAW BOOKS, INC.

DONALD A. WOLLHEIM, FOUNDER

375 Hudson Street, New York, NY 10014

ELIZABETH R. WOLLHEIM

SHEILA E. GILBERT

PUBLISHERS

http://www.dawbooks.com

DAW Books Collector's No. 1559.

DAW Books Inc. is distributed by Penguin Group (USA).

First Printing, September 2011
1   2   3   4   5   6   7   8   9

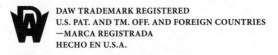

DAW TRADEMARK REGISTERED
U.S. PAT. AND TM. OFF. AND FOREIGN COUNTRIES
—MARCA REGISTRADA
HECHO EN U.S.A.

PRINTED IN THE U.S.A.

to Margot.

ACKNOWLEDGMENTS

My heartfelt thanks to Estara Swanberg for overseeing my German,
Pilgrimsoul for help in envisioning London,
Emily Feeley for reading the first few chapters,

And
Rachel Manija Brown, Beth Bernobich, Hallie O'Donovan and Kate Elliott
for trudging through raw draft.

ONE

I WAS SPEED-MARKING a stack of French grammar finals, trying not to think about Marius Alexander Ysvorod, Crown Prince of Dobrenica, when the office phone rang.

One phone was shared by four foreign language teachers, so it could have been for any one of us, but by the second ring I had a really bad feeling.

Okay, I have abilities some would call weird, but premonitions aren't among them. So what was this dread? The phone's ringing broke with the norm. In my three months of teaching in Oklahoma, students usually called with excuses before quizzes and tests, not after. And definitely not the Friday night after finals, when the entire college campus had gone home for the end-of-year holidays.

I stared at the phone as if it were going to bite me, then picked up the receiver.

"Yeah?" I grimaced, remembering slightly too late that I should have answered in a more professional way: *Fort Williams College, Foreign Language Department, Kim Murray speaking.*

All that zapped out of my head when a woman said, "This is College Hospital. Are you related to Ronald Huber?"

Ron was the other newbie, teaching French and Spanish, whereas I taught French and German. Since we both covered beginning French, we'd graded the exams together, earlier this evening. He'd finished, left, and should be home by now, taking over baby care while his wife worked the night shift. I'd learned all this not two hours ago when, after three months of mutual reticence, we finally broke the ice as we tiredly ground through test corrections together.

The hospital calling? This was not good. Why didn't they call his wife? But I was so worried that I didn't ask. "Yes," I said instead, "what is it?"

"There has been an accident," the woman said.

The rest of her words filtered through a shockwave, and I only comprehended a few: *intersection . . . emergency surgery.*

"I'll be right there." I grabbed my purse and ran, not even stopping to lock the office door.

The hospital was at the other end of campus. People surrounded me, talking in clipped voices. I tried to take it all in: *drunk driver, jaws of life, cell phone smashed, driver's license from a small town in Iowa, only legible thing a record book of grades with a phone number.* Our shared office number. *Are you his wife?*

"His wife's name is LaToya," I said, and on pure instinct added hastily, "I'm his sister."

Wife's number? Last name?

Did his wife use his last name? I'd only met her once, my first day, but that memory was a blur. As I'd been a blur to Ron: *What's your name? Cami? Kerry? Kim! Geez, I'm sorry, I'm crap with names. Great thing in a teacher, eh?*

I banished the memory of the gaunt, earnest, gentle fellow whose pen still sat on my desk, and gave them what little I'd gathered from Ron during our marathon session correcting finals. "She works for Child Protective Services. Duty therapist nights at Grace Morton Children's Home."

Last name? Phone? someone repeated insistently.

I grimaced. "Uh—uh—"

Someone else called out from further away: *I've got Grace Morton Home on speed dial. There can't be more than one LaToya on the night staff who's married to a Ronald Huber.*

I looked down at the bloody wreck of my office mate, whose blond hair and skinny form resembled mine just enough for the harassed staff to accept us as relatives. The instinct was to not leave him alone among these businesslike hospital people exchanging unintelligible exclamations in medicalese.

I spotted a loose hand dangling beyond a blanket and slid my fingers into Ron's. I felt a faint, convulsive grip, human to human. He clung, and I was glad to be clung to, as hospital people circled us, speaking in the tight, clipped voices of adrenaline-fueled competence.

One by one machines came to life, displays bouncing and bleeping. I could not bear to look down at Ron's mangled flesh, so I stared beyond him through an observation window, at a bad reproduction of a Cezanne bolted to the beige wall of the corridor. I tried not to breathe the amalgam of cleaning fluids, antiseptics, and the sticky-sweet smell of blood as some of the flow of words worked their way into my comprehension.

Then three things happened. The fingers in my hand loosened their grip, the air around me took on a bone-deep chill, and one of the machines shifted from *bleep-bleep, bleep-bleep* to *wheeeeeeeeee!*

And suddenly Ron stood next to me, looking around in a puzzled way, his glasses winking with reflection of the bright lights. *Kim, what's going on? Why are you crying?*

"Don't you see yourself?" I said.

A nurse cast a distracted glance my way, then muttered, "Sorry," as she shoved me aside. I had to step back, my grip on Ron's hand lost, as they closed around Ron in a huddle.

But the ghost didn't waver. *I have to go*, Ron said. He still had his nerdy shirt on, though I could see the bloody remains of it in the waste receptacle ten feet away.

"Where?" I whispered

"Now!" someone said—or something like it. There was a sickening thumping noise as Ron's body jolted.

The Ron next to me began to blur. *Cami, I think I need to . . .*

"Ronald Huber." I hissed the words voicelessly at that image suspended a yard away, through which I could see a technician bent over Ron's chest, and beyond him that machine going *wheeeeeee*. "Look at me! *Look at me!* No you don't. You can't leave LaToya. You can't leave that baby. Don't you *dare* go, or I'll kick your booty from here to Mars."

Ron looked at me—really looked—his watery blue eyes gazed into me, and through me, and then my tear-blurred eyes blinked, and I was glaring at the machine that had reverted to *bleep-bleep, bleep-bleep.*

"Got him!" A doctor shouted, and then began uttering a stream of incomprehensible orders as I stood there staring at the bleeping machine until someone elbowed me toward the door, saying, "Gabble-gabble, quack, quack." At least, that's what it sounded like through the rushing sound in my ears.

I zombie-walked into the hall, dropped onto a bench, and put my head between my knees.

The next thing I was aware of was a deep female voice. "His *sister?* But—"

"She's right over there."

I raised my head. There was LaToya, a large, curvy woman whose hair, eyes, and skin were the same dark hue. She stopped right in front of me, lowering her voice. "Aren't you the other French teacher? Katie? Cami?"

"Kim. French and German."

"Right." The word had a thousand invisible questions attached.

So I took a deep breath and started in. "A drunk broadsided him in the intersection outside of campus. All they could find was our office number. He told me you worked nights, and your families are out of state, like mine. So I thought he shouldn't be alone. . . ."

I remembered the ghost and shook my head, my words drying up.

A nurse appeared. "They're going to begin surgery."

LaToya spun around. "I want to see him."

"As soon as we're finished. Please sit down. There is a waiting room right past that door." The nurse nodded toward the other end of the hall, then vanished inside the emergency room.

LaToya's phone burred. She pulled it out. "He's in surgery. No. No. No. Yeah. Call you as soon as he's out. You tell everyone else, okay? No, Olivia's with the sitter. I don't want to talk until I know something." Her Chicago accent was strong. She and Ron were strangers to Oklahoma, as was I.

She clicked off the phone, dropped it into her bag, then leaned against the wall. Somewhere a clock ticked, and behind the nurse's station there was a continuous low murmur of voices. LaToya's breathing was tight with suppressed tears.

After a pause that stretched painfully, I said, "Want me to go? I'd be glad to stay, but not if you'd rather be left alone."

She wiped her eyes on her sleeve. "I can't figure out why you came in the first place."

The words were a cold shock, but her tone wasn't hostile. More . . . wary.

"I was afraid they wouldn't . . . that it might take a while, and I didn't . . . want him to be alone. There should be a familiar face. Even if it was only mine." I was babbling, and shut up without saying what I was really thinking: *I didn't want him to die alone.*

She said abruptly, "I cussed him out for leaving a peanut butter knife in the sink." She wiped her eyes again. "Dammit! I don't want to remember that as the last thing he heard from me."

"Actually, as it happens, he mentioned that," I said. "While we were correcting finals. He wasn't mad. He was laughing about it. I hope that helps. I mean, that he wasn't mad."

She slewed around. "What did he say?"

"We were trading jokes the way you do when work is really tedious. He asked if I lived with someone. I said no, and he said, 'Then you don't make anyone mad when you forget to wash off your peanut butter knife.' And I told him . . ." I stopped.

"Go on," LaToya said as she stared at me. "You told him what?"

That I hate living alone. That the guy I love is married to a second cousin who looks just like me, half the world away. "How much I hate coming home to my own messes."

She was still regarding me with that unreadable look. She switched her gaze to the observation window, beyond which there was nothing to be seen, then back to me. "Cami," she said. "He thought all this time your name's Cami. You didn't give us ten words at the faculty meet-and-greet in September. He said you come and go. Don't talk to anyone." She said all this with a puzzled frown while she stared at me at an odd angle, as if trying to bring me into focus.

"I got into town that very same day," I explained. *After running away from California.* "After a seven-hundred-mile drive, with four hundred the day before. I was a last-second hire to replace someone who got a last-minute, tenure track gig at a big university."

"Yeah, I remember that."

"And I'm not good at parties." *I'm not good at dealing with the fact that you can't run away, that the memories come right with you.*

"You read," she said slowly.

"Read?" I repeated.

Her tone was odd, someone still trying to figure out a puzzle. "Ron says, you're always reading during office hours. Like you don't want him talkin'."

"No, that's not it at all," I said, though it was kind of true. But I didn't want to explain how painful I found the normal chatter around the office: *Are you dating? Where are you from?* And the worst one of all: *What did you do over the summer?*

"So what *is* it?" she asked.

There we were, two total strangers, both far away from home, sitting in a hospital corridor in the middle of the night. Somehow it seemed natural, even right, to cut past the protective layer of meaningless small talk into intimacy.

But what could I say? *Last summer I went searching for my grandmother's family, and ended up masquerading as Ruli, a doppelganger cousin who I hadn't known existed, and falling in love with Alec, the guy she was supposed to marry. Oh yeah, and Alec's father was supposed to be crowned king on Alec and Ruli's wedding day.*

And, by the way, I see ghosts.

I was unaware that the natural pause of question and answer had stretched into an extended silence until she said, "Looks to me like you've got some issues."

Issues! "Yeah. You got that right—"

The door opened and a doctor appeared. "He's stabilized, but in critical condition. We've repaired . . ."

LaToya cut into the flow of medical jargon. "I want to see him."

"For a minute."

She got to her feet. I was not going to follow unless asked. She walked swiftly to the door, then skewered me with a look. "Go fix it," she said.

"Fix it?"

"I've been listening to people for ten years." LaToya flashed five fingers twice. "You helped me out, so I'm helping you out. I'm getting the sense that you left a peanut butter knife lying around somewhere. Go clean it up."

"It's too late for that," I said.

"Then you deal." She tipped her head toward Ron and shut the door.

How do you deal with the fact that you've fallen in love with the right person at the wrong time, in the wrong place? No, Dobrenica was the right place, it just wasn't *my* place. But I wanted it to be my place. . . .

The familiar round of questions I couldn't answer closed in. I'd been trying to ignore them for three months without success. So how *do* you deal?

Start by going home.

By the time I got back to the office, it was a quarter to three in the morning. By the time the sun came up I'd finished the tests, and logged the grades.

By seven I had my stuff thrown into the back of my car and locked up my crummy studio apartment.

I stashed two thermoses of super-strong tea in the cup holders, jammed in the Beatles' *Revolver* CD to blast at top volume, and hit the road.

When my overheated, bug-splattered car rolled up my parents' quiet Santa Monica street, it was one a.m. Sunday morning.

I pulled into the driveway, killed the engine and sat back, flexing and wringing my hands. During the 1100-mile, five-state drive, I'd been battered by snow through the Rio Grande National Forest, then rain as I flashed past the spectacular geography of the Colorado River country, and finally hot desert wind, and here I was at last. The house was dark, the December air dry, and with nightfall, the fitful, hot gusts had died down.

Everything looked exactly the same, as if nothing had happened, as eerie a feeling as the preternaturally clear air of Southern California in December.

The front door was not locked. I saw a light in the kitchen at the same moment I smelled fresh coffee.

I leaned against the kitchen door. My head felt detached from my body, like a balloon on a string. Dad sat at the table with the innards of one of his clocks scattered before him, and tools neatly lined up. The coffee pot rested on an old clock manual, steam drifting upward in misty tendrils. Around the pot, half a dozen mugs clustered like chicks to a hen. The rhythmic lyricism of Irish folk music played softly on the radio.

My father's fingers shifted in patient, minute movements as he tweaked the tiny gears. The yellow light overhead made a nimbus of his long, untamed, gray-frosted hair, and his chest-length, straggly beard. He made a last adjustment, then lifted his head and smiled. "Rapunzel," he said, as though I'd only been gone a few hours instead of three and a half months.

I was too tired for surprise. "Any of those cups clean?" My voice sounded dry and strange—as if it came from somebody else's throat. My gaze went to the small dish of M&Ms next to the coffee pot, and absently I started picking out the blue ones, though I was too tired for the burst of chocolate to do much for me.

"All of 'em, as it happens. I wash 'em in a bunch after I've used 'em up, then I start over again. How was the drive?"

I dropped into my old chair and poured coffee, since I was too tired to make tea. Elbow placement required some attention, for the table was covered with delicate clock innards. But at last I was looking at Dad from a comfortable angle.

I thought about the close calls, the traffic snarls, and the spectacular Southwest scenery, all stitched together by the black and yellow ribbon of the road. "Okay." My throat hurt. I swallowed. "How's Gran? Mom already crashed?"

Dad squinted down into the clock, pausing as he made another tiny adjustment. "Your grandmother is fine. Asleep, of course. As for your mother . . . answering this question would entail broaching the forbidden *It*."

It covered everything that had happened to me last summer.

On my arrival home from Europe, I'd told them the whole story, but a couple of days later, when reality hit me along with the blazing heat of a Southern California September, I'd asked my parents not to talk about *It* anymore because it hurt too much.

But I couldn't forbid my grandmother, who was the reason I'd gone in the first place. She'd been in a deep depression that had gradually slipped her into a coma by the time I left for Europe. It was hearing me speak Dobreni on my return that brought her out of it. When she began asking entirely natural questions about the changes in her homeland, the memories hurt so much that I accepted the first job that would get me away from having to provide answers . . . and you see how well that worked.

I stiffened my spine and thought of LaToya's sad eyes and determined face as she stood outside the room containing the mangled body of her husband. "I'm here to deal with *It*," I said to Dad.

"Good. In October Milo invited your grandmother and your mother to visit him. Gran wasn't up to traveling yet, but your mother went. She's been there ever since."

"Mom's in *Dobrenica*? With Gran's *ex*?" I was so not ready for that.

"London." Dad wiggled his brows.

"London, as in England?" I repeated, as though there were fifty Londons. Maybe there are. "I thought Milo was crowned King of Dobrenica back in September. Finally. After seventy years. I saw him in Dobrenica the day before I left."

"Apparently some old duke who was about to leave England for Dobrenica had a stroke instead. Milo returned to England, and something or other has kept him there ever since."

"Something or other? An earthquake? A revolution? Redecorating the palace with bees?"

Dad grinned at the Napoleon reference, then shot his forefinger at me, Mick Jagger style. "Dobreni politics. You know how much interest your mother has in politics."

"That would be zip."

"But apparently she's been a big help in other ways. Still able to deal with more *It?*" Dad asked, and on my nod continued. "Your grand-mother decided a couple of weeks ago that she's through with physical therapy, and she's going to join them for the holidays."

"Wait. Wait. Gran is not going back to Dobrenica, she's going to see Milo in London?"

"Yep."

"The guy she dumped seventy years ago."

"The very same. I offered to go along as wingman, since your Gran's never been on a plane."

Obviously a whole lot had changed while I'd been grinding my way through interminable days teaching elementary French and German, and wasting night and day thinking (or dreaming) about how I didn't want to think (or dream) about Alec, nor the Wicked Count Tony (well, not *really* wicked, was he?) nor the castles and mountains of Dobrenica.

"I'm on a plane to Heathrow tomorrow. Which is why I'm up till all hours." He gestured at the clock. "I want to have this finished before I go."

"This isn't a sale clock?" I asked.

"For Milo," Dad said. "Christmas gift from the family."

Silence built, broken by the low mutter on the radio, and the tinkle of a tiny clockmaker's hammer on the worn sixties' Formica.

Dad poked a ruler through his beard to scratch his chin, then said, "Alec won't be in London. He's too busy in Dobrenica."

Pop! went the balloon of exhaustion that had made my head feel like it was floating. Now it felt like a bowling ball on my shoulders.

Dad looked up, scraggly brows climbing toward his wild hair. "Was it the holiday that brought you back?"

I sipped coffee, trying to find words. Then I started talking. "There was a call on the language department phone, and when I picked up, it was the hospital. . . ."

Dad listened as he delicately wielded one tool then reached for another.

When I ran out of words, a gust of hot wind rustled the tree outside our big kitchen window, and the chair beneath my dad creaked. He said, "It's the first time you ever heard a ghost talk, right?"

I closed my eyes. "He was not a ghost," I whispered. "I don't know what he was but . . . ghosts are dead. His heart had stopped, but . . ."

"I believe that is the definition of dead." Dad wiggled his eyebrows. "Let me rephrase: Is it the first time someone has talked to you . . . without their body?"

"Yes." I dropped my hands flat to the table. "Dad, there were two things I thought about on the long drive back. One, what happened with Ron scared me bad. I didn't want it to be true, because I don't want the responsibility of thinking that maybe I talked someone out of dying. But I believe that I did. That is so *very* scary. What if next time I screw it up, and someone . . ." I shook my head, and discovered I was actually shivering, in spite of the warm air.

Dad took my hands in his. "Second thing?"

"I kept thinking about how I grew up with pretty much just us."

"Are you saying your childhood was unhappy?"

"No! I had a great childhood. You *know* that. But . . . maybe what seemed perfectly normal to me, really wasn't?"

Dad laughed as he let my hands go and picked up his tool again. "What's normal?"

I shook my head. "I mean, I never thought about how Lisa Castillo's house was always noisy with people. Her siblings, her cousins. The neighbors. But Lisa never came over here. I never realized that until the drive home."

Dad said, "She came over once or twice around the time you two started kindergarten. But there was a time . . ."

"Go on." Tired as I was, somehow I needed this conversation. Maybe the exhaustion made it easier to deal.

"You probably don't remember. Your grandmother made the two of you lunch, and Lisa said, the way little kids do, *Why does your grandma talk funny?* She wasn't being mean, and she probably meant the accent, but your Gran took it hard. So after that, she stayed in the back room when Lisa came over, and I think your little friend found it strange that you and she were always left alone, so she stopped coming. You didn't seem to mind. When you wanted to play with other kids, you went up the street to the Castillos'. The rest of the time, you had your books and your ballet as well as us. And you seemed happy with your grandmother's company when your mom and I were on the road."

"But it really was just Gran and me when you guys traveled for work. Gran didn't have any acquaintances, much less friends. Did she ever try?" I slurped more coffee and grimaced at the taste.

"Well, we know now that her accent was Dobreni, but it sounded German to California ears. And you have to remember, after the war, Germans were not exactly popular. Your Gran stuck hard to the French myth, probably in self-defense, but she really hated lying as much as she hated having to speak English."

"So she closed herself up," I said, following his train of thought, "with her piano, and books, and us. Okay, so let's leave aside the question of what's normal. LaToya told me to clean up the peanut butter knife, and I swear her words cut worse than . . . worse than memory." I finished on a sigh. "Dad, why does love hurt so much? It hurts every time I think about Alec or Dobrenica."

He placed a tiny screwdriver on the table, then scratched his chin through his beard again. "Rapunzel, think how hard it is going to be for your grandmother to face Milo again, the guy she dumped. And she hasn't your strength."

I looked up. "So you agree with LaToya. I need to deal. I guess I don't know where to begin."

"You can start by going with us to London. The invitation included you as well, you know. Milo liked you when you two met, last summer."

"Is Gran strong enough for a flight to England?"

"The physical therapist said yes. The doc said it was her decision. She is determined to go. Feels it's her duty. If you could handle going with us, I think it'd be a good deed," he went on. "You wouldn't have to stay long, if your job doesn't leave you much free time."

I grabbed at my one last hope. "They'll never have tickets this close to the holidays—"

For answer he reached under a welter of papers, pulled out three airline packets, and dropped them in my lap. "I don't know if this will actually work, but I tried to time it so we'd see the lunar eclipse from the plane. Wouldn't that be cool?"

I paid no attention to eclipses, lunar or otherwise. "Dad, you told me you don't see ghosts or have any arcane powers."

He grinned and rubbed my shoulder. "No. I hoped you'd show up. Go get some sleep. I'll unpack your car."

TWO

D AD'S GREAT PLAN for some family astronomy fun was a total
failure, since most of Europe was being hammered by massive
snowstorms, as were parts of the East Coast. For us, that meant short
flights and long delays in airports that all blended together into a nightmare of loudspeakers, plastic chairs in horrible colors, and the endless
rumble of rolling suitcases as people streamed back and forth.

Gran sat between us, quiet and focused on *Lettres de Madame de
Sévigné.* Her way of dealing with stress was reading. I tried—I had Dad's
copy of the latest Robert Harris novel about Cicero, which he'd loved—
but I couldn't concentrate on the pages. Not Harris's fault. I still wasn't
caught up on my sleep, and I was horribly distracted.

It was right around midnight New York time when I got so restless
that I left my stuff with Gran and Dad and prowled around, looking
for . . . I still don't know what, because I don't get premonitions. All I can
tell you is what happened.

I was walking past one of the shops and caught my reflection in the
glass. I turned to check myself out—you know how you do—except my
butt-length mane wasn't in its looped chignon on my head; it was short,
trailing untidily on my shoulders in total bed head. My long-sleeved T-
shirt and jeans had turned into a fashionable shirt and slacks that had to
be straight from Paris.

My gaze shifted to my eyes. No. Those were not my eyes, though
they were the same brown, they were—

"Ruli?"

The last time I'd seen Ruli, she'd driven me to the first town past the border of Dobrenica, after I talked her into going through with her marriage to Alec.

"Help me." I heard her voice inside my head. She said it in French, and then again in English. "*Help me.*"

"Help you? How? What—"

"Ma'am, are you okay?"

I looked up, right into the face of a security guard. She gave me that wary look people get when they might be facing a crazy person. I sneaked a peek back at the window. There I was. No, it was still Ruli.

I glanced back at the security guard, who frowned at the window and then at me. She didn't see what I did.

One quick glance. Now I could see us both, but Ruli was a double image, growing more faint by the second, until she was a blur.

"Ma'am?" The voice was more insistent.

"I'm all right." I smiled, doing my best to project normalcy. "Jet lag."

Other bored, tired passengers eyed us from their uncomfortable seats. The security guard asked me a couple of questions, my answers were sane and boring (we've been up for hours, waiting for the flight to London, see that old lady over there? That's my grandmother) and she let me go.

My heart was still beating hard when we boarded our flight a short time later. I didn't tell Dad or Gran what I'd seen, because I still wasn't sure what to think.

Real or not real? I thought in frustration, as the plane bumped down the runway. Though the security guard and the gawkers hadn't seen anything, Ruli's appearance felt way too real, the way that Ron Huber had been real. But Ruli's appearance had also been different than Ron's—he'd vanished in a blink, like most of the apparitions I'd seen.

So why did Ruli fade slowly? Either this was some kind of weird form of communication, or something drastic was going on . . . maybe in her dreams. So was Ruli really talking to me? Ron had definitely been talking to me.

I'd only met Ruli twice: once when I rescued her from her family's castle and again on my last day in Dobrenica. She had rich friends, a high ranking family, and she was married to Alec. Given all that, it made no sense for her to be calling to *me,* especially in that ghostly form. But nothing about apparitions made sense.

Thinking such things at thirty thousand feet made me kind of squirmy. But we landed at Heathrow in perfect safety. It was a relief to find Mom waiting at Heathrow, looking bulky and unfamiliar in cold weather gear. She hugged us each, then said, "Milo is feeling funky. The cold. He asked me to apologize for not being on hand to greet you."

Gran murmured something polite and proper, but in French. When she didn't even attempt English, she was upset, though you would not have known it to look at her. Her tension was another reason I kept Ruli's apparition to myself. At first I'd thought it was due to her flying for the first time, but if anything, landing made her more so.

Yeah. Because she was about to see Milo again; that is, Marius Alexander Ysvorod senior, whom she was supposed to marry back in 1939. Instead, she ran away from Dobrenica with Ruli's and my grandfather, Count Armandros von Mecklundburg, when she was sixteen and Milo was around twenty.

This would be their first meeting since the eve of World War II.

Dad took Gran's arm and walked ahead. Mom gave me a humorous roll of the eyes and whispered, "Milo was bummed about how it'd look not to meet her, but I told him she'd hate a public reunion."

"Bet he'd hate that, too," I muttered back.

"Big time." Mom grinned.

When we got through customs and made our way outside, there was Emilio, the dapper, gray-bearded little man who had been Milo's aide-de-camp for many decades. And Alec's for nearly two.

Beaming with hearty good will, he bowed to Gran and welcomed her in Dobreni. "So good to see you again, Mam'zelle," he said to me. "How was your trip?"

I mumbled something and then stepped back as Mom introduced my father. Emilio gazed up into my father's face. No two men could have been more dissimilar than the short, trim Dobreni and my rangy, rumpled father with his wild Rasputin look.

"Whoa," Dad said with his usual cheer. "Winter is *cold*. Nobody ever told me that cold is cold."

Emilio chuckled. "Is this your first visit outside of California, Mr. Murray?"

"Call me George. 'Mr. Murray' makes me think I've been busted, or worse, I'm back in a suit and tie. Yes, I did see snow once, when I was a kid, but. . . . Here, let me help forklift the kafuffle," Dad said, pointing to the bags.

Dad made easy weather chat as the porter got tipped, and the suitcases, along with the box containing the clock, got shifted to the trunk of a beautifully maintained Bentley Mulsanne.

Dad and I were glad to get into the warm car. Although we'd separately made sure that Gran had several choices of outer garments, the weather had been hot when we left, and I'd overlooked the possibility that I might need anything beyond my denim jacket (which had been fine, so far, in Oklahoma). Dad had relied solely on his ancient fringed suede, which had lasted for four decades thus far because in Southern California, you wear a coat maybe three times a year.

Conversation during the drive was a three-cornered question and answer session on what plays were running in London. Dad cheerfully outlined his plan to see everything he could, Mom told us what she'd seen and done, and Emilio made recommendations. I sat next to Gran, equally quiet as I fought against the vertigo induced by traffic on the wrong side of the road.

Finally I shut my eyes. I had to get a grip. When I next saw Milo, I knew it would be his son I'd be thinking about.

I gave Alec up for the sake of the Blessing, and there is no Blessing.

Supposedly, there was this magic protection, the Blessing, that happened around Dobrenica's borders if the five ruling families met in peace on September 2nd for a marriage between two of their members. The little country would be shifted outside of our time-space continuum into something called *Nasdrafus*, which I didn't understand well enough to try translating. ("Fairyland" isn't quite right.) Anyway, peace was a political necessity in a country still recovering from the old Soviet hold, and as for magic—or *Vrajhus*, as they called it—well, all I can say is, once you've seen Dobrenica, you could totally believe it exists.

But I guess it doesn't exist, after all. September 2nd had come and gone, Alec and Ruli had married, and Dobrenica was still here. If they hadn't married—if there had been some last-second reprieve—then surely, *surely*, Alec would have shown up on my doorstep on September 3rd.

But no call, no letter. No visions. Nothing.

"Here we are," Mom said.

We'd already reached Hampstead. When I looked up, the headlights glowed on two rows of snow-dusted trees as we drove down a long driveway.

The house was a Georgian three-story, mostly hidden by trees. The Bentley drove directly into a spacious garage that had probably once been a carriage house. It was only slightly warmer than being outside.

Emilio sent our bags off with a couple of servants and escorted us to a parlor where tea awaited, steam rising invitingly from the spout of the silver teapot. Havilland cups and saucers sat on a silver tray that looked like it had been etched around the time that Paul Revere was learning his trade on my side of the Atlantic.

My recent life having been measured out in daily doses of Styrofoam-encased teabag caffeine reluctantly sloshed out in the faculty nook, I appreciated the marriage of culture with art. Mom set about providing tea and coffee as if she'd been handling this kind of porcelain all her life, instead of our old stoneware at home.

Gran accepted a cup of tea, her back straight, her shoulders tense. She had dressed formally for the plane, in her customary widow's black, her long silver hair pulled up into its bun. Her pulse beat softly, visibly, in her neck as she held her cup and saucer.

A pair of double doors opened. In came a thin elderly gentleman in an expensive suit, leaning on a gold-topped cane. Marius Alexander Ysvorod's face was craggy and lined. If gravitas had not been supplied by his DNA, it had become so habitual that Lord Chesterfield might have used him as an example of it in those letters to his son.

Gran set aside the tea things.

Dad, Mom, and I stood up politely, but we could have been yodeling and swinging from the chandeliers for all the notice the not-yet-crowned King Marius took of us.

"Lily," he said softly, advancing on Gran, who stood up.

Gran and I (and Ruli) shared the same first name—Aurelia—which none of us actually used. Gran's nickname had been Lily. Her twin sister Elisabeth, Ruli's grandmother, had been known as Rose.

Milo stretched out both hands.

Gran laid her trembling fingers in his, and as he bent down to kiss them, she clasped his hands and offered her cheek. He acknowledged it with a peck then said, "Welcome. How was the journey?"

"Please sit, Milo," said she. Her English was heavily accented.

Only then did he take his place in an armchair, and that was the mode for the entire dinner: old-fashioned manners ruled them both. Each move, almost each word, had been inculcated by careful tutors and governesses almost a century ago, in lessons meant to get one through any eventuality in a civilized manner. They spoke in carefully enunciated English, a language not native to either of them. It, like this house, was neutral territory.

But they couldn't quite hide the effect of seeing one another after seventy years, a major war and several minor ones, relocations, births, and deaths. She had dumped him in front of the entire kingdom to run off with Armandros (who later returned and married Rose), leaving Milo duty-bound to take up Lily's rejected crown as the Germans rolled over the border.

The conversation was correct, and killingly boring, though Dad did his best to lighten things up by introducing easy subjects: the clock he'd made for Milo, the history of timekeeping, cultural views of time. Literature. Dad, who is a Roman History buff, ranged back and forth from Vergil to Voltaire, writers chosen to include my grandmother, though she scarcely spoke. Mom threw in a comment here and there, though she'd never been much of a reader. She's more into movies, opera, and folk tunes. She prefers image to text.

For me, the occasion exuded a false neutrality because from the moment I walked in, it was inescapable that Alec had been there. He had breathed this air, he had walked upon the polished hardwood floor where I now stepped. *He's married to Ruli.*

As I sat in a cabriole-legged Chippendale chair on which he might have rested, the present unraveled around me, blending with the evidence of his past. There was the Edwardian era portrait of a dark-haired woman with Slavic features; in it, the painter had reproduced, with inexorable detail, the Ysvorod diamond necklace that Alec had put around my neck the night of the masquerade ball. Opposite her hung a painting of a young woman in Regency era lace, ringlets, and puffed sleeves, who bore a strong resemblance to the Swedish princess, Sophia Vasa, whose genes were visible in several of us.

Superficially, everything was pleasant, and the *Linguine aux asperges et saumon fumé* delicious, making me wonder if my mom had a hand in menu planning, or even supervising. But it was a relief when we rose at last, and Emilio said that coffee would be served in the parlor.

As we followed Milo through a comfortable sitting room with great leather-backed chairs and floor to ceiling bookcases, my mother whispered into my ear, "We've got to get them to mellow out. I've never seen him that stiff, even at the duke's funeral."

She stopped talking when Gran touched her arm, murmuring in French, "I think I had better lie down. Will you make my excuses?"

"Of course, *Maman.* I'll show you your room."

Mom walked away with Gran as the rest of us moved to a pale green salon with high ceilings, pastoral cornices, and Queen Anne furnishings. Emilio began serving out coffee and tea. I offered to carry around the cups and saucers, finishing as Mom returned.

Dad and Milo were talking about London plays. Under cover of that, while she fiddled with cream and sugar, Mom muttered, "All she'll say is that she's tired, but I think she's bummed."

"I think it took major guts to come here and face the guy she dumped," I muttered back.

"It took major guts for him to face her," Mom's smile turned wry, "being the dumpee."

There was a pause in the chat as Dad and Milo sipped coffee, so Mom said to Milo, "My mother asked me to beg your pardon. Jet lag. She'll be fine after a night's sleep."

Polite chatter resumed, but the atmosphere was easier. Weird, when you consider that Gran hadn't said much. The conversation had switched to different versions of *Hamlet* (original versus movies) when the phone began to ring somewhere beyond the tall doors carved in a sylvan scene.

I said I don't get premonitions, and I still believe that's true, but one does sense patterns, even in a new situation. The back of my neck tightened as the housekeeper came to the door. She whispered to Milo. We all heard the word "Statthalter," that being Alec's official title.

At that very moment, someone rapped the knocker at the front door. Only three times, but loud enough for the sound to carry all the way down the hall to us. The housekeeper went to answer it as Emilio helped Milo out of his chair. Milo excused himself with his customary grave courtesy and left through another door.

The tea wasn't doing me any good. I tried to calculate how many hours I'd been awake and gave up when I realized I was too tired to figure in the time zone jumps. If we were expected to stay awake and be polite, I needed to splash cold water on my face.

So I got up and headed for the bathroom right across the hall. I almost ran into the housekeeper. She had someone right on her heels. A tall someone, with long, curly blond hair.

"Uh," I said intelligently.

The tall man drawled, "Cousin Kim." And laughed at the expression on my face.

It was Ruli's brother, Tony.

THREE

THE LAST TIME I'D SEEN Lord Karl-Anton von Mecklundburg, a.k.a. the Possibly-Wicked Count, he had put himself under the gun of a pack of real villains, in order to get me out of his castle alive. That was definitely not wicked. These villains, by the way, were his one-time allies and operated under the dubious leadership of a total obnox who called himself Captain Reithermann.

The time before that, Tony tried to abduct me from the middle of a masquerade ball. That qualifies as just over the edge into wicked territory, though I had to admit it had been swashbuckling in a typically brazen way. The time before that, however, he'd tried to sweep me off, with a characteristic combination of charm and *force majeure*, to his ancient castle on the Devil's Mountain. That one definitely landed in the wicked category—though I'd escaped by diving off a bridge.

Oh yeah. And at the masquerade, he'd kissed me.

I was still debating the wickedness quotient of *that*.

He looked the same only taller, somehow, his black eyes tilted like a Byzantine icon, his long, curly blond hair wilder than I'd remembered. He was dressed much the same: an exquisitely made white shirt over old jeans, single-seamed riding boots, and—worn carelessly open over all—a handsome long black duster.

The crooked grin he gave me I'd seen in countless dreams. "Which is it, love, a tip or a kiss?"

"What?" I said, rattled.

"Which one will get me in the door? Or is this a delicate hint that old Milo's got the wind up and barred me at last."

"Oh!" I realized I was blocking his way to the parlor. As I stepped back, the housekeeper excused herself with a word and walked on down the hall. Tony and I were alone outside the parlor, but with my parents sitting side by side in view, watching.

Tony bent to kiss me.

I turned my cheek so his lips pressed beside my ear, cold and warm at the same moment. His coat smelled of wood smoke, wool, and leather, and his arms were as strong as I'd remembered.

"Now, is that a welcome kiss?" he asked, chuckling as he passed inside to my mother. "Hullo again, Marie."

"Tony," Mom said, sending another shock wave through me. *Mom knew Tony?* "This is my spouse, George Murray."

As they said polite things I tried to deal with this astonishing turn of events. How weird this was—Tony and my mother in the same room, knowing each other, apparently on friendly terms.

". . . Milo?" he was saying.

"On the phone with Alec," Mom replied.

"They'll be at it all night, no doubt. Nothing gets in the way of their riveting discussions over whether they should build street lamps or wind machines. Your mum? Came to pay my respects, all right and proper, before I head back to Paris for Christmas."

Mom chuckled. "Very proper. But she's gone off to bed."

Tony refused coffee with a casual wave of one long hand, then he said to Mom, "Tell you what. How about I take Kim out for a quick tour of London. Maybe stop somewhere for a bit of night life."

I did not trust him for a heartbeat and was thinking up a polite way to refuse when my mother shrugged, as if this happened all the time. "It seems Milo might be on the phone for a while. Go ahead, Kim. We hadn't planned anything else for this evening. Come on, George, I'll show you our room."

"Mom?" I asked, and when Tony laughed—and I knew he knew why I was aghast—I added clumsily, "Are you sure?"

My father yawned as he followed Mom out the parlor door. "Time for the old folks to go horizontal." He shot his forefinger at us. "You kids have fun."

Leaving Tony and me standing alone in that pretty parlor.

I put out a hand. "Reality check time," I said. "Last time I saw you . . ." No. The last time we'd seen one another he'd saved my life. So I skipped back a bit farther. "What about that night you tried to grab Alec and the government? May I take it you and Alec aren't enemies anymore?"

He flashed the grin that I had not forgotten. It, too, had figured in my dreams. "You want the long version or the short?"

"I want the truth. Or maybe I should go in and ask Mom, since *she* seems to know you."

"We've met several times, but she doesn't know what happened in Dobrenica after you left."

"Okay, so tell me." I stood with my back to the door, arms crossed.

He lifted a shoulder. "After they took you off the mountain I hid out in the hills until things cooled down a bit. My plan was to wait until after the wedding, and then move back into the Eyrie—figuring Alec's wedding present to Ruli could be a royal pardon for the conniving brother."

"Is that what happened?"

Tony snorted a laugh. "No. We were sitting out under the stars one night, half of my people drunk and the other half working on getting there, when Kilber walked into our camp."

I got a vivid image of the big, burly old man who served as Alec's lieutenant, as he had served Milo during WW II and after. As tough as he was silent, he was also extremely loyal. "I'm surprised your guys didn't shoot him."

"Shoot Kilber?" Tony said, his eyes widening. "I was terrified of him when I was growing up. Somehow never believed that mere bullets or steel could stop him. I sat there with a jug in one hand and a rifle on my knee—we'd heard wolves down in the valley—and hoped he wouldn't grab me by the scruff of my neck and shake me like he used to when Alec and I were fighting schoolboys."

"So then what happened?"

"Stopped right in front of me, squinted down, said, 'Statthalter wants to talk to you.'"

"So you went?"

Tony grinned. "Well, of course I did. That's hardly the sort of invitation one refuses. I figured Alec had cooled down by then. If he was still after my blood, he wouldn't have sent Kilber, he would have come himself. We agreed to regard the past as error and continue on with our praiseworthy attempt at family unity."

It sounded reasonable. If one knew them both. Meantime, Tony was here—he'd met Mom. Alarms were stilled. So he wasn't The Enemy any more.

There was no way I could sleep now. Intensely curious, I said, "In that case, let's go." I pulled open the door, felt a blast of cold air, and stopped. "I better go unpack my parka," I said.

"No need." With unhurried grace he removed his long coat and dropped it over my shoulders.

"Then you'll be cold," I said, acutely aware of his warmth captured in the silk-lined coat, and his scent.

"We won't be outdoors long."

He opened the door to an Aston Martin roadster. Soon we were bowling along on the wrong side of the road at a pulse-pounding speed, and I couldn't help but remember—vividly—what had happened the last time I went driving with Tony, in the mountains of Dobrenica.

I must have moved, or stiffened, or shown some kind of expression, because Tony said, "Cheer up, coz. You won't be diving off any bridges. I promise."

I reminded myself that he was welcome at Milo's, that Mom seemed to like him. And the chances were pretty good that Tony wasn't conspiring to take over any governments. "Awesome," I said, trying for lightness. "This is not the weather for floating down the Thames."

The Hampstead streets widened. As the car nosed onto a main road, I had to close my eyes against the traffic coming at me from the wrong side.

Tony's cell vibrated with that *brrrt-brrrt* noise, quiet but insistent in the small space of a car. He ignored it as he pointed out various sights with famous names: Finchley Road, St. John's Wood, Regent's Park, Hyde Park. There were neo-classical Nash-like terraces dominated by the enormous British Telecom tower. We sped past monuments, bridges, old and new buildings, dramatic against the skyline. His phone kept burring, but he ignored it as he answered my "What's *that* building?" questions.

When last we saw each other he'd said, *Au revoir*, before he ran off, a knife wound in his shoulder. *And that's a promise.*

"Didn't you manage to see anything?" he asked. "I thought you stopped here before flying off to Los Angeles."

"I did, but I barely had enough for bus money. So I walked around a lot, and once or twice treated myself to the tube. You don't see much from the tube." I didn't say that I'd spent most of the time holed up in my B&B, feeling sorry for myself.

"I know what you might like, then. See it all at once. If you don't mind heights, we can take the champagne flight on the Eye. I've never been up on the damn thing. Should do it once."

"Sure," I said. "Sounds like fun."

We were stopped at a red light. He pulled out his cell, which had begun to vibrate again. He sighed. "Hell. What's my mother want, calling fifty times? I'll see her tomorrow." He thumbed the *ignore* and brought up a search engine. By the time the light changed to green, he'd found the Eye and the time. "Good. Last flight in half an hour. If we stop at the flat, we can borrow one of my sister's coats. She must have a hundred of them upstairs."

Now that I felt safe, I was wildly curious to see the von Mecklundburg London house. Tony drove up a quiet street lined with handsome street lamps. The Georgian façades looked unchanged from the days of Horry Walpole. Tony parked in front, and as we walked to the door I pulled his coat close against the icy air. His cell phone vibrated three times.

Tony unlocked it and led the way down a hall into a cavernous room, where he moved around quickly, flicking on lights. The air was still—

stuffy in the way rooms are when they've been closed up for months. There was no heat, and I was cold.

"Sorry about the lack of welcome." He indicated the covers on all the furniture. "We've someone who comes in, sweeps out the spider webs, and plunks down the mail. Otherwise no one is here anymore."

"You usually spend Christmas in Paris?"

He shot me a fast look, then flashed his grin. "Not usually. This year, yes."

There went his cell again.

"Go ahead and answer that if you have to," I said. "I'll wait in here while you get the coat."

"I should chuck this thing out the window." He pulled out the phone. "Make yourself at home." He vanished into the hall, saying, "*Ja?*"

A few seconds later a door shut somewhere upstairs.

I didn't want to risk sitting on some chair that would turn out to be three hundred years old and fragile, unused since it received the royal backside of Prince Somebody in 1734. So I walked around the room, idly looking at things.

In spite of the Enlightenment era architecture, what I could see of the shrouded furnishings turned out to be vintage 1920s, right down to the light fixtures. Here and there were jarring touches: a sixties stereo console, and in a corner, a big screen television that reminded me of Ruli.

Ruli.

I'd tried for three months not to think about her. I knew I should wish her well in her huge, cold palace in Riev. But keeping your rational mind civilized doesn't fix the hurt.

I was examining the art deco-framed nineteenth-century racing prints on the walls when I heard Tony's footsteps clattering down some stairs, much louder than he'd gone away.

Then came the ringing, shivery sound of drawn steel, and Tony advanced, still in his shirt sleeves, carrying a dueling sword in each hand, his eyes narrowed.

"Uh—" I said.

He tossed a rapier to me. Cold, blue-gleaming steel rang softly as the blade whooshed through the air. Instinctively, I put my hand up and caught the elaborate hilt.

Tony whipped his blade back and forth so it voomed a low, unnerving sound. For a moment he held the blade horizontally, tip resting on his flat palm, the steel glinting below those black Byzantine eyes. "I never did get a good look your skill when you fought your way down the ancestral staircase." He brought his blade down in *seconde*. "*En garde.*"

"There's no button on this thing," I protested, flashing my blade in an automatic beat and riposte.

The swords rang—my bones jarred down to my heels, and I backed away a step.

"No." He took a step toward me, swinging the sword back and forth. And struck again, in tierce.

"It's sharp," I yelped as I blocked.

"Yes." His grin was crazy. No, it was *angry*. "So you had better defend yourself, hadn't you?"

"Have you gone out of your freaking *mind?*"

Whoosh! His blade arced in indirect then straight at my head.

"I can't *believe* it," I yelped.

There was no answer except the whoosh of his blade. I was about to point out our lack of padding and practice clothes, but he smashed aside my blade and lunged, the smile gone.

This maniac is gonna kill me.

I parried. The shock of the hit—no easy hit—sent a sting up my arm. Tony was taller than me by at least half a foot and in superlative condition. The last time I saw him with steel in hand he'd pulled a knife out of his own shoulder and then nailed that horrible Reithermann square in the throat. During my time with Tony, I'd seen him laughing, curious, evasive, even idly amorous, but except for a brief moment when we'd both been under Reithermann's gun, I'd never seen him really angry.

He was angry now.

"Time for some questions," he said.

"Questions," I repeated in an *I-do-not-believe-this* voice.

We exchanged a rapid series of blows, each pressing for the advantage. I held him off. Barely. He advanced step-by-step. "First. Why are you here?"

Whang-g-g! Zing! Lunge, beat, riposte—lunge.

"To see the Eye? To see London? Because Mom and Dad said, 'Go and have fun.'" I blocked, attempted a bind, disengaged, and hopped back, deflecting a lunge straight at my gut. "*You* said I wouldn't have to dive off another bridge." The expensive coat fell to the floor behind me. "Why are you *doing* this?"

"Why." He kicked the coat out of the way. "Are you here? Today?"

Zing! We exchanged *prises de fer* as we each tried to shift the other out of line, his strength forcing me back step-by-step. When I tried a flashing cut-over, he responded with a vicious circular parry that took all my strength to disengage. The wicked blades, sharp as death, whished through the air. His knocked a vase over with a *thok!* Mine caught in long brocade drapes, the material hissing as I ripped my point free.

"The curtains!" I squawked as my hairclip, put in for comfort against a long plane flight, came loose. A loop of hair drooped in one of my eyes.

"Why," he swung a cut at my head, "are you in London?"

"Because my dad bought me a ticket." I blocked, jumped back, and almost tripped over a footstool, whirling around it to catch his blade at the last second.

He leaped over the footstool, and for a moment we stood chest to chest, guard to guard, blades pointed upward. "Because?"

Pulling force from all the way down to my heels, I ripped my blade free, nearly taking his ear off.

He twitched his head aside, disengaged, backed up—and kicked that footstool out of the way.

Neither of us looked when it hit something with a metallic clang, followed by a crash.

Cold as the room was, sweat broke out on my brow as I worked to keep his blade away, but I was still backing up little by little. Tony lunged in a powerful *croisé*, forcing my blade from high line to low, his black eyes narrowed with murderous intent, and I remembered Alec's stories of him running about as a teenager, chasing armed Soviet soldiers with little more than crossbows and steel.

When I reached a point where I fought for breath as hard as I fought him, he finally spoke.

"Last time." He flicked the tip of his blade down. *Whang!* I gathered the remains of my strength and tried a feint-and-lunge attack that used to rattle my opponents. Two loops of my hair flapped against my cheek and back, and his hair hung in his eyes.

He deflected me with a flick of his wrist, then stepped up *corps à corps*, his breath stirring the top of my hair. "Why are you here?" he whispered, soft as a lover.

"Dad and Gran were going . . . Argh! Put the sword *down*," I yelled as his blade slid along mine in a metallic *coulé*, sending me nearly stumbling over that same footstool. I scrambled around it, leaped over whatever it was I knocked down—oh lord, one of those antique tulip lamps. "I'm not talking until you do."

"I'm not stopping," he said as he kicked that footstool against the wall. "Until you tell me the truth."

"I've never lied to you."

"You lied from the first day you showed up in Dobrenica," he retorted. "And kept it up until you took off. Why did you leave?"

"I was in the way." *Zing!* "In Ruli's—in *their* way. You yourself said I was trouble." *Whang!* "It seemed leaving was the right thing to do."

"It was the wrong thing to do." Tony's mouth flattened into a line as he attacked again. My arm shivered as I deflected his blade—all art gone, my form along with it. I fought to defend myself. He kicked a chair my way, which skidded, rumpling up a fabulous Persian rug. "Damn it! Disappeared in a day." *Crash!* "No word to anyone except my sister." *Clang!* "Ruli whinged about having to drive you to the border like she was a chauffeur, and how you nagged her to do her duty." *Slash, zing!* "No reasons." *Zang!* "Nothing—" *Whoosh!* "—that made sense."

Another feint, a lunge that he smacked out of the way, and then a lamp rocked, teetered, went over with a crash. Tony never gave it a second glance.

My hair clip fell out at last, and my hair swung down in ropes, tangling with my arms.

I whooped for breath as I slung my hair back. He wanted the truth? Fine. "Honor."

"*What?*"

"And I couldn't bear it." May as well get it all out.

His hand dropped, that point swinging aside, out of the line of attack. "Bear what?"

I let my point fall slightly, my arm throbbing. I was furious with him and furious with myself for actually trusting him enough to get into that car. *Never* again.

"I thought you were better than that." He held his point steady but still out of line.

"I *am* better than that," I retorted. "Months of no practice, and your reflexes wouldn't be as fast, either. Once my shoulder healed up from that bullet hole, I was at my new job: *teaching French*. They didn't have a fencing team." He was rubbing his own shoulder. To forestall some irritatingly superior comment about how he'd had to recover as well, I said, "And about that bullet hole in my shoulder."

He paused. "What about it? You're going to say it was worse than Kilber's bull's-eye on me?"

"I was going to say that when I went to the doctor to get it checked out, he said the wound was so cleanly placed it hadn't done any bone damage. I figured, if Reithermann's guys were going to shoot point blank, they would have hit me somewhere far worse. I think I was shot by one of your guys. In fact, I remember his face. I've seen it a lot in nightmares."

"Niklos," Tony admitted. "He was very careful."

"Yeah, I figured that out. He shot me in the shoulder before one of Reithermann's slimes could shoot me in the head. That way, it still looked like you guys were his allies. And I bet Kilber threw his knife in exactly the same spot on you for some of the same reasons."

"True." He rubbed the spot again, then said, "Couldn't bear what?" A little of his old sarcasm was back as he said, "What was it sent you off so suddenly, an American distaste for the depravity of monarchy?"

"Look, last summer, when I finally realized that my showing up in Dobrenica was an epic mistake, the least I could do was not force Alec to have to choose between Ruli and me—knowing the Blessing would only work if he married her. So I left." I wiped my forehead with my sleeve, then said fiercely, "And I couldn't stand by and watch it happen."

Tony squinted at me. "Who said the Blessing wouldn't work if you married him?"

"You did. Explicitly. When you talked about bastardy. Everyone else only hinted: Gran not being legally married, my mother born out of wedlock. Alec's marrying Ruli was to bring peace between the five ruling families, which meant—"

He spun around and flung his blade across the room so it stabbed the priceless silk wallpaper next to the door and stayed there, vibrating violently. "I didn't tell you that," he said. "I said you were trouble, yes, a problem, yes—but only because it was becoming clearer by the day that you, and not my sister, were the necessary component. And I wanted you up the Eyrie with me so I could use you as a bargaining chip—no, not only against Alec, though that was true in part, but against my mother. Dammit. *Damn* it."

"What? Make some *sense*." I waved my sword in an arc.

"My mother lies when it's to her advantage. Like sending me to London on this so-called urgent law question, when I should be. . . ." He stopped, his profile shuttered. Then he flashed the nasty grin. "Let's say there's trouble at home. Today. This particular day. *Now*." His voice lowered, oddly gentle. "And I don't believe in coincidence. Yet here you are."

FOUR

6 6 I T'S ENTIRELY COINCIDENCE," I said. "I didn't even know I was coming until day before yesterday. And my parents didn't know I was going to drive home. My dad got me a ticket just in case."

He frowned. But at least he was listening and not attacking.

We were still standing in the middle of the trashed room. Since his sword was stuck in the wall, I dropped my point and leaned against the table as I tried to recover my breath. "Look. From my view, everything that happened last summer was a personal disaster. So when I got back to L.A. I told my parents never to mention Alec again. Or Dobrenica. Or . . . anything about any of you. I took a job five states away."

"Your personal cock-up wasn't as bad as the one you left behind." He swung around and paced across the room, stopping in front of the wide screen TV, which had a long sword scrape across the surface. "I know you think fast on your feet. Like the rest of us in the family," he added over his shoulder as he regarded the sword still stuck in the wall, then he moved away. "It happened to me once," he flicked a hand at the sword, "being attacked at sword point for the truth. It worked. I was too busy to lie." He grinned unrepentantly. "So were you."

Swordplay to get the truth was insane, but then, when one is furious, there's little or no sanity at work. I could tell that he was still very angry. "If you don't want to tell me what's going on 'this particular day, now, today' fine," I said. "But it's your turn to at least answer some questions." I laid some heavy emphasis on the *at least*.

"We called a truce. Milo still holds my father's ring." He gazed across the room at me, his mouth twisted sardonically. "Save your breath, I know what a fine upstanding democrat thinks of that."

"Don't." I shook my head.

"So you *did* have a reason for taking off so suddenly last September, even if it was barking mad?" He looked at me and went on, mockingly, "I wasn't the only one wondering. That's why Alec sent for me—in case I'd grabbed you again and Ruli'd lied to him about your leaving. His theory made more sense than what actually happened, what you actually did."

"Wait," I said, pressing my hands over my eyes. "Wait, wait. I don't get it. He did marry Ruli, right?"

"Of course. Had to, since you'd scarpered. Neither of them wanted it, which might be the reason why whatever was supposed to work didn't. Or maybe it was because everybody else in that cathedral was angry: with him, with my family, with one another, with you. Or maybe there isn't any Vrajhus left, if it ever existed."

"But you say you've met vampires."

He waved an impatient hand. "Please . . . vampires have nothing whatsoever to do with the Blessing."

"How can you say that? Isn't everything . . . connected? Isn't Dobrenica . . . ?" I retorted feebly.

"You see ghosts," he shot back, twirling his hand skyward. "Does that mean you have fairy dust, Tinkerbell? At the end of August my father suffered a stroke. He sent for Milo, who was still there when he died on the tenth."

I remembered Dad's mention of *some old duke.* "So that was your father who died? That's what you meant by Milo holding your father's ring?" I dropped into one of the chairs that had been kicked aside. "I'm so sorry," I whispered.

He made one of his lazy gestures, probably meant to mask his emotions. "He was older than Milo by four years. Drank like a fish. He wasn't close to any of us, though he and my sister shared a taste for breakfast cocktails."

I said, "So you're now the duke?"

"Yes. Well, technically. As technically as Milo is king." He glanced at the once-elegant room, now pretty well trashed. "What remains is all this." He waved a hand in a lazy circle. "I always hated those damn tulip lamps." He wiped a hand up over his face, then pulled his sword out of the wall and laid it on the table. "I was supposed to go back to Paris tomorrow, but all things considered, I'd better do that tonight. Where's that coat I brought downstairs? I'll take you back to Milo's."

I stood there with the sword still in my hand, wishing I could high-handedly say that I'd take a cab, that I'd walk, that I'd do anything but get into a car with him again. But I'd been up for nearly thirty hours, and I didn't have my purse with me, or even Milo's address. Yeah, I could have held out my hand for some cash and demanded the address from my lofty stance on Mt. Moral Superiority, but there was so much pain in his absent gaze, that I thought, *His father's death hit him harder than he wants to admit.*

So I laid my blade next to his on the table and said, "Let's go."

Tony was preoccupied pretty much the entire way back. When he pulled into the driveway, and I started shrugging out of Ruli's expensive silk-lined coat, he said, "Keep it. She'll never wear it again."

His caustic tone surprised me, then I remembered his mention of "a hundred coats upstairs," which reminded me of Ruli's super-wardrobe last summer.

"Okay," I said and slammed the door. There was no use talking to him anymore. He'd only tell me what he wanted me to know, not what I wanted to know.

He zoomed off, the tail lights vanishing at jet speed.

Milo's front door was unlocked, and the parlor lit. I found Mom sitting with her laptop, cruising the net. Her earphones were on. I sank down next to her, catching a few notes of Victoria de los Angeles singing *Madama Butterfly.*

"Kimli," she said, pulling off the headphones. "You look weirded out."

"Very weirded out. Things are definitely weird."

Mom clapped her laptop shut and set it aside. "What's going on?"

"It started at JFK. I was passing this shop window. No, it really started at Fort Williams, when I was grading papers . . ." I filled her in, ending with Tony's attack. I repeated everything he said, finishing with "this particular day."

"What does he mean by that?" I asked. "Do you think there's some connection? I don't mean with my officemate, necessarily, but what about some crazy connection with Ruli? Only why would he attack me to 'get the truth'—" I made air quotes, "—just because I arrived today?"

Mom shook her head. "No idea. It isn't like Milo kept your grandmother's arrival a secret. She's been planning this visit for a month."

"No one knew *I* was coming," I said.

"True."

I sighed. "The oddest thing is, he didn't go ballistic until after he answered one of his mother's fifty million calls. Maybe the duchess got mad that he was making nice with me, especially when you consider she once did her best to get me killed. But would that make him attack me?"

"Can't even guess," Mom said. "Can't ask Milo, either, as he's been on the phone the entire time you were gone."

Dad came in then, his wild hair and beard wet from the shower and slicked down. "Back already? That was a fast tour."

I gave Dad the short version. He rubbed his chin through his beard, which was beginning to fluff out as it dried. "I know one thing," he said. "If Tony's steely form of interrogation has any connection to Milo's being on the phone all this time, the last thing anyone is going to want is visitors underfoot. What's been going on with Dobreni politics, hon?"

Mom shrugged. "Milo and Emilio don't talk about Dobreni politics much, since I've never been there. But you can't help picking up vibes when you're around people, and I get the idea there's something or other happening with the mines."

"A big part of the GNP, mines, right?" Dad asked. He sank into a satin-covered chair, then said, "How about this: If things still look bad in the morning, we'll vamoose and hole up in some tourist hotel. Leave Milo a polite note, make some excuse. We can hang around in London for a few days, and if their problem clears up, we come back here for the Christmas bash. If it doesn't, we can always go back to LA, and try again in spring, or something. How's that sound?"

"My mother would probably think it's the right thing to do," Mom said. "I just don't know if she'd be relieved or disappointed."

While this conversation was going on, I was only half listening. *Deal with it*, said LaToya's image.

Help me, said Ruli's image.

I looked up at my parents. "Mom. Dad. I think I need to go back."

"To Los Angeles?" Dad asked.

"To Dobrenica."

"Whoa." Mom set her laptop on the coffee table. "Whoa-ho."

"Look. I'm beginning to wonder if Ruli got into some kind of trouble, and Tony's family thinks I'm to blame. Then there was that . . . vision? Apparition? Hallucination? Anyway, she begged me to help her."

Mom tipped her head to one side. "Hey, maybe all that astral plane stuff we talked about in the seventies is true. Ruli sure doesn't sound like she's got much in the way of support from that family of hers."

"Astral planes make as much sense as ghosts." I sighed, wishing I didn't have to deal with this stuff while under the influence of mega-jetlag. "Then there was something Tony said: 'The cock-up you left behind.' You guys know I thought I was doing the right thing, for all the right reasons. But if he's telling the truth, nothing worked out like it was supposed to. So maybe, *somehow,* my leaving is mixed up with politics, and Ruli's caught there in the middle."

Dad grimaced, then coughed, trying to hide it.

"Spit it out, Dad."

"What if it's not politics, but personal, Rapunzel? If it's something like her having had a royal fight with Alec, what if she wants you to trade places with her, like she suggested before you left Dobrenica? Without the hassle of divorce and remarriage?"

That gave me a sickening jolt, especially when I had to admit to myself that deep down (or maybe not all that far down) I wanted just that.

But daydreams and reality seldom match up. When Mom was a baby, Gran broke up with Armandros partly on ideological grounds but partly because she had found out their marriage was fake. Though Gran and I are at either end of Mom's generation, we are a lot alike. And my mom is more like her dad. I looked at my parents sitting side by side, representing yin-yang perspectives on how relationships worked.

If Alec wanted a divorce, who's going to stop the acting head of state? Also, it's not like he doesn't know where my parents live. If he'd wanted to find me, he could have.

But he hadn't, because he's a married man.

"If she wants me to be a stunt double or something, then I come right back here." I paused, because thinking about Alec always required me to stop and get a grip. "Anyway, this whole vision thing . . . like I said. She asked for my help. Twice. I think I need to go there, find out what trouble she's in and, if it's connected to me in any way, I have to fix it."

Nobody had any argument to make with that. I could see that the apparition thing unsettled the parents nearly as much as it did me.

"Okay," Mom said finally. "So when do you want to go?"

"Right away. If I can get tickets, first thing in the morning."

"Do you want to talk to Milo about this?" Mom asked.

I thought about what Dad had said and made a face. "What if Ruli's thing is personal? No, I really don't. She came to me on the GhostNet. Let me scope it out myself. Sooner the better."

"Christmas is four days away."

"Do you have plans I'd screw up? You couldn't, since you didn't even know I was coming."

"No plans that you'd screw up. Hon, I'm not standing in your way, I'm trying to get my head around it. Okay." I caught a whiff of Mom's familiar, comforting patchouli as she reached forward to grab her laptop, her lopsided grin flashing. "One thing I'm real good at now is tickets. I don't think you know that Milo and I went to Paris in October? I can tell you all about it tomorrow morning. Before I put you on any plane, boat, or train, we're getting you some winter clothes. I don't know how successful I'll be in finding flights what with the snowpocalypse and the holidays, but one way or another you should be out of London by afternoon."

"You two do that," Dad said, "and I will heroically postpone my personal geek-fest at the Worshipful Company of Clockmakers and hold the fort here."

FIVE

MILO DID NOT JOIN US the next morning.

Emilio was also absent. Either he was still asleep, or the poor old guy had been sent on errands, because it was us alone at the magnificent breakfast table, with formal apologies offered by the staff.

"Right. We're out of here," Dad said, and as Gran put down her cup, looking worried, he said, "I'll go scout out a hotel." He picked up a piece of toast and vanished, leaving Mom and me to bring Gran up to date using our typical mix of French and English.

At the end, Gran said only, "Aurelia Kim, you must remember that in Dobrenica, personal *is* political."

"Are you saying I shouldn't go?"

She gave her head a definite shake, the morning light turning her silver hair to pewter. "*Au contraire*. I think you should keep your covenant with your cousin Ruli."

This was my grandmother, who had firmly denied there was any such thing as ghosts. Or visions. Or magic. Until I came back and told her that I'd personally encountered two out of three.

She paused, then patted my hand as she said gently, "You ran away to Oklahoma in part because you could not bear how politics and the personal are inextricably intertwined. You will probably have to address that if you go back to Dobrenica."

Mom said, "Let's beat feet."

Mom had the use of a car, and she'd gotten accustomed to the left-hand driving situation. We crammed in a fast morning of shopping and talking a mile a minute. Too soon it was time to get on the boat to Ostend, as the planes were all booked and overbooked.

At last we stood above the briny-smelling dock and stared at the round-bowed boat riding at anchor in the choppy gray seas under a cloud of mewling gulls. Mom said, "Shall I get you a European prepaid?"

"Cell phones don't work in Dobrenica, remember?"

"Oh, yeah." Her brow cleared. "But they do have land lines. When I got this English cell phone, I picked an easy number." She touched her purse. "Remember Dad's birthday and the license number on your old junkmobile, if you need to call."

"Got it."

Mom searched my eyes. "I'm glad you're trying to do the right thing. But sweetie, if it's going to hurt you to see Alec, don't."

"I don't plan to go anywhere near him. It's Ruli who tweeted me on the woo-woo net. Once I know what's up with her, I'm turning right around and coming back. In and out. See you in a couple days."

Mom and I hugged, and she took off.

Because of the holidays and the heavy weather, my trip back to Dobrenica turned out to be a lot like my exit, only in reverse, switching between a bunch of different types of conveyance.

I spent most of that journey trying to catch up on the sleep deficit caused by jetlag and my drive from Oklahoma. I was only moderately successful, and it wasn't until the train began its slow, creaking climb into the mountains that I began to feel human again. As it squeaked and screeched around a tight bend below an ancient crag topped with a mossy ruined fortress, a line from Wordsworth came to mind: *The immeasurable height/Of woods decaying, never to be decayed—*

Wordsworth. I'd probably read more poetry in the past three months than I had in the previous three years. Alec loved poetry. He'd memorized yards of it. I knew that by following his steps through his favorites I was trying to find *him*, which is always a danger. Natalie Miller, Alec's

American-born doctor friend, had insisted that Milton's poem "Lycidas," Alec's favorite, held the key to understanding him. I had that poem memorized by now, I had studied it so closely. Yet I could not grasp that key.

Was it because I didn't understand Dobreni politics? He wasn't always the elegantly dressed Alec I'd seen everyday as we drove along the Adriatic, or attended Tony's mother's high-toned parties while pretending to be Ruli. Late one night, just when I'd finished reading Milo's WW II journals, we had an unexpected encounter. Alec was dressed in jeans and a black sweater, grinning like a boy as he admitted he'd returned from the mountains after "poking around where he had no business being." He had to have been trying to get near Tony's castle, to figure out Tony's plot. That was Dobreni politics—all in the families.

The train climbed above a lacy waterfall, foaming and splashing in terraced ledges. *The stationary blasts of waterfalls/And in the narrow rent, at every turn. . . .* It seemed a thousand years ago that I'd dived off a bridge into a rushing river, leaving Tony leaning on that bridge and laughing, surrounded by milling sheep. He'd tried to kidnap me as a move in the chess game he was playing with Alec.

Personal and political. *Got it, Gran.*

When we reached the last little station before the border, the three people left in the train car put away their electronic stuff like it was old habit. A couple hours later, I spotted the Eyrie, Tony's enormous castle, high on a mountain peak, briefly lit by a slanting ray of bluish-white light until the slow tumble of clouds closed it into sinister silhouette again.

. . .Winds thwarting winds bewildered and forlorn,
The torrents shooting from the clear blue sky,
The rocks that muttered close upon our ears,
Black drizzling crags that spake by the wayside
As if a voice were in them. . . .

I pressed my face to the window, watching the castle slide out of view.

Tumult and peace, the darkness and the light . . .

Tumult and darkness. I remembered Ruli mentioning off-handedly that "some say Tony knows the wild folk." I'd have to ask her what she meant by that, but in the meantime, at least, he was safely in Paris. He and his dueling swords.

A few hours later the train pulled into the Riev station with a screech and great goutings of steam. I gripped my suitcase in one gloved hand and pulled my collar up around my ears. I could see that the air was freezing; clouds of breath came from the people on the narrow concourse.

And I felt self-conscious. Normally, it would seem egomaniacal to worry that I'd be recognized and that word would spread of my arrival. But to the Dobreni I was a granddaughter of the Dsaret princess. I'd paid little attention to this paradigm when I was first here, and with disastrous results. So this time, I'd thought out my approach more carefully.

As the train slowed to a stop, I wrapped my new scarf around the lower half of my face, pulled my new wool cap down to my eyebrows, and hunched into my new coat. I followed the other three people off the train and shouldered through the bitter wind to the cab station, where I was startled to discover, next to the single ancient car, three sleighs pulled by honest-to-Santa, shaggy gray and brown reindeer. Alone of all the beings there, the reindeer seemed to be impervious to the cold. They stood placidly enough, older males tossing heads that looked oddly bald, having recently shed their antlers.

"Waleskas' inn, please," I said to the first driver in line.

This was the second thing I'd thought out. I was making a low key, anonymous approach. No driving straight to the palace and asking for an interview. I would scout the territory first and discover the rules for citizens who wanted to talk to Madam Statthalter.

The one hitch in the low key, incognito aspect of my plan was staying at the Waleskas' inn. There had to be other hostelries, but I resisted the idea of trying to find them. My reasoning was that either I go back to lying about who I am or else risk my name being recognized. The Waleskas would recognize me, but I planned to make that work for me by asking them to keep my presence a secret.

The sleigh hissed and jiggled over the hard-packed snowy streets. Now I understood why the houses all had front doors that were up a few steps, off tiny porches. In winter, there was a whole lot of snow, and it came right up to the doorway.

The inn was exactly as I remembered it, minus the flowering window boxes, and with a blanket of blue-white snow on the slanted roof. The triangular terrace was obscured by heaps of slush piled alongside the steep corner where two streets met, one high, one lower.

The downstairs windows of the inn glowed a warm gold, throwing me back in memory to the wedding of Anna, the oldest of the Waleska girls, when I was last here. Inside, the restaurant was packed. There was a gasp when I entered, and a thin girl with dark braids bustled forward.

It wasn't high-school-aged Theresa, who'd helped me a lot during the summer, but the middle Waleska sister, Tania, a tall, twig-thin girl. Maybe not a girl anymore, as she must be nineteen or twenty. I was surprised to see Tania in a white apron; when I knew her, she worked for a lens maker.

She halted when she saw me, and stepped back, her face lengthening, almost in horror.

"Tania?" I asked. "Is something wrong?" I looked behind me, to make certain there was no monster ghost, or creepy guy with a gun.

No one.

When I looked back she was breathing easily again, her face flooding with color. Relief.

"Mademoiselle," she said in her careful French, "it *is* you. What can we do for you?"

"I'd like to get a room. If you're not full up."

Madam appeared, wiping her hands on her apron. She stared at me, took a step back, then smiled broadly.

"Welcome." No French for her! In Dobreni, she said loudly, "For you, we always have a room. You shall have your old chamber, yes? We make sure it is fresh. And you have the bathroom at the end of the hall, yes?"

I stepped close, turning my back to the busy room. They were quite a contrast—the short, round mother with her triumphant smile, and the tall, thin daughter with the serious face. "I don't want anyone to know I'm here," I said. My visit will probably be short."

Madam pleated her apron, her honest expression going from delight to puzzlement. Tania sent a quick look at her mother, then said, "Of course."

Madam jerked her head toward the stairs, and Tania fled.

I couldn't imagine them having to clean the room. The inn was always spotless. I hoped Tania wasn't throwing some hapless guest out.

As I tried to find some diplomatic way of finding out, Madam chattered away. I learned that the place filled up for Christmas, which fell on a different date from the Russian Orthodox Christmas. Many mountain families came to the city for the holidays as well as for great events.

Madam offered me tea, but I did not want to sit alone and face that crowded room. In any case, there was no use in postponing what I had come all this way to do, and not if I wanted to be gone again before gossip could start a *Princess Aurelia's Granddaughter: the Sequel.*

Tania reappeared and took me upstairs to the room I'd had before, at the end of the hall, with windows overlooking the snow-covered terrace. The slanted roofs of the houses on the street below the terrace, last summer slate-colored, were now smoothly blanketed with white.

Tania brought up my suitcase, giving me another of those worried glances. Wary. Then she closed the door, leaving me alone, except for the quiet hiss of a very old radiator below the window.

I took in the familiar room. So weird, how much had changed since I first stayed here.

Traveling light meant it took about two minutes to unpack. In the wardrobe I hung up my carefully chosen clothes—all new, bought at Harrods—and stashed the rest in the two big drawers below. Then I looked around again, feeling this sense of weirdness. I couldn't tell if it was just being here, or something more dire.

"Stick to the plan, Murray," I muttered and kicked my empty suitcase next to the wardrobe.

The third stage of my plan, the scouting-the-territory part, meant going to the person I was sure could be trusted not only to fill me in on the latest news and local custom, but also to keep quiet about my presence: Alec's doctor-midwife friend, Natalie Miller, who had repaired my shoulder when I was shot. She had also filled me in on *things.*

I wintered up and went downstairs to the street. The late afternoon sun barely cleared the mountain tops, its light weak and watery and gray-blue. Warm golden glows lit the windows of the well-remembered buildings, so old and charming and distinctively Dobreni. The hot California sun seemed impossibly distant, especially when I slid on mushy snow that was humped over the sidewalks to the edge of the street. Sleigh cabs hissed and jingled down the middle. There were very few wheeled vehicles.

I hadn't expected the commercial look of American Christmas, but the decorations here seemed exceptionally discreet, in the form of fir wreaths on doors, with a tiny silver or glass star hanging in the center; I remembered that the customs centering around fir trees at Christmas and New Year's actually came from this part of the world.

It was a relief to know my way around somewhat. It had taken me some time to discover that Riev had a single streetcar line, running up and down Prinz Karl-Rafael Street, the longest and broadest east-west street in the city, starting where the Friday market met from spring through fall, and ending at the top of the mountain, at the traffic circle below the triumphal arch.

Before I entered the post office, I yanked my hat down to my eyebrows and pulled my scarf up to my nose. Then I walked in, changed euros for Dobreni currency, and asked for a few streetcar tokens.

"They are cheaper if you buy them in lots of twenty," the old woman behind the counter explained.

"Won't be here that long," I muttered, hoping the scarf muffled any accent I had.

"You can also use them with the *inkri*." She pointed at the window.

It took me a moment to understand the word for the sleigh cab whizzing by, its runners hissing over the snow. Remembering the moment of juggling money with the inkri driver, I nodded, and bought a pack of twenty.

Then I walked one street over and caught the streetcar going past piles and piles of slushy snow. People seemed dour, not surprising considering the weather. Mindful of my wish to stay unnoticed, when Mom took me out to buy winter things, I'd picked out a sturdy coat, hat, and scarf of dull charcoal. They fit right in with all the black hats and scarves I saw around me.

I rode the streetcar all the way to the big traffic circle. When I climbed off, I looked around, a surge of pleasure warming me. This city was as beautiful in winter as it was in summer.

At least . . . I stopped and stood there, though the wind cut through my coat and mittens as if they were beach clothes. Something was wrong. I did a slower sweep of the fountain, turned off for the winter. The young shepherdess looked as graceful and free with her snow decoration as she did when seen through rainbow-hued sprays of water. The animals, mythical and normal, were blurred by the snow. I gazed outward at the traffic circle, to the winter-bare trees. That was it: one of them looked gray, the branches brittle and broken. As if it wasn't hibernating but dead. I shifted my gaze, hoping I was wrong.

The buildings framing the circle had the corbels I remembered and here and there a gargoyle. I spotted at least three eras of architectural styles, punctuated by tall windows, many of which glowed golden in the bluish winter light. As I plunged my way up the half-remembered narrow street leading to the northern end of town, I passed through a low, mossy, medieval archway attached to a Renaissance building that reminded me of photos of Italian villas. Juxtaposed was a half-timbered building, in its turn annexed in yet a different style. The original Renaissance symmetry had long since been amended to a jumble that I found immensely appealing.

I looked more closely as I walked by, or I might not have spotted an intriguing anomaly—a door, painted so realistically that at first I thought it was three dimensional. I back-stepped a couple of paces, and yes—it was a painted door with beautifully rendered hinges that looked like stylized flowers of a type I did not recognize.

An impossible door! The sheer absurdity cheered me right up. I jumped over a thin slushy stream winding its way down the cobblestones, and climbed a steep hill lined with older houses, slipping and sliding on the cobblestones. The icy wind buffeted my face. Dobrenica was colder even than London had been, and I'd thought *that* the equivalent of the North Pole, after California's endless summer.

As I neared Natalie's familiar door it opened and a young Dobreni woman stepped out. Her eyes lowered modestly as she walked away.

From the doorway came a slow American drawl: "I do not believe my eyes."

There was Nat. Her short, curly brown cap of hair was tucked up into a kerchief, and she wore a floor-length dress of some thick material that hid most of her generous contours. "Look who's blown back into town." She leaned against her door frame, arms crossed.

What kind of welcome was that? "At least," I said, trying for humor, "you didn't make the King's X and spit three times, like Dobrenis no doubt still do to ward off the devil."

I might as well have saved my breath.

Her lips tightened, then she sighed. "You may as well come in, since you're here."

Her living area was as cluttered as ever, the mismatched furniture piled with knickknacks, the walls mostly covered with wooden crate bookshelves, all of them overstuffed. She waved me to the ancient, sagging armchair as she dropped onto the scruffy, equally aged couch bed, stretched out her legs, and propped her feet on an end table. She was wearing jogging shoes and heavy sweats under the old-fashioned skirt.

Her smile was caustic. "I expected you'd return within a week. Or never. No word, even! I thought about placing a bet with someone that *your* granddaughter shows up and pulls the same stunt in fifty years' time—"

I rubbed my eyes, feeling sick inside. "But it's different than Gran—"

"Who was to know that?" she cut in roughly. "Not a friggin' word, a postcard, even. Jeez, dude, was it revenge, or just a royal snit?"

"Go on." I got to my feet, hands out. "Take your best shot. A week ago somebody I don't even know told me I needed to fix things, and I'm trying."

"*Fix* things?"

But when I started for the door, she said hastily, "Sit down, sit down. I'm sorry." She shook her head. "Hell! I promised myself if I ever saw you again I'd be cool. None of my business. But—hell!"

"Then it *was* bad. Tony said I'd left behind a cock-up, but if he said noon was daylight I'd be busy looking for the moon."

"Tony?" she repeated.

"Saw him in London. When I flew over with Gran to stay with Milo."

She waved her hands at me to stop, then pressed the heels of her hands against her eyelids. "Okay, one thing at a time. What exactly did Tony tell you?"

"That I left behind a mess."

"Nothing else?"

"That his father was dead, and the Blessing didn't work—which I'd already figured out. Oh, he also told me that he and Alec made a truce. He'd obviously been at Milo's a lot, as he'd met my mom."

"When was this? Date, day, time." And when I told her, she said, "Jeez, I can't believe this."

"Can't believe what?" I said and added, "Does your 'this' have anything to do with the phone calls that Tony and Milo got? After which, Tony, I might add, then attacked me with a sword."

"What?" This time it was Nat who stood up and then sat down again. She set her elbows on her knees and covered her face with her hands. "I was normal when I woke up today. Do I look normal?" The hands dropped. "No, don't answer that. You shouldn't even be here."

"But I am," I said, getting impatient. "Look, if this is a bogus idea, then I'll go home again."

"What's *your* 'this'?" Nat asked.

"To find out what's going on with Ruli. Because I saw this weird apparition where she—Nat, are you all right?"

Nat's jaw had sagged.

"So you really don't know?" she whispered.

"Know. What?" I said with careful patience.

"Ruli," Natalie said as carefully, "is dead."

SIX

"**D**EAD? WHAT HAPPENED?"

"The car brodied off a cliff, because . . . no. There's enough rumor going around."

Every nerve in my body zinged with that painful internal shock then went cold. "Okay. Tony did *not* tell me that. If he knew. But . . . he had to. After his mystery phone call, he came out and said 'this particular day.' Then he said he doesn't believe in coincidence. What coincidence, and why wouldn't he *tell* me, for heaven's sake, instead of attacking me like a lunatic and calling me a liar?"

Nat sighed. "I *really* don't want to get into rumors. I wouldn't say this in front of any of them." On the last word, she jerked her thumb over her shoulder, in the direction of the southeast end of the city, where the aristocrats had their city houses, along with the rest of Dobrenica's VIP crowd. "But I think there's something hinky about the whole thing. However. I said I wouldn't do rumor, so here's the Wikipedia on what's been corroborated. On Monday, Ruli wanted to leave for Paris. Family shindig for the holiday. Alec took off with her down the south road toward the border in that cool ride of his."

"The Daimler?"

"That's the one. Usually they do the border run with a couple of Vigilzhi on motorcycles, you know, going in front. But they left without them, straight into a snow flurry. See what I mean about hinky? Anyway, the roads get dangerous fast. When the Vigilzhi went looking for them, they saw a column of smoke. Discovered the car had gone over a cliff."

I thought my heart would stop. "Alec?"

"Fine, he's fine." She waved me down. "When the guys got off their cycles to take a look, they found Alec lying on an outcropping a few yards down. No broken bones, though he was pretty bruised up. Ruli's purse was there with him. The car was on fire below, and the purse made them fear the worst because there was no sign of her. But there was no way to climb down. They took Alec back to the palace and rushed a team with rappelling stuff back to the spot, but by then the car was burned out. They found Ruli's bones inside." She grimaced and shook her head.

"What caused the crash? Ice?"

"He doesn't remember the accident. Clocked his head on a rock, and came to when they got him onto one of the motorcycles." She hesitated, rubbed her eyes again, then dropped her hands. "And that's all I know for sure."

The mental and emotional jolt was like a 7.2 earthquake at 3:00 a.m.

"My turn," she said, "'Apparition'?"

"I guess she was a ghost, then," I said, numb with shock. "But it was so *different*." I told her what I'd seen. "She faded so slowly that I didn't think she was actually dead. Not *dead* dead. I mean, the one I saw a few days before that survived—oh, never mind that. This stuff is so new to me! Look, tell me this: What time would that have been here? Was it when the accident happened?"

"Around midnight in New York . . . that would have been . . . um, early Tuesday morning, I'm pretty sure." She counted rapidly on her fingers. "And the accident happened Monday, late in the day."

"Okay, then already my theory is bust. About her ghost, or apparition, appearing when she died." I thought again of Ron, and shook my head. "I really do not understand how that stuff works, because last summer I saw ghosts of people who lived centuries ago. Geez, and I thought it out so carefully. Stay with the Waleskas, who I know. Swear them to secrecy. Come to you and find out how to contact Ruli without hassle. Then . . . find out why she appeared in a window reflection to ask me for help."

Nat waved away the window reflection. "Coming to me was good, but the Waleskas? You still don't have a clue, dude. Your being here is probably all over the valley by now."

"But they promised."

"Sure." She shrugged. "Look, I don't want to say anything against them. I checked them out after you left, when I was trying to figure out if you'd really busted out of Dobrenica. The young teen I'd trust, Theresa? And the older teen, what's her name, Tania? Yeah. She's an odd duck—someone told me she used to sit on the roof ridgepole and talk to imaginary friends when she was a kid. Played with cats and rats. Actually, I kinda like the sound of that! Anyway, she's gotten locked into the Salfmatta sorority, so you can bet she'd keep her lip zipped."

Salfmatta sorority—the Salfmattas were the ones who were kind of like healers and kind of like mages, near as I could tell. My grandmother's old governess, Tante Mina, was one. I'd stayed with her after I escaped from Tony, and she'd clued me in about the Blessing, among other things.

"I'd also trust the married sister," Nat went on. "But the mother is a businesswoman. I'm sure she promised you. I'm sure she even meant whatever she promised. But my guess is she couldn't resist telling her sister. They have this sort of rivalry thing going. The sister owns the laundry at that end of town—you know how electricity has been. Even with the dam, few people have washers and dryers. The laundry is like a social center. That goes back about ten centuries. And Madam Waleska's sister has the fastest mouth east of Frankfurt."

"So what should I do? I'd better get on the first vehicle I can. I do not want Alec to find out I was here. Not with his wife barely cold. It's way too sickening."

"Safe bet he already knows," she said and leaned forward, elbows on her knees. "Kim, I would agree normally. But this isn't a normal situation."

"Do you mean politics, or something else?"

She grimaced and looked around her cluttered room as if seeking clues.

"Okay," I said, striving to sound reasonable. "So tell me this, Wikipedia. What would be worse: For me to go away without seeing him, or to see him?" And when she hesitated, still not meeting my eyes, I asked, "What did Alec say when I left last summer?"

Nat faked a surprised look. "Alec? Say anything?"

I rubbed my knuckles across my burning eyes. "Oh, crap, I thought I'd cried the last tears in September."

Nat yanked a box of tissues from among her welter of pillows and blew her nose defiantly. "Twit!" She eyed me, her own face flushed, eyes pink. "Yeah, it was bad. For about a week. He was here every day, ostensibly in case you sent a message, but I knew it was ol' Mama Nat's American accent he wanted to hear. Then he stopped coming after the wedding, and I've only seen him once since—public appearances don't count—when I was lunching with Beka and he showed up at her place."

"Beka?"

"Ridotski. I told you about her."

I remembered now. During the summer, Tony's mother, on the pretense of being the loving aunt welcoming the new niece, had controlled my social schedule, making sure I never met any of Alec's friends. I knew three things about this Beka Ridotski: that she was the granddaughter of the Prime Minister; she taught at the Temple School; and, at one time, she and Alec had been an item.

I squashed questions I had no right to ask, and said, "I left so Alec wouldn't be forced to make a choice."

"Very honorable and noble, but it didn't occur to you that he might not want it made for him?"

"Tony said that, too."

"*In*-teresting. Well, there's no knowing what's going on in Tony's pointy little head, so we'll forget him for now. I've got five minutes left before my next patient. Kim, I think, all things considered, it would be better if you get the straight scoop directly from Alec. Since you're here."

"So what's the protocol?"

"Get your keister over to the palace. Oh, it's already too late today. He usually leaves there by this time, and I have no idea where he goes these days."

"You mean he's not in the hospital?"

"Alec?" She threw up her hands in mock surprise. "Take R&R like a normal person? He was back at work the next morning. All things considered, probably better if you don't go chasing all over the city trying to find him. First thing in the morning, go to the main gate. My guess is the Vigilzhi will wave you right in, and direct you to the right place."

Wave me right in. So much for the anonymity of winter clothing.

"Got it," I said, rising.

She grinned and bopped me lightly on the shoulder. "Despite my having hexed you steadily for months, I think you're good people. Go for it. Anything I can do—"

"If you'll promise me one thing?"

"Yeah?"

I put my hands to my heart. "You'll pick up the pieces after, whatever happens."

She laughed again. "Dude. Report back. I want the full Monty."

I might not get even a partial Monty, I thought as I bundled up and left. But I was going to try.

Darkness had descended during the short time I was inside, and the temperature had dropped even farther, which I hadn't thought possible. I found an empty inkri at the bottom of Nat's street and, with gratitude, hailed the driver. As the sleigh skidded downhill toward the Waleskas', the frigid air carried the melodic rise and fall of singing, sweet and pure as the shivering of crystal. Somewhere, people wandered about singing carols. The smell of braised or baked pork was pungent, and I wondered if some strata of Dobreni society celebrated a version of the Romanian Ignat.

When I reached the inn, Madam offered to serve me dinner and brought enough food for a platoon of marines. I ate, read until my eyes swam, and went to bed early, listening to the faint sounds of carolers walking up and down the streets.

The chill that had gripped my bones when Natalie told me Ruli was dead did not fade. When I got out of bed to figure out how to turn up the radiator, I discovered that my room was icy. I burrowed down in the thick coverlet and shut my eyes . . . and spent the rest of the night waking up from heart-pounding nightmares. Car crashes, fires, a horrible dream about standing in a garden looking up as snow fell, my limbs gradually freezing as the air got colder and colder.

I woke to the bleak, watery light of a winter dawn. My hands and feet were numb with cold. I felt the radiator. Warm. But the warmth seemed to dissipate within inches.

My head throbbed, my skin hurt. Noises were sharp, almost distorted. I went to the bathroom, relieved to find it empty in spite of all those guests. As the hot water slowly filled the tub, I wondered if I was getting sick—not only my body, but the entire world seemed askew. Guilt for coming here? I peered in the small mirror on the old plaster wall, glaring at my own bloodshot eyes.

Help me, Ruli had said.

I got into the tub, concentrated on my tai chi breathing as I soaked, and when I got out of the bath, I moved through some of the tai chi forms I'd been learning, as I had not found a fencing club in Fort Williams. Then I went down to a good breakfast and, after eating, felt human enough to face the interview I wanted. Dreaded. Wanted.

How could I help Ruli now? How could I help *him*? Because one thing I was sure of: There was no way that he would cause an 'accident' just to get rid of an inconvenient wife, no matter what rumors might be circulating. Rumors, I was willing to bet any sum of money, had to have at their center Tony's mother, the evil duchess, who had once smilingly asked me to call her Tante Sisi.

By ten I reached the great gates of the Royal Residence.

Its walls gleamed warmly gold in the wintry sunlight, reminding me again of Schönbrunn Palace outside Vienna. The snow-covered grounds were smooth either side of the pathway. Few people were around—no tourists lined up at the gate or shuffling behind a guide. A Vigilzhi in the well-remembered blue-piped-with-scarlet uniform, caped and gloved, peered at me. I hadn't tried to hide my face. Sure enough, his eyes widened. Then his expression went all official and blank as he saluted me and opened the ornate carved door.

"I wish to speak with the Statthalter," I said in Dobreni. I could see my breath.

He gave me a short bow. "Please. Go to the double door there, in the south wing."

The palace is shaped kind of like an E with a bent spine. The south wing lay to the left. Inside that door waited a young guy with a shock of curly black hair resolutely tamed. He, too, wore a Vigilzhi uniform, but with no insignia and no cap. Maybe a cadet. His eyes widened when he saw me. They were startlingly green. "Good day, Mam'zelle," he said in careful French that sounded rehearsed. "Please to come this way."

I followed him into the business wing of the palace, where the parquet floors were covered with rugs to protect the old wood, and where ceilings were smooth plaster above rococo molding instead of fabulous wood-carvings and paintings. As we walked, I considered and reconsidered what to say to Alec.

Then the cadet opened a set of double doors that had to date back to the seventeenth century.

By that time, I felt as if my nerves had poked through my skin, and though warmth emanated from the enormous china stove in the corner, I shivered. In the middle of the room was a splendid baroque era rosewood desk. A woman was seated there, and standing behind her, his arms reaching around her to rest on the tops of her hands, was Alec.

My brain shut down, and I stumbled to a stop.

They looked up as one. For about a hundred years I took in those shocked honey-brown eyes the same shade as my own, and Alec's enigmatic blue-gray gaze above.

Then Alec straightened up. I was peripherally aware of the woman putting something in her purse as he said, "Kim. Welcome back." It was almost a question.

The woman's expression smoothed to blandness.

"Uh." My voice came out sounding like someone else's. "I'm intruding. I can . . ." I waved my hand in a circle.

The woman got to her feet—not that she had far to go. She was short, built in the petite version of the pear shape, with a pointed face, a broad forehead, and a cloud of curly dark hair twisted up simply but in a way that framed her face with wispy tendrils. She wore a plain pearl-gray shirt-waist dress, but it was so stylish it had to have come from Paris.

Alec pinched his fingers to his forehead as though his head hurt. "Kim, this is Rebekah Ridotski. Beka, Kim Murray."

Beka smiled at me. "Hello." She flicked a glance at Alec. Her English was French-accented. "I'll see you tonight, then?"

He assented with a gesture. She stepped around the desk and whisked herself out, leaving a whiff of expensive scent as the door shut behind her with a decisive click.

I approached the desk but stayed on my side of it.

Alec looked exactly the same—wearing slacks, a good shirt, a hint of a tie at the V neck of a dark woolen sweater-vest. His eyes, the color of clouds on a rainy day, were steady. But he wasn't exactly the same; there were healing bruises on one side of his forehead and along his jaw. The cobalt Ysvorod signet ring was on the little finger of his left hand, and on the ring finger of his right he wore a plain gold band.

And he stayed there, on the other side of that huge desk.

I stood poised to close the distance between us, though I knew it would be wrong, that whatever his relationship had been with Ruli, he'd just lost her in a horrible way. "Alec, I'm sorry about what happened. I really, truly did not know. Until I got here. And Nat told me just now."

"You just got here?" Alec repeated, sounding distracted the way you do when way too much is going on at once.

"Well, yesterday. On the train. You knew I was here? I told the Waleskas not to blab about—"

He was catching up; he gave me a look, with a hint of the old humor.

"Okay, old news before I even got to them. But how? I'd swear no one could have recognized me after I got off the . . . oh. Right. The train conductors. I'm sorry, Alec. Nat did warn me. But the whole concept of my being 'a person of interest' seems totally alien to me. Anyway, I came because . . ." It was difficult to get the words out, because modern life makes it too easy to scorn what we don't understand. But it was too important not to try. "The other night. On our way to London. I saw a vision of Ruli."

He stilled, almost a recoil. It was like I'd hit him. The words *Help me* froze right there in my mouth. What if he took them as accusation, and hard on that was the betraying thought: What if he *was* the cause?

No. Every cell in my body revolted against that notion. No matter how disastrous a marriage it might have been, Alec would not do something so evil as to cause an accident.

Or so stupid.

"A vision?" he repeated.

The instinct to avoid that was as overwhelming as the instinct to talk to him, to regain the understanding between us. But where to start?

I looked around wildly for any subject to break the nightmarish silence stretching out into *infinity*. "Vision. Hallucination, maybe, caused by jetlag. Do you know now *long* I have been traveling?" I babbled. "This country is beautiful even in winter. On the ride up I kept wondering if Wordsworth had ever been here—'Black drizzling crags that spake by the wayside—'"

His smile flickered, and the quote came automatically. "'As if a voice were in them. . . . '"

He stopped himself before *the sick sight*.

Urgh. Only *I* could commit a poetical faux pas! I said quickly, "It figures you'd know 'Simplon Pass.' Did you think of it when riding the train up here, when you were a kid?"

But it was too late. The smile was gone, and I knew without any mysterious visions that we were right back where we'd started, no matter how much either of us would rather have avoided it: Ruli. "Yes," he said, neutral and polite.

I said, "I saw Tony in London."

I may as well have hit him. He didn't quite recoil this time, but his chin lifted, and if possible he tensed up even more.

I blundered determinedly on. "He came over to meet my grandmother, but she was—your dad was—Tony and I were touristing around when he got a phone call, and—something was very wrong, but he wouldn't tell me what it was."

I couldn't bear to see that painful question in Alec's tense face, the beautiful, dear face that I had tried not to think about even though I was reading the poetry he loved and practicing his language. And dreaming about him at night.

"Kim," Alec began. "We should probably—"

There was a polite knock at an inner door, followed by muffled words in Dobreni: "Statthalter, they are all here but the Prime Minister."

"A moment," Alec called.

Noooo! Not with us like this, on opposite sides of the room, and the tension, the *questions* between us.

I said quickly, "Alec, before anything else, I wanted to apologize for leaving last summer without talking to you."

Our gazes finally met, and personal space made that seven-points-on-the-Richter-scale shift to intimate space. The urge to run to him was almost overpowering. I watched his eyes, his hands, for the green light . . . and he looked down at the papers waiting on the desk, his long eyelashes effective shutters.

The last time we'd seen each other, I spent the night within the circle of his arms. The chemistry between us was as powerful as ever (and I discovered that I was gripping the edge of the desk) but something was definitely wrong, horribly and painfully out of balance.

Because his wife just died, and you have her face. Doh!

I finished numbly, "I really thought I was doing the right thing."

"I know." He made an effort I could feel in my own bones and muscles. "You thought you were sparing me from . . ." He pinched his fingers between his brows again. The signet ring glimmered, a cobalt blue teardrop. "You thought you were doing the honorable thing," he said. "I know you well enough to have been fairly certain about that."

"Could I have possibly called it more wrong?"

As if the words were wrung out of him, he said, "Kim, I do not want you to take this the wrong way, but I wish you had not come."

Sick and miserable, I gazed at him, completely unable to speak.

"No." He flung up his hand in a sharp gesture. "No, I take that back. Please don't walk out of here thinking. . . . A week ago, I would have welcomed you more than—" I'd never heard him speak so wildly, so disjointedly. I felt the effort he made to stop, to take a deep breath. "Kim. I am afraid there's going to be trouble. I don't yet know how much, but one thing I want to prevent if I possibly can, is your being dragged into it."

"Alec, I would do anything to help you. I hope you know that."

"I do." He dropped his hand and moved to a rosewood Louis XV cabinet in the far corner. "And I want you to know how glad I am to see you. In spite of . . . everything going on. But I—"

Another knock, more insistent than the first.

Alec's head lifted sharply, the fine skin over his cheekbones tense. "I can't make them wait any longer. We'll have to talk later. It's the best I can do at the moment."

"Alec."

He opened the glass door in the cabinet and removed a crystal decanter. At the sound of his name—perhaps at the sound of me saying his name—he jerked around, as though I'd reached inside him and yanked.

"If you want me to leave Dobrenica," I offered, "say the word. You're the one in crisis mode right now. What's best for you?"

"The Prime Minister has arrived," came that muffled voice from behind the inner door.

"It's too—"

Late?

He didn't say the word. I felt it and so, heard the sidestep in his tone. "It's too confusing right now. That is, there is too much going on. Let's talk later, shall we?" As he spoke he poured something from the decanter into his coffee mug.

Logic insisted I should get out of the country—go to the air field, since the train only ran once a week or so. But instinct clamored for me to stay, to fight against whatever it was that threatened him, to take a stand at his side.

"I'll be at the inn," I said and opened the door to the hall.

I slipped out—

And found Rebekah Ridotski waiting for me.

SEVEN

"**WHY ARE YOU HERE?**" Beka's English flared with a strong French accent.

"I . . ." Though I had no right to complain if Beka and Alec were an item, I also didn't owe her any answers. "Why do you need to know?"

"Because it is I who must pick up the pieces after you—" She made a little shrug, then finished with the French verb *déguerpir*.

It means "take off" or, closer, "ditch." *Ditch Dobrenica? Ditch Alec?* "Pick up the pieces" was what I'd said to Nat.

I answered, "What makes you think I'll do anything of the kind?"

I expected her to dismiss me or, worst case, shoot back something hostile. Instead, her chin lifted slightly. "Permit me another question. Have you seen Natalie?"

"I was there yesterday."

"Perhaps we should visit her together."

I hesitated, then thought, *I came here to help.* I made a "lead on" shoot with my forefinger, then followed Beka down the icy hallway and through the servants' door to the side of the palace, where there was a half-cleared parking lot. From the haphazard look of the clearance, it was evident they did not have any snow plows. The work was done by grunt force.

Last in a modest row of examples from over five decades of auto manufacture was a sporty French model. It felt unreal to climb into a car with the woman who had had Alec's arms around her.

It felt more unreal that Ruli was dead.

Beka negotiated slowly past the mounds of slush onto a slippery cobblestoned street that had been cleared, then asked polite questions about my journey. My replies were equally polite efforts, barren of content but crammed with phatic cooperation as the car slid on the icy street then caught, slid and caught.

She nosed down the boulevard leading to the huge traffic circle built around the statue of St. Xanpia, where the streetcar looped around. From there, we continued under the triumphal arch and on past nineteenth-century buildings with the ubiquitous tall windows, iron grating, and Palladian embellishments. Our struggle at conversation was drowned by the clatter of tires on cobblestones, and we abandoned talk—no doubt as big a relief to her as it was to me.

We reached the Khonzhinya District, where Nat lived. Most of the houses dated back to the eighteenth century, with a few newer. There were fewer cleared streets.

Beka parked around the corner from Nat's with the ease of habit, and we crunched into the crusty slush alongside the road, chins down into our coats. From the low sky, flakes of snow dropped. I wondered if it was still ninety degrees in LA.

An older woman was leaving. Nat looked past her at me and said, "Did you chicken out?" Then she saw Beka, and her brows shot up. "Dude!"

Beka said with a hint of irony, "You can offer us some of your vile coffee."

"Get in here before all my warm air escapes," Nat replied.

She shut the door, and we stood in the tiny vestibule, again in one another's personal space as we shed gloves and scarves and hats and coats, hanging them on the row of hooks Nat had bolted to the bare plaster wall. Beka's face was turned away, so all I saw was her profile, her expression closed.

Nat called, "I'm finishing a patient. Grab a sitz."

Beka gestured for me to take the armchair. I did, then noticed that the other two would be sitting side by side on the couch, staring at me like a two woman jury.

I made a business of looking around so I wouldn't have to sit there staring, or not-staring, at the person Alec was going to meet later tonight.

From the back Nat yelled, "Kim! Tell her who attacked you in London."

"Tony," I said, and when Beka's lips parted, I added, "With a sword."

Her eyes widened. "La la!"

Two sets of footsteps went down the outer hall. The second pair was Nat, who reappeared holding a tray, trailing the mixed aromas of astringent soap and fine black tea. "Water was already boiling for washing up my instruments."

Beka put her chin on her hands and studied me, eyes narrowed.

"I gotta say, I thought nothing I ever heard about that guy would surprise me." Nat flopped down next to Beka, then handed her a cup. "But that wins the coconut. Try this, Bek. It's concentrate from Hawaiian coffee." She waved at me. "He attacked you. Like that. Out of the blue. Does he have swords all over the house? *Of course* he's got a stash of swords. Probably guns and grenades, too."

"Maybe he's just nuts," I said. "Like his insisting there's no magic, but vampires totally exist."

"They do." Beka sipped. "Ah. Much better."

"Vampires?" I repeated, turning to Nat.

She shrugged, hands out. "News to me. I thought they were part of the hill myths."

"I hope they remain unknown. I would love it if they faded to myth," Beka said, and turned to me. "Did he say why he attacked you?"

"He said it was to make me tell the truth. I guess I earned that, lying like a rug to his family last summer. Though he knows why I did it."

Beka and Nat each looked the other's way, just for a second. I couldn't read anything from that brief meeting of eyes, except that whatever I'd said carried some significance that they were not going to share, because then Nat chuckled, a pleasantly rusty sound. "They were being buttheads. Especially his mother. Geez, she tried to have you offed!"

"I have not forgotten," I said, and was going to say that I hoped she was still in Paris, but of course she wouldn't be. Not after her daughter's accident. "Is the duchess in the country?" I asked.

Beka said, "Sisi von Mecklundburg? Alec told me this morning that they are . . . expected." She glanced at her watch. "Within an hour."

Nat hoisted her mug. "Usually this time of year there are parties, balls, concerts, right up until the twelfth day of Christmas, or what the Eastern Orthodox gang call Theophany. When there's a really snazzy ball, we minions gather along St. Mihal Bridge to watch the sleighs cruise by. People decorate 'em up."

Beka uttered a soft laugh at the word "minions." "We have canceled the parties, at least through the date of the funeral. We are waiting to see what the von Mecklundburgs will say about the New Year's Eve gala they were organizing in honor of the new opera house. Ruli was to host it. Her first formal gesture as Madam Statthalter." Beka got up and said to Nat, "I did not have time to visit the ladies' at the palace. May I?"

Nat jerked her thumb over her shoulder. "You know where it is."

When she was gone, I discovered Nat staring at me with a puzzled, wary expression. Nat said, "You tracked her like you're a bomb sniffer and she's about to plant a nuke."

"I can't figure her out," I said.

Natalie thumped her elbows on her knees. "Geez, you're not going to go all high school catfight on me, are ya?"

"Like I have any grounds," I said. "And if you knew how I grew up . . . but you don't. I'm trying to understand where everyone is coming from."

"Okay, that's cool. So how did it go with Alec?"

"It was horrible." I told her what he'd said, then finished, "It was like it actually *hurt* him to see me. That's even worse than 'I'm over you.' Something is really wrong."

"Ya think?"

"I mean, besides the accident. Because I know that was an accident. I don't believe for a second it could have been anything else." I shivered again, glanced at that empty spot on the couch and said, "So in the nature of figuring out what's going on in his life, are Alec and Beka close?"

"Close, yes. How close, no idea." Nat started piling the dishes together. "Yeah, she's over here often, and yeah, we talk about him, but like I said, I haven't seen him but once, and she doesn't tell me everything."

"Got it."

"What was that about your growing up?" she asked.

"Mom was a hippie. Free love, drugs, rock and roll. Except she liked Wagner and Puccini."

"Wow. Just your Mom?"

"Dad was too much of a geek," I said. "Mom didn't settle down until she was forty. That is, she got married. Let's just say she was in love with being in love. But she always came home after her romances."

Nat's brows rose. "Your mom was a player? Well, if she hit her twenties during the sixties, yeah, I guess that would make sense. I somehow didn't picture that, you know, with your grandmother added in. The princess thing and all."

Her tone wasn't the least nasty. Natalie had told me during the summer that monogamy was not her style. So I said, "Dad once told me that people are going to do what they're going to do, and that jealousy means you've got some self-esteem issues of your own."

"Heh."

"As for Gran, I don't know how she felt, but she and Mom have always been tight in spite of being completely different in pretty much every way possible. There was no drama. Everything mellow. It took until pretty recently for me to see how hard everyone worked on their relationship. Including Mom."

The distant door opened, loud enough that I wondered if Beka had done it on purpose, as a polite warning, in case we were dishing the dirt on her. I was feeling weirder by the second.

"I think I'd like to meet the 'rents," Nat said.

"I can't picture them here," I admitted. "I still have trouble believing *I'm* here."

Beka reappeared. She sat down, her movements neat, even fluid. I wondered if she'd had ballet training. Like me.

Now I had the two woman jury looking at me expectantly. Waiting for testimony? "Okay, here's where I'm coming from," I said. "You may not believe me. I sure can't prove it, because both times in the last week that I saw. . . someone not in their body, I was around other people, and nobody saw what I saw."

I paused. Neither of them said anything.

"One of these apparitions was Ruli. Monday night, around midnight, Ruli appeared in a store window reflection and asked me to help her, and I'm wondering if maybe I should try to do that in spite of . . . her accident. *Because* of her accident. But I keep thinking, Why would she call to *me*? Where do I start?" I couldn't make myself look Beka's way.

"Is that question rhetorical, or is it 'Dear wise Nat, what do you suggest I do?'"

"Dear wise Nat, what do you suggest I do?"

"Oooh, say it again!" Nat crossed her arms across her chest and hugged herself, then she leaned forward, serious. "Aside from questions of apparitions, ghosts, and vampires, none of which I can help with, the problem seems to be that you don't know anybody but me and Alec, so doing a Sherlock Holmes is going to be tough."

Nat and Beka both glanced at the clock ticking on a cluttered side table. It was a wind-up clock, because electricity was still unreliable in Dobrenica. Or people believed it was, though the hydroelectric dam that Alec and Milo had struggled to finance had been supplying the city for almost ten years.

Nat went on, "Seems to me that you'd have to start your investigating with her relatives." She sat back, making the king's X with her fingers. "Better you than me."

Beka said, "I was going to suggest that you come to my wreath party tonight. They will all be there."

"The von Mecklundburgs or the vampires?" I asked.

Nat said wickedly, "Is there any difference?"

EIGHT

B EKA GAVE NAT one of those looks that teachers give the kid who just threw a spitball as I asked, "What's a wreath party?"

"A mourning custom in our country."

"Tell me about the mourning customs," I said. "I don't want to do something wrong." *More wrong than showing up in the first place?*

They exchanged another of those quick glances, then Beka said in that neutral tone of a teacher, "The country people gather at dawn each day to sing laments for Madam Statthalter, until she is buried. The city people all have fir wreaths on the door, with a star."

"I saw those," I said. "I thought they were Christmas decorations."

Beka said, "In this part of the world, there is an old belief that for every person there is a tree and a star. You put a replica on the door when someone in the family dies, or a friend. Or a leader."

"Okay," I said. "And tonight?"

"Traditionally, the others of the five families host a wreath-gathering for the bereaved family, and on the sixth day is the funeral. This custom dates back to . . ."

The five families. Those were the highest ranking clans, the ones who'd been kicking the crown around between them for centuries. The highest number of kings came from Gran's family, the Dsarets. Second runner up was Alec's family, the Ysvorods. Tony and Ruli's gang, the von Mecklundburgs, had mostly hooked up with royal princes and princesses. Remaining were the Trasyemovas and Beka's family, the Ridotskis. I knew zip about either of these, having only met one Trasyemova, a teenager, at the masquerade ball last summer, before Tony abducted me right off the ballroom floor.

I shifted my attention back to Beka. ". . . disrupted by the war years, and the absence of the Dsarets. There are of course two bereaved families, but as Milo's health has kept him in London, Alec is alone of his, so there will be only one party. My grandfather is co-hosting tonight's event, with my mother." She raised her perfectly groomed winged brows and tipped her head. "I invite you as my guest."

"But won't they be talking about Ruli? Won't that be horrible if I'm there? They wouldn't expect me to give a testimonial, would they?"

"No, no," Beka said. "Sometimes the person is remembered, but it is entirely informal. Wreath parties were meant as social cheering for the bereaved—a chance for the five families to be together. The formal testimonials, as you say, are done at the vigil, the night before the funeral."

"I think it's a great idea!" Nat exclaimed, then gave me a scrutinizing glance. "Even though there won't be any dancing or whoopee, Beka's crowd isn't quite the thrift store types. You got any fancy clothes?"

"I bought two nice outfits in London. In case. That'll have to do," I said quickly. "I'm not borrowing any more of Ruli's clothes. It's too creepy."

Beka looked surprised. "We do have stores in Riev." Then she made a slight grimace of regret. "Ah, I beg your pardon. I thought . . ."

You thought about the Dsaret Treasure.

Which wasn't supposed to exist, as far as the world was aware. Milo and a handful of old folks knew what Gran's dad had done to liquidate and hide the royal treasure before World War II. Alec had been put in charge of it. Tony wanted to find it.

I knew that the Prime Minister was in on the secret. I wondered if he had told Beka—or Alec had.

That opened up a whole new can of wigglers, but I forced my mind back on topic. "I only brought enough cash for a couple days. I do have a credit card, but something—" *Alec said* "—that those are rare around here."

"Try useless," Nat said, grinning.

"I would think . . ." Beka's brows rose, and she started again. "These things can be arranged. In any case, come to Ridotski House at eight."

"Is dark green okay, or do I need something black? I noticed everyone wearing dark colors."

Beka and Nat both nodded, and Beka said, "People will wear subdued colors—gray is most common—until after the funeral. Dark green will be fine."

She rose. "I had better return, for there is much to do."

Nat waved at us both. "And I've got three patients coming in this afternoon."

Beka and I crowded into the little vestibule in forced proximity once again, as we loaded on all that winter gear. She offered me a ride—I showed her my tokens—each of us determinedly polite. Then she was gone with a quick lift of her hand, and I started slipping and sliding toward the street car or an inkri, whichever came first.

As soon as I stepped on the streetcar, my mood plunged. I knew how to handle a sword, even if I was out of practice. But the social duel was so not in this Los Angeles girl's training. Well, at least I wasn't pretending to be Ruli, like last summer.

That made me wince.

When I opened the door to my room, I entered a cloudbank of *cold*. There was my reflection in the wood-framed mirror on the inside of the wardrobe door. In the bleak, thin light, my face looked bleached, almost skull-like.

This wasn't winter cold. The radiator was burbling along contentedly. It had to be the refrigerator-ice of ghost air, only it snapped the hairs on my arms and the back of my neck like the shock of static electricity.

"Ruli?" I said. No visions, no flickering lights answered me. "Ruli, if that's you, I came to help you out. I don't know if that makes a difference."

No ghost appeared, but the numbing cold gradually faded, leaving pleasant warmth and the sound of the radiator hissing to itself. "Okay, so that was . . . weird," I said. "I really wish you'd do something ghostly. Let me know you're listening, so I don't feel like a complete dork standing here talking to an empty room."

Zip.

So I went downstairs to get some lunch.

Madam beamed when I appeared, and she happily bustled me to the corner table by two windows. Then, with a flourish, she pulled out a chair, giving me the table all to myself. After, she went straight back to the group who'd shoved two tables together at the front of the room.

As it was early afternoon, and the regular lunchtime was pretty much over, I'd figured that these had to be Madam's relatives, and maybe some of her local friends.

Anna's husband Josip headed toward me, bringing a plate of savory pork-stuffed baked cabbage leaves, aromatic with caramelized onion and garlic, and a couple of slices of the sweet bread made with layers of ground nuts and raisins soaked in rum.

I dug in. At the long table Madam lowered her voice to a rumble. For such a small woman, she had an amazingly deep voice. As she spoke, I could feel the eye-tracks.

Then her characteristic bustling step approached.

To my surprise, it wasn't more food or drink. "Mademoiselle Dsaret."

Dsaret? This was her idea of protecting my identity? Way to be unclear on the concept! Since I'd blown the whole anonymity thing anyway, there was no use in correcting her.

"May I trouble you with a question?" she went on, hands folded before her apron. "I would not ask, but this is from my own cousin's sister-by-marriage."

"Certainly." To save her from having to act as go-between (though I realized later she might have relished that very thing) I got up and headed for the long table.

Most of the people looked like they were related to her—narrow skulls, dark hair with that reddish tinge, dark eyes. One old woman was fair-haired. The youngest one there, a boy who looked about nineteen, had curly black hair and the sparse beginnings of a mustache.

"Hello," I said in Dobreni. "I understand you have a question for me?"

From the shiftings and exchanged looks, I got the sense that I'd made a mistake. Of course. It's always easier to nose into the business of a total stranger if your question is carried by someone else, and no one is face-to-face.

Trying to get past the social fumble, I said, "Well, I have a question for you. I love Dobrenica. But I didn't see much when I was here before. What do you suggest I visit?"

The smiles and bright looks made it clear that I'd said the right thing.

The grandfather spoke first. "You must see the museum. It is on St. Ladislas Street, next to where we are building the opera house. Did you know that we shall have our own opera house?"

The others looked at me with expectation, so I said, "You didn't have one before?"

Madam Waleska's old father, who lived at the inn, said, "The palace did. We in service could stand in the gallery, but before the war, the city's only public spaces were the cathedral and the temple."

"Now Riev will have its opera house, where anyone can go," a younger woman put in.

An older one added in an undertone, "If they can get chairs."

There were some significant looks exchanged. "You must hear the children's choir at midnight mass," the dark-haired grandmother said, and the subject of the unfinished opera house was closed. "Children from the mountains as well as the valley are chosen."

"Oh, you must hear the concert at the music school on New Year's Eve."

"You must have the special cheesecake at Branduska's Bakery . . ."

". . . the Roman church on the mountain . . ."

"You must visit the Capuchins. They sell the best *zhoumnyar* in the . . ."

". . . old ruined Ysvorod castle, where they held off the Swedes all winter in sixteen thirty—"

"—before we left the Polish kingdom and had to make our treaty with the Hapsburgs," the grandfather said, with as much sorrow as if it had happened three months ago and not three centuries.

The suggestions came so fast they overlapped.

I went to get my food, and they squeezed up, freeing a space between the black-haired boy and a solid woman Mom's age whose voice was even deeper than Madam's.

The suggestions were still coming: this shop, those glass windows at Something House, the catacombs near the ancient mine, the new dam.

Finally the woman to my right said politely. "Did you hear about the death of Madam Statthalter from the radio? The news was broadcast all the way to Paris?"

They still think I grew up in France. When I'd first arrived at the inn, I'd signed the register as Mademoiselle Atelier—the name I'd grown up believing was my mother's maiden name. These people seemed to have accepted that as an incognito.

I was saved from having to answer by the appearance of Theresa, the youngest Waleska girl, a coltish, sober-faced teen who had been of enormous help to me during summer. She wore a skirt of robin's egg blue, a blouse embroidered with holly leaves and buds, and a silk rose tucked into one of her dark braids. I wondered if this was Dobreni teen fashion.

She gave me a happy smile. "We have been decorating the cathedral for tonight. Will you come to the midnight mass?"

"I'm invited to a gathering tonight."

"Yes, the Ridotski wreath gathering. Everyone knows about that. But they will end by eleven, so that those who wish may attend mass," Theresa said.

Attending a church service was not my idea of fun, nor did I see how it would help anyone, but I couldn't say no to that earnest face.

My hesitation prompted them into speech again—as, and all the while the black-haired boy twiddled his fingers, shifted one bony shoulder then the other, and shuffled his feet under the chair. When his elders let him get a word in, he spoke in a voice still breaking, "Why did you leave Dobrenica, Mademoiselle?"

The man across from him beetled his brows. The woman to my right made a scandalized noise. But they all waited for me to answer.

"The only thing I knew before my first visit was that Aurelia von Mecklundburg was to marry the Statthalter. For the Blessing."

Chins lifted, eyes flicked, little stirrings and murmurs indicated that the word *Blessing* had a lot of meaning, if not power.

"Once I met Aurelia, I figured it was better if I went away. I thought it wasn't good if there were two of us here."

"Will you stay, now?" the oldest grandmother asked.

"If it's the right thing to do. I'm not sure about that."

I could see that they wanted to ask me things I couldn't answer, so I got up. "Will you excuse me? I need to get ready."

By the time I got to the top of the stairs. the adrenaline spikes from the morning jaunt followed by this lunch had died away, reminding me how tired I was after a long night of restless non-sleep.

The prospect of Beka's party was filling me with anticipation (seeing Alec) and dread (everyone else). What would be worse? Seeing Alec and Beka together, or Aunt Sisi showing up with Tony in tow? And with sword in hand, in case I wasn't thoroughly humiliated enough.

I swung my arms. That's what I needed, a good workout. For years I'd divided my energies between ballet, fencing, and school. Now I had none of those. My brain felt like a fuel-injected hamster racing around its wheel, and my body was stiff and sluggish.

I dropped and tried a hundred pushups, but my muscles had turned to string by forty-nine. I used to do a hundred just to warm up! Disgusted, I got up and used the back of the little desk chair to work through a full set of barre exercises. I was drenched by the time I forced myself through a set of *battements, grand* and *développé.* My legs shook. It was time to get back into shape.

That used up an hour, leaving a full afternoon and early evening stretching out before me.

"Ruli?" I said to the air.

Nothing.

Can you call a ghost? Ghosts—*Salfmatta*—Nat's careless words: *She turns out to be part of the Salfmatta sorority*—And Tania's shock when I first arrived at the Waleskas' inn. It hit me then, her look of horror—she thought I was Ruli's ghost.

Maybe it was time to have a little talk with Tania.

I went downstairs. The dining room was empty except for Theresa in the middle of changing the tablecloths and setting up for dinner. "Theresa, where's Tania?" I asked.

"She is at the shop. They close at five today," she said, her dark eyes round with question.

"She works for a . . ." I searched my head and did not find the word for optometrist. "She makes lenses, am I right?"

Theresa said somberly, "She is *still* the assistant."

I didn't understand that emphasis on *still*, but I swept right on. "Where is the shop?"

"Go down the lower street." She waved behind her, beyond the terrace. "It's at the first corner." She looked around carefully, then whispered behind her hand, "The lens maker married in September. Tania might not be free to talk."

"Thanks."

The inn was built on a pie slice of land, the pointy part of the triangle being the terrace. The inn fronted on the high street. I pulled all my winter load back on, scarf up to my nose, hat pulled down to my eyelids, hiding my hair. Then I forced the front door open against the fierce wind. In the summer, that sharp corner and the gate were a few steps. In the middle of a snow storm, it seemed a mile.

At least when I got around the corner and started down the lower street, the wind was somewhat blocked by the wall below the inn's terrace. There was my room, high up. It passed out of sight as I made my way down a curving, cobblestone street so narrow a car could not have passed along it. A couple of people struggled against the wind, one clutching a basket. Gender was impossible to detect. We were all bulky shapes, lurching like the zombie apocalypse.

Of the row of shop fronts, only one was lit. The rest of the buildings were plain-fronted boarding houses.

The lens maker displayed various types of wire rimmed glasses in the shop window, as well as photographic lenses for the old-fashioned analog types of cameras. But those weren't all. In the corner was a pretty little lamp with crystal prisms hanging down.

Crystals. I remembered what Ruli had told me on my last day in Dobrenica: crystals were protections. She'd thought the idea of protections mere superstition.

I opened the door, and chimes tinkled above.

Tania Waleska came out, a thin figure in a plain dark brown dress. She looked like a college-age Wednesday Addams. She stopped in surprise when she saw me, then her long, sober face smoothed into politeness. "Mademoiselle?"

Polite caution. She'd been far more friendly in summer. "I have a couple of questions that I think you might be the one to answer," I said,

"TAAAAAn-ya," came a high voice from the back room. "TAAN-ya! Did I not tell you to sweep up these—oh." A short, solid woman appeared, her pale hair pulled up into an aggressive knob squarely on the top of her head. "A customer. The polishing is waiting. I'll tend to her." She shooed Tania with her apron and showed me a lot of teeth.

"I have a question for Tania," I said.

The pale eyes swept over me from knit hat to the hem of my charcoal coat, then the smile vanished like a light put out. "Very well, very well. Tania, you'll tend to the polishing after you help this person." Snap! Went the inner door.

"May I help you?" Tania's manner was polite, not inviting.

Ghosts. Ruli. Crystals. Ruli had told me that her crystal bracelet was a gift from Beka Ridotski. "I was told on my last visit that these crystal prisms are more than decorations."

"They are traditional protections. It is a custom to take them out in sunlight and say novenas over each before we affix the prisms to a lamp or window decoration."

"Protections? Against what?"

"It is a custom in our land. Visitors find it charming, so we sell many."

Visitors find it charming. Was I being fobbed off, or shut out?

Time to try my original question. "When I arrived at the inn yesterday, did you think I was the ghost of Madam Statthalter?"

Her face tightened as soon as I said *ghost* and then flooded with color. I hadn't merely trespassed some boundary, I'd trampled it like a centipede wearing jackboots.

"Sorry, Tania. I know you're busy. I'll, um, go now." I yanked open the door and left.

The cold wind was a relief. Wondering if that disaster of a conversation was a harbinger of the evening, I toiled uphill to the inn.

I found the shared bathroom empty, but when I turned the hot water spigot, there was only a tiny dribble. So I shivered through a barely lukewarm sponge bath. On my way out, I nearly ran down Anna, carrying bedding to an empty room. "Is there a reason this bathroom is always empty?" I asked. "I know you've got a ton of guests."

Anna looked surprised then puzzled. "Is it not understood, you pay extra for it to be yours?"

"Oh."

"Mama says that is what rich people like," Anna explained. "You may bathe as many times in the day as you wish. Though our boiler is not always so good late in the day," she added apologetically.

I was about to explain that I wasn't rich, then thought: *by whose standards?* Instead I asked, "But where do the other guests go?"

"Oh, they come downstairs to ours," Anna said. "Or go up to the new bathroom in the attic. It is all family. They do not mind."

Rich people. Did I act like a privileged snot without knowing it? The problem is, I thought aggrievedly, we are all the hero of our own story, and behavior we think reasonable can look arrogant to someone else.

Finally I stepped back and stared at myself in my forest green dress. Was it properly "subdued?" My hair was in smooth coils, pinned with a beautiful silver leaf clasp my mom had spotted on our shopping foray and gave me as an early Christmas present. Besides my travel boots I'd brought one other pair of shoes, a wickedly expensive pair of black ballerina pumps. Those should be subdued, I thought. Ready or not, here I come.

I said to the air, "Ruli, it would be great if you could appear and give me a hint about the help you needed. Need. Even a ghostly hand pointing in the right direction would be awesome."

After about thirty seconds, I walked downstairs to get my coat.

NINE

———————⚜———————

A S SOON AS I appeared downstairs, Madam was scandalized, waving her arms. "You cannot wear those in the ice!" She pointed at my shoes.

Already I was off to a great start. I grumped upstairs and exchanged the good shoes for the boots. I put the good shoes in a carrier bag and tried a second time to leave, hoping I wouldn't be criminally early—or late. I didn't know how long the inkris took to cross the city.

I bent into the flensing wind and thought about Tania as I tromped along the street, glad of the boots. Even in those, my toes were fast going numb.

There were small covered kiosks like bus stops at certain corners. When I reached one, I was not the only person waiting. A couple muttered softly, and a little boy stamped his feet, either to warm them or to hear the crack and snap of the ice film over the snow. An inkri came along and scooped them up.

The next inkri came along almost immediately, and I climbed aboard. It was only then that I realized I hadn't asked Beka for directions. The cowardly part of me hailed hope for non-comprehension when I said, "Ridotski House?"

The driver gave a short nod, and that was that.

The upper, or southwest, slope of the mountain below the palace was the Beverly Hills of Riev. I knew that Ysvorod House, Alec's home, was a few blocks from Mecklundburg House, which was about ten blocks from the palace. The streets were broad with only a few houses on each, as they had extensive private gardens, by city standards. Ridotski House turned out to be a couple blocks north of Alec's street, along the cliff above the river that bisected the city.

Little of Ridotski House was visible from the street. It lay uphill behind a screen of tall hawthorn interspersed with rowan. Long golden windows spilled light in bars on the snowy driveway, which had been cleared off. Three or four cars were parked to one side, and I glimpsed what seemed to be a stable down a hedge-walled driveway, from which arose the sound of convivial voices.

I paid the inkri driver, who looked at me curiously as he tipped his hat. Then he shook the reins, and the reindeer tripped daintily through the crunchy snow, and away.

Leaving me alone before the carved front door, I had that stomach-sinking sensation I used to get before a ballet performance when I wasn't sure of my steps, or I hadn't had time to warm up properly. But I was here. Ruli had asked for my help, and I was going to try to find out how and why.

As I reached up to rap the door knocker, I felt exactly the way I did the night in the Eyrie when I pulled the rapier off the wall: There was no turning back.

The door immediately opened, and a young man in white jacket and serving gloves smiled a welcome. He led me to a side room where I could take off my coat, and sure enough, there was a bench and a couple of stools for people to sit on and change their shoes.

After that, an older woman led me through an oval entryway that featured two circular ascending staircases at either side, the supports for the banisters carved in patterns of hawthorn branches and leaves. I thought them pretty. I had no idea of their significance.

Beyond the entry lay a long salon that evoked the Renaissance with its restrained Classical Greek and Roman lines. The furnishings had that classical feel, the silk cushions in shades of buff and camel. The rest of the room was decorated with Byzantine high-relief ornaments, tapestries and silk runners in burgundy, gold, and hints of green.

So far, there were maybe eight or ten guests gathered in a cluster at the far end near the fireplace. My eyes zeroed in on Alec, seated on a couch covered with sand-colored raw silk. His head turned, and our gazes met. His lips parted—he seemed on the verge of a smile, but then his expression smoothed into politeness.

Sitting close on one side was Beka, and on the other Cerisette von Mecklundburg, Tony's cousin, who was even thinner and more elegant than I'd remembered.

"Welcome, Kim," Beka said.

"Kim. Glad you could make it," Alec spoke at the same moment, their voices blending.

Cerisette had apparently seen that almost smile, for she gave me a polite nod with all the warmth and welcome of the Antarctic in a deep freeze.

"Thanks for inviting me," I said to Beka, and to Alec—painfully aware of Cerisette's laser-glare—"Hi."

Then I stuck to my resolve and faced the laser. "Hi, Cerisette."

"*Bon soir*, Aurelia." She wore an elegant dress in a properly subdued pearl gray, which flattered her new hair color, a warm auburn. She had made it plain how much she despised me during summer.

Aurelia. I was now going to give her the benefit of the doubt, and assume that she was using my first name because she didn't remember that I went by my middle name. Time to start over. "Call me Kim. Sorry about my part in all the misunderstandings last summer."

"I understand," she said, with a heavy air of *You should be*.

Thud went the old conversational ball, as I struggled against an angry reaction. I wanted to add, *And if you hadn't been such a total snob, things might have been different*. But that wouldn't help anybody.

She reached for her drink, the movement enabling her to turn her shoulder, effectively shutting me out as she murmured, "Remember when Ruli gave that party in Paris just after . . ." Her voice sank, too low to hear. Leaving me standing there feeling very stupid.

For one second.

Then I found at my side a short, elderly gent in a suit who I belatedly recognized as the Napoleon from summer's masquerade ball.

"Mademoiselle . . . Murray? Have I that correct?" He pronounced my name with a French accent.

"You're Prime Minster Ridotski?" I asked. I'd had no idea who the Napoleon was that night, except that he'd been kind to me just when Aunt Sisi had tried to prevent me from meeting anyone except von Mecklundburg connections.

"This is a private affair, not one of state." Beka had gotten up and joined her grandfather, leaving Alec to Cerisette. "He's *Grandfather* to all of us."

The old man chuckled. "Even in my family, they do not call me Shimon. That is the cost of passing down the same name. Nowadays, 'Shimon' is my great-grandson. What can we offer you to drink? We have seasonal mulled wine."

"Or if you prefer the modern, there's everything from cocktails to *limonade*," Beka put in, using that tone that I was beginning to understand as her way of asking a question. In other words, on the surface was the fact of drinks, but underneath: *Do you want to stay away from liquor?*

Gratefully I said, "I'll go for the *limonade*." I was tense enough without worrying about the effect of alcohol while trying to negotiate social pitfalls.

It wasn't until Cerisette made a little movement—no more than re-crossing her long legs—that I noticed the subtle twist to her mouth. The tinkle of ice in Alec's hand drew my eye. He was also drinking *limonade*.

Beka said, "Come with me, Kim. I will introduce you."

She led me to the bar at the far side of the room where another servant in white jacket tended the drinks. As I watched, he stuck a mulling rod into some wine, sending up an aromatic waft of cloves, cinnamon, and red wine.

Two guests took silver-framed mulled wine glasses as Beka reeled off names. First was Beka's mother, who I'd learned had been widowed during the bad old Soviet days, right after Beka was born. Behind her, talking to Beka's forty-something older brother and sister, was Honoré de Vauban—another of Tony's cousins. I'd thought that my Aunt Sisi's preference (if not affectation) for speaking in French was one of her little quirks, but now I was hearing French all around me.

Honoré lifted his glass slightly in salute, his heavy eyelids narrowing with cynical humor that reminded me instantly of Tony. This guy was somewhere between my age and Alec's, tall, slender, graceful, his suit tailored by an artist. Last summer I'd mentally tagged him as a cross between Bertie Wooster (for the wardrobe) and Christopher Lee (for the cool, slightly sinister face and dark, slicked-back hair).

Noise from the entrance caused a shift. With a quick "Pardon me," Beka left to greet the new guests.

When I turned back, Honoré was watching me. Time for try two. "I'm sorry about last summer."

Instead of winning the male version of the Cerisette blow-off with my apology, I got an intent gaze. "Sorry in what sense?"

"That we got off to a bad start," and when he didn't make an immediate reply, I tried a new topic. "Why does everyone speak French instead of Dobreni?"

"Habit, I expect."

"Most of us were raised outside the country." Cerisette had joined us. "I'm told one thinks in the tongue one used most as a child." She reached past Honoré, a fine diamond bracelet on one skinny wrist catching the light. She claimed a glass of mulled wine, then gave me a look like my eyelashes were crawling with bugs. "What language did you grow up speaking . . . Kim?"

That hesitation was like a needle-jab. "I grew up speaking English and French. They mix in my mind."

Honoré asked, "Were you taught Dobreni?"

"I am pretty sure my grandmother talked to me in Dobreni when I was little, before I knew how to read and write. But then she stopped, and I forgot. It came back to me last summer, all at once. But I've still a child's vocabulary."

I discovered why Cerisette had joined us when Alec spoke from behind me. "Your grandmother wasn't much older than a child herself when she left."

"It's true," I said. For the first time with these cousins (for they were my cousins, if twice removed, as well as Tony's) I was in an actual conversation, not a fake one with me pretending to be Ruli. "Most of Gran's education had been in French and German, and Latin as well."

Cerisette asked: "Is your grandmother planning on a journey?"

Journey? A socially neutral term, neither *return* nor *visit*. Her expression was polite, but the way her smile did not reach her eyes, the angles of her stance, betrayed her hostility.

"I don't know her plans."

Cerisette's bony shoulder lifted as she cast a quick look behind me.

I knew it was Alec before he stepped up beside me. Desperate for some topic of conversation that wouldn't stick like old gum on the social shoe, I hefted my glass, looked at his, and said (inanely), "I didn't know you like this stuff."

Alec looked down into the half-empty glass, his lashes shuttering his eyes, his expression withdrawn into his Mr. Darcy look. I hadn't managed to step into the gum, I'd stuck to it.

In other words, I'd said something wrong, and I had no idea what.

Beka touched his arm. "They're asking for you."

Alec followed her back to the couch. I took a step, meaning to join them, but Cerisette expertly cut me off, leaving me following her elegantly knobby back. I slowed as she calmly took her place beside Alec, sitting slightly sideways, legs crossed, preventing anyone else from sitting on that couch besides the two of them.

How could it get any worse?

That was the moment the door opened on the noise of fresh arrivals, and in came the principal von Mecklundburgs—minus red-haired Percy, the only one I'd kind of liked.

Tony's uncle Robert, Cerisette's dad, strode ahead of the others, looking more than ever like a Russian emperor, though in an expensive double-breasted Italian suit. Now that Tony was the duke, this guy was technically Tony's heir, which would make him the new count. His wife, the countess, drifted at his side, as thin as a wraith.

The last set of cousins, Morvil and Phaedra Danilov, were right behind, walking on either side of Tony, who was dressed up for the first time I had ever seen. He wore a black suit with a black mandarin collared dress shirt, no tie. It was startling to see him in formal wear. He'd even pulled his wild hair back into a ponytail, revealing the fact that he wore a diamond in one ear.

They were clustered around the duchess, who had once asked me to call her Aunt Sisi—before she tried to get me killed. She looked like a Parisian version of Mom in her a mourning suit of silk, the glitter of diamonds on one hand and at her throat.

Aunt Sisi air-kissed Beka's mother and grandfather, bestowed a fond pat on Beka, greeted everyone else. By then the entire party had reformed with her at the center.

That's when she saw me.

Her stare was like glass, then her brows lifted in perfect polite surprise. Then she came smack up with a smile and a cordial, "Aurelia Kim, *chérie*. Someone said you had returned. What a charming surprise."

The last time we'd seen one another, she'd sent me up a tunnel in her castle to rescue her daughter. After which she slammed the door in my face.

Could she *possibly* not know that I knew?

"Here I am," I said brilliantly, and choked off a *How are you?* remembering in the nick of time why she was here. "I'm very sorry about Ruli," I said, flashing prickly heat with embarrassment and awkwardness. "I just found out—" I choked off *or I wouldn't have come.*

"Thank you, chérie." She took my hand. Hers was warm and soft, the skin fragile over her delicate bones, as she nodded toward Alec over on the couch. "Alexander must have invited you for the holidays, then?"

"No," I said, and when she lifted her brows in question, I said, "Nobody knew I was coming."

"A surprise? You wished to visit him as a holiday surprise?"

I wasn't going to see him at all. I couldn't say that, but I really did not want to tell her about her daughter's ghost asking me for help. "No," I said. "I, um, eh, thought I should come."

Even in my own ears that sounded painfully unconvincing, though it was the truth. From the direction of the couch came the faint ring of crystal, and a titter from Cerisette.

I forced myself to meet Aunt Sisi's brown eyes so much like my own—to discover she wasn't looking at me at all. Before I could figure out who she was checking out, her gaze shifted back to me, and she smiled. "How very generous, my dear. Is your family with you?"

"No. I came alone."

"It was probably a wise decision on Alexander's part to leave them to a peaceful holiday in London," the countess drawled, her soft voice giving me those prickles of implied extra meaning. Then she flashed her invisible dueling sword and went for the kill. "If you will forgive the curiosity of an old woman, if you didn't know about . . . the event of my daughter's death, why *did* you come?"

The silence was profound. They were all waiting, and it was then that Nat's hints, Tony's *I don't believe in coincidence,* Beka's wary politeness, and Alec's tense *There is going to be trouble* punched past the days of jetlag and travel, the cascade of surprising changes, and most of all, my own conviction of my good intentions, which I had never thought to question or to think anyone else would.

The duchess, and no doubt many of these others, not only thought that Alec had caused that accident, they thought I was in on it.

For an endless second all I could do was stare at her in horror.

Then I thought: the duchess will never believe me no matter what I say. But I had to kill that rumor dead, if I could, with all these others.

I raised my voice and glanced around. "When I left last September, it was because I believed it to be the right thing to do. Ruli and Alec were engaged, which was supposed to bring peace between the families. I saw myself in the way. So I returned to the States and found a job."

No one was speaking.

I took a deep breath and went on. "Last Friday, I finished my semester of teaching and drove home to see my parents. When I discovered they were going to London for the holiday, and my father had bought an extra ticket in case I came home, I decided to go with them rather than spend Christmas alone."

I paused, looked around—and discovered that at least half of them weren't looking at me at all, but at someone behind me. Were they bored? Except they weren't talking.

So I gritted my teeth and slogged on. "Shortly after our arrival, Tony appeared, and invited me to take a trip on the Eye. Then he got the bad news, but he didn't tell me what it was. So I decided to come here, alone, and see what I could find out." There. Let them deal with that, every bit of which was true.

Again, at least half of them were watching someone behind me. It wasn't Tony. He was standing three feet away from me, drink in hand.

He raised the drink in salute to me, and said, "My part is true." He grinned, and I knew he was thinking of that sword fight. Maybe even daring me to mention it.

I turned away from him to find the duchess smiling thinly. She said to Baron Ridotski, "May I request one of those glasses of mulled wine, *cher* Shimon? The air is so chilly."

She walked away, and everyone was in motion again, leaving me once more alone in the middle of a floor. I used the opportunity to take a look behind me to see who everyone had been checking out, to discover the only person there was Honoré de Vauban leaning against the bar, a glass held loosely in one hand.

Why would they be staring at *him?* No clue. Perhaps someone else had been there? *Oh, well.* I turned my mind back to Alec, behind me on the other side of the room. Now I understood his reaction when I showed up at the palace—that exclamation, seemingly wrenched out of him, that he wished I had not come. How many people in this room were watching us both, gleefully waiting for the least sign of friendship and affection between us, to verify that we'd conspired against Ruli? I shut my eyes, furious, sickened. *You're right, Alec. I should not have come.*

Except Ruli had appeared in a window and begged, *Help me.*

"I don't think we've met." I opened my eyes to discover a handsome man in a Vigilzhi dress uniform, complete with epaulettes and a ribbon across his chest. Instead of the small gold captain's stars on either side of his collar, the pins were stylized falcons, like those the Vigilzhi wore on the fronts of their hats. He was a well-built man with sandy brown hair and light eyes. "I am Dmitros Trasyemova, at your service." Here was the duke I hadn't yet met, the leader of the fifth Important Family.

"Kim Murray. Glad to meet you," I said, as a boy of about ten tugged insistently at Dmitros' uniform tunic. The boy's heart-shaped face and general resemblance to Beka and her siblings made it clear that this was the youngest of the many Shimons.

"Uncle Dmitros, you *promised* . . ."

With an apologetic smile, Trasyemova excused himself and was pulled away to where a bunch of kids waited in the door to a far room. I was alone, and *so* not feeling the love. I chugged down the *limonade*, just to have something to do, then came a deep voice.

"Permit me to say it is a surprise to find you here." There was Tony's Uncle Robert, he of the Russian emperor costume and the octopus hands last summer. "Did old Milo send you, is that it?"

"*No* one sent me," I said. I couldn't prevent my face from heating up.

"He doesn't know you are here?" Robert's bushy brows rose.

"I don't know what he knows. All I can tell you is that I left London without telling him. He was busy."

Robert's disbelief was so obvious I might as well have saved my breath. He then cleared his throat, giving me that false smile I remembered so unfondly from summer. It was more a leer than a smile, a brandishing of teeth below angry eyes. "I believe you are an opera connoisseur?" he began.

What? Had I fallen down a rabbit hole? "That would be my mother," I said, shooting my forefinger toward the west as I edged away from him.

"Kim. I was wondering if you'd like to—" Tony came up and, mad as I was at him, he was still a thousand times preferable to his Uncle Robert. Before he could finish his sentence, however, a thin, elegant blonde stepped between us.

"Take this. You need it," drawled Tony's cousin Phaedra Danilov in her high voice, while pressing a tinkling glass into Tony's hand.

Beka came up on my other side with her short, salt-and-pepper-haired older brother—another Shimon—who gave me a rueful smile before he deftly intercepted the countess, Robert's wife.

Beka was equally deft in cutting off Tony's uncle and passing him to her older sister Malca, saying smoothly, "May we tempt you with something at the buffet, Count Robert? We've also freshly mulled wine . . ."

Malca then escorted Robert firmly away.

Phaedra gestured impatiently to her brother, and as he and Honoré joined us, Tony shifted slightly to let them in. Honoré said something under his breath that caused the cousins to laugh as Tony stepped closer to Beka. While everyone else's attention was on Honoré, he gave her a private smile, then ran his hand up the back of her neck to cup the back of her head.

Here's the weirdness of human nature. That gesture of tenderness, from someone I had extremely ambivalent emotions about, gave me a real jolt. Beka whispered something, and his hand dropped.

I looked away quickly, suspecting I was not supposed to have seen that. Since I did not want to be caught staring at Tony, I found myself face to face with the Danilovs, like a pair of golden bookends and about as friendly-looking. Morvil Danilov's blond hair was perfectly barbered in the same style as Alec's and Honoré de Vauban's, and Morvil, like Tony, wore a dress shirt with a mandarin collar (though his was white, with a hint of pleat showing in the V of his beautiful suit coat). Like Tony's coat, his was beautifully cut, exquisitely evoking the Edwardian era. The wink and glitter of diamonds drew my eye to his cufflinks.

Then Phaedra gave me a forced smile and cooed in her high, kittenish voice, "Tony and I were just talking. I hear you are adept with the rapier. Why don't you come to a practice at our *salle?*"

"Say yes, Kim," Tony coaxed. Then he grinned. "You know you need it."

Was this friendly invitation a gesture of apology?

"As soon as the sun rises," Morvil Danilov said. "Day after Christmas."

"It will be warm." Phaedra added with another of those glances, "Quite warm."

Wary, curious, gratified, wary again. "I don't have any fencing gear," I said.

"We have plenty." Phaedra's brows lifted.

"*Dienstbeflissenheit,*" Honoré muttered softly, from just behind Phaedra. I mentally translated that as German for "fuss," but just as I was wondering if it was aimed at me, Phaedra flushed.

I could refuse and learn nothing. In that case, I may as well go directly back to London. But would that look like I was running away out of guilt? It was that flush of Phaedra's, the first human expression I'd ever seen from her, that decided me.

"Okay. Thanks."

As Phaedra leaned toward Honoré to murmur something, and her brother reached past her to pick up a fresh drink from the end of the bar, Tony said low-voiced to Beka, "Want to come watch?"

"You don't need an audience," she whispered.

Tony laughed softly, his smile intimate. The chemistry between the two was totally guns and roses.

During the brief lull in conversation, I heard an old councilor on the other side of the room: "Statthalter? You will forgive a moment of business, but I must ask . . ."

How was Alec dealing with this horrible party? I did not dare look, though I fancied I could feel his tension. As Phaedra and the rest of the von Mecklundburg gang chattered, I ducked around them and wandered in the direction of the buffet, concentrating on the voices at the other end of the room.

The foremost voice was the duchess—Aunt Sisi—probably at the center of a circle, as was appropriate for the bereaved mother. But when I focused, I realized she wasn't reminiscing about her dear departed daughter; she was in the middle of an amusing anecdote about the disastrous dinner she'd served before she left for Paris. Then she went on about the troubles she was having finding a decent cook who was willing to relocate to the middle of nowhere.

I busied myself at the buffet as Beka's niece and nephew led a pack of middle-grade kids in a raid on the edibles, bouncing between fast, idiomatic Dobreni and French, with a smattering of Russian. I tried one each of the marinated mushrooms, the *caponata parve*, and *baba ghanouj*. Delicious. When the kids moved off toward some inner sanctuary with their loaded plates, I found myself alone.

Okay, I'd done what I'd come to do, I'd even made a date with the von Mecklundburg cousins at which I could (at least theoretically) do some sleuthing. Though I longed to talk to Alec, just to see him, eyes meeting eyes—I was not going to give the gossips any more fodder. Time to leave.

I took a step here, ducked there, and a minute later reached the foyer.

I changed back into my boots and was just picking up the bag with my shoes when Beka appeared. "Thank you for coming," she said politely.

"Thank you for inviting me," I said politely.

"How long are you staying here in Dobrenica?"

Whoa, what to say? "I don't know."

Okay, this non-conversation could stagger on until the polar cap melted. She seemed to want to know where I was coming from, and I wanted to know where she was coming from. To test her out a little, I said, "There are a whole lot of things I'm not getting. But. One thing will get me on the next train, and that's a conviction that my being here is bad for Alec," I said, and waited for her to smile, to tell me how my departure would be for the best.

She looked back toward the gathering then gave an impatient sigh. "I don't think—no. I dare not say anything." She tipped her head as though considering, but an older woman appeared with one of the white-haired council guys behind her—and behind him, Robert von Mecklundburg, drink in hand, his eyes on me.

"Bye!" I said, and hustled through the door into the cold night air, with the lung-expanding enthusiasm of a dungeon-escapee.

TEN

S EVERAL INKRI DRIVERS had lined up along the street below the driveway, like cabs do at home, hoping for business. I jumped in the first one, and we set off. The cold was a shock. The runners of the sleigh hissed and cracked over the thickening ice as we zigzagged from street to street. From a distance I could see the cathedral lit up, and I sighed. I was exhausted. The thought of sitting through an incomprehensible Latin church service with the Waleskas was as welcome as air so cold it hurt to breathe.

But when I reached the inn, there were two anxious faces side by side in one of the frosty front windows: Wednesday Addams, aka Tania, and her little sister Theresa. When they saw my inkri pull up, Theresa's somber face lifted in a relieved smile.

I paid, bolted up the steps, and promptly skidded on the ice. As I caught myself on the iron handrail and picked my way unsteadily to the doorstep, Theresa flung open the door.

I began, "I'm late ? I'm sorry—"

Theresa shook her head. "We have a quarter of an hour, Mademoiselle. We must take the streetcar, as everyone else has gone ahead."

"I thought the streetcar stopped at sunset."

"Not tonight. It will run before and after Christmas Mass."

Tania stood behind her sister, gaze on the floor. Theresa took charge, gesturing toward the corner table, as if that little distance from the entrance and the front desk afforded extra privacy in an empty house.

We sat down, and Theresa leaned forward. "Tania says you asked about . . . the protections."

"Protections?"

"The prisms. The charms, we say to visitors." Theresa went on in that calm, helpful tone of the carefully prepared speech, "It is a very old custom here, in winter, to wear the faceted stones as protections. The wealthy wear diamonds, but faceted crystal is said to be as good to ward off the magical beings who mean us harm."

I sat back so I could see them both. "I really went there to ask about ghosts."

Tania looked away. Theresa shot her a fast glance. "Perhaps we should start for the streetcar."

In silence they turtled up into their winter gear (I was still in mine) and bent into a chill that was doing its best to enter the next Ice Age. In the distance, the cathedral bells tumbled melodic peals into the starry night. The last note sang brassy shivers through the air as we followed the last arrivals into the cathedral, where we were handed a candle by an apple-cheeked, earnest choirboy.

The cathedral, like most medieval buildings, was luminous with architectural beauty meant to draw the eye upward. The hundreds of candles painted the gilding on the vaulted ceilings with rich light, though the long stained glass windows were dark, sending down glints of gentian blue, cadmium, and malachite green—hints of sunlight's full glory.

There was a Byzantine feel to the murals representing the Stations of the Cross. The huge decorated fir was not loaded with tinsel, fake snow, and a zillion ornaments as I was used to. It was hung with tiny crystal stars. There was also an Advent wreath with three purple candles representing the first three weeks of Advent, and the single bright red candle for the fourth.

When the service began, the white candle at the center was lit, and someone passed down the aisle with it to touch flame to the first candle in each pew, after which people held their wicks together, passing the light until the entire space glowed.

While that happened the singing began: children's voices first, then women's clear, beautiful tones, and then the men joined in, some voices so deep, they resonated through the wood of the pew.

I was prepared to be bored. I was not prepared for the power of song, color, scent, the feel of the candle in my fingers, the charged air as the antiphonal responses echoed back and forth like a carillon, the sight of smiling faces, young and old, all made beautiful by the candles' warm glow: the cumulative effect was to break apart the habitual enclosure of the "I" and join it with the community—and with spirit on a different plane.

I don't remember when my gaze was caught by the reflection of my candle flame in the diamond pin securing the hat of the woman in the pew in front of me. I recall gazing at that tiny flicker, likening it to the star in the song currently being sung . . . and then I saw the reflections of hundreds of pinpoints of light, held by up by arms covered in velvets and brocade. . . in woolens . . . in slashed sleeves . . . in uniforms not seen for a century or more.

I'd fallen into vision. I recognized it, and though the periphery of this vision glittered, and my body seemed unmoored, instinct caused me to narrow my focus to 1938 as I stared at that first pew.

And there was a row of three kneeling teens beside several old folks. There were the twin girls, their corn-silk hair gleaming in the ruddy light.

My Gran and her twin had looked exactly alike, but their personalities had been completely different, and I saw the evidence before me as one glanced around, her lips parted with barely suppressed mirth. The other knelt soberly, head bent, eyes closed. The sober one had to be Lily, my grandmother, and the one looking idly around was Rose.

With them was a tall, thin, dark-haired boy in a blue cadet's uniform, only with epaulettes . . . Milo. He, equally sober, had never interested Rose. It was Armandros who had flirted with both sisters, which had deepened their rivalry to a serious breach.

The pangs in my head thundered to my heartbeat, and the vision smeared into flickering colors. I blinked, gasped, and clutched with one hand at the pew as Tania sent me a frightened look, and on my other side, her grandfather blinked at me in sudden concern.

I forced a smile that was probably as convincing as Prometheus on the rock saying, "No, I'm fine. Really."

I kept my eyes closed, rising when the hiss and rustle of people around me indicated I should, and sitting again when they did. I opened my eyes when they began to snuff the candles, filling the air with the heady scent of honeybee wax smoke.

As we streamed out of the cathedral some began to sing Christmas songs with unfamiliar rising and falling melodies. The singers' breath clouded and froze in tiny sparkles. Gradually my headache lessened, leaving a profound exhaustion.

The return trip was not via streetcar. Tania and Theresa fell in on either side of me, each taking an arm to guide me to an enormous sleigh drawn by two heavy horses.

The ride wasn't long. When we reached the inn, there was warmth and light and the delicious smell of the Christmas day meats slow-braising. The Waleska relatives gathered in the dining room, as Josip and Domnu Waleska brought out trays of wine and red-glowing mulling irons.

As soon as I got rid of my winter gear, I slipped between the chattering Waleska relatives and headed for the stairs, pausing when I sensed a quiet step dogging mine. It was Tania, her expression one of mute question.

I waved for her to join me and continued up to my room, which was blissfully warm and cozy. Tania refused to sit down, so I collapsed on the bed, as she said without preamble, "When I was little I talked to ghosts. Many ghosts. I see them all around, though most are silent and like fog. But my family, they thought I lied, to gain attention."

I sat up again. "You *talked* to them?"

She brought her chin down in a single nod.

"But no one believed you?" I began to pull off my boots.

"No one but my sisters. Theresa because she loves the stories about ghosts. Anna because she knew I never lied."

"But your mother didn't believe you?"

Tania looked away, a thin shoulder rising. "Mother is very practical. And my aunt, well, she said I made up ghost friends to get attention. It brought shame to the family. So I lied, to make peace. I said that I did not see ghosts, and I was forgiven. This was many years ago, when I was seven or eight, so it is now forgotten, except sometimes in family jokes."

I grimaced in sympathy. I knew how cruel some jokes could be, even if they were supposedly meant in fun.

"But I learned everything I could about Vrajhus," Tania continued, "about the magic and the Nasdrafus."

"Thank you for telling me." I got up to put my boots away. "My mind is filling with a million questions, but I'll limit myself to two, and if you don't want to answer, that's okay."

"Ask."

"First, how do you talk to them, and second, what made you decide to tell me these things?"

"I do not know how I speak to them," she said, her slender hands open as I reached for the wardrobe door. "It happened more when I was small. Rarely since. No one else could hear them. It was not always about things that made sense to me. As for why I'm telling you this, it is partly because of what you said when you came to the lens maker's, but also because of this man." She pointed at the wardrobe.

"What?" I jumped back as if I'd been electrocuted, leaving the wardrobe door ajar. "What man?"

She pointed. "He stands there, with a cigarette."

I whipped around, but all I saw was the wardrobe door, with its mirror on the outside, and inside the wardrobe my clothes hanging exactly as I'd left them.

"I've felt coldness in here," I said, examining the outside of the wardrobe, then stood on tiptoe to peer upward, as if a ghost crouched like a vulture atop it. "I thought it might be caused by my cousin Ruli."

"No, this is a man." Tania's eyes narrowed. "He wishes to speak to you. But I cannot hear him."

The air now whiffed of refrigerator, but I could see nothing weird. "What do I do so he will let me see him? Or get him to talk?"

"I don't know how to explain," she said. "The Salfmattas have asked. It is the way I see, and hear. But it was easier when I was young. I am told that the young do not see what they expect to see, they can . . ." She made a gesture of sweeping something aside. ". . . make their minds ready." She raised a hand to hide the tight jaw of a suppressed yawn, and her eyes watered.

I forced back the questions—I'd asked more than my two. Time to let the poor kid gets some rest. "Thank you, Tania. You've been a huge help."

She looked doubtful at that but only wished me good night and left. I shut the door, and—it's embarrassing to admit this, but I didn't want to undress. Neither did I want to turn out the light, knowing that the ghost of some guy was hanging around. It was that cigarette. The first thing to mind was that horrible Reithermann, killed by Tony at the Eyrie last summer.

So I hopped into bed still wearing my good dress.

My eyes burned. My body was so tired I felt as if I had been turned to stone. I stared at that wardrobe until my eyelids drifted down, then jerked wide open. It felt like hours had passed, but when I checked my watch, it had been two minutes.

"Oh, to hell with it," I said, and got out of bed to turn out the light. I saw nothing by the wardrobe—but when I reached to shut the door, which was still ajar, a flicker of movement in the mirror froze me.

There I stood in my good dress, my hair straggling down . . . and behind me, Tony leaned against the bedpost, smiling lazily.

ELEVEN

I WHIRLED AROUND.

No one was there.

So I whirled back and found him reflected in the mirror, but he wasn't really leaning because I could see the bedpost through him. Also, he wasn't Tony. His eyes were light brown, the blond hair straggling unkempt along his forehead was short and wavy, not long and curly like Tony's. The scruffy tunic looked a lot like pictures I'd seen of the general issue field uniform of the German Army after 1915. The shoulder tabs were outlined in red, which indicated Lancers, and the two pips were the insignia of a captain. The uniform was frayed at the turned-back cuffs and much mended.

He held a cigarette. Smoke that I could not smell drifted up from its tip. He had the lazy, crooked smile that belonged to my mother and me, as well as to Tony and Ruli.

I was staring at the ghost of Grandfather Armandros.

I gazed in the mirror at him, trying to meet his eyes, but his face blurred . . . and he was gone. I peered in the mirror then examined the room, rinse and repeat. No sign of him.

"You're not going to make it easy, are you?" I asked the air.

No answer.

I hung up my good dress, changed into my nightgown, hit the light, and fell into bed.

This time I didn't waken until the weak winter light filtered through the curtains. It had to be late morning. I'd missed breakfast—but then it was Christmas day.

My first thought was of Grandfather Armandros's ghost. I glanced into the wardrobe mirror, but he wasn't there. "Ruli?" I asked, without much hope.

Zip.

"Hey. Anyone on the GhostNet? What's the deal?"

No answer.

So I thought about that horrible wreath party and, once again, dread tightened my middle. Here I'd come back to Dobrenica, this time not pretending to be anyone. Determined to tell the truth. And what happens? The same crowd who thought I was some kind of con woman seemed to have leaped straight to the assumption that I was part of some murder conspiracy.

Had I just made things worse for Alec?

I *had* to see him. But how? If all my movements were gossiped about over the entire country . . . and there I was yesterday, knocking at the palace gate in front of God and everybody. He'd said, *There's going to be trouble.*

I groaned and threw back the covers.

As soon as I got out of bed, my gaze fell on an envelope that had been slipped below the door, with my name neatly printed on the outside, and the inn's name and street below. Mail delivery on Christmas? No, there was no stamp.

I tore it open. On a single sheet of heavy paper was written in fountain pen, *Meet me at Zorfal at three? A.*

Happiness and relief flooded through me.

What time was it? As if in answer, the distant church bells began ringing: noon.

I forced myself through a full set of warm-ups, my muscles twanging in mild protest. Overall it felt good, though my mind was well aware that I was going to get trounced if that prospective fencing practice really happened, but . . . oh, well.

The downstairs was full of Waleska relatives, local and visitors, sitting down to the big midday meal. From the loud, cheerful conversation it was apparent that half of them had recently returned from church.

Madam's voice boomed out, "Mam'zelle! Come, here is a place for you!"

She was beaming with welcome as she ushered me to a place right by the window. Everyone else smiled cheerfully, even proudly. Surely they didn't think I conspired to murder! I breathed in the heady fumes of mulled wine as Anna, with a triumphant air, brought in pork stew, rolled breads filled with cinnamon, nutmeg, and ground nuts, along with peppered vegetables, and a cake layered with custard.

I could no more refuse any of it than I could reverse the weather. Hoping that this mysterious *Zorfal* (which sounded like the word for 'hedge' in Dobreni) wasn't a restaurant, I dug in.

Talk flowed around me, people at first self-conscious, sending me looks as if to gauge my reactions. Gradually they forgot about me as I ate and gazed out the window into the snowy street. Like generations of ancestors, I listened for the cathedral bells for the time. At two, I rose to go.

Madam appeared out of nowhere, and said, "You will stay for the *tantzias?* The dancing?"

"Dancing?"

"We clear the tables at three. We have music and dancing. We thought you might—"

Anna appeared at her mother's shoulder, her arms laden with a tray full of dirty dishes. "If you would like to join us," she said, then glanced at her mother.

Madam beamed at me. "Yes! If you will join our dance, and give us more French ballet?"

Anna flushed, looking apologetic.

It would be stupid to get mad at Madam's efforts to turn me into a show pony. My background might be responsible in part, but the rest was my having danced at Anna's wedding. "If I get back in time, I will," I said. "But I have somewhere to be at three."

"Oh yes. We saw the messenger." Madam put her forefinger to her chin, and winked at me. "When you return from your important business."

Anna grimaced slightly, and my ready ire died down. Weird how sharing your irritation makes it bearable.

I went upstairs and got ready, putting on my secondary nice outfit. It was a plain but well cut wool dress of periwinkle blue. Was the color too loud for mourning? I looked at it doubtfully, turning this way and that, trying to see the blue as subdued, then gave up and put the forest green one back on. When I got outside, braced for the ultra-deep freeze, I found a relatively mild day, with feathery high clouds in the sky.

"Zorfal," I said when I found an inkri.

The streets were largely empty. I hoped my driver, a young guy, was not missing his family or holiday as we jingled and slid across town and over the bridge into the Beverly Hills section of town, where I'd been the night before. Instead of turning left down one of the three or four grand streets lined with linden trees, the inkri kept on going past the fine houses and started downhill to a part of the city I'd never seen.

The houses gave way after one of the many pocket gardens to an older neighborhood of smaller, steep-roofed houses along a street below a spectacular cliff. The street ended in a *cul-de-sac* on its own cliff. Most of the buildings had shops on the ground floor, judging from the broad windows and the swinging signs outside.

He pulled into a narrow driveway beside a rambling half-timbered, half-stone building with every window lit. People stood outside chatting, or walking to and fro, and I saw a lot of Vigilzhi uniforms. In the back there were cars from six different decades, a bunch of unhooked sleighs, and a hay wagon with a huge shaggy horse munching in a feed-bag, apparently oblivious to the cold.

My driver nosed between the wagon and what looked like a leftover World War II German field vehicle of some sort, with additional siding that made it look like a giant, weird kind of camper. The broad stone steps leading down from a door were worn into ovals: this building was *old*, whatever it was.

I gave the driver a double tip for having to work on a holiday and made my way over the slippery slate stones. To my right several young guys, two of them in the blue Vigilzhi uniforms, were flirting with some young women. One of the guys slipped and fell on his butt, cussing a blue streak in Russian. The others laughed and made sympathetic noises as I passed.

An enormous shape loomed on the porch, then faded back. Kilber? It was hard to be sure with all that hat and scarf camouflage. Judging by his size, it could be Kilber.

A guy barely out of his teens leaped down the stairs and blushingly approached me. "Will you come this way Mam'zelle?" he asked in terrible French. His shapeless dun coat flapped open, revealing a Vigilzhi uniform beneath.

Inside, the building was timbered and had plaster walls, decorated with very old shop signs. I wondered if the place had been an enormous barn back in the days when everyone drove carriages. There was a central stage, and tiers of tables built along the four walls, clear up under the roof.

The place was hopping with business, but no one disturbed my guide as he led me up some narrow stone stairs to the second level, which was railed in rustic wood carved in knotwork patterns.

He showed me to a little alcove fenced off by old-fashioned screens, a hanging plant overhead obscuring the table from the gallery opposite. It was completely secluded though, from it, we could see the stage below.

Alec rose politely. He wore a dark suit, his handsome face subtly marked with exhaustion. "Merry Christmas," he said.

"Same to you." My entire body flashed with warmth, but I took my cue from him and sat down without making any demonstration. "You didn't send Emilio or a minion to pick me up," I said.

Alec flicked me a slight smile. "Gave you the chance to refuse. And to avoid public notice."

True. If I'd gone to Ysvorod House, or to the palace . . . um, like I had yesterday. "Nothing as private as a public spot, eh?" I asked. "Are you able to get around without being noticed?"

"I can. If necessary. But it's difficult." Once again I felt the fuel-injected, super-powered chemistry, but with it came tension. I could see it in the taut skin of his forehead, in the line of his shoulder beneath the fine suit coat, in his hands. Though he didn't make a fist or tap or twitch, light winked, a tiny blue pinpoint, in the cobalt stone of his signet ring. His heartbeat.

On his other hand, the wedding band gleamed in the golden light.

"What is this place?"

"Do you remember the night after the concert in the cathedral, the music we heard?"

"Yes."

"It was coming from here. In the summer, the car park is a terrace. They hold open air concerts. Ysvorod House is up on the cliff above us." He jerked his thumb behind him. "Zorfal is usually booked months in advance. But on Christmas Day, any group who wants to play can take the stage, first come first served."

The young Vigilzhi had reappeared.

"I hope you haven't eaten yet," Alec said. "They make an excellent paprika stew."

"I did eat at the inn, but I'll have dessert if they've got a good one. And I'll take some of that mulled wine I smell, if you're having some."

Alec ordered and the fellow vanished, leaving the tension to close right back in.

When I set out, I couldn't wait to get right down to important matters, but now that I was face to face with Alec, it was unexpectedly difficult. How about something easy, then? "Outside the door as I arrived, some guy slipped. He was cussing in Russian, but his friends spoke Dobreni, which he switched back to when he got up. I remember you doing that. Cussing in Russian, I mean." *As well as Tony, but let's leave him out, shall we?* "I thought it was an idiosyncrasy."

"You have to remember that Stalin required that only Russian be spoken in the schools in this part of the world. Speaking Dobreni was punished. Children were to grow up as happy Soviets. Not to be a happy Soviet was to commit treason."

"Oh, yes. I've read about that."

"They gave it up by the nineties, but people still have a habit of reserving Russian for invective."

"Not whimsy, but intent. Okay, I completely missed that."

Alec gestured in apology. "For the sake of our Russian population, I've tried to cure myself of the habit. Most of the time I remember."

The food and drink appeared then: paprika stew with dumplings, cabbage rolls over hot fisherman's soup, and rice with ewe-cheese for him. An apple-cinnamon tart kind of thing for me, with a buttery hard sauce over it. Two mugs of mulled wine were also set down, aromatic with spice.

"The duchess last night," I began. "After she grilled me, I mean. All I heard her talking about was how tough life was without a chef. She didn't sound like any grieving mother to me."

Alec closed his hands around his mug. "She'd consider a display of grief vulgar. Unless. . . ." He loosened his grip on the mug and picked up his fork.

Last summer, perhaps because we'd behaved so decorously during my masquerade as Ruli—around everyone except Ruli's family—we'd gotten into the habit of talking. We'd fallen into a natural rhythm that had become as precious as life to me.

"Unless it suited her purposes?" I said, striving to recover the rhythm. *Take it easy, no demands.* Didn't take mysterious powers to see how much stress he was under. "How much contact have you had with the duchess since the accident?"

"None until yesterday."

"How about the rest of them?"

"Very little. Robert was the first, the day after the accident. He said he'd been at the Eyrie. The staff told me that Magda Stos, Ruli's personal assistant, had called the von Mecklundburgs' family doctor to deal with removing Ruli from the wreckage. I endorsed that as soon as I was conscious enough to understand what was going on. When Robert called, he corroborated that decision as well." Alec paused, his face tight, then said, "Robert didn't want to try identifying her any more than I did."

"Ugh." *I hope she died at once.* I didn't quite want to say it.

"I didn't see any of them until Tony showed up at the airstrip the day you came in on the train. He was with Danilov. Came straight to the palace, demanding to know where I was keeping his sister's body."

"That must have been grim."

Alec set down his fork and pressed his fingers between his brows. "I told him what I knew."

"And then?"

"And then he left. Didn't hear another word until I saw him last night."

"He showed up with Morvil Danilov?"

Alec almost smiled. "Don't use his given name. He really hates it."

"They didn't tell me that last summer. But then he and I scarcely exchanged two words. Can't say I blame him. Dorky name, Morvil."

"Morvil Ilyich, to be more precise. Even Phaedra calls him Danilov."

"Phaedra . . . Ilyichna, right?"

"She kept that patronymic a deep secret when we were all teens."

Below, the first group of performers started tuning up. At first I took them to be a Romanian *taraf*, but the men wore the vaguely Cossack-like, long belted shirts of the Dobreni, and there were three women, two old and one young, all wearing long fringed scarves to hold their hair back, that were crisscrossed and tied at their waists over contrasting colored layered skirts. The instruments were balanced, three woodwinds—panflute, clarinet, and recorder—and three stringed—violin, viola, and codza. The oldest woman, the braid dangling from her mourning-gray scarf set a tambourine on her stand, and softly sang scales, major key, minor. Major, minor.

I sipped the warm, rich wine. In the deceptive quiet, I leaned toward Alec. "Last night, Grandfather Armandros appeared in my—"

The word *room* was lost as a wild, wind-driven ribbon of music snapped more strongly than any mere magic spell around every person in that room. The strings carried the difficult melody under the singer, the winds cascading in counterpoint. By the time they'd played the melody through, feet and hands tapped and bodies swayed or bounced gently to the beat. On the second verse, the winds braided the melody as the lute-like codza and the violin dueled in cascading cadenzas. A third round, half a chord higher, a little faster, caused people to clap and stamp. The musicians faced one another for the last verse, improving wild counterpoints as the entire audience joined in on the chorus.

A huge cheer rang off the walls as the musicians bowed, flushed and sweaty.

"What was that song about? I couldn't understand a word."

"It's a Russian dialect. The song—what else? Love and war."

"What else?" I echoed, thinking, *We're almost back to where we were last summer* . . .

Alec's smile was brief, but genuine, and the tension seemed to ease as he asked, "Did Grandfather Armandros say anything?"

"No. He was there in my mirror, then faded out. Why was the duchess going on about her cook, anyway? Oh yeah, didn't you take the famous Pedro away from her last summer?"

"It became official when Ruli moved into the palace. It was what Pedro had wanted all along. His ambition extended to state dinners and diplomatic affairs."

"Don't send him back."

"I won't. Though if he wants to return to the von Mecklundburgs, I won't try to stop him. But I don't think he will."

"You treat him better?"

"She treated him like a king, except the duchess only permitted him to cook for her and her chosen few. After he came to us and realized that state affairs and diplomatic dinners would seldom be on the scale of the *Ancien Régime*, I gave him his second dearest wish, to hire his services to a fine restaurant."

I thought, *fine restaurant? Here?*

Alec must have seen it in my face, because he flashed his rare grin. "We have two. La Maison, which is mainly French cuisine, and Hanging Gardens, which is kosher, its cuisine chosen from Jewish communities all over the world. Hanging Gardens has the edge on popularity—it was one of the few places Ruli liked in this city. And Pedro, who was born in the south of France, sees it as a patriotic imperative to improve La Maison." When Alec mentioned Ruli, his voice dropped a note, and there was the tension again.

Okay, one step back, try another step in a different direction. I looked down at the stage, where the first group was busy collecting their things. "You'd think music would be part of Vrajhus, if anything works."

"It is, I'm told," Alec said—like anyone else would say, *Summer is warm*, or *I need new toothpaste*. "Problem is, that same power to stir emotion makes it exponentially more difficult to control."

The second group came out. These were younger, two of the guys in jeans, though they too wore the long belted shirts, but these were brightly colored, one with a falcon embroidered in piratical detail, the other with a gryphon on his. The third guy, also young, wore the traditional loose trousers stuffed into low boots, and a plumed hat. They had one female, a teenager who carried a panflute.

The first group had brought the audience together. This second group got them rollicking. Two boys played strings—violin and codza—improvising in round as the girl on the panflute set the melodic line. The other two boys played tambourine and hand drums.

When the song had finished, I said, "I was only in London a couple of days and scarcely saw your dad. Why is he still there?"

Alec gazed down at the stage. "You understand how nebulous our government has been."

Government. I shifted in my chair, trying to hide my impatience. Last summer, the night before I left, when Alec and I were alone on a hillside above the city, he'd said that he could never really get away—that was both the joy and the pain of his position. I wanted to get to the personal, and then I remembered what Gran had said. For Alec, government *was* personal.

"Right." I counted on my fingers. "When you came in as Statthalter, the Soviets controlled things, but you were building a government under their noses." Another finger. "The last ten years, you've been slowly getting rid of the Soviet governmental controls and restoring the old ways."

"Not all the old ways," he said. "Right before the war, your great-grandfather had seated the first Great Council, which included elected officials through the guilds. When I came in as Statthalter, the election was Soviet controlled but instituted on our old model. We're still using that model now, with emendations."

His voice eased incrementally, and I felt that as a victory: There was the rhythm again, beckoning. *If you want him, you have to take the whole deal, and that includes the Council, the offices, the millions of meetings, and how, with even trivial moments, history intersects.*

Like car wheels slipping on ice?

I shut down that train of thought hard, and gave Alec my best smile. "Old ways and new. Got it."

Alec sat back, his hands loose for the first time that evening. "If my father comes back, even as a symbolic king, then whatever government he comes back to gains legitimacy."

"So?"

"So before you arrived last summer with the news that your grandmother was alive, the biggest conflict remaining was Dsaret mountain, our oldest and most important mines." Alec idly turned the wine cup around and around in his fingers. "You know that there's a Russian consortium claiming those mines. I've been negotiating on behalf of the country. Since we believed the Dsarets were dead, my father and I thought: when we recover those mines from the consortium, we want the mountain to belong to the country. And I think we're going to regain control, whatever the von Mecklundburgs think. We've steadily been decreasing production there, and it's costing the consortium too much to maintain the mines."

"I remember. But does Tony still want to send his guys to take them over by force?"

"Well, the von Mecklundburgs have lost a great deal of revenue, because the consortium also controls roughly half their territory. And the von Mecklundburgs felt that they should inherit the Dsaret holdings through Rose and her daughter, the duchess."

"Uh oh, I think I see what was coming. Your marriage with Ruli was supposed to settle that, right?"

"Since they seemed, at the time, to be the only surviving Dsaret descendants, half for them, and half for the country."

"And then I showed up, with the news that my grandmother is still alive, right?"

"Right."

"So Tony tried to capture the government last summer because if Gran was really alive, they would lose that half?"

"Something like that. I don't think he really expected to become Statthalter and mire himself in council meetings and bureaucracy. And to give him his due, I don't think he wants to strut around as a tin king. His plan was to ram through a treaty in favor of his family, once he regained control of the mines by a fast attack. A plan which had the enthusiastic support of his people."

"Yeah, I remember that much."

Third up was a single player, a short round geeky-looking kid with dark hair. The buzz of conversation dropped dramatically to a few whispers as the boy took his time checking his taragot, which was a sort of clarinet.

"Is that thing ancient?" I asked.

Alec smiled, shook his head, and leaned toward me. "Modern. Descended by way of politics from the Hungarian *tárogató*, which was forbidden by the Hapsburgs two or three centuries ago."

"An underground instrument," I whispered. "I didn't know there was such a thing."

"The old version was loud and not very musical, in fact. I think it was primarily used as a battle horn—"

The boy lifted the instrument to his lips, and the audience hushed in expectation. The only sound was the quiet tread of servers moving about, then they, too, stilled.

The sound of the taragot was reedy yet mellow; the melody catchy and compelling in the way of folk music. When the player reached some of the higher flourishes in that compelling tritone sequence once called the Forbidden Chord, I flashed back to the mountain picnic with Tony last summer, and a talented young flautist. This had to be the same kid.

Questions piled up as the song appeared to ascend by changing keys, a half-step at a time as voices joined in ones and twos until there was a powerful chorus. The player then let loose, brilliant flourishes dancing around the melodic line like larks braiding heavenward.

"*. . . open the door to my heart,*
Love and laughter, mercy and justice,
Honor and peace, solace for grief . . ."

The boy bobbed, eyes closed, as he bound them together with a scroll-work of splendor.

"Misha's father wanted him to become a carpenter," Alec observed. "Until Tony offered to fund an apprenticeship."

Tony again. Time for a change of subject.

"... *close the door to my heart,*
Hatred and sorrow, malice and perfidy,
Greed and strife, the weak betrayed ..."

"Someone at the inn said there's a music school. Connected to the synagogue—is that right?" I asked.

"Yes. Mainly involves teaching the students to read and write music. Most of them come already trained by ear, with enormous repertoires in their heads, and years of experience improvising."

The chorus rose to a crescendo:" ... *light the way, Xanpia, share us your wre-e-e-e-ath!*"

The long last word dissolved in pounding, foot-stomping applause that resonated through the wooden gallery. The boy bowed, grinned at the audience, then walked off.

As the next band walked on playing a Greek ballad, Alec fell silent, his profile lit by the lamp on the next table. Fine strands of his dark hair drifted down onto his forehead, and I sensed that the wall of tension between us was melting at last, shifting us to the intimate space I so cherished.

I said, "Have you recovered your memory yet?"

"No." Alec stared down into the lights winking in the dark ruby liquid, then suddenly lifted it and drank half. He sat back, eyes closed, and let his breath trickle out, and the tension in his voice was back, the words wrung out of him, "No, I have not. Kim, how could I not remember driving her to her death?"

"How much do you remember?"

His eyes stayed closed. When he opened them, Mr. Darcy was back: the shuttered face of good breeding, the cultured voice. But I was beginning to sense the terrible cost he paid for that appearance of cool and elegant detachment. "Ruli was going off to Paris for the holidays. We had . . . a disagreement." His voice was so low I had to bend close to hear him. "This is what few know. Her boyfriend, Marzio di Peretti, came up here. She said she'd arranged it with him so she wouldn't have to make that long journey alone, but I suspect she wanted to introduce him around, maybe to test the possibility of moving him in. I told her he had no place in our society, not the way things are now."

"Because it would look bad?"

"I can hear you trying not to say hypocrite. Which she said outright. Not that I blame her. The marriage was based on appearances. But there is too much strife, and I don't think Marzio di Peretti would have been content to lounge around in the background, pouring wine at Ruli's parties and sitting next to widowed baronesses in order to make up the table. He has ambitions."

"Oh."

"So I told her what she did in Paris was her business, but here, in Dobrenica, where people still talk about two hundred year old gossip as if it happened yesterday, he would have to cool his heels in one of the guest rooms until she was ready to leave—if I had to assign a Vigilzhi to sit on him until she'd packed her bag."

"Okay. I'm not passing judgment, by the way."

"I did. Marzio is an ass." Alec's smile was brief, and ironic. "He's never had a job. Or rather his job seems to be leeching off of rich, titled women, while gassing on about his great plans for internet publishing, once he gets enough funding. He's been gathering funding for ten years. Not even a website to show for it." He stared at the mulled wine, then he sighed abruptly. "Ruli and I shared a drink to seal our agreement. We must have had more than one. I don't remember. In fact, that's all I remember."

Must have had more than one. I remembered how much liquor we'd slapped back the summer before and wondered if they'd had more like six. But I kept my lip zipped, because I also remembered that when he'd been drinking over a certain amount, Alec didn't drive. He'd have Emilio or Kilber take the wheel.

He went on. "According to what Magda Stos told the staff, as soon as Marzio heard Ruli and me clinking glasses, he got pissed off. Ordered Magda to take him to the nearest civilized city so he could fly to Paris. That much is corroborated by the fact that one of the service vehicles was gone as well as di Peretti and Magda."

"So then what happened?"

"Apparently Ruli insisted that we go after him. I don't remember offering to drive her myself, but I must have. She always did prefer me to drive. And that's my car down at the bottom of the gully, with no one in the driver's seat."

He looked down, his face so tense and unhappy I felt sick. "I don't remember it," he whispered. "I don't remember any of it. All I remember is waking up with the world's worst headache, bruised from tumbling down a cliff, the contents of Ruli's purse scattered underneath me. I probably would have frozen to death but for my usual outriders' discovering the Daimler gone and coming after us. They saw the smoke of the burning car." He glanced away, at the stage, but I had a feeling what he was seeing was that horrible smoke. He made a quick gesture, as if pushing something away. "There is no use talking further about it until I remember."

"Of course," I said, with another worried glance at his tense face. It was clear that dragging out the story again was not helping. Time to change the subject. "Tell me instead how are things going in the country otherwise?"

He took a deep breath, like someone had lifted a boulder off his chest. "Incremental progress." But his fingers were still turning that mug around and around. "You know I want to get wind turbines up in the mountain passes where there is always wind."

"That's clean energy. Who objects to that? Or rather, why? Is it the cost?"

"The cost is one factor." Now he was back in territory where he was sure of himself. "There is a solid phalanx of old-fashioned people who feel that we don't need such frivolities as electricity. We did fine without it for centuries. I think I told you how long it took to get the hydroelectric dam built. That was partly the cost, partly because we used its power to run the city's waste management system, which is also new, and partly because there was so much resistance to these innovations, which are relatively benign."

"Water power is considered green," I said, thinking, *Keep him going on hydroelectricity, if it eases that burden.* "Is the resistance fear of flooding or environmental damage?"

His smile was brief, automatic rather than warm. "No. We're not that sophisticated, here. It was resistance to change. The underlying worry is that should we need the Blessing, we won't be able to reach the Nasdrafus if we're riddled with the poisons of electricity."

"Do you think that's true?"

"It doesn't matter what I think." He lifted his head as, below, another group began to strum a minor key fanfaronade. "The mountain people are difficult to get to, and even more difficult to convince. I can tell you this, however: Magic, or whatever it is, is not destroyed by electricity. Yesterday when you walked in, Beka was demonstrating magic-or-whatever-it-is on a tablet computer."

"She knows magic?"

Alec looked away, then back. Again he was turning his mug around and around. "I'll leave Beka to answer that question for herself. Perhaps I shouldn't have said anything, though I see no danger in it. If you stay here, Kim, you're going to get mired as deeply as the rest of us. You'd better consider what that means for you."

I'm here because I love you. I spent the past several months studying every word of Milton's poem "Lycidas" because Nat told me before I left that she thinks it holds the key to understanding you.

When are such confessions welcome, and when yet another burden? There was that wedding ring, still on his finger. It had to mean something, because he'd stood beside Ruli and made her his wife.

"Here's what I know," I said. "I want to help you. Any way I can." I gave in to my own desire and reached for his left hand, meaning it as an encouraging gesture. "We don't have to talk about whether or not there's a 'you and me' until you've had as much time as you need."

His left hand lay under mine unmoving, but his right gripped that mug like it was a hand grenade. "Are you going to come to the funeral? It's at noon on the twenty eighth."

"Do you think I should? Will my presence make this conspirator gossip about us any worse?" I casually lifted my fingers so I could hold my mug with both hands. And he didn't stop me.

"That gossip would have been just as bad if you hadn't shown up," he said dryly. "It was all over the valley that your grandmother was visiting Milo for the holidays; and then the rumor reached me that you were expected to show up as well. That was the morning before the accident. It was merely news of interest then. Until the night of the accident."

"Sheesh. So no matter what I do, I'm toast."

"Just continue what you are doing. Don't worry about the gossip. You can't. There's always gossip of one sort or another, and worrying about it can drive you mad."

"Okay. I'm so used to the anonymity of the big city that . . . well, anyway. Tell me about the funeral, what's expected."

"I can't tell you all the details. Aunt Sisi sent a message requesting that she be permitted to organize the funeral."

"That sounds more like a grieving mother."

"That was my thought. As for you, anything beyond showing up at the cathedral is . . . optional."

"I suppose I ought to be there as the Dsaret representative, then. But hey. If I stay much longer than that, I should probably call my folks, and you know the cell phone issue."

"You can always use the phone in my office at the palace. Natalie could take you over there, if I am tied up. That's how she keeps in touch with her medical suppliers in London."

"Thanks." And because personal issues worsened his tension, and I was feeling protective, I tried for something light. "Do you ever get time to go to a movie? Watch TV? Read a book?"

"All three. During those long drives to the border, I've been listening to Patrick O'Brian's series."

"You like those?"

"Excellent," Alec said, and pushed the mug aside as he leaned toward me. "Excellent evocation of the time, of characters, of the world of wooden ships. They have nothing to do with modern day politics, and there is no vestige of magic, or of ghosts."

"I don't know," I said. "There are some hints of liminal space in some of Stephen Maturin's scenes."

"True," Alec said, and the Mr. Darcy mask eased fractionally. It felt like a victory. "True. But then Stephen Maturin seems to exist in liminal space."

There we were, off again, just like summer. Liminal space. Vrajhus. Was the Nasdrafus liminal space? Napoleonic times and why the appeal. The conversation was like a tennis match without a score, as he hitched his chair closer to me, so our talk wouldn't disturb the other listeners.

A chance glance up, and we'd slid from personal space back into intimacy. I could hear his breathing and see his pupils dilate. I could feel the chemistry again, as powerful as summer.

I don't know what he saw in my face, but his expression lengthened, for one heartbeat, into pain, or regret, or maybe it was a longing to match mine. He grabbed the mug and tossed back the rest of his wine in a sudden, almost violent gesture.

When the waiter came back, he refilled both our mugs. Before either of us could touch the mulled wine, Kilber appeared, a huge presence. He didn't say anything, but Alec got to his feet. "I have to get back," he whispered.

"Okay. Bye."

Alec brushed the tips of his fingers on the top of my hand and then was gone. I kissed the place on my hand where he had touched and stayed there staring at his empty chair until my eyelids ceased to sting.

When I got back to the Waleskas' inn, the dining room was heady with the fumes of various mulled drinks. People sat tightly packed around the perimeter of the room. I stood in the background as three very old people played instruments with somewhat rough enthusiasm, one on accordion, another on violin, and the third playing a cimbalom.

In the center of the room, two older men and a teenage boy danced with their arms entwined across each other's shoulders, feet stomping and twisting in complicated rhythms as everyone clapped on the beat.

They finished with a yell and a leap into the air. The claps dissolved into applause, somewhat shortened; it was clear that this had been going on for some time.

Several young girls jumped up, a couple of them giggling self-consciously. I was going to move past, but Madam Waleska had been on the watch. She popped up by the counter and boomed, "Here is Mademoiselle! She has promised to give us French ballet!"

The applause was loud and enthusiastic, the waiting faces mostly friendly, some curious, some expectant. What did dance mean to them? What would *my* dancing mean?

Theresa watched me, her entire body radiating urgency, and I knew it wasn't at the prospect of watching me dance. That meant there was a question of face, or reputation. Maybe if I bowed out the Waleskas would look bad.

So even though I hadn't warmed up, and I was dressed completely wrong, and I felt a little ridiculous, I started humming the first thing in my mind, which was what Misha had played on the taragot at Zorfal; the song with the distinctive minor-key tritone. I hummed as I dance-walked around in a circle.

My singing voice is somewhere between computer-generated flat-tone and a chipmunk's, but enough of the melodic line managed to convey itself that several gasped. What did that song mean? Yet another hidden pitfall?

I whirled into a pirouette.

Someone picked up the melody on a recorder, and then several girls began to sing. Interpretive dance had never been my thing. My ballet was corps level, never soloist, and I was no good at choreography. My favorite type of free dance is ballroom, with a partner to respond to.

".*. . hear us O Xanpia, open the door!*
Give us the light, Xanpia, bound in your wreath . . ."

So I used the easy beat and began a Highland step-dance. I'd taken several courses in high school, mindful of my father's Scots background.

The song came to an end at last. I did a double pirouette, took a bow, and sat down, figuring it would be rude to perform and then vanish. The teenage girls jumped up, and began a vigorous folk dance. One of them tried some innovations, working in a few of the Highland steps I'd done. Cool!

After that some guys kicked and leaped in place, Georgian-style, with a lot of masculine flourishing. I wondered if Tony knew any of those dances. If he danced at all, he'd be good at it—far better than these fellows, one of whom was drunk, and the youngest, on the end, was behind the beat just enough to nearly step on his partner's toes.

Did Alec know the dances? I tried to imagine him—the sorrow and yearning I thought I'd successfully suppressed was back, stronger than before, as I thought about Alec's rare grin, pictured his hands loose and easy as he whirled and kicked.

In the distance the cathedral bells rang, and Madam came out, clapping her hands. The party reluctantly broke up. I began to tramp upstairs, then paused, looking back. Madam and her daughters and several young cousins were tiredly stacking dishes and hauling them to the back. Josip and several men were busy moving tables and chairs back into place.

Tania paused before lifting a tray full of crockery, giving a huge yawn. When she met my eyes, I ran down to meet her. "I don't want to keep you," I whispered. "I only wanted to know if that ghost, my grandfather, lives in that room, or began to appear when I arrived a few days ago."

Her eyes rounded. "He's always been with you."

"Always?"

"He was there when you first arrived. I thought you were . . . I thought you were the ghost of Madam Statthalter."

"I know. But you say there were other ghosts with me?"

"This man arrived with you. After Christmas Eve Mass, there were several of them."

I put the heels of my hands straight out before me, arms rigid, as if ready to halt an oncoming train. "Wait. They follow me around? So when I'm eating breakfast, a pack of ghosts is watching?"

"It's not quite like that . . ." Another yawn took her, fiercer than before, "they come and go."

"Thanks, Tania. Good night."

I refused to worry about ghosts hovering in my room. I had a fencing match to mentally prepare for. A match, or maybe it would be another duel.

TWELVE

I F THE GHOST OF Grandfather Armandros was really there (for any definition of *really* that you prefer), I saw no sign of him either in my room or reflected in the wardrobe mirror.

I dropped straight into sleep but kept waking up intermittently, restless and worried about oversleeping. At the first faint blue of dawn, I got up, bathed, and then confronted the wardrobe problem.

I'd packed for a very few days. The forest green dress for fancy, the periwinkle blue one for backup or not-so-fancy. My usual jeans and three long sleeved shirts, a nightie, one leotard for stretching, tights, socks, and undies. I had no fencing clothes, and what I had were fast running out.

Time to ask Auntie Nat's wardrobe advice. But *after* the fencing session.

Tony had dropped that hint about the Danilovs keeping their place like an oven, so I pulled on a sleeveless leotard over my tights and then a long-sleeved cotton tee and jeans. I wasn't about to fence in a sleeveless leotard, but I could finish warming up in it, and if the practice space was really sauna-like, strip down to it between bouts.

Last thing, I pinned my hair up in a tight ballet bun, then went downstairs to wait for my ride—who had better be Danilov, I thought. If Tony was driving, I would get the address from him, and take an inkri. Twice, I'd gotten into a car with him and regretted it. I was not going three for three.

In the dining room, I found bread, cheese, preserved fruit, and cold meat pies laid out next to a small stack of plates and silver. When no one appeared, I helped myself and sat alone by a window, looking out at a white world as I ate. I'd finished breakfast and stashed my dishes on the waiting tray when I heard a muffled *vroom*.

A short time later the door opened, then the inner door, and a tall, elegant feminine figure entered, looking around with a haughty air. For the first time in my life I understood the phrase *dressed to kill*. That pants suit and the great coat with its huge fuzzy collar and trimmed sleeves were from Paris fashion houses, and she wore them well.

An equally fuzzy snow hat hid her hair, and sunglasses hid her eyes, so I wasn't sure of her identity until she lifted the glasses, and there was Phaedra Danilov.

"Ready?" she asked. "Or have you changed your mind?"

Her tone made her ambivalence about me clear, but it was better than Cerisette von Mecklundburg's outright hostility. I grabbed my coat.

A few seconds later I sat for the first time in a Maserati. The sporty coupe model was bright red, built low to the ground. As soon as I was in she jammed her muscle car into gear and zoomed up the street.

The snow gave the stone buildings a stippled effect. The cobblestones roared under the wheels. I gripped my hands as she downshifted in surging spurts.

When she downshifted on the approach to the huge traffic circle at the start of Prinz Karl-Rafael Street, I said, "All right, I'm impressed with your car and your driving. How about taking it easy, before you nuke a pedestrian or a sleigh driver?"

She pulled the car into a skid, sending a sheet of snow flying up. I thought we were hydroplaning on ice, but she controlled the car perfectly as we came to a stop facing the central fountain with the young shepherdess.

She shot a glance my way. "There are no inkris, or streetcars. There will be little traffic, as today is the Stefan-Zarbat, the—"

"St. Stephen's Day, or Boxing Day. Right. I thought that was the day after Christmas, though."

"It is, but it's generally recognized on Monday if Christmas has fallen on Saturday, here. Your inn will not provide hot meals or service, but you will pay for the day."

Her tone mocked me. Her expression was impossible to see, what with the huge glasses and the fuzzy hat obscuring a lot of her face.

"Thanks for explaining," I said, trying for neutral corners.

Her grip on the steering wheel tightened, then loosened as she faced straight ahead at the whirling snow that barely obscured the fountain. The figures seemed to shimmer, almost to move.

I shifted my gaze from the fountain to Phaedra. She had been frowning at the steering wheel. She said to it, "Your being here right now looks unfortunate. Again."

"I can't help that." I couldn't see her eyes behind those bug glasses, and I wasn't sure I wanted to, especially sitting so close to each other. It didn't take magic powers to feel her antagonism.

So I peered through the windshield at the fountain. They'd shut off the water, of course. The wind-swirled snow was relentless, partially obscuring the dancing figures, but that did not explain the giddy sense I had that the fountain figures were moving.

"I didn't talk to anyone but my parents before I came. There was no conspiracy of any kind, at least, not with me in it," I said. "But I'm beginning to think you don't want to believe that."

I blinked. Ghosts I'd come to terms with. The idea of the possible existence of another plane, the Nasdrafus, I was getting used to. But what possible use would be moving fountain figures, even within the weird logic, or lack of logic, of magic?

Phaedra said, "No one knows what to believe. Except that your timing is . . ." She shrugged.

"Is this you dis-inviting me to this fencing *salle* of yours?"

Now the central figure, the little shepherdess (who I understood was also St. Xanpia) twirled on her toes, smiling as smoke-hazy animal shapes gamboled about her, tongues lolling, short horns glinting, plumed tails high. I blinked and she froze. The ghost animals were gone.

"Do you wear any diamonds?" she asked, as abruptly as before.

"Diamonds?" I struggled not to yelp: *What have you been smok-*

ing? "Does it *look* like I have any diamonds? I thought this was fencing practice."

Did she really think that I would wear magical charms to fencing practice? No, much more likely this was her way of digging around for the truth about the rumors of the Dsaret Treasure.

That treasure did exist. The king had liquidated the last of the royal treasure on the eve of World War II, by melting it down in secret, after which it was formed into golden statues. Those were covered by plaster and hidden in the oldest church in Dobrenica, the Romanesque one high behind the city—the one dedicated to St. Xanpia. Alec had been in charge of slowly getting them replaced, without anyone finding out beyond the original conspirators.

Some of this was Gran's inheritance, faithfully kept by Milo all these decades, just in case she hadn't died in the war. Emilio, acting on behalf of Milo, had sent Gran's share to us at the beginning of September. In fact, it had arrived in Los Angeles the day I returned.

But as far as I was concerned, that was Gran's (and Milo's) business. So I said, "I don't own any diamonds. Or pearls. Or rubies. Argh, I wish they wouldn't do that. It makes me dizzy."

"Who is doing what?" Her high voice had sharpened. If drawling hadn't been habitual she probably would have sounded shrill.

"Xanpia and her animals and fauns. On that fountain." I pointed. "They're dancing around."

Phaedra's shoulder jerked back so she could face me, but all I saw were the greeny-black bug eyes of the sun glasses. Then she rammed the car into gear, and we took off.

Why so upset about the dancing animals at that fountain? She didn't speak again as we jetted over the bridge and up the hill to the posh area. The streets were empty. I remembered from summer that the Danilovs lived a block away from Ysvorod House, but these were long blocks, what with the extensive gardens surrounding each mansion.

Phaedra turned up a narrow driveway that had been shoveled, but was fast filling up again. When I caught sight of the front of the manor, I recognized from summer the winged lions and dancing fauns carved into the pediment. The rest of the Danilov home was obscured by the garden, unlike Mecklundburg House, which had a more shallow front garden that afforded a splendid view of the mansion's Palladian lineaments from the street.

As Phaedra pulled up close to a side door, I wondered if Mecklundburg House had been designed with public entertaining in mind, because this house seemed more isolated, if not reclusive, its exterior Renaissance-era.

We entered. The hall opened into an enormous complication of arches and vaultings in the Renaissance style. Like at the Eyrie, the center was a dome rounded with windows, and below it a glassed-in conservatory. Halls led off in every direction. They were not the smooth plaster of so many Renaissance buildings, but gorgeous boiserie, complete to gilt moldings.

The conservatory was filled with reflected light. As we walked by it, the sight of lemon trees threw me back to UCLA, on my way to fencing class. The sense of dislocation in time and space sharpened when we entered a long gallery.

Warm? Tony wasn't kidding. The heat nearly blasted me back out into the snow. The room was a picture gallery of paintings going back centuries, with a complicated rosewood ceiling carved in knotwork patterns, and a roaring fire in a stone fireplace big enough to park a car.

The zing and clash of steel echoed. My gaze arrowed straight for Tony, who looked up expectantly as Phaedra and I walked in, shedding coats and gloves and hats as fast as we could.

It could have been summer again. He sauntered toward us, wearing his usual loose white shirt over a black tee shirt, jeans, and boots.

Danilov lifted his saber in casual salute, then resumed lunge stretches. Honoré was a few paces away, dressed entirely in black and looking more like Bertie Wooster's evil twin than ever as he warmed up by practicing footwork. He was tall, slim, and impossibly elegant in those tailored fencing duds.

Phaedra led me to one side, where racks of equipment had been lined up next to a long table. We set down our armloads of winter gear, and I hesitated, wanting to strip to my leotard, but not sure if I should.

A few paces away a good-looking guy in old jeans shrugged into a white fencing coat—not the rumpled general issue ones I was used to at my university fencing class, but fitted, coming down mid-thigh like a military tunic. He had curly dark hair. I recognized him as Niklos, Tony's main aide-de-camp.

The guy who'd shot me.

His gaze lifted, our eyes met, then he advanced. "You are Mademoiselle Murray, yes?" he asked in French-accented English. "I must tender apologies, me, for my actions at the castle. I trust that your bones, they were not involved? No damage, one could say, serious?"

"Nope," I said, trying for ultra-cool. When I caught Tony grinning at me I added, "Except now I'm way out of shape."

Niklos made a large gesture, smiling. "We must make the amends for that."

"Tea?" Danilov drawled. "Or coffee?"

I wanted to say *Iced tea, and heavy on the ice*, but I didn't want to be rude as he gestured with his sword toward the side table set with a splendid tea service, and Russian-style glass cups in silver holders.

Phaedra was dressed in ski clothes that showed off her thin, taut body. She was in splendid shape, her clothes so snug they were the next thing to a leotard. In relief, I shrugged out of my long-sleeved shirt, then sat on the floor to take off my boots and socks. I felt their gazes, quick, then away. Something was going on, and it had nothing to do with my togs.

Whatever. I kept my jeans on over my tights, and began some ballet stretches to warm up.

Phaedra said to me, "You will find extra jackets here. There are also gauntlets, but mostly men's sizes. I have an extra pair."

"Women don't fence here?"

She lifted a shoulder, her mouth tight. "Some do. But this is our private *salle*."

She stood next to her brother, who wiped his damp brow. Phaedra whispered something to him. Tony backed up, taking up a lazy stance next to the fireplace, in spite of the blast of Hades roaring out.

Danilov gave Phaedra one of those sharp shrugs with covert facial expressions, like, *This was your idea.*

The welcome I'd hoped for—a truce, maybe even the hand of friendship—had vanished like smoke going up the chimney. Instead, I felt that uneasy, crawly sense along the back of my neck; something that happens when I think people are talking about me, and not in a good way.

Phaedra whirled around and advanced on me.

"I don't suppose you'll tell us the truth," Phaedra drawled, "but I will ask. What are you doing here in Dobrenica?"

I got up from the floor and took first position in ballet, as if beginning a set of warm-up *plies* would somehow force the incipient interrogation into becoming the fencing practice that I'd been invited to.

They were all watching me, except for Honoré, who practiced fully extended lunges into a target on a wooden post some five yards away, his profile completely absorbed, as if he existed in a different space.

I made myself do right foot through all five positions. They waited for me to speak. So I said, "First tell me why I owe you any answer, seeing as how you've offered me nothing but hostility ever since you laid eyes on me?" When she didn't shoot back a hot retort, I tried to get the better of my temper. "I apologize for my lies at the duchess's party last summer, but you know, I wouldn't have done that if you people hadn't acted like I was going to rob you right down to your underwear the second I walked through those doors."

"What we heard, before you walked through those doors, was someone chatting up Alec and doing her best to take Ruli's place." Phaedra leaned against the table laden with breakfast.

"What?"

She crossed her arms and gave me a level stare from her assured place on the moral high ground. "You were using her name while shagging Alec up and down the Adriatic coast, last summer. Then you came here, and we thought—Tante Sisi thought—she said she thought—you were doing your best to take Ruli's place and marry Alec. You certainly had him by the—" She stopped herself.

Honoré muttered something and lunged at his target. He skewered the center of the one-inch circle inside the painted heart.

I couldn't quite hear him, but it sounded like he'd spoke the German word for fuss again, *Dienstbeflissenheit,* and the others turned his way with complete attention. Odd.

When Honoré went on practicing, Danilov poured coffee, then shot me a speculative glance across the table. "It appeared to us that you'd done something to Ruli," he said, his tone light, as if it didn't much matter. "You used her name. Shopped at her favorite places. Flirted with di Peretti and those *connards* on the coast."

"Yes I did. To flush her out of hiding—we thought, we hoped. And then I came here. Without Alec knowing. I didn't pretend to be Ruli here, in this city, until Alec and the duchess, your Aunt Sisi, asked me to. So why didn't you bring these questions to either of them?"

The Danilovs cut fast glances at Honoré.

He was busy lunging at the target.

Phaedra said, "We did. Alec said it was to flush Ruli out of hiding, and Tante Sisi agreed."

I jerked my chin at Tony as I began the *grandes plies.* "*You* tried to kidnap me the next day and haul me off to that castle of yours, where you had Ruli locked up as a prisoner, so do *not* try to scam me about my conspiring against Ruli."

Tony raised his hands, palms out. "I'm not saying anything here."

I shot a glare at Phaedra as I jerked my thumb Tony's way. "*He* knew I was here to find out about my grandmother's background. As for the shagging, there wasn't any. Alec was a perfect gentleman on the Adriatic coast." *Worse luck.* "And during the entire time I stayed at Ysvorod House, he camped out somewhere else."

Danilov leaned his hands on the breakfast table. "Tante Sisi said that you and Alec were observing the surface proprieties to stop gossip. She convinced us that going along with your pretense would lead to exposure."

Of me and my supposed plot. At least he didn't say it.

"Yes, about that," I returned cordially, as I used one of the target posts as a barre and began warming up my legs with low kicks, then high. "What exactly did she say to you? Considering the fact that she knew that Tony had Ruli up at the Eyrie all along?" I did a *battement fondu développé* with full extension, toes pointed Tony's way as I said to Danilov, "So you didn't know that Tony was planning to hijack the government?"

The fire crackled. Porcelain clinked as Danilov set down his glass cup. I worked through both legs, and began a set of *grandes battements* as *Smack!* Honoré's rapier point dug into the target's heart.

Tony leaned against the stone fireplace, damp strands of hair across his brow, and smiled.

Then Phaedra took me by surprise. "I didn't know," she said flatly. As though still angry. "I knew there was some conspiracy, and it seemed that Alec was either a party to it, or pretending not to see it. Everyone was aware that he didn't want to marry Ruli."

I looked at her, amazed that even after knowing what Tony had done, she still blamed me through this "Alec conspiracy" theory.

As I snapped my feet out in hard, fast *frappés*, Honoré muttered again—this time in Ancient Greek. Then he set aside his rapier with a precise movement and smoothed a black lock of hair off his brow with his other hand. When his hair wasn't slicked back, it reminded me a lot of Alec's—thick and fine, with a natural wave.

I said, "By the way, who's di Peretti again? Seems to me I've heard that name before." *Oh yeah, the boyfriend Ruli was going to install at the palace.*

"Marzio di Peretti?" Phaedra said, eyes wide in disbelief. "You met him, in Split. You *danced* with him."

"I told you why I did that—to flush Ruli out of hiding." I paused and took in the Danilovs' skeptical faces. "But I don't think you want to believe anything I say."

Whoosh! A welcome draft of cold air swirled in. Honoré had opened the far door and a window beyond that. Within seconds the temperature inside became more bearable, the fresh, chilly air welcome.

Phaedra crossed her arms. "No. Yes. There is the matter of Tante Sisi's actions. But the only person you talked to besides Alec was Ruli, and then you left the country. Tante Sisi said you left because you discovered there is no Dsaret treasure. Not that any of us believed there's still such a thing, but we could see how *you* would."

A fast glance back at Tony. I remembered what I'd said just after he'd killed Reithermann. In spite of the fact that I'd been shot, I'd figured out where the Dsaret Treasure was hidden. Then I had to go and retort like a six-year-old: *I know where the treasure is, and I won't tell you.* How dork-tastic can anyone possibly get? Granted I had a bullet in my shoulder and a raging fever.

Tony smiled gently at me, like we were the only two people in the room. I bet myself all the treasure in the bank—in the world—that he was thinking of it, too, and that he was going to pick up this unfinished business when he could pick the place. And the time.

I'd have to make sure that there would be no place and time.

I forced my gaze away from him. The others were watching Honoré again. Last summer I'd thought of them as a kind of monolith of elegant snobbery, indistinguishable except in looks, equally uninteresting. Now that I was seeing them up close, and the only similarity between them was this undercurrent of tension. This much I was sure of: Whatever Tony's motivation had been at that horrid wreath party at the Ridots-kis', the Danilovs had brought me here for their own reasons; not as a friendly gesture but for this interrogation in an overheated room.

I was not going to tell them about Ruli's ghost. But I could tell them what she had caused me to decide. I said, "I came to try to reason with Ruli, because I heard she wasn't happy. I didn't know she was dead."

The Danilovs turned Honoré's way.

He raised his weapon. I braced myself for another odd mutter, but all he said was, "*En avant.*"

Let's go.

As if released from invisible ties, the others pulled on fencing tunics. Within a few more minutes my expectations took another hit. This wasn't merely a setup to grill me. At least, it had been partly that. But not wholly. It was clear from the ways they fell into familiar patterns of warm-up, then paired off, that this gathering was habitual.

I finished a few combinations, then hunted through the available clothing in search of a tunic that more or less fit. It felt different from the fencing jackets I was used to, but it was sturdy and quilted. As I sat on the floor to put my socks and boots back on, Tony spoke up from behind me.

"If there was anyone wanting evidence you were raised in California, those bare feet would convince them."

I shrugged as I pulled on the gauntlets. They fit in length, though they were tight in width, which wasn't surprising. Phaedra was a tad taller than me.

Tony tipped his head toward the rack. "Pick a weapon."

"Are you too cool for warm-ups?"

He snorted. "No. If I do have to defend myself, no one is going to stand aside while I stretch."

"I'm half warmed. I usually do some lunges."

"We'll take it slow," he said.

"Bad guys won't do that, either."

He shrugged.

I said, "Where are the helmets?"

"We could dig one up for you, if that makes you feel more comfortable."

"I take it no one worries about lawsuits any more than they worry about poked eyes?"

"What can I say? We're backward here. Danilov says his family used this room as a *salle* in days of yore, until his great-great-grandmother put a stop to it when she noticed the boys' spurs cutting up the floor." He pointed to the parquet a few yards away.

"Where did you practice before?" I asked, as I sorted through the blades. I found a fine rapier, what we called a saber in competition fencing. I tested the length. Perfect.

"My place," he said as we squared up. "When I was in town."

"And you can't anymore because?"

"The way the estate is tied up. Robert has that wing of the house now. Goes to the heir. He chucked us out. My mother still has hold of the duke's wing."

"What's Robert turning it into, a torture chamber?"

Tony laughed and struck, easy and slow. I parried, and we worked through some exchanges, neither of us moving fast, as he said, "Restoring the grand gallery. His big project is the opera house."

"Opera house? Robert? That has to be a front for something sinister."

"No more sinister than having to listen to opera." Tony flashed a grin. "Robert got infected by it while studying in Italy." He increased the pace. "So you came to talk to my sister?"

"Another third degree?"

"No, it's fencing practice."

"It was the third degree—and a slaughter—back in London."

He grinned and attacked in the high line. "So?"

"Why didn't you tell me Ruli was dead? Nevermind, you obviously thought Alec and I were up to some evil plot, just as you were last summer. Do you really see the rest of the world as conniving liars?"

He didn't answer the question—or the implication that he was a conniving liar. Instead, he pressed an attack on my right, which I warded with a snap. "So answer this instead," I said. "Phaedra stopped near a fountain. I think she was going to begin her third degree then, but she changed her mind when I told her the fountain figures were moving. Why?"

"I think you spooked her."

"Why?"

"Family secret."

"I thought I was a member of the family."

"I'm wondering about that." Tony whipped the blade around, attacking in the low line. "When we were at Sedania. Did you see something through that old portal?"

"Yes," I said, recalling golden light and strange faces. I whistled my blade up in a fast block, then lunged high. "For about a second."

"And you've seen that sort of thing before?"

"Yes." Mentally I vowed to redouble my pushups as I leaped back. "Your turn to answer. Did you know that Grandfather Armandros has been following me around?"

He checked, his eyes widening. "No. You've seen him?"

"Briefly. Reflected in the wardrobe mirror. But someone else has seen him around me."

"Heh."

"You told me after Niklos shot me that you have seen ghosts."

"Yes. Up at the Eyrie. Ever since I was small. But not here in the city. And I've never seen our respected grandfather."

Clashes and clangs resounded to my right. Danilov was fighting against his sister. Clearly they'd been working with one another for a long time. They were superlative fencers.

Tony whacked me on the shoulder. "Warmed up?"

Warmed up? My arm felt like string! "As good as it gets."

And mayhem is what I got. Though my strength was sorely lacking, at least I wasn't pole-axed by jet lag after a thousand mile drive, as I'd been when he attacked me in London. I had enough of my old speed to land a couple of good hits, causing Tony to laugh out loud. Other than that, he demonstrated with pitiless detail not only how out of shape I'd let myself get, but how much of an advantage height and strength had. I would have to recover my flexibility as well as my speed, which had been more than a match for the tall and strong when I was doing serious competition.

Finally I lifted my blade, wringing with sweat. "Break."

He sauntered over to Honoré, who leaned against the opposite wall, sipping coffee as he watched Niklos and Danilov finish. Phaedra gestured to Tony, who walked her way. To discuss me? No, to fight: they squared up. I reached the breakfast table, wiped my damp forehead—and there was Honoré's considering gaze zapping me from the other side of the room, from beneath an enormous portrait of some guy on the back of a rearing horse. The guy was tall and thin and blond, wearing a variation on the Vigilzhi uniform.

Most of the other noble figures in the portraits were dark-haired. As I recovered my breath, I wandered along the walls looking up at the various styles of clothing and painting. I could guess when this family had first married with the von Mecklundburgs, judging from the variations of my own genetic markers that began appearing in the portraits. It looked like they'd been closely allied since the Vasas brought in pale hair. One of Queen Sofia's daughters, maybe?

When I returned from my perusal of the gallery, the others had changed partners. They were all extremely good, but Niklos and Honoré were world class fencers, playing ten-moves-ahead chess with their blades.

When the matches broke up, Tony sauntered back in my direction. "Up to your speed?"

"Those two are amazing." I jerked a thumb at Honoré, who was demonstrating something with his point as Niklos observed.

"Honoré used to do competitions in Germany a few years ago."

"Before what?" I asked. "Do Honoré and Danilov have jobs? What do they do? Or if that's a state secret, tell me this: Have you ever included Alec in these private meets?"

Tony's brows rose. "He used to practice with us, when we were young. Over at our house. This was while Ysvorod House was still occupied by the Soviet captain, and he was still stopping with his father at the Dominican Friars, who had been sheltering Milo for years. That all changed when Alec became Statthalter and got his house back."

"He had no time after he became Statthalter, is that what you're saying?"

"Partly that, but also my mother objected to the inevitable streams of messengers and minions running through our house. Actually, I think she hated having Klaus Kilber lurking around. So Alec started going to the Vigilzhi officers' gym at the old convent."

"The Vigilzhi kicked out a bunch of nuns?"

He laughed. "The Soviets did. They made us build an up-to-date gym for their officers, and the Vigilzhi took it over when they left. The Clares who used to live there now live behind the hospital."

"Do any of you have actual jobs?" I asked, as Niklos took on Phaedra, pressing her hard.

"Danilov and Honoré sit on the High Council—began as soon as they reached twenty-five."

"*High* Council? I thought it was just the Council."

Tony looked across the room in Honoré's direction, then shrugged. "We usually call it the Council. As opposed to the General Council, whose members are elected." He gave me one of those sardonic looks.

"So Danilov didn't run for his Council seat?" I couldn't imagine the elegant Danilov stooping to campaign, even a low key campaign of the sort Alec had told me about during summer.

"The five families have hereditary seats, as does the mayor of Riev, the guilds' rep—you could think of him as the unions' rep. Then there's the bishop, the chief rabbi, and the Orthodox metropolitan. There is actual work involved. Whether we tend to that work or appoint someone to serve as proxy is a matter of . . . negotiation." He dropped his voice and continued in English, "Phaedra has always wanted to be an officer in the Vigilzhi. Alec once promised her that the Vigilzhi would be open to women—with Dmitros Trasyemova's full support."

"But it isn't?"

"No. I also promised," he added with a humorous shrug, "and also failed to keep the promise. In Alec's case, the change was to have been initiated after Milo's return, at which time the Statthalter would be retired. As Statthalter Alec has one vote. If Milo returns, Alec would have two votes: as the Ysvorod on the High Council and as heir. The old generation is mostly holdouts for the old ways. His two votes would have broken the deadlock, and opened the Vigilzhi to women."

I glanced at the others. Phaedra was still fencing Niklos. Danilov leaned casually against the wall between a gilt portrait of a Renaissance matron and an oval picture of a family group in eighteenth century satin, posed in a sylvan setting. Danilov offered highly technical commentary on the match.

I pointed my blade Phaedra's way. "She's good."

"She's a first-rate sharpshooter, and she rides like a Cossack." Tony grinned. "She's usually my tango partner. You know the tango?"

"Oh yes," I said. "Used to do it a lot."

"Interesting." Tony's brows lifted again. "I'm glad you told me that."

"What's so special about tango?"

Tony said, "You must be aware that it is . . . seduction without words."

I snorted. "Tango is a dance. A fun dance, but it's a dance."

He said mockingly, "Yours must be a very weak style."

Stung, I retorted, "I won some awards, as it happens."

"Your partner was a lover?"

I laughed. "Hardly! My favorite partner is gay."

Tony looked up sharply as a young guy entered. Though he didn't wear any special outfit he had the air of a messenger. He headed for the Danilovs.

Phaedra and Niklos broke off their match. Tony caught up with them in a few long strides. The messenger spoke, then Tony said something to Danilov, who gave a short nod. Tony issued some orders to the messenger, who left even more swiftly than he'd come.

During all this Honoré lounged at the other end of the table, as though he existed in a separate sphere, until Danilov beckoned and talked to him in a low voice.

Tony came back to me, his mouth tight. "It looks as if our day has filled up, so we'll have to call it quits."

"What's wrong?"

"A summons from my mother." His voice was clipped as he sent a questioning glance at Phaedra.

Before she could speak, Honoré said, "I will take Kim."

THIRTEEN

T HE OTHERS GAVE HIM these looks that not only revealed their surprise—with subtle clues such as narrowed eyes, interrogative angles to their heads—but also hinted at some meaning or message that I couldn't decipher.

"It's almost noon," Phaedra said, drawing the word out in an *are-you-sure?* sort of tone.

"I know what time it is," Honoré said, and to me, in perfect English, "They know me for a creature of habit. It's a curiously civilized comfort, to perform certain tasks at the same hour each day, and from noon to four I work on a project. But it can wait."

"Sure," I said. "Thanks."

Honoré gave me a polite nod. "I will return shortly." He left through one of the side doors.

Danilov went to the double doors and called out to someone. A couple of guys, one young, one old, appeared to take away the tea service as Danilov wiped down the blades himself. Phaedra hung the jackets over the racks to air out.

Honoré reappeared a few minutes later, his hair damp, his clothes changed. He pulled on a snow cap and shrugged into a coat over shirt, woolen vest, and dun-colored jeans.

By then I'd wintered up. He led the way out.

To break the lengthening silence, I said, "What's your project? Of course, if it's a big secret—"

"Not secret at all." His smile was fleeting. "You might have noticed that the old library building is being restored."

I had no idea where the "old library" was, but I made an affirmative noise. He gave me a glance that recalled last summer and said with gentle reproof, "It's above the park named for King Alexander. Across the bridge from Ridotski House."

He obviously didn't care for white lies, so I said, "I know you all live fairly close together, but I don't know the streets at this end of the city. Last summer I spent most of my time holed up in Ysvorod House or being driven around."

"Fair enough." His equable tone was back. "The library was burned, of course—"

"By the Germans?"

"Actually, it was by the Soviets. The Germans left it alone once the Gestapo determined that we did not have any Jewish texts. As those had been removed and hidden, they believed our claim that we'd expelled the Jews two centuries before, and they took no further interest, other than seeing that the schools were all supplied with copies of *Mein Kampf* and similar rubbish."

"Ech. We had to read it for a history class."

"An amazing trifecta of evil, mad, and boring," he said over his shoulder as he opened the door. "The library was destroyed on the order of the first Soviet commander. We were to become good Soviets, you see, so they systematically attempted to eradicate our history. My paternal grandmother tells of how they woke up at midnight thinking the sun had risen early and discovered the library in flames."

We cleared the eaves of the house and bent into the wind. The snow was thicker than ever. Honoré's car was a sturdy Swedish model built for snowy driving—it had no problems bumping gently down the driveway, which was visible mostly as a pointillist landscape in a thousand shades of silver, white, and gray.

As he eased slowly into the street, I said, "So tell me about the project."

"What with that fire and many of our elders having fled their homes, we actually have relatively few historical documents left. Just for the amusement of our families, I've been reconstructing an annotated genealogy. The sort of thing that would bore anyone else, but is highly satisfactory when it's your own forebears."

"That sounds cool."

He sent me one of those considering looks, and then came the smile. "Most of the family have tired of hearing about it. I will have it printed and suitably bound, where it will look handsome on their shelves, and probably remain untouched once they've read about themselves and the most scandalous of their forebears."

He chuckled softly, and I grinned. There was no use in denying the obvious.

"I've been at it ten years, you see. If you'd like to have a look at it, I can stop at my house. You might recall that I live on the next street over."

"Are you kidding? I'd love to see it."

Another of those long glances, then he gave a little nod and swung the car around. We reached his place a minute later and turned up the driveway. He flashed his beams a couple of times and slowed. The garage door opened so promptly it was clear someone was waiting on his arrival.

We drove into the garage. When we stepped out, Honoré said, "Thank you, Zoldan. Please. Go join your family."

A red-cheeked middle-aged man in a quilted coat looked from Honoré to me, hesitating.

Honoré said, "I believe I will not perish from tending the garage door when I take Mademoiselle home. Go enjoy Stefan-Zarbat."

The man touched his cap and shut the garage door, closing himself outside.

Honoré opened the inner door, and we passed through a plain white hallway. I'd noticed that the insides of most of the buildings whiffed of wood smoke. Fireplaces were still in use for heat, and they had plenty of wood. Honoré's place had the same smell, but slightly sharper—a chemical scent. I was wondering if that was normal when Honoré sniffed, and frowned. "Smells like one of the fireplaces is smoldering. Zoldan must have shut the windows tight against this weather—"

The click of toenails on the polished parquet floor preceded the exuberant appearance of a chocolate brown wolfhound, who bounced in, flagged tail wagging, tongue lolling, until he sniffed me. Then he went on alert, gaze fixed, tail lowered.

"This is Shurisko," Honoré said, ruffling the dog's long ears. "Shurisko, Kim is a friend."

I held out a hand for him to sniff as Honoré said, "Our ancestors lived with that stink year round, apparently. Every other letter, and most of the diaries, complain a lot about smoky fires, especially at the start of winter. My theory is that the stork nests would drop twigs, which singed then burned away."

Shurisko gave me a tentative tail wag—permission to touch. I ran my hands down his back, scratching his spine. He stretched his muzzle upward, his eyes half shut with pleasure. When I straightened up, I was rewarded with a quick lick, and then the dog bounded out again, pausing only to sniff an enormous tortoiseshell cat, who paced languorously across a hall, tail high, ignoring the dog with disdain.

"This way," Honoré said as the dog vanished somewhere down one of the long halls.

We passed quickly through the empty house. During summer my visit had been confined to the formal salon, which was another of those eighteenth-century sitting rooms. The rest of the house was much more interesting, I discovered. Some relative had loved Art Deco, and so there were long, languid lines. Most of the furniture was black. The bookcases were made of a very dark wood, with gilding in art nouveau motifs. Throughout were Tiffany lamps with multi-faceted crystals worked in.

On each bookcase rested a pair of marble busts of famous figures from Greek and Roman times. On one bookshelf there appeared to be two busts, until I saw that the extra was actually a living black cat in meatloaf pose, back hunched, front paws curled neatly. In the long windows, crystals hung from curtains, catching light as they winked and gleamed.

We passed through two or three small sitting rooms, each with at least one bookcase, and then up a beautiful sweep of stairs and onto a long hall with doors on both sides. We walked to one end, and he opened a door to reveal a very narrow stairway. "The secret room is up here. I made it over for the Project."

"Secret room?"

His quick smile was lopsided like mine, like Mom's, like so many of us descendants of Armandros. Yet it wasn't Tony's pirate grin. The lifted corner gave it a whimsical charm.

"One of my great-great grandmothers was the mistress of a prince. She had the old secret passage fitted up. He tipped quite generously, so the servants maintained that he merely came to call. A steadfast assertion for forty years."

"Forty years!"

"And when the princess died, he married Karolina in secret. Here we are."

He opened the door to a cool chamber, a librarian's dream. It was solid books—the tastes of a sophisticate of a hundred years ago on one wall, and two hundred years ago on the next. Signs of ancient passion were long gone.

"Is that the secret passage?" I pointed back at the narrow stair, as the big tortie walked daintily in, followed by another cat, a young, lanky Persian.

"No." He smiled as he shut the door. The young Persian began to wind around his ankles, its purr loud and rusty. "That was the stairway for the servants' quarters. This room became the upstairs linen closet during the years of Karolina's grandson, who had six daughters before he got a son to inherit. The scandalous passage was covered up. It lies beyond that wall." He tipped his head toward a short bookcase on which sat a bust of a man with a Vigilzhi high collar. "Here's the Project."

He indicated the only pieces of furniture, a fine rolltop desk with a zillion little drawers, and a comfortable chair. Neatly stacked on the desk were several piles of papers. The Project was completely handwritten, in a beautiful old-fashioned italic hand.

I looked closer and read: . . . *the bullet holes can still be seen in the wall outside the shop, which is now a shoe repair. The fire fight continued down to the intersection with St. Marcos Street, where Shimon was able to dodge into the alley, and gain the cellar at Litvak's (St. Marcos) Wine Shop. Milo and Kilber kept them running*

And there it broke off.

"I hope you've made copies," I said, hesitant about touching.

"We haven't copy machines here. And I don't need copies. I am careful when I take notes, then the books are put back—though taking notes is tedious because I want all the details to be right. In this particular incident, the Soviets were going to shoot some nuns caught teaching catechism to the children and Dobreni history to the teens."

He tapped a small, very battered, bound book: a journal or diary.

"Shimon Ridotski, the current Prime Minister, heard about the order to execute the nuns. He contacted Milo and decoyed the MGB agents—forerunners of the KGB—while Milo and his aide-de-camp, Klaus Kilber, extracted the women."

"Into a cellar? Wouldn't that be a dead end?"

"Ordinarily," Honoré said.

"What do you mean, ordinarily? Oh. There are tunnels?"

He hesitated, which was an answer in itself; I was an outsider again.

So I went on, "I remember that incident from reading Milo's journal last summer. Though he gave no details."

Honoré said, "Milo's reticence is well known. Not loved by archivists. His journal is useless for much of anything other than a memory device. He and his people were excellent, however, about seizing leftover files whenever one set of invaders gave way to another. I promised on my life that these records will never leave this room until they go back to their various archives. We lost so much during the past half century."

He gave me the whimsical smile again, as he touched a sheaf of thin carbons so aged the faded ink on them was barely legible.

"That diary belongs to one of Kilber's agents. These here are carbons of MGB orders, stolen from their office by the old woman they employed to clean."

"Didn't they discover the missing carbons?"

"Of course. But by the time they caught up with her, she was about to be buried after a heart attack. Or so they thought. Another elderly woman who had recently died was substituted with the collusion of both families. The MGB forced their own people to do the cleaning after that—" He paused, raised his head, and sniffed. "Does it smell stronger to you?"

"Yes, but everything smells a little like fireplace smoke in your houses, to me." I hesitated, unsure whether I should mention the other smell that tugged at memory. I couldn't quite identify it.

"*Cum tacent, clamant,*" he muttered under his breath as he lifted his nose. "I'm going to look around. Feel free to examine any of these materials if you wish, but please do not take them out of the room."

"Got it," I said, dredging up the familiar quotation. Oh yes. *Although they keep silent, they cry aloud; their silence is more expressive than words.* "Cicero?" I asked.

Honoré gave me an odd look. "It's habit," he said slowly, then with a sudden, whimsical smile, "I promise I did not intend to be irritating this time."

He left, closing the door on the sharp scent of wood fire. *This time?* Because he wasn't there to ask, my mind moved on to wondering if the servants had left something in the oven. The smell reminded me of barbeques. Except it wasn't roasted meat.

I bent over the fragile carbon copies, careful not to touch. The blurry purple was in Cyrillic, already difficult for me to read, so I switched to the diary, which turned out to be written in a hodgepodge of Dobreni, German, and Latin. No wonder the project had taken ten years, if these were the sorts of sources Honoré had to work with.

But as I pored over the diary, my hindbrain was supervising the wrestling match between memory and subconscious until I recognized what I was smelling. "Lighter fluid," I said to the Persian cat, who had settled on one of the piles of papers as if it was a nest.

We'd never been a barbeque sort of family, but the Castillos had invited us often enough for me to have sensory memory. It took longer to identify that scent, as it was so unexpected in this house, with fully operational electricity, which was, to many, still a futuristic concept. But it was that same incongruity combined with the *flee!* instinct that goes with the whiff of burning, that caused me to shut the diary.

I went to the door. "Honoré?"

Was that a faint smoky haze?

Panic ripped through me. "Think!" I said aloud. Fire drills are common in Southern California, where there is a serious fire season from August through November.

If there was a fire, it might be small. It was possible that Honoré was busy putting it out. I had to make sure. Only which way to go?

I carefully closed the door behind me, mindful of The Project, and slipped down the stairs.

In my panic, all the rooms looked alike. I ran from room to room. No fire—good—but the stink of burning was getting stronger. So was that chemical smell.

I dashed through a circular dining room and through one of three doors, and found myself in the formal salon I'd seen before. I backed up to leave, casting a last glance around. Something was out of place. I forced myself to take a couple of steps inside the room, though the odor of burning made my eyes water. I heard a faint, high keen.

Was that a dog whining? I stepped in a little farther. There was Shurisko, shivering with his belly flat to the ground. He didn't move. Was he injured? I stepped around a satin-covered loveseat and stopped in shock.

Honoré lay sprawled on a beautiful rectangular carpet, the side of his head gory. A yard or so away lay one of those marble busts. It had obviously conked him on the head.

Was he dead? No, the wound was bleeding sluggishly, and I'd learned through reading plenty of mysteries that the dead don't bleed. Relief washed through me as I bent over him. His chest rose in a shuddering breath. He was definitely out cold.

As soon as I crouched down, the dog leaped up and ran around the room, uttering sharp barks that hurt my ears.

"Honoré, wake up!"

The room seemed blurry, almost diffuse, and the reek clogged my throat. Smoke!

"Hey, wake UP! I think a spark got loose in the next room!"

He didn't stir.

Trying to ignore the frantically yapping dog, I grabbed Honoré's arm, and hauled him to a sitting position. He slumped heavily, and one of his knees looked odd. What now? I knew that female fire fighters could get a guy twice their weight out of danger. The trick (so I'd read in those mysteries) was to get the guy over your shoulder in a fireman's carry.

I got both hands under him and tried to lift. He flopped loosely, too heavy and too lanky for me to manage. I sneezed. The haze was worsening.

I looked around wildly, wishing the poor dog would *shut up*, though I wanted to howl, too. Gray-white tendrils fingered under the nearest door, reaching up to dissipate in the gathering haze. I looked back in desperation at Honoré, lying there full length, framed by a beautiful rug in shades of crimson, scarlet, gold, and tiny hints of blue and green.

Oh.

He was lying on a *rug*. On top of a beautifully polished hardwood floor. Doh!

I straightened him out, crossed his hands over his chest, and wrapped the rug around him. A couple of tugs and he slid along the polished parquet floor.

Okay, so where to? Away from the door with the smoke, obviously. The door I'd come through led to that circular dining room. And . . . double doors on the other side.

I threw them open. Another formal chamber—the sitting room from summer! Across it were the French doors I remembered that opened onto a terrace. I ran to them—and the door jammed against the piled snow outside. Some frantic digging and shoving on my part got one open wide enough for me to drag Honoré through. The black cat leaped over us and across the terrace toward the trees beyond. Shurisko followed, whining and running about.

"If you were Lassie," I muttered, "you'd be doing this."

Shurisko barked.

Honoré bumped over the icy snow. I took him all the way to the other end of the terrace and stood there, my chest heaving, and sweat running down inside my clothes in spite of the bitter cold.

Great. We were safe . . . but I should call 911. Did they even *have* 911?

And then I remembered that secret room with the Project, and two cats I'd carefully shut in.

FOURTEEN

RUNNING BACK INTO A HOUSE with a room on fire is a stupid idea. You don't have to watch TV or read mysteries to know that. On the other hand, there was no way in hell that I would leave live creatures to burn to death if there was a possibility of saving them. And so far, only one room was sending out smoke.

I said to Shurisko, "Guard him."

The dog barked, ran around in a circle, then plunged off the terrace into the snow.

So much for my animal command skills.

I ran back inside. The smoke haze had increased, but I didn't see any flames. Somewhere crystal rang on a high, sweet, yet almost painful note, or maybe it was merely my brain gibbering at me.

I shoved my nose into the elbow of my coat sleeve and plunged off in the direction I'd first come, stopping long enough to scan each table or nook for a telephone so I could try to call for help. If Honoré had one, it wasn't anywhere obvious.

I'd taken a couple of false turns before I spotted that narrow stairway. Up the stairs four at a time, and into the little room, where I found the cats going crazy, yowling and scampering about. When I tried to pick one up, it hissed at me and leaped up onto the desk to get away, skittering on papers and sending them flying.

Papers. *I promised on my life . . .*

I grabbed up the diary, the carbons, and everything else on the desk, and stuffed them down inside my shirt. "Come on, cats, follow me."

Not that I expected them to listen any better than their dog friend had, but I dashed to the door—and backed up as a huge billow of smoke whooshed up the stairs. What? I was just there!

I crouched low, and crept out onto the narrow landing, but as soon as I put my foot on the first step, I saw the orange flicker of flames in the doorway at the bottom of the steps. The cats scampered back inside the secret room.

I backed after them and slammed the door. What now? The room had no windows. It was a secret room—it was a *secret room*.

I moved to the short bookcase with the prince's bust on it. I hefted the bust, which caused the papers in my shirt to crackle warningly, and dumped it onto the desk. Then tried to pull the bookcase out. It didn't budge—it was nailed in!

I picked up the bust, held it over my head, and threw it at the wall with all my strength. It made a huge dent in the plaster. I picked it up again, and smashed it into the dent. It crashed through the plaster into blackness, and clunked down a stairway.

I swooped down on the big tortie, which promptly tried to bite me, and tossed the cat through the hole. The Persian leaped up onto the bookcase in front of the hole. "Go on, Kitty," I said, and shoved it through. I heard it land lightly and skitter off. Good. Passage intact, at least for cat feet.

Using both hands, I pulled at the plaster until there was a human-sized hole. Smoke was now streaming under the door. I climbed up onto the bookcase, and swung my feet through the hole. Back to tunnels with spiders, I thought as I felt around with my toe . . . and found purchase.

I got through the hole, and felt my way down a stairway, hoping that whichever room it led to (assuming that the other end was not blocked off) wasn't on fire.

I almost tripped over the bust, which I picked up and cradled against me like a football. When the passage dead-ended, I felt around for a latch or knob. Nothing. I hefted the bust and bashed at the wall. This time it was more difficult: I was smashing through wood as well as plaster.

The wood splintered in slats. I yanked and kicked my way free, emerging into . . . a closet stuffed with clothing, smelling of mothballs and a florid perfume. I fought my way past the clothes into a room full of swirling smoke. A cat yowled at my feet. Coughing, my eyes streaming, I fell to hands and knees, groping for a wall. When at last I found one, I swept my hands up and down, up and down until my knuckles bruised painfully against a window sill.

I reached behind me for anything, found a lamp, and heaved it through the window glass. The air rushing in caused a roaring behind me, but I didn't stop to look. The younger cat leaped through, no more than a blur. I found the big tortoiseshell puffed up to the size of a small car, running back and forth in a tiny space against the wall below the window. I grabbed the cat and tossed it outside, hoping it would be all right, but I couldn't stop to look.

Tiny zaps of hot pain needled me as I picked up a rug from the floor, flung it over the jagged glass in the window, and climbed out. I was on the second story, but there was a tree branch not far away. I did my best to launch for the tree branch—and missed.

Snow and wet, twiggy branches slapped at me. I bounced painfully off something, then landed on my back in a snow bank. My coat hissed.

I was safe. I was alive. I lay there sobbing for breath and coughing up acrid smoke, until the snow began to melt around my neck, making my skin numb. All of a sudden I was cold all over, my body shivering violently.

I forced myself to sit up. Then I got my feet under me. Dizzy, coughing, I made my way around the side of the house. It seemed a thousand miles, but I found the terrace. There lay the rug with Honoré inside. There were foot prints all over, like little wells with soft edges. How had I made so many? Dog prints dappled the entire terrace, though the dog was nowhere in sight. Neither were the cats—which was good, I thought, as I looked around. No cats meant live cats.

The terrace reflected an orange glow. I lifted my head, and froze in shock: every window showed bright orange. A window cracked, glass tinkling down as flames gouted out.

A surge of adrenaline got me moving again. I grasped the rug, and discovered that my gloves had ripped—my hands were bleeding.

Grunting and yanking, I dragged Honoré's rug out into the snow, and toward a stand of enormous cedar and spruce and fir. Once or twice there were loud cracks like rifle shots. Sparks whirled out of the windows, some flying far enough to land in the trees. In California, that would torch the greenery, but here the sparks fizzled out in the snow-laden boughs.

When I reached a little space between two spruce, I let go and dropped beside the rug, breathing hard as I coughed up more smoke. I checked Honoré. He was still out, but at least he was breathing. What now?

He'd had no phone that I could find. Cell phones didn't work. From the total lack of response, my guess was that the neighbors were too far away to see the smoke in the blizzard—if I peered away from the fire, I couldn't even see the next house.

His car! The garage was attached to the house, but the fire seemed to be burning upward.

I pulled his papers out of my shirt before I ruined them completely, and laid them on the rug next to Honoré. Then I got to my feet and lumbered back into the snow, past the terrace, and to the other side of the house. The garage was still intact. I shouldered the door open. Heat blasted out—and flames licked at the door to the inside. But the car was right there!

I dashed in, yanked the car door open . . . and sure enough, the keys were in the ignition. I turned it on, threw the car into gear, and backed out into the snow as the flames ate through the door and hungrily spread. I backed up until the car was well away from the house. It plowed up some of the fresh fall. I was afraid it would get mired, so I stopped it, yanked the keys, and flailed my way back to Honoré through wind-whirled snow.

Shurisko had returned from wherever he'd been. He crouched down beside Honoré and licked his face.

The rug had a thin ridge of snow on it, which slid off as Honoré began to shift about. He groaned and made a vague swipe at the dog's muzzle.

Then he opened his eyes, and stared at me uncomprehending. "*Gespenstisch*, Ruli," he observed in a whisper.

"I'm not a ghost," I said in German back to him. "I'm Kim."

His eyes closed. He seemed to be processing. I could imagine how bad his head hurt by how long it was taking to grasp this fact.

"You got clocked by one of your marble poets. There was a fire."

"A fire?" he repeated voicelessly, then struggled up on an elbow, his fine hair dark against his pale forehead. Thin, brittle lines of blood had matted into his hair, frozen into reddish-brown wires.

My stomach heaved, and I looked away. "Maybe you should lie down again."

"I have to . . ." He lay back, his face pale and moist. He swallowed several times, obviously fighting nausea. "Shurisko?"

"He's right here. And three cats got out. I hope that's all you had," I added.

"Three." He winced, then made another effort, checking when he inadvertently put his elbow on one of the papers. It crackled, and he jerked his arm up, then fell back with a groan, his fingers scrabbling restlessly. "Tell me. What . . . happened." He closed his eyes.

"A marble bookend fell on your head, I think. At least, I found it lying next to you, and you've got a huge knot right there behind your ear."

He tried to shift, and halted when one of the papers crackled again. His eyelids flashed up and he froze. "What . . ."

"It's your sources. And the Project. I grabbed them when I went back for the cats. I had to stuff them in my shirt. Got kind of messed up. Sorry about that. Look, I couldn't find a phone, so I should go find someone, but I wasn't sure who I should get. I'm not even sure where your neighbors are—I don't want to get lost in the snow."

His hands brushed over the diary, and touched a couple of the carbons, now creased and rumpled, a few, regrettably, from melted snow. His jaw lengthened with pain.

"Here. Let me help with that," I said, and began to pick up the scattered papers. They were all still on the rug, but I didn't know how much longer it would stay dry. The snow beneath us had to be melting from our combined body heat. I scrambled the papers together then said, "Let's go. Your car is waiting."

His voice was slightly stronger. "Garage?"

"Gone. But your car is in the driveway."

He began to move, then fell back, his face blanching. He brushed his fingers over one knee, which was so swollen his jeans looked like a tube.

"I can't bend it," he whispered.

"Get the other under you. I can pull you to your feet," I said as I picked up the papers and once again stuffed them inside my shirt.

It took a couple of tries, his face so pale it was nearly green. He hauled himself up, and I pulled his arm over my shoulder. For a step or two he tried not to lean on me, but that changed fast. We staggered clumsily into the snow, followed by the anxious dog.

It seemed to take forever. Honoré's pace was slow, and a couple of times he stopped, either from dizziness or because he was compelled to look at the stone shell of his house, smoke billowing from every window and blending into the heavy snowfall.

At last we reached the car. He eased into the front, teeth gritted as he maneuvered his leg in. That knee had swollen into sausage-like distortion, and the cut on his head was bleeding again from his efforts. I hoped his skull wasn't fractured.

Shurisko leaped into the back, filling the entire space as I fell into the driver's seat. I cranked the engine. Warm air blasted from the heater. Within a minute the car began to smell like wet dog. "Where should we go?"

"Ridotski House. Go this way . . . past second house . . . left turn onto Mathilde Street."

During the summer, it would have taken maybe a minute to get there. Possibly two. But the journey seemed endless, with me crouched white-knuckled over the steering wheel, as if proximity to the windshield would improve visibility. The car bumped over the snow well enough, but my progress was slower than an amble, I was so afraid of ramming into another car or a tree or even a house. I was so flustered it took forever for me to figure out how to navigate by the street lights. They seemed miles apart.

I wasn't sure I'd recognize the Ridotski place when we reached it, but Honoré took care of that. "Turn here," he said, his voice slightly stronger. "Up the hill."

I remembered that steep little hill. The car was a good one, but not a sleigh pulled by animals with sturdy hooves. It shuddered in the mass accumulation of white, then slid gently back down the hill as I spun uselessly at the wheel, until we came to rest against a snow bank that blocked the entire driver's side.

I killed the engine and clambered out the passenger door. Shurisko leaped past Honoré, prancing about anxiously. The car heat had wakened up the cuts all over my hands, which were stinging in little jabs of red heat.

Getting Honoré out of the car was tougher than getting him in. I wanted to leave him there and get help, but he insisted on going with me, so together we plodded grimly up the long white-shrouded driveway. The house seemed miles from the road, emerging at last from the white curtain. A puff of wind stirred the snow, and there was the front door, not twenty feet away. Fifteen. Thirteen. Nine. Trudge, trudge, and at last I reached for the knocker. My throat hurt. I discovered I was crying.

The door opened, and there was the shocked face of a housekeeper. A few moments later Beka appeared.

"What is this?" she exclaimed, then threw the door wide. "Enter!"

Shurisko galloped in, shedding snow in every direction.

A crowd of servants appeared behind Beka. At a gesture from her, two men took over from me. "Upstairs," she said, "the yellow room."

They helped Honoré toward the stairway to the left, leaving us to follow up in a long spiral. At the top, the housekeeper opened the door to the first room in a long hall, then yanked an embroidered satin bedcover off the bed as the men eased Honoré down.

Beka gave me a questioning look.

I rejoiced at every sign of normalcy and got control of my shuddering breathing. My lungs still burned, and my breath smelled smoky. Or maybe it was my clothes. "There is a fire at his house." I moistened dry lips. "Something fell on his head."

Beka said quickly, "How bad is the fire?"

"Very."

Beka turned to someone behind me. "Call the brigade."

Footsteps ran off. The housekeeper had produced a cloth from somewhere and bent over Honoré. He clapped the cloth to his head and lay there, shivering. "Let me be."

The dog bounded in and leaped on the bed.

Beka snapped her fingers. "Shurisko!"

Honoré gave out a groan of relief, holding out his hand, which the dog frantically licked as he trampled lovingly (and no doubt painfully) all over his human. But when Beka snapped her fingers a second time, Shurisko obediently leaped down, and sat, head at an alert angle, as if he was relieved that someone was in charge. Or maybe that was me, projecting my emotions onto the dog.

Beka ordered one of the guys to take Shurisko to the laundry to dry him off and feed him, then turned to me. "Kim, the guest bathroom is at the end of this hall. Make use of the bathrobe in there—it's fresh. You might want to get out of those clothes. I will be back shortly."

She went out as I set the papers carefully on a little table against the far wall, out of the way.

The housekeeper, with a furtive, wondering glance at me, beckoned and led me to a bathroom that was the most modern thing I'd seen in this country. I shucked my clothes while the bath filled with steaming hot water. Soon I was soaking my aching body in stinging heat. The headache I hadn't even noticed began to throb less. The lassitude was such bliss I caught myself on the verge of falling asleep, and sat upright. Whoa.

I used the waiting shampoo and soap, then climbed out and wrapped myself in the bathrobe. It only came down to mid-calf (Beka was probably five one in heels), but it was warm and soft. I felt as heavy as a stone, and yawn after yawn seized me as I dried my hair, ran the waiting comb through it, and left it to hang down the back of the bathrobe.

From the guest room came a yell of pain, then Natalie Miller's familiar voice. "That's it. No more torture. Your kneecap was kicked out of alignment. You'll be glad to know I just fixed that. But it might be fractured, which would need more attention."

Honoré muttered something, then Nat laughed. "No, now I'm going to wrap that sucker up, so breathe easy."

Beka peeked out of Honoré's guest room. "Ah, Kim. There you are. Honoré wishes to speak to you."

I joined them, intensely self-conscious in the bathrobe, though it covered more of me than the average evening gown would have. So much symbolism in clothing, I thought as I approached the bed, where Nat was laying out bandage stuff next to Honoré's leg. She'd already cut his jeans up to the thigh. The sight of his swollen, discolored knee made my stomach curl, and I looked away from it.

Honoré squinted at me past Nat's shoulder. Sweat stippled his face as he slowly unclenched his teeth, and his body relaxed incrementally. Nat had obviously given him some kind of pain killer.

His bloodshot eyes narrowed as he made an effort to speak, "I don't understand."

"There was a fire," I said. "I'm sorry about the house." And to Nat, "I looked for a phone, but didn't find it. Do you have 911 here?"

"Fire brigade," Nat said. "Beka called them."

Too late. But I wasn't going to say it.

Honoré whispered, "Cats . . . did you say the cats got out?"

"Three did," I said, holding up three fingers, and he relaxed a little.

Beka said to Honoré, "What exactly were you doing?"

Honoré took a deep breath. "Showed her the Project. Smelled fire. Went to check. Don't remember anything more."

His eyes closed as Nat finished bandaging his leg. She straightened up. "That will do until you can get your own doctor to look at you." She turned to me. "How long was he out?"

"I don't know. It felt like hours, but it must have only been a few minutes."

"How did you get him out?" Beka asked.

"Dragged him on a rug."

Honoré opened his eyes again. "The Amaranth rug?"

"It was mostly reds."

"Then it survived."

Beka whispered to us, "The Amaranth rug is a family heirloom."

"I left it lying there in the snow under the firs."

Beka opened her hands. "That won't hurt it. But fire would."

I didn't want to say that the rug was all he had left of his house, but from the faces around me, I was not the only one thinking it.

Nat said to Honoré, "You're definitely concussed." Then to Beka, "I suggest getting some ice for his head. He needs to stay flat and quiet. His pupils are normal, at least, so we're ahead on that front, but we need to keep checking. And he needs to see a doc to make sure there isn't more damage under the hood." She tapped her own skull. "As well as see to that." A jerk of her thumb at his knee.

Beka said, "You hear, Honoré? You need to rest."

Honoré's lips whitened. "I need to know what is happening . . ."

Beka hesitated, then gave a firm little nod. "Then we'll have something to eat in here. You may lie flat, we can check on you, and you can listen all you like. I'll make arrangements."

She ran out, and Nat beckoned me out into the hall. She took up a station by the door so she could watch Honoré, and I stood at the other side. "You look like you lost something. Got an injury?" Nat asked softly.

"I'm wearing somebody else's bathrobe. And there's nothing to change into but my smoky clothes."

"Relax. Bek's probably got her people on the hop with the laundry."

"Okay." I peeked in at Honoré. He lay quiet, his eyes closed, so I whispered, "Speaking of injury, I don't mean to stick my nose in your business, but shouldn't Honoré be hospitalized? Check that. *Is* there a hospital here?"

Nat grinned. "Sure is. Nice one. Or will be, when they finish redoing it. One of Alec's first projects. But by our standards, it's little more than a sanatorium."

"What, the so-called guardian families can buy Maseratis but can't see their way clear to setting up a modern hospital?"

Nat laughed. "You sound like me when I first got here. Alec did get them a state-of-the-art x-ray setup, but no one would use it. You gotta remember how removed they are here. X-rays, in most people's views, are a cross between death rays and superstition. Wouldn't go near it. Had to get an ultrasound, and even then. . . ." She shrugged.

"Superstition!"

"Sometimes, a good part of any medical treatment is in the mind of the treatee. The fact is, there are only four of us doctors trained outside the country, and we all had to adjust to the realities here. We learn from the midwives and horse doctors, and they learn from us. So anyway, Beka will probably get their Dr. Kandras over here later on, and he'll feel the knee, and nod, and maybe throw in some Latin—though he usually doesn't try that on with the toff set, who've lived in the West. But Honoré will be happy if the guy says, 'Stay off it and you'll heal.' Ah. Here they come. I could use a cuppa."

Beka's servants appeared, one wheeling a cart loaded with food and two steaming pots. We stepped out of the way so they could go into the bedroom. On the other side of the bed was a coffee table with two armchairs. One servant loaded dishes onto the table as another fetched a pair of ladder-backed chairs.

"Another question, and this is entirely personal," I said low-voiced. "If I stay any longer, what do I do about laundry? I mean, I'm sure Madam Waleska would arrange for it, but you said her sister is a blabbermouth, and I don't want my bra size being a news flash all over the valley."

Nat chuckled. "And that's exactly what would happen. Bring your stuff to me. I've got a great gig, and she's quiet." Nat shook her head. "I'm just glad I got back from my sweetie's last night. I wouldn't have missed a free lunch from Bek's cook for the world. Wait till you taste it."

"Cook? I thought today was Stefan-Zarbat."

Nat grinned. "This is a Jewish household. They get a different day off. Works out," she added. "The Jews do essential services on the main Christian holidays, and the rest cover on the Jewish biggies."

"I wondered about those inkri drivers on Christmas Eve."

"The only time it can be a hassle is when the heavies fall on the same day."

"Then what do they do, get the nonbelievers to step in?"

"Good question."

Beka reappeared, and we walked in behind her. Honoré's eyes opened when Beka approached him with a cup of water. Nat and I sat down at the table.

The talk was easy—food, Pedro, his new restaurant, and his favorite dishes—as we dug in on the spicy fisherman's soup and cabbage pancakes. Honoré lay quietly, listening.

I'd finished my soup when the housekeeper appeared at the door, eyes wide—and right behind her came Alec, dressed in a long coat with a suit under it, a narrow white silk scarf hanging down on the outside of his coat. The parallel lines of the scarf somehow made him seem taller.

His face was distraught as he met my eyes. He blinked, and I could feel the effort he made to turn his attention to the others. "I am afraid I have bad news," he began, then his gaze reached Honoré and widened. He let out his breath. "Honoré. What a. . . . We thought you were dead."

FIFTEEN

HONORÉ'S EYES OPENED. He spoke faintly but with a hint of his customary suavity. "Who was it . . . who said, 'News of my demise . . . has been greatly exaggerated'?"

"Mark Twain," Nat and I said together, and Nat muttered under her breath, "It's 'reports of my death.' I'm a Twain freak. No one gets it right."

Honoré smiled briefly. I didn't know if he even heard us. "I am alive," he began. "Though I don't know how long that will last. When my brother hears. What I managed to do to the house."

Beka extended a hand toward an empty seat at the table, and Alec sat down. "I thought he hated that house. The last thing I remember him saying was that your great-grandparents ought to be shot for renovating a dozen rooms without adding a bathroom."

Honoré flicked the fingers of one hand in a semblance of a Gallic shrug. "He has not been home. Since. I put in the upstairs bathroom."

"The house gives Gilles prestige," Beka said to us, smiling. "'My brother Honoré, the baron, and his mansion in Old Riev.'"

"He has a brother?" I said to Nat.

"Twin. Some kind of film guy, in France. Never comes here if he can help it."

Alec said to Honoré, "I hope your people were away."

"Yes. I sent everyone home. Stefan-Zarbat. How did you . . . ?"

Alec indicated the windows. "We got several calls as soon as the storm passed on. There's quite an impressive smoke cloud hanging over the—"

The door banged open, and Tony strode in, eyes wide and angry. When he saw us, he stopped dead. His face whitened, then shuttered, and there was the old careless Tony as he leaned in the doorway. "You, too?" he said to Alec.

"I didn't want Anijka finding out through town gossip," Alec said. "Bad enough about the house."

The two sounded normal, but the back of my neck tightened. They were watching one another as if no one else was in the room.

"Anijka?" I mouthed to Nat.

"Honoré's sweetie," she said. "And Beka's cousin."

Beka explained to Tony: "I sent first for Dr. Kandras, but I was told he was at Mecklundburg House. I hope everyone is all right there?"

Tony shifted his gaze from her to Alec and then back. "No one has told me much, *draska mea*, but I think he's been employed for matters of *après*. The Danilovs went over in search of your animals, Honoré."

"Shurisko is here," Beka said, and to me, "The cats?"

"Got outside. But vanished."

Tony glanced from me back to Beka. "Then I believe my job is to see that the good news outruns the bad." He vanished in a couple of long strides.

Draska mea—'my darling' in Dobreni. Color heightened Beka's cheekbones, but she said nothing.

Nat turned to Alec. "'After' in French, I got that much, but what was he saying without actually saying it?"

"Forensics, I suspect." Alec got to his feet. "The duchess, or Robert, probably wanted a report from the doctor about the aftermath of the accident, and the doctor was gone all last week, it seems. This is the first anyone has seen of him since the 21st. Beka, hold that coffee. Damage control is a good idea. Honoré, if there is anything I can do for you, let me know."

He was gone as quickly as Tony.

"Well, that was sufficiently weird," Nat said, looking around the table. "What's going on?"

Honoré had closed his eyes again. Beka lowered a tiny spoon of sugar into her cup with the care of a scientist handling nitro.

Natalie studied Honoré with a doctorish eye. "I think you might try to get some rest now."

Beka had been eyeing me. "You also look pale. Are you certain you did not take harm?"

I ached in every bone and joint, but there was no use in whining. "Here's my biggest problem. If I stay much longer I'm going to have to buy some more clothes. I am seriously out of wardrobe." I didn't want to add, Especially for funerals.

Beka said easily, "How about if I take you shopping tomorrow, yes?"

Beka's Great-Aunt Sarolta arrived right behind the housekeeper, who brought my outfit back.

The tiny old woman was grave, kind in face, listening with eyes closed as Nat told her what she'd done to Honoré's knee and what things to watch out for—dizziness, disorientation, nausea, unconsciousness. The old woman responded in the same polite, old-fashioned French that Gran had taught my mother and me.

Then the housekeeper apologized for the fact that my coat was ruined. She held it up, and everyone stared at the rips from glass and wood, but scariest of all were the holes in the back where sparks had landed on me, probably right before I launched myself out that window.

The sight of those creeped me out so much I made excuses and retreated to the bathroom to change. When I came out, the bedroom door was closed, and Nat and Beka stood in the hall, waiting.

Beka asked me, "See you at nine tomorrow morning?"

"I'm going to have to do something about money. What I've got was for my return trip. Can we stop by a bank? I'm sure *they* can handle credit cards, even if everyone else is back a century or so."

"We can discuss that on the morrow," she said. "Would you like to borrow a coat and gloves? Shimon's wife is tall, too, and I know she will not mind if you take one of her coats."

"Great. I can return it tomorrow after I get a new one. Thanks. "

Beka brought me a coat, then Nat and I left.

We climbed into the waiting car, and the driver took off at a sedate speed. Someone had swept the driveway and plowed the icy streets. As the car bumped slowly past the walls of banked snow, I peered through the back window. Though the time was something like five, and it was already dark, there was a thin gray stream of smoke against a black night sky studded with stars.

"Tell me about *draska mea*," I said in English, hoping the driver didn't speak it. "I've never heard Tony use that kind of language before."

"And you know him so well," Nat retorted, grinning. "Look, I'm not going to yap about Bek's personal life, but put it this way. All of them have had on and off again affairs with that guy. Like I told you last summer, he's the king of on-again off-again."

"Got it." I lowered my voice. "Look, you're a doctor."

Nat chuckled. "Last time I checked."

"Honoré got a concussion, right?"

"Minor, I think. I'm more worried about that knee."

I lowered my voice even more. "Here's what I'm getting at. He doesn't remember what he was doing when the bust fell on him. So . . . is it possible that the same sort of concussion happened to . . . someone . . . if he were thrown clean out of a car?"

Her smile vanished. "Yeah, I see where you're going, and yeah, that *has* been talked about. In fact, that's pretty much where we are. Especially as the dude we're not naming has been ram-jetting around ever since, and if he gets more than five or six hours of sleep a night then call me Ishmael. *Ishmael.* Geez, what kind of parents would ever land that name on a defenseless kid? Even in the olden days. It's that *ish*. Too much squish in it, you know what I mean?"

In other words, end of subject. Not that there was anything more to say. My big insight was old news.

When the car reached the Waleskas' inn, I ran inside, shivering.

I had one thought: going horizontal. But there was that whiff of refrigerator air in my room. A glance at the mirror, and adrenaline shot through me like a geyser: there was Grandfather Armandros, staring straight at me, that cigarette glowing at the tip. And behind him, several other people, their outlines blending and overlapping. When I tried to bring any of them into focus my head swam.

I slammed the wardrobe door and sat on the bed, hands pressed to my eyes. "Can you talk to me?" I asked.

Nothing.

Reluctantly, I got up, opened the door, and squinted at the mirror. They were still there.

"Talk to me! What do you want?" I tried variations on that in four languages, with no result.

So I slammed the door again and was about to flake out on the bed when someone rapped at the door.

When I called out "Enter," Theresa came in, her eyes wide. She said with muted excitement, "The duke is here to see you."

Her eyelids lifted on the word "duke" as if she'd said "Santa Claus is here to see you." Or maybe "the devil."

I swung my feet down and followed her, wondering if it was Tony or handsome Trasyemova duke. I couldn't imagine why a Vigilzhi, duke or not, would want to talk to me.

I would rather have had the Vigilzhi arrest me, I thought when I saw Tony prowling around the empty dining room. Theresa looked from him to me, then vanished through the door to the private quarters behind the counter.

"Can we go up to your suite?" he said abruptly.

"Suite? I have a room." The idea of being alone with him in that tiny space was way too unnerving. Not because of the wayward attraction so much as because I didn't trust him as far as I could toss an elephant.

"Oh yes," he said. "I've seen that, haven't I? About the size of a kitchen-maid's room, and you probably don't have hot water."

"There's plenty of hot water." *In the mornings.* "I like it here."

"Why the hell didn't you hire a house?"

"Because I forgot to pack a suitcase full of cash," I retorted.

"But you . . ." He made a dismissive gesture. "The point is, why don't you come stay with us? No, forget that." He raised a hand before I could give him both barrels about that idea. "Stay with Danilov. They've plenty of space."

"Even I, with my gold digger rep and my bastard background, have better manners than to invite myself to someone else's home where I know I am one-hundred percent unwanted—no matter how much hot water they have. I'm fine here. Drop it. General question. Is there a Dsaret House? Or was that made into a garage during the war?"

"Dsaret House would be the palace."

"Uh, right. I should have thought of that."

"Speaking of Dsaret . . ."

Here it comes.

"Just before we parted last summer, you said you knew the whereabouts of the Dsaret Treasure—"

"I know what I said," I interrupted. "I was out of my mind with pain, and it was the best I could think of to snap my fingers under your nose."

He gave me that slanting black gaze, smiling faintly. I braced myself to take it without wavering.

"Don't you think," I asked, ignoring how heat crept up from my toes to my hairline, "if I'd found a treasure I'd have hired the house you mentioned?"

"I'm not sure what to think," he said slowly.

In less polite words, *I don't believe you.* The way his smile deepened, he knew I knew it. And that's the trouble with lies—it's like a neverending mirror, because I knew he knew that I knew it, so did he mean for me to know that he knew that I knew it? But then if I knew that he knew . . .

Argh.

He glanced at the door behind the counter. "Damn it. Let's go outside."

"Nobody is in here," I said. "And they don't speak English."

"Every ear is probably pressed to that door," he shot back. "And how do you know what languages they speak?"

I hated his implication, but there was no use in arguing, especially as I didn't know if any of the Waleskas spoke English. "Let's go sit in my car," he said.

"Oh no, we've been here before," I said, backing away.

"Yes, about that. After our fencing practice, I took off from Danilov's to the news that Magda, Ruli's assistant, had at last been reached, if only by telephone. By the time I got home Magda had hung up, and then I wasted the next couple hours trying to get through to her in Paris, until Uncle Jerzy came in with the news that Vauban House was in flames, and Honoré had burned to death. What the hell happened?" He added, "The rumor *now* going around is that you tried to off him."

"Rumor going around where?"

He lifted a shoulder. "My house. The servants must have been talking to their mates at other houses. You know how fast talk spreads." He indicated the door. "Want less of an audience for this conversation?"

The Dsaret Treasure was buried. For now.

I held out my hand. "If you give me the car keys."

His brows slanted up. "You're not serious."

"Try me."

Uttering a soft laugh, he dug in his pocket for the keys and dropped them into my hand. Then, with a mocking bow, he opened the door, and I followed after a quick glance at the area beyond the front desk. I pulled on Shimon's wife's coat and promptly skidded on the icy steps. Tony caught my arm, and I clutched at him. For a moment we were chest to chest. I thought, *If he tries anything more I'll clock him.* Yet I wanted him to try. Just so I could smack him.

"Thanks." My voice came out a croak as I jerked free.

The waiting car was the same red Morgan I'd driven to his castle the summer before. He'd parked the wrong way on the street, so the passenger side was next to the sidewalk. The snow on the rooftops was blue-white in the starlight. It was so cold that every shift of my shirt felt like someone pressed ice against my skin. I fumbled with the driver's door—which was where the passenger would be in an American car. That just contributed to the sense of unreality.

I jammed the keys in the ignition and started the engine as Tony sank into the shotgun seat. Hot air blasted out of the heater. I leaned my face into it and then held my hands out.

Tony said, "The Ridotskis are guarding Honoré in the upstairs citadel until it's time for Ruli's vigil, and I doubt he will be there. So I can't ask him what happened."

I stared at Tony. "You don't think it was an accident."

His mouth twitched, sardonic and impatient. "Nobody thinks it was an accident. Though officially it was an accident until . . ." His gaze shifted away, then back. "Someone finds proof otherwise. So. Back to the rumor."

I glared at Tony. "So *I* whacked him, and then set his house on fire, and then dragged him to safety? Wow, that makes so much sense."

"Since the rumor also says he's dead, yeah. Tell me what happened."

"We stopped at his place to look at his history project in his secret lair upstairs. We smelled smoke. He went to check. When the smell got stronger I went downstairs. Found him lying on a rug. Fire in the next room. So I wrapped him in the rug and dragged him onto the terrace."

"The rug fought you?"

"Nobody fought me."

"What happened to your hands?"

I looked down. My hands looked like someone else's. In the reflected light from the inn windows, the scabbing welts looked dark and worse than they were.

"I went back in to get the cats from the upstairs room."

Tony frowned. "Tell me exactly."

I sighed, but there was no reason not to.

I went into detail by talking to the steering wheel, but when the silence grew, I dared a glance. He was so . . . so close. I glared at the scabs on the backs of my hands. "He can show you the papers tomorrow, if you don't believe me. Why would I knock him on the head then set his house on fire? And by the way, why do you think it was no accident? It seemed pretty clear that the bust had fallen down."

Another silence, during which Tony peered out the windshield. His profile was unreadable. The light from the street lamps emphasized the hollows under his cheekbones, and the more subtle marks under his eyes. At last he said, "At this point it's difficult to determine what you know and what you don't."

"You being the model of truth," I retorted.

"So . . . were you wearing jewelry today? Diamonds, maybe?"

"You're the second one who's asked me that. Why?"

"Nobody," he said slowly, studying my face through narrowed eyes, "has told you that there are . . . charms woven into certain crystals, and into diamonds?"

"No! Wait. Yes. Tania mentioned something about charms and crystals. And . . . and your sister also did, last summer. She was complaining about—she said that she thought the charms were superstition. But she wore a bracelet that Beka had given her. I thought all that was . . . um." I scowled at him. "Are you telling me that magic works? After all that you said during summer about how it doesn't? Who's the liar here?"

It was his turn to look away. Finally he said to the windshield, "The truth is dodgier than you might expect."

"Truth is truth."

"So we're told as children." He paused, then dropped the sarcastic tone. "I've never seen the charms work, but Honoré insists that they do. You know how one will see a ghost and the next person doesn't."

"You could have told me that last summer."

"You could have told me your real name and where you came from."

"I would have, if you hadn't been such a jerk, trying to drag me to that castle of yours. But I don't want to argue about that. It's over. Tell me this: Magda was Ruli's assistant, but who *is* she?"

Tony's face was in shadow, difficult to read. "Family employee. Since Alec apparently remembers nothing about what happened, we'd left a call at the Paris house for when she reached it. Took her a few days to get there, as she customarily takes the train."

"You don't believe Alec? Considering how out of it Honoré is with a small bump, how much worse would concussion be after Alec was thrown from a car onto his head?"

Tony's eyes narrowed.

"You don't believe him?" I repeated.

Tony's shrug was sharp. "It would be an easy way to get rid of an inconvenient wife—get her wasted, put the car into neutral, shove it over the edge with one door swinging open, then throw oneself down onto that ledge to get some convincing bruises."

"It would be a *stupid* way," I retorted. "If Alec really wanted to get rid of Ruli, there must be a couple hundred easier ways, including just asking her for a divorce or an annulment. And all without totally hosing a classic car."

"It *is* stupid," Tony said, in a slow voice, as though he was choosing his words. "And whatever else Alec is, he's not stupid. But back to Honoré. Unfortunately, by the time I got home from Danilov's my uncle had helpfully finished the conversation with Magda, and my mother had taken to her bed. From what I can gather third-hand, Magda doesn't contribute much toward solving the mystery, other than establishing what we'd already figured, that Marzio di Peretti got pissed off with Alec because he wouldn't let Ruli parade him all over town. He arsed off, using Magda as a chauffeur, since he's never driven in snow."

"You think Alec was wrong about him, too?"

Tony lifted a shoulder. "Ruli gassed on about how much di Peretti loved her, when it was apparent to everyone else that what he loved chiefly was her money. And her proximity to a title, even in a country so small nobody has ever heard of it. So I have no opinion." He gave me one of those looks and the crooked smile. "Other than that, love is illusion."

Love is illusion. I was *so* not getting into that. "So where is Marzio di Peretti now?"

"No idea. Magda unloaded him at an airport outside the border then continued on to Paris, as ordered."

"You said she called. I thought phones didn't work. Long distance, I mean."

"Mobiles don't. But the trunk lines do. The few we have. Until 1990, the extant lines all went east." He glanced at his watch. "The vigil is in an hour."

I was going to ask if I should be going, then thought, *If no one invited you, the answer is clear, isn't it?* So I said, "One more thing. Your phone at Mecklundburg House is connected to same system as the one at the palace? I remember that Alec's house phone was only local calls."

"My mother insisted on a separate cable." Tony laughed. "The family was furious at the cost. We also had a cable up at the Eyrie, laid by the Russians. We cut it on them, they cut it on us. Then laid it again. Alec was with us when the twins and the Danilovs and I blew it up. We were barely in our teens." He laughed again, shaking his head. "We blew out half the mountainside that night. Still haven't fixed that cable yet."

SIXTEEN

I GOT OUT OF THE CAR after that, and he took off.

I plodded upstairs, my entire body one big ache. The room smelled like beeswax furniture polish again, and I did not bother checking the wardrobe mirror. I fell asleep as soon as my head hit the pillow.

I woke the next morning to the sound of girls singing.

The song passed slowly down the street. I got up to look, my body protesting with needle-zaps of pain. Below the window an open wagon passed, drawn by four horses. It was packed with girls well wrapped up, each holding a candle. They sang *a capella*, not quite on tune, and when the wagon jolted, there was a corresponding jolt in the flow of their song, but the melody was poignant, deceptively simple, and I was to find that it lingered in my mind through the day.

I went back to bed.

At eight-thirty, Madam Waleska knocked on my door.

I forced myself to my feet. Everything hurt. I opened the door, and Madam's gaze went to my hands, which, in the light of day, looked like I'd lost an argument with a weed-whacker.

"There is a letter from the Statthalter for you, brought by special messenger."

That explained the tray. "Thanks." I took it. "Um, is everything closed again today?"

"It is a half day, in honor of Madam Statthalter's funeral," Madam Waleska said. "Most will open after noon."

She left, and my heart began a drum solo against my ribs as I ripped open the heavy envelope. There was a note card inside with handwritten words:

Kim: any expenses you incur can be drawn against the Dsaret account at the bank. A.

Oookay, so Beka and Alec had been talking about me. Probably after Ruli's vigil, to which I'd not been invited . . . and afterward, whoever had been offering comfort to Alec wasn't Yours T.

I sat down on the bed, trying to deal with the surge of regret, resentment—and jealousy. My lizard brain wanted to hate Beka, to pick apart her appearance or personality for something to despise, as if that was going to keep Alec away from her.

There are few things more futile in life than jealousy, my dad had told me when I was in the throes of my first crush in high school, around the time I'd become aware of my mother's occasional disappearances. After a couple of dates the guy I was obsessing over lost interest in me, and a week later I saw him sitting with someone I knew, with whom I had nothing in common. She was skinny as a stick, with frazzled black hair always flying every which way, and her complexion was a mess. But though I mentally picked apart her appearance, and assured myself with how boring she was, nattering about her flute lessons and Girl Scout camping at Catalina Island, the inescapable truth was that he'd seen something in her that he didn't see in me.

Dad had said, *No matter how hard you love, you can't make anyone love you back. It has to be freely given, and it has to be their style of love.*

I glared at the ghost-free wardrobe mirror. In my life's story, I was the heroine, and I'd chosen my actions out of honor, and wow it had hurt. But in the von Mecklundburgs' story, I was still the flaky Ruli-wannabe who'd taken off when she didn't get a treasure, and then conspired to off Madam Statthalter. "So suck it up and deal," I told my reflection.

Having regained the high ground, at least in my own mind, I marched off to the bath. I shucked my nightie and stared in horror at my reflection in the narrow mirror on the back of the door. From the collarbones down, I was a rainbow of heavy duty bruises, in addition to the scratches. I lowered myself into a hot bath and splashed about in an ocean of self-pity.

When I got out and put on my last set of clean clothes, I reminded myself that at least it wasn't *my* funeral today. And yeah, it could have been, the inner me whispered, when I remembered those burn holes in the back of my ruined coat.

The dining room was half full, Madam and Anna whisking around in white aprons, bringing breakfast to everyone. Madam greeted me with such a happy booming voice I figured that Tony's visitation the night before, and Alec's messenger today, had given her at least ten gossip points over her sister.

Most of the guests were reading the newspaper, which was about the size of the smallest section of the *Los Angeles Times*. When I went to the tea urn, I glanced down at the open paper a man was reading and was shocked to see my face staring back at me, stark in black and white.

But it was not my face. It was Ruli in her wedding gown, standing side by side with Alec for what was obviously an official photo.

I had to read it. There was a pile of papers on the counter. I took one, and sat down with my breakfast.

The lead article gave the superficials of Ruli's life: where and when she was born, a little about her exalted family, where she'd been educated, and notes about the wedding. All the places she'd been, but nothing that was about *her*.

The quotations were the usual compliments—her beauty, her good taste, her presiding at charity functions—but those were standard obit language, without giving any hint of the real person. The extensive quotes from Aunt Sisi seemed to be about someone else altogether, an ideal daughter who dedicated herself to good works, had excellent taste in opera and chamber music, and who was the favorite of her entire family.

I scanned rapidly for something about Alec. No quotes from him, nothing but a final paragraph saying that the paper joined the Dobreni people in commiserating with him on his loss.

By the time I'd read that, I'd finished my scrambled eggs and a couple slices of fresh-baked bread with nut filling.

Beka arrived as I finished my tea. I was glad to leave that paper behind.

She greeted me with a distracted air and waved me to her car, which was a recent hybrid. I grabbed Shimon's wife's coat, and we were off.

I waited until she'd pulled into the slow traffic, then said, "I take it you told Alec about my cash flow issues. Can you tell me what it means, 'draw on'?" I quoted Alec's note. "Do we have to go to the bank and show them all my papers and my credit card?"

"Not necessary. The store will bill the bank directly, if you tell them to."

"How do I know if I've run out of money?"

She slowed for a huge cart pulled by oxen with some kind of boots on their hooves, and threw a quick smile my way. "You won't. In fact, you could buy up a street or two, and you wouldn't run through it all."

"How is that possible? I thought . . ." Did she know about the Dsaret Treasure? Of course she did. "I thought my family already got their share," I finished, leaving it at that.

"Your family was sent your grandmother's portion of the Dsaret inheritance," she said calmly. Yep, she knew. Then came the part that *I* didn't know. "But that was the royal treasury. You forget that your relatives also had their holdings. Not only the Dsaret mines, but here in the city. My family was instrumental in the rebuilding during the baroque era, with the result that, between the Ridotskis and the Dsarets, we own pretty much everything east of the cathedral, and as far south as the river. Even though rents have risen very little over the centuries, and it's only been about fifteen years that we once again got control of those funds from the Soviets, it nonetheless adds up."

Her voice had flattened to calm and matter-of-fact, the way a teacher strives to remain neutral before the classroom, especially when introducing a potentially hot topic. I wondered for the first time if she felt about me the way I did about her: wary, not sure about trust.

I wondered if we both felt the same way about Alec. And what about *draska mea?*

I said, "Do *you* think I was conspiring with Alec to kill Ruli?"

"You? Alec?" She shot me another look, her brows up. "Killing Ruli? Impossible."

"You seem angry."

"I am angry. But with someone else. Not with you."

"I don't understand," I said.

"Last night, my cousin Anijka came to see Honoré, while the rest of us were at Ruli's vigil. He saw her out. He insisted on using my great-grandfather's old cane to walk her out. On the way back, he reached that turn at the top of the stair . . ." She closed her mouth tight. "He fell. He got one hand on a banister, and so he only crashed to the steps, while the cane tumbled all the way down."

"Did he trip over the cane?"

"That's what we thought, except for three things. First, his impression that something got between his foot and the cane."

"You mean like a trip wire?"

"Or something stuck between the two, from between the banister posts. The second thing, Shurisko was in his room not ten meters away, barking in madness. That's what we came home to, actually. And third, the door to the garden was unlocked, and my mother distinctly remembered locking it herself."

"So . . . you think someone did it on purpose? Tony thought the fire was on purpose. He came over to accuse me last night."

"So I understand." She looked down, her lips compressed.

"It sounds to me like the vigil meant to honor Ruli wasn't all that healing?"

"It was horrible, so full of traditional words, so meaningless when spoken with smothered anger. So many are angry with one another. Angry with Alec. Yet there are so many questions one cannot ask outright." She flicked the fingers of her hand upward, rattling her bracelet as if waving goodbye to an unhappy topic. "It was very formal, very stiff, and very, very short. Let us talk about something else."

"Is there a Dobreni history book?"

"Both the city and the palace libraries were destroyed by the Soviets. Although some books were secreted, they are seriously out of date. We're in the process of doing something about that."

"When Honoré told me about his project, he mentioned what happened to the library."

"We're still recovering from those years, in many ways." She paused as she negotiated through the snarl of traffic around the enormous traffic circle where Prinz Karl-Rafael street ended. In the center was the shepherdess fountain. The figures were not moving. I watched as we threaded through people, carts, horses, autos ranging from the forties on, and the streetcar. "I hate driving the Xanpia roundabout," she commented, "but it's the quickest way to Ladislas, and we don't have a lot of time. So. Even if you know nothing about us, what do you think 'Dsaret' means?"

"Oh." *Never saw that coming!* "'Tzar' or 'Caesar' is at the root?"

"Yes. The oldest legends have it that the Dsaret family were custodians of the oldest mine. What was in that mine . . . has been debated." Her tone was odd.

As she turned again and slowed in search of a parking place, I considered her words. "You don't just mean the usual things you find in mines. You mean something to do with the legends about Vrajhus and the Nasdrafus?"

"It might. Or it could be that this oldest mine that no one seems to be able to point to just means Dobrenica."

We'd arrived in a neighborhood where the buildings had grand Edwardian fronts. This had to be the Rodeo Drive of Riev. She pulled up in front of a marble-fronted shop with fine lace curtains in the windows and discreet lettering in old-fashioned script: *Été*. Summer—a lovely thought.

There was barely enough space in front. Beka put the car into park and put her hands in her lap with a faint rattle of her bracelets. She was frowning at the steering wheel as if it was speaking a language she almost remembered.

Then she said abruptly, "You didn't tell us that you also saved Honoré's work. As well as the cats."

"Sure I told you."

Beka's smile was brief. "Perhaps we did not comprehend. Honoré certainly did not until this morning."

I looked out at the shop, trying to deal with a weird mix of gratification and intense embarrassment.

"I would like to tell you how much that means to us all, but we really don't have the time," Beka said, now brisk. She glanced at her watch, then sprung the car door, exclaiming, "Come."

"Lead on."

We went inside the shop, which was completely different from shopping experiences I was used to. There might be places like this in LA, too, but in areas where I couldn't even afford to park. We sat down, and the sales women showed us examples of all kinds of dresses. I picked out ones I liked. Then they took my measurements, and we talked about colors and fabrics.

Beka suggested a subdued silvery mauve shirt dress of soft wool for the funeral. It was very simple, few seams in the whole thing.

The sales woman promised it would be delivered before I finished my shopping. When I gave the address, she blinked once or twice, but made no comment. Her only expression was a minute smile, mostly a relaxing of the skin around her eyes, as I piled up the orders. I've always preferred one stop shopping, and if I like something, I grab it and go.

The woman thanked me, everything in French, as discreet as could be. The only reminder that I was still in Dobrenica was the greeting on leaving, an elided version of some kind of blessing, somewhat like the Austrian "Grüß Gott."

After that, we rounded a corner and went up narrow stairs to a shop that didn't even have a sign. One glance at the swatches of fabric on display, and I suspected I was in one of those super exclusive places where the clothes are not only bespoke, but in some greater sense designed for the wearer.

As we mounted the stairs, Beka said casually, "I am assuming you shall attend the gala on New Year's Eve."

"What gala? Oh yes, you mentioned it before. At the Opera House? I haven't been invited to that, either."

"They've thrown the celebration open to the entire city, as so many have been working to get the opera house ready. Though Ruli was not particularly fond of life in Riev, one thing she loved was the Black and White Ball on New Year's Eve. It's a tradition here. Everyone wears black and white, in celebration of the old year ending and the beginning of the new," she said. "This year the von Mecklundburgs were to host it—we trade off—and they had intended to combine it with the opening of the opera house. Even though construction isn't finished, they are holding it there anyway, to show the progress. Perhaps to inspire contributions. Anyway," she said as we entered, "you need a ball gown. But getting one made in a few days, especially with everyone wanting one, is . . ." She glanced at the shopkeeper, a small, stout woman with a broad face who reminded me of some Russians I'd seen. The two exchanged gazes, a heartbeat too long. A signal.

Beka asked, "Madam Celine, is it too late to make a gown?"

It was like she was giving a cue, and on cue the woman replied, "We might be able to achieve something." Her French was decidedly Russian accented.

I said, "I'll take any old thing off the rack—I don't really care."

Beka was trying not to laugh. "There is no rack here. Ball gowns are made for the wearer, works of art."

Madame Celine said, "If we might measure . . . ?"

Beka's lips pursed. Then she flicked a look at me.

I said, "What's going on? I'm not being set up for something nasty am I? No, wait—is this a place Ruli used to come to?" I was completely squicked out by the idea of them hauling out some fancy gown of Ruli's.

"She hadn't even come in for the first fitting. It was made up on her pattern. The gown is based on something Ginger Rogers wore in a film," Beka said.

I stopped in my tracks. "Which film?"

"*Swing Time*, I think it was called. I know I've seen the film, but I don't remember it very well. It was a favorite of hers."

"Not the gown from 'Never Gonna Dance'?"

"That's the one."

Okay, I had to have that dress. *Ruli, if you don't want me in it, now's the time to speak up*, I thought.

The silvery-white gown was deceptively simple in design but made up of many thin strips exquisitely stitched together, broadening out from the hips into a filmy skirt. The fabric was a marvelously supple, floaty, silk on silk, brocaded in the pattern of a stylized flower. Where had I seen that flower? Oh, yeah. Woven into the pattern on the Amaranth rug where Honoré had lain. And it was the same one carved into the hinges of that wonderful fake door I'd seen on my first day. A long chiffony black scarf draped in a scoop across the neckline to fall over my shoulders in two streamers to the hem.

I postured and twirled before the mirror. The skirt had the necessary swoosh for waltzing, but it wasn't poofed out with miles of petticoats, the way my eighteenth century ball gown had been for the summer masquerade. I wouldn't feel like a ship under sail when trying to walk.

So I agreed to everything and promised to return for a second fitting.

As we left Beka insisted on elbow length black silk gloves, so on we went to the anticlimax of underthings and accessories. We made our way down the street until we reached a shoe store. Beka said, "You won't find anything adventurous here, but the shoes are comfortable and classic in design."

"Since my interest in footwear has been pretty much confined to sandals, ballet slippers, and fencing shoes for competitions, this is not a big disappointment."

She laughed. "I wish I could take you to Italy. You would discover the beauty of good shoes." It was the first genuine expression I'd heard from her.

The shoemaker measured my feet. I picked out one pair of high heeled pumps, which the earnest young man promised would be ready in time for the ball, and several pairs of satin covered flats that could be delivered later. A shawl, two coats—one a full length, incredibly soft thing and one short and practical—a couple of hats (a fuzzy one like Phaedra's), and a couple of new suitcases. I wondered what Madam Waleska was going to make of this stream of deliveries.

After the suitcases, Beka looked at her watch. "We have forty minutes."

Back to the car we tramped. She maneuvered us into the thin but steady stream of sleigh, auto, foot, and occasional shaggy-horse traffic.

We drove down a street parallel to the cathedral and the temple, pulling up in a tiny cul-de-sac with shops so small the doors and windows were about the same size. One was a café.

Inside, it smelled like fresh-ground coffee and onion-braised meats and steamed cabbage. Beka led the way between tiny tables where people sat eating, talking, or reading. No cell phones, no computers. The late Victorian décor had Corinthian pillars and flourishes against the ceiling. A wave of giddiness rippled through me, as if I'd slipped back in time. I had a sense that this café was very old.

So I focused on Beka's curly head directly in front of me as we passed the customers in the narrow shop, even though there were two tables free. We went through the back door into a corridor barely wide enough for us in single file. I caught a brief glimpse of a kitchen and of someone taking rolls out of a brick oven. Beka led us down a narrow hall to a small parlor with a single window overlooking a small court-yard. Central was a tiny garden, snow-mounded, except for a bare tree that reminded me of the one around the shepherdess fountain; only this tree didn't look withered and dead. Snow covered the rest of the court, drifted right up against the window.

Our private little parlor had two chairs with iron legs, and on the little round table a coffee service had been set minutes before, judging from the stream rising from the pot.

"If you would like something to eat, I will open the door. Otherwise, we can talk here without being overheard," she said.

"I had a huge breakfast two hours ago."

She poured out coffee for us, and I looked down at it, wishing it was tea. Enough cream and some sugar made it palatable.

She cradled her cup, brow slightly furrowed, then said, "Will you please tell me exactly what happened at Honoré's house?"

This time I went into detail, from Honoré's pulling into his garage to the moment when his car slid down the hill as we tried to reach Ridotski House. She did not interrupt, nor did her gaze waver from my face.

At the end, she leaned forward, hands clasped. "You didn't mention lighter fluid yesterday."

"Yeah, well, maybe I *didn't* smell it. Maybe I smelled something else that reminded me of lighter fluid. But that's what got me downstairs. For what it's worth, I did not set that fire, and I did not drop that bust on his head."

"I believe you. It makes no sense whatever to hit a man, set his house on fire, drag him to safety, then plunge back in to save his cats and his papers." Her gaze shifted to the backs of my hands, then away as her fingers tapped lightly against the handle of her cup. Finally she said, "But somebody did those first two things. Natalie came to check him last night, since they couldn't reach Dr. Kandras. He has left the city again. After she examined him, she asked us how a bust could fall on his head, then bounce high and hard enough to fracture his kneecap. Because she thinks that's what happened to his knee."

"I don't know. The closest I get to detective work is watching *NCIS*. Does Honoré remember anything?"

"Yes. Here is where things get difficult." She squared her shoulders. "When he woke up this morning, he said he remembers bending down to pick up the bust."

I stared at her. "Then . . . it wasn't the bust at all? Falling on his head, I mean."

"Tony thinks that while he was stooping down to pick up the bust, someone brained him with the fireplace iron, then took out his knee on the back stroke." Her cheeks colored at the mention of Tony's name, but her voice was smooth as always.

I wasn't sure what was more disturbing, Tony's ability to assess that kind of injury, or the fact that Honoré had been hit on purpose. "But not hard enough to kill him outright."

"That's the puzzling part. I mean, aside from the motivation. Either someone was not strong enough to smash in his skull, or else the attacker wanted him to be alive when he burned."

"Ugh!" I gasped. "And so Tony accused me."

"He doesn't believe it any more. No one knows what to believe."

"Okay, so next question, why would anyone want to kill Honoré?"

Her fingers played with the bracelet on her wrist. It was made up of tiny, beautifully faceted diamonds on a chain of thinly braided gold hung with polished wood pendants in the shape of a stylized flower—it was those that made the rattling noise. It was the same flower woven into the fabric of the Ginger Rodgers gown, and Honoré's Amaranth rug. Hmm. Coincidence or significance?

"All right," Beka said, breaking through my distraction, and leaning forward, her gaze intent. "Here is what is important. Honoré asked me to tell you something that he seldom shares. And that is: he sees what you might call auras."

"Like New Age-y auras? You know, green if you're into peace and love, and that sort of thing?"

"Not as . . . defined as that. He perceives scintillations in color around people. The colors coruscate in hue with emotional alterations. He thought everyone saw them until he and his twin discovered that Honoré perceived such things and Gilles didn't. By the time he was ten or twelve, it became clear that he could tell when people were lying. You can imagine how unpopular he became in our small circle, for a while." Her smile was mordant. "Then Honoré's and Gilles' parents vanished— word came of a car wreck in Greece—and they were adopted by the duke and duchess. Gilles pretty much lived at his French boarding school, but Honoré became more reclusive. The von Mecklundburgs hired tutors for him. He never talked about the auras outside the family."

"So that's why everyone keeps looking at him, when they ask nosy questions?"

"He hates that, being used as a lie detector. He hates the necessity." She tipped her head, then added quickly, "I believe this is why he has a habit of hiding his own truth behind obscure quotes and the like."

"Whoa." I thought back over the summer, and my lying from the first moment he saw me. No wonder he disliked me. And would his "emotional spectrum" also have revealed how I was falling for Alec, who was supposed to marry Ruli? "Oh." I fought past the tide of embarrassment and said, "But if that's true, last summer, how could he have not known about Ruli being kept up at the Eyrie? The duchess lied about that from the get-go."

"You say 'the duchess' and not 'Tante Sisi,' I notice."

"Any woman who tried to off me, I'm not going to call 'aunt.' No matter how many ways we're related."

Beka's smile widened to a brief, impish grin, then she sobered. "This is another thing that is seldom known, but I think it might be time. The protections?" She touched the discreet diamonds at her ears. "One of the ways they work is to mask auras. They are intended to ward off *inimasang*."

"Spirits of the blood?"

"The more common term is Shadow Ones, or sometimes Wild Folk—but the latter term is inexact, because it can mean others who are said to live in the Nasdrafus, the were-creatures, the fae. Anyway, when people wear the charmed diamonds or crystals, Honoré cannot perceive their auras, except vaguely."

So *that* was why the Danilovs set up that sauna in the fencing *salle*, they were hoping I'd strip down far enough for them to see whether or not I was packing diamonds.

She must have seen my reaction because she said, "Yes, Honoré told me about yesterday. He was quite annoyed with his cousins."

"Okay, so getting away from me for a second, and the von Mecklundburg gang thinking I'm some sort of supervillain—those diamonds everyone wears: they're to ward off vampires? And that big fat diamond the duchess always wears kept anyone from knowing she's a liar?"

Beka touched her bracelet again, hesitated, then gave a quick shrug. "You must understand how confusing last summer was for Honoré. The duchess has always been his champion. Gave him anything he wanted, like those expensive tutors, when he could not bear the proximity of other boys at their school."

"And Tony knew where Ruli really was, last summer. Didn't Honoré know that *he* was lying?"

She looked away, her lips tightening briefly. "Tony claimed to be keeping Ruli safe. They saw you as . . ."

I raised a hand. "I know what they saw me as."

So did Beka believe Tony, or excuse him, or what? And how could I ask? *I didn't know you were involved with so-and-so* is seldom perceived as a neutral statement. If you say it to a lover, or to someone involved with someone you are interested in, it can be seen as a challenge.

We all have "someones" in our lives. And it's not always easy to fit them into neatly labeled boxes. Even ex-lovers. There's the ex you curse and want to scrub your brain out if you even think the name. Then there's the ex who's still part of your life—a kind of friend. But you look at them, and they look at you, and there's always some memory of the time when you weren't exes. I didn't know what Beka's relationship with Tony was, any more than I could define whatever was going on between her and Alec, but I had this sense that if Honoré was looking at her now, he'd see a sun's worth of emotional fusion.

"So, what now?" I finally asked.

She had been frowning down at her bracelet as she turned it on her wrist. "So there remains the possibility that someone wishes Honoré harm. But we have no idea why, or who. There are very few who know about his ability."

"I know you don't want to speculate, but if someone is trying to get rid of Honoré, it's because of his ability? I thought there was no prejudice about magical stuff in Dobrenica."

She flicked her fingers outward in a quick gesture. "Not so simple. Some disapprove of his relationship with Anijka."

I stared at Beka. "Not because she's Jewish? Isn't Dobrenica fairly free of religious prejudice?"

"My second-cousin Anijka is not a Ridotski, has no rank or fortune, and works as a teacher." She tipped her head, her mouth sardonic. "Yes, we Jews have existed in relative amity in Dobrenica. But there are always contingencies, as some say, and class prejudice is one."

"Go on."

"Very well. Perhaps it is important for you to understand. You are aware that the Ridotskis are regarded as one of the five guardian families."

"Right."

"Did you ever stop to ask why the head of our family does not share the ducal coronet with the other four?" Beka's brow puckered.

"No." I felt that guilt one always feels when discovering unexamined prejudice. Then I said, "Not to excuse myself or anything, but the way I was raised, well, I don't ordinarily ask myself anything about dukes."

"Fair enough," Beka said, and then added: "So tell me this. How much do you know about the von Mecklundburgs' past? Specifically Aurélie de Mascarenhas?"

"Only what Alec told me, that she married one or another of the crown princes. Oh yes, that there was some sort of gossip about her past."

Beka said, "Have you ever looked at Tony's black eyes and wondered what ancestor is peering back at you? There is some evidence that Aurélie was not the daughter of a Spanish marquis, but the illegitimate granddaughter of an exiled Englishman and a runaway slave from the Caribbean."

"Wow! She must have an awesome history."

Beka regarded me askance. "So this doesn't bother you?"

"Why should it? My mother, it turns out, is legally considered a bastard, and as for the race thing, aren't we all pretty much from Africa, if you go back far enough? Okay, look, I know we all grow up with all kinds of hidden pockets of prejudice. Sometimes not so hidden. That particular subset doesn't happen to be mine, so go back to the dukes. Is there prejudice against Jews after all?"

Beka checked her watch, then cradled her cup in her hands. I got the sense that, once again, she was considering what to say and what to leave unsaid.

"Tradition in the Holy Roman Empire was strong," she began. "Jews were not landholders. They didn't form the aristocracy. In Dobrenica, Jews did not build castles on great tracts of land, but we could invest money in the building of the city. The landholding was quietly arranged with the crown. The barony happened after Emperor Francis elevated the Rothschilds to the nobility in the early 1800s. My family had done as much, more actually, for this kingdom, and the queen knew it. As did her son. So on his accession, he raised the Ridotskis to their current rank."

"And the world didn't end?"

She smiled briefly. "The world didn't end, as you say. But the court at that time was . . ." She tipped her head. "Well, you would have to read about Aurelia, as they called her, and the young king. Though you will find intermarriage here, and children usually chose which tradition to follow, everyone grew up knowing that if you had political ambition, you stayed Christian."

"Yeah, I know my history. But why hasn't that changed?"

"It was one of the things Milo had long promised Grandfather," she said, "once Dobrenica regained its sovereignty. Can you guess who objected?"

"Aunt Sisi, of course. No-brainer. But why? This can't be a class thing, as you're all toffs. Religious prejudice?"

"If my family is raised to the dukedom, then one of us Ridotskis one day could be king or queen. It is solely a matter of power and influence. As for you, your mother was baptized a Dsaret, so if she returned, she could establish herself as Duchess of Dsaret. There would be muttering, but the name, the tradition, is so strong that people would accept it. Especially if your grandmother appeared with her."

I paused to consider the comic picture of my mother in her old hippie jeans, arms elbow-deep in pastry flour, prancing around in a tiara, and had to laugh. "Mom would make an awesome duchess," I said. "But what about that other family, the Trasyemovas? I know they have dukes, but I don't recall any kings with their name, when I took the tour."

"They gave up the right to kingship by treaty when they chose to inherit the leadership of the Vigilzhi. Even centuries ago, our various ancestors knew that whoever controlled the armed forces could control the kingdom. The Duke of Trasyemova is also Jazd Komandant . . . I'm not sure how to translate it. The closest rank is the old German *Rittmeister*."

"Cavalry commander."

"Which for us here is the equivalent of a general. And so Dmitros, who is Jazd Komandant, can never be king."

"Got it."

"But their daughters can marry princes, and some of them have produced kings through the maternal line. Ever since Maria Theresia ruled the Empire, the maternal line has become increasingly important. Daughters can inherit the throne. Your grandmother would have."

"Okay, so back to Honoré. Someone doesn't want him sniffing out something?"

"That's the strongest possibility."

"Truth about what?"

"That we don't know. Maybe he's not supposed to discover that someone is lying." She laid her hands flat on the table, fingers pressed together, as if she was keeping the furniture from leaping into the air. "Here is what bothers us most," she said to the table.

Us? Her and Alec—or her and Tony?

"If it is true that someone struck Honoré and set his house on fire, and that person was not you, then it was someone who Shurisko knows. Because he never would have permitted a stranger in the house."

SEVENTEEN

"**O**KAY," I CONTINUED. "So you said the dog was barking like crazy when Honoré nearly fell down the steps after Anijka's visit."

"Yes. That *could* have been because Honoré exclaimed when he fell, it *could* have been because someone was there who did not belong. Or . . . it could be nothing more than the fact that Shurisko wanted to go outside to relieve himself. *Vachement!* You see why I hate speculation, it is endless, yet with no answers." She looked at her watch, and exclaimed under her breath. "And we are out of time. The memorial singing finishes at noon."

"Memorial singing? Those girls I heard from my window?"

"They made their way around the city this morning, singing the Song of the Dawn."

"Was that the *Roman* Song of the Dawn? Wow. I thought that melody sounded . . ."

"Ancient. Though the words have altered slowly over the centuries. In spring and summer, for state funerals, girls are chosen out of the religious communities, otherwise it's family. In winter, they circle the city from sunrise until noon."

"It was beautiful. So where's the funeral?"

"At the cathedral. All the other places of worship will hold a state memorial. At the temple, we will sing a *nigun* in Ruli's honor. She would have liked that." Beka's expression was troubled. Then she said briskly, "I would say come and hear it, but I think you should probably only attend the funeral proper."

"Is there some kind of procession?"

"No." Beka sighed. "It's been so very long since there was a state funeral, and because of the circumstances there was no lying in state at the palace, therefore no procession. She didn't even lie in state in the cathedral for three days, because of the holiday. Her casket was relegated to the smaller chapel."

Poor Ruli, I thought. Always shoved aside, by family, by politics. I thought of Alec wearing the wedding ring, and conflicted as I was about how we were going to work things out (assuming there would even be a "we") I was glad he had that much respect for her.

And how was I supposed to help her?

Beka went on, "Grandfather will be at the cathedral, as he has been asked to the ceremony at the vault." She paused, then said tentatively, "You look surprised."

"It's the first I've heard about this vault thing," and I remembered that Alec hadn't wanted me to take to heart what was obviously a snub, as the duchess had not invited me. "It's separate from the actual funeral?"

"It takes place after the funeral, when she is entombed. It's traditional for at least one person from each of the five families to be present." She gave her coffee a wry glance, and I knew she was thinking of the duchess's snub. But she neither rubbed it in nor commiserated with me by referring to it. "If you wish to know more about the prisms, my Great-Aunt Sarolta says that you may use her name. You can go to Tania Waleska for what they call the test."

"Is your aunt's name like a password or something?"

"Nothing is ever written down about these matters. People are taught one at a time. One layer at a time."

"Got it. Thanks."

"*On se casse.*"

When I got back to the inn, I found that the mauve dress had arrived before I did. As I changed I thought about that conversation, specifically about how carefully we'd tiptoed around the Alec-shaped elephant in the room.

A short time later, I slipped into a crowd walking into the cathedral. My skin felt rough inside my fine new dress, and my entire body ached, especially my head. It wasn't the sinus throb of a smoggy day. My skull felt sensitive, as if I'd lain out in the California sun and my brain had taken sunburn.

When I saw Alec alone in the front pew, the sensitivity sharpened. He sat not ten yards from where the magnificent casket lay, surrounded by hothouse flowers limned in the peaceful golden light of a Paschal candle. He was dressed in a fine black suit, and he was so straight and so still I didn't need any psychic powers to sense the stress he was under. Madam Aradyinov, his gentle, maternal great-aunt who had been my nominal chaperone during summer, stood by his side, wearing a hat and a veil over her black dress. Otherwise Alec had no other relations with him—his father wasn't there.

Behind the mostly empty first pew sat the Trasyemovas. There was young Sergei in a black suit, handsome Dmitros in full uniform, and another man in uniform—had to be Sergei's father—next to a fortyish woman who I recognized as Queen Eleanor of Aquitaine from the masquerade ball last summer. Beka's grandfather, the Prime Minister, sat with them.

Of course, there were no Dsarets.

Should I go up front? I hung back uncertainly until there was a stir at one of the side entrances. The door opened, and in came the von Mecklundburgs, like a group of elegant black and gray swans. They stood around the door, partially obscured by marble pillars and decorations, but because of where I stood, I could see them all.

The Danilovs and Tony stood out, their light hair contrasting with the somber colors of their clothing. With them walked red-haired Parsifal, his sober expression making his long-chinned face look even more horse-like. But he was not the only redhead. Walking next to the duchess was a tall man with short, curly, silver-touched red hair. He wore a fine black suit. As the duchess peered around the cathedral, I snuck a good look at him and wondered if I was seeing Percy's father. But no, an older version of Percy trailed behind the family. And then I remembered meeting Percy's dad, a baron, at one of the parties the summer before. Someone had mentioned that he rarely came down from the mountain, where they had a small castle.

My attention returned to the duchess. I had so visceral a desire to avoid that black veil's turning my way that I slid into a pew midway along the aisle.

As soon as the von Mecklundburg contingent sat down, the choir began to sing from the hidden galleries above. I recognized the *Requiem* by Gabriel Fauré and closed my eyes to listen.

Beautiful music can be painful, and so it was now. I hadn't known poor Ruli for more than five minutes, though I'd worn her clothes, fallen in love with her intended husband, and spoken for two seconds with her ghost. The song evoked the pain that transcended this moment, enveloping everyone who has sustained loss.

Next was the *Pie Jesu*, sung by children's voices. I opened my eyes—and there were the ghosts. Hundreds of them, drifting, blending, some as diaphanous as a curl of smoke, others clearer, faces and forms etched in white and silver and gray, children drifting upward like a skyward rain of angels, as above us in the gallery the living children sang. Like drawn to like.

Blink.

One wall of the cathedral had dissolved into a stippled white, like a blizzard, into which the ghosts ebbed and flowed. I searched among the faces for Ruli.

She was not among them.

So I looked for Gran's twin Rose, who I'd seen in a vision of the past. I didn't see her. So I looked for Grandfather Armandros. Was he there, behind the tall blond woman?

Though the mass had flowed around me, it was the half-choked, wrenching sob that broke the vision. Percy gulped, hands covering his face. The duchess's thin shoulders shook.

The bishop had finished the Prayer of Commendation, and the world around me reasserted itself in magnified sounds—the shifting of cloth, the shuffle of feet and scents—incense, the blended aromas of perfumes and soaps and, to my right, mothballs, probably from a stored funeral outfit. I gripped my hands together and gradually those, too, subsided into normal. In the first pew, the silvery-red head next to the duchess bent toward her protectively, and the duchess lifted her veil to drink a tiny glass of water that the man with the silver-touched red hair thoughtfully offered.

"You okay?"

A whisper on my left. It was Natalie. I didn't remember her sitting beside me.

"Fine."

"You didn't get bopped on the head by a marble bust, did you?" She leaned around to look into my face.

"Nope. Weird mental space."

"Okay. I gotta say, though I'm not one for church, that was a beautiful service."

Up in front, pall bearers were stationed all around the casket, waiting for some signal. Obviously from here on the ceremony was private. People were leaving—I'd missed it all, except for an elusive memory of the music. "They've had two thousand years to find what works," I muttered as we filed out of the pew.

"I'll grant 'em that."

Sound carried in spite of the lofty ceilings. As we reached the aisle I heard the duchess say, "But you must. I insist, dear boy."

I whipped around, and almost stepped on Nat's toes. She backed up, hands raised, and I mumbled, "Sorry. I thought she was right behind us."

"Acoustics." Nat jerked her head backward.

At the side of the first pew, the entire von Mecklundburg clan was gathered around Honoré, who leaned white-knuckled on a beautifully carved cane.

"It's no trouble. I can stay with Danilov," Honoré was saying.

Danilov said from his place as a pall bearer, "I sent a message over last night."

"But I insist," the duchess replied in caressing tones. "It will be like old times. Such a comfort, to have young people around me."

"We have plenty of room," Phaedra drawled, her high voice sounding like a little girl's in that vast space. "We can have the guest wing warm by sunset."

"Your own room awaits you." That was the older, red-haired man. His voice matched his charming lopsided smile. "And it is already warm."

"No one has touched it. Everything in that suite is the way you and Gilles liked it when you were boys." Count Robert spread his hands, a huge diamond glinting on his little finger. He looked like Henry VIII in a Brioni swallow-tailed jacket.

"They sure are piling it on," I whispered, remembering Beka's revelation about Honoré.

"Popular, isn't he?" Nat grinned, and whispered behind her hand. "My guess is, they don't want him contaminated by his low-class girlfriend when he's vulnerable. Or maybe they're worried because some think he's a taco short on his combo plate." She tapped her forehead.

"Crazy?" I stared. "He's not."

She shrugged. "You were alone with him. Did he pop obscure German at you? And watch out when he starts hurling Latin around, Beka says. Sure sign that he's seriously pissed."

He hates being used as a lie-detector, I wanted to say. But I didn't. Whatever other secrets Beka shared with Nat, the aura thing couldn't be one of them. While I was thinking that, I almost missed the decision, it was so subtle.

Honoré lifted his head, Tony made a gesture, and then Honoré said, "Very well. Thank you, Aunt Sisi. Robert."

"Come, dears." The duchess sounded pleased. "We must not leave poor Alexander standing in the cold vault. Honoré, dear boy, you should not attempt those steps. Anton will see you home."

"Want to go with them?" Natalie asked.

I grimaced. "I wasn't invited."

Nat chuckled. "Big surprise, eh?"

"What surprises me is the duchess sending Tony away, if this is all about appearances."

Nat shrugged. "My guess is, everyone will assume he was there. But one thing for sure, Honoré ain't getting down those steps into the vault any time soon."

The von Mecklundburg posse and their chosen few from the Ridotski and Trasyemova families vanished through another side entrance as Tony bent to pick up Honoré's long coat from the front pew.

I turned my back on them and started up the aisle. "Where is the cemetery? I don't think I've seen it."

"Catacombs right below us. Royal families only. Otherwise the posh set pretty much have their own vaults at their estates."

"So why isn't Ruli being buried up at the Eyrie? Oh, because there's more points to being stashed with all the kings?"

"That would be my guess."

"Where's everybody else get put?"

"Up on the mountain, near my neck of the woods." She jerked her chin toward the north end of the city. "It's really pretty up there."

We followed the last of the crowd through the great double doors, carved with medieval scenes of saints and angels. "Are the catacombs open to the public?"

"No, but you could get permission from the bishop if you want to take a gander. Also, it's pretty much fifteen hundreds and up, I hear. Around here, that's practically postmodern. The medieval kings are in a crypt in that rose garden between the cathedral and the school over on that side. There are a bunch of little gardens with high walls built all around it."

"Theresa and her friends showed me one of those gardens last summer."

"Probably the Nuns' Walk, behind which the teaching sisters live. That used to be where the schoolgirls hung out, before the gym was built. Girls eat their lunches there during good weather."

As we walked, I was hyper-aware of the ring of heels behind us: Tony and Honoré.

"Anyway," Nat said. "If you want, I can go back with you. Pick up your duds for my laundry connection. I have to drop off my own stuff."

"Kim."

We turned. Honoré was right behind me, his face strained. "Did Beka talk to you?"

"Yes," I said. "Hey, did your cats show up, I hope?"

Tony's gaze cut from me to Honoré and then to Nat as Honoré said, "The neighbors took them in. Thank you for saving them, and thank you again for saving me." To Nat, "I neglected to thank you for your medical aid."

"That's what I do." Nat waved her mittened hand at his knee. "Did you get that looked at by your own guy?"

"Dr. Kandras has gone on holiday. I can wait upon his return. It's not as if he can do anything."

Nat had been right. Honoré was going to tough it out, guy-style.

Tony's gaze was back on me. "Introduce me to your friend? Didn't we meet somewhere recently?"

"Dr. Natalie Miller. She's the one who patched up Honoré right after the fire. Um, do I list all your titles for a formal introduction?"

"Tony will do."

"Nice to meet ya." Nat's American accent was a contrast to Tony's Britspeak and Honoré's French air.

"Question," I said to Tony. "The tall guy with red hair, who came in with your family then left: Couldn't place him, but he sure looks like you."

"That's Uncle Jerzy. Listen. Uncle Robert asked me to find out if you're attending the gala at the opera house."

I thought of that dress being made. "I guess so."

Tony said, "In that case, there will be a sleigh to pick you up at half past seven."

Before I could frame an answer, Honoré shifted, grimacing in pain. Tony lifted his fingers in a casual wave. "I'd better get him off that leg. Tomorrow will be rough enough."

"Tomorrow?" I said.

"Council meeting. He insists on going." Tony shook his head.

"*Summum ius summa iniuria*," Honoré muttered, head down as he walked past.

"What did I tell ya?" Nat made a face. "I have no idea what he said—my Latin is strictly medical—but phew."

"I know it only because one of my history teachers had a crush on Cicero. It basically means, 'More law, less justice.'"

"And what does that mean when it's at home?"

"No clue. Honoré is on the Council, so it can't be a crack at them," I said as we hiked through the churned-up slush toward the streetcar stand.

"One thing I do know. They sure make good-looking guys here." Nat whistled softly under her breath. "Tony is even hotter up close then seen across a park when he zooms by in his candy-apple red chick-magnet, or across a restaurant. It's those eyes. And Honoré is Raffles, the gentleman thief, in the flesh. Woo-ee! Anyway, what was that about Beka talking to you?" Nat asked as we joined the queue at the streetcar stop.

The sky was streaky with clouds, the snow mushy on the ground. I shivered, though I wasn't that cold.

"She gave me the lowdown on some history and told me a little about magical charms."

"Heh." Nat chuckled, her breath clouding.

"You told me once that some charms work," I said, edging close to the subject of Honoré, in case she knew about his gift. "You said they weren't superstition."

"Yep. I've seen both. What I mean is, I see superstitious behavior all the time. Like pregnant women putting a knife under the bed during childbirth to cut the pain. The mountain women still do it, partly to cut the pain, but partly in case the Wild Folk are drawn by the smell of blood. The knives they use all have hawthorn handles, which are supposed to be great for offing vampires. Then there's the superstition about doctors and diamonds—that one cracked me up when I first heard it."

"Diamonds?"

"Like I ever owned one! But let me tell you, especially in the mountains, I don't dare wear diamonds or crystals when I examine or deliver."

"Do you know why?" I asked. If Beka hadn't told Nat about Honoré's aura thing, then I probably shouldn't, either. It wasn't my secret to share.

She shrugged. "The old midwife who first trained me warned me that people assume you're hiding bad news. How did they get to bad news from anti-vamp action? Anyway, those old Salfmattas praying over wounds? I swear I saw them stop a bleeder once."

We'd been talking in English, but the word "vampires" caused some of the people in line to give us sharp looks.

We climbed on board the streetcar. As we sat, I said, "Did I hear Beka say something about being lucky to find you home?"

"She knew I was spending the holiday with my sweetie. But I got in the night before because they were predicting that heavy storm. You can get mired in the mountains for a week if you aren't a skier or a sled or sleigh driver, and I can't do that to my patients."

"A sweetie! How does he rate against Tony and Honoré?"

Nat snorted a laugh. "Just as hot but a different style. He's got more of the Greek in him. Works as a joiner up at St. Josip's. But his Greek profile isn't what snagged me. He's a singer with the temple choir. He'll be doing a solo at the New Year's concert—Britten's *Choral Dances from the Gloriana*. Ordinarily I'm not that into classical music, but his voice will melt your socks off."

She continued easy talk about her guy, music, the concert, and not much else as we rode down the street then walked to the inn. There she looked around with interest as we trooped up to my room. We piled my dirty clothes into the shopping bag where I usually kept my good shoes, then I said, "Want some tea or something? My treat." I was so grateful she had a "laundry connection," as she put it.

She grinned. "You look like you could use a nap, and I've got to drop this stuff off before my afternoon appointments." She stood with her back to my door and dug through her purse. "Here's a couple of aspirin. When that wears off, have them make you some bark tea." She used the Dobreni words. "It's as good as aspirin. Better, in this weather. I'm not kidding, dude. All of you look tense as hell. I don't know if it's for the same reason, and I don't want to know. I'm interested in people, not politics."

And I'm interested in both, Tony's voice said in memory.

I put Dobrenica above everything, and therefore I get trapped in politics, Alec had said.

"Something's going on. Doesn't take mysterioso magic to see it." Nat hefted the bag of laundry. "Catch ya later."

EIGHTEEN

S HE LEFT, AND I SWALLOWED the aspirin with water from the
jug that always waited for me on the little nightstand.

I took off the funeral dress, hung it up, put the good shoes back in
the wardrobe, then lay down. I meant to take a nap. The room was warm
and quiet, and there was no sign of any ghost. But when I lay back on the
quilt, my brain kept buzzing from one thing to another, always centering
around Alec. What was he feeling? What was he thinking? Did he want
me to stay, or not? He'd sent me a message, but why couldn't he have
come himself, even for ten minutes? Maybe I should go find him.

I put Dobrenica above everything, Alec had said, *and therefore I get
trapped in politics.* Something was missing. Something was *wrong*.

I thought again of the turmoil he'd betrayed when we first saw one
another. He'd wanted to see me, and yet he'd said that about wishing I
hadn't come, and that he didn't want me dragged into "It." Except, whatever "It" was for him, I had a nasty suspicion I was already hip-deep, and
the tide was rising fast. The first splash had apparently happened before
I even arrived from London.

The problem wasn't me, then, it was *him*. What was this pain I
sensed in him? He hadn't loved Ruli, nor she him. Was it guilt? No, I
could not believe that. I could easier believe the world was flat than that
Alec had deliberately murdered Ruli. Anyway, he wouldn't have to be
guilty to feel guilty. In fact, he could be full of self-reproach *because* he
couldn't remember what had happened. I hated the thought of him all
alone, wracked by guilt and remorse.

So why wasn't he talking it out with me? I remembered that tension on Christmas day, the ambivalence during our first interview. Something was sure wrong.

I got up and did a set of ballet warm-ups. Then I did a set of lunges at an imaginary target, left hand and right, left and right.

Muscles loose as string, my skin damp with sweat, I lay down again. No nap. What I really wanted to do was go straight to the palace, march into Alec's office, and say, "What's this wall between us? Is there a door for me?"

Except I knew I'd find him surrounded by government flunkies, who would then do the Dobreni equivalent of tweeting . . . whatever happened.

His days didn't belong to him. So, what about nights?

I hit the bath (there was hot water, yay!) and put on one of the two outfits that had been delivered. When I descended to the dining room, I found Josip, for once, not confined to the kitchen. He was sitting at a table with a group of men, talking and drinking.

Theresa was also there, hanging fresh holly wreaths in the windows. I noticed that hanging in the center of each wreath was a flower-shaped piece of cut glass. The flower was the same basic shape as the one on Honoré's prize rug Ruli's Ginger Rogers dress, and the wooden pendants on Beka's bracelet. What had they called that rug? Amaranth. A word that appeared in Milton's poem, "Lycidas," which I'd studied hoping it would furnish the key to understanding Alec.

Connection or coincidence, I wondered, staring at the way the wreath's crystals winked and gleamed.

One of the men shoved back his chair, startling me out of my reverie. "Midday already gone! Back to work before my rascals fall asleep or 'borrow' my tools."

Voices rose in agreement, and Josip's group broke up, leaving him to pile cups and plates on a tray.

"I will clear the table, Josip," Theresa said, and sidled such a furtive look my way my interest jumped.

"I can clear it." Josip smiled. "There is nothing for me to do until the meats are finished."

"Go help Anna with the breads," Theresa said. "She would like that. I don't mind clearing things away. I am here, anyway, to do the wreaths."

"Maybe you should get the wreaths up first." Josip chuckled. "Just in case, I'll have my cleaver at hand." Still chuckling, Josip left her to it and vanished into the back room.

"Something going on?"

Theresa made a quick gesture. "My aunt says that the kosher butcher's wife's sister heard at the Habsburg Street weavers that some of the old protections have blown down in the wind, or broken, or been defaced. Then someone else said Shadow Ones have been seen along the edge of the city, where Friday market is held."

"Vampires?"

Theresa tossed her head, her braids swinging. "My aunt, she loves talk. No one else has seen them, but many are renewing the protections. My mother insists on fresh holly, with her great-great-grandmother's charms brought out, to keep them away." She joined me in the alcove and lowered her voice, her manner one of suppressed excitement and secrecy. "Speaking of talk. A man was here at breakfast today, asking many questions about you."

I paused. "Is this a good or bad thing?"

Theresa looked around. "I do not know that. Here is what I know. My second cousin's father, Uncle Tadenz, who first brought you here last summer in his horse cab? Uncle Tadenz met this same man at the train station and took him to Mecklundburg House a week or two ago."

"Does anyone know his name?"

"No, but he was very friendly. But he asked so many questions! Mostly about you. Who visits you here. If the Statthalter ever visits, or sends messages." She looked around again, then lowered her voice so I almost couldn't hear her. "Mother was very proud of yesterday's message. You know her way. She means nothing ill toward you in telling him all about it! But I felt you should know."

"Thanks, Theresa."

I tried to dismiss my irritation as I pulled on my gloves. Why couldn't whoever it was talk directly to me? Maybe he'd meant to, but that would have been when I was shopping with Beka. It didn't sound like he'd been exactly secretive—not if he'd joined the daily breakfast blab.

Still, when I got outside, I took a good long look around in case there was someone lurking. It was a half-day for most workers. There were plenty of people on the street, anonymous in their bulky clothes, but they all seemed to be going somewhere.

I pulled my hat low, yanked my scarf up to my nose, and bent into the wind. My experiences last summer, and that picture of poor Ruli plastered on the front of the newspaper, made me feel outlined in neon.

I scurried my fastest, skidding once or twice, but I didn't slow until I reached the intersection. Tania's lens shop had three customers inside. Waiting on them was Tania and a tall, thin man around my dad's age, the latter helping an elderly man, who peered at the alphabet chart on the opposite wall. Tania's customer was a gawky girl of about thirteen, her mother hovering behind her. The girl was trying to decide between the various wire-rimmed frames. They were kind of pretty, though definitely old-fashioned by Western standards.

As I shut the front door, the little bells tinkled.

The blonde bomb barreled out. "Tania? Tania? Do not keep custom waiting!" she said shrilly then peered at me. Her nose lifted. "Tania, I will take over here myself. You help the lady."

"I can wait," I said.

The woman shooed Tania with fussy movements of her small, plump hands and cooed at the mother in a sugary voice. The daughter eyed her for a moment, looking mutinous as only thirteen-year-olds can when adults are trying to coax them into something. Then she whispered to Tania.

I wandered along the shop walls, peering at the astonishing array of glass and crystal prisms as Madam Lens-Maker urged the mother toward the most expensive frames. The mother sturdily asked the price of each, and the girl peppered Tania with anxious questions about which of two pair looked most flattering.

I worked my way to the shop window. In it were large shapes of welded glass with water inside, some of it colored. Below, positioned to catch passing rays of sunlight, were prisms in pyramid, cube, and other shapes. And hanging from tiny beaded strings were many styles of chandelier prisms. When I got close to some of these, the glitter of refracted light made my head pang.

Behind me, the drama steadily escalated as the two women were now carrying on a kind of battle conducted in rigidly polite voices. The girl peered into the hand mirror, her nose about an inch from the glass.

Tania said in a low voice, "The octagonal ones frame your eyes so nicely."

"The square ones are much more practical," the mother stated.

Madam Lens-Maker cooed, "The *hill* girls *all* wear *these* with the decorative silver chasing."

"I will have these." The girl touched the ones Tania had suggested.

"They will be ready tomorrow." Madam Lens-Maker said, giving up. "Taaan-ya! Take them to the back."

Tania was already doing that. Madame turned away from the mother and daughter, elbowed in front of the man—presumably her husband— leaving him to collect the money, and cooed up at the elderly gent: "And now, dear sir, which frames would you like?"

I went up to Tania. "I was told to say that Salfmatta Sarolta requested you to test me."

Her eyes widened, then her expression changed to one of focused intent. "Come into the back."

I followed her to a tiny room crammed floor to ceiling with various tools and simple machines for glass grinding and making, and cabinets filled with tiny drawers. She indicated another, narrow door. "We share this room with the photographer."

She picked up a prism from a small work table, and then opened the narrow door to the photography room, which smelled like an old-fashioned darkroom.

"I have learned to make charms, which we sell in the shop," she said. "I say the Novena over each, on days when there is sun, with the protective light held in mind." She touched her forehead. "We are taught that

Vrajhus makes the simplest covalent bond with light. Sound is more difficult, though it can be very powerful. As is scent, like that from our protective trees, such as hawthorn, rowan, and rose."

"You're talking about quantum mechanics," I said, trying not to goggle. Physics and magic in tandem did not compute in my brain.

Tania said, "The teachers try many words, some from the mathematics. We lost so very much during the war, and slowly we try to recover. Sister Franciska tells us the language is changing."

"So . . ." I was thinking fast. Vampires—*inimasang* in Dobreni—also called the Shadow Ones, as well as Wild Folk. "Do vampires use darkness in some sinister way?"

"The bending or absence of light. Some can see them, even though they try to hide in shadow. Have you?"

"I don't think so. How would I know?"

"You would know." She sounded definite. "I can feel them, I think. I know my cats feel them."

"Your cats?"

"Not really mine." Tania flushed. "The neighborhood cats." She almost smiled. "You know how one does not actually own cats? My family lets me live in the attic, where I have a little door so the cats can come and go freely. I bring the leftover food up there for the street cats, in winter. Anyway, we know they see the Shadow Ones, even if *we* don't. But I am straying from what I am to tell you."

I picked up the thread. "So these crystals and diamonds, are not only worn, but hung in windows, where they catch the light, and that wards off vampires."

"Yes," she said. "We understand that it makes our spaces harder for them to perceive."

"Is it always crystal or diamond?"

"Anything that reflects light, though the Salfmattas say that the more light refraction, the stronger the Vrajhus. But highly polished pure metals are also used."

"Do they use prisms for the same thing?"

She hesitated, then said slowly, "Those with the Sight can use prisms to . . . to see across the border. At times. I don't know how," she added. "I do not have the Sight."

"So seeing ghosts isn't the same as the Sight?"

"No. Though there are those who see both. Now for the test."

She set the prism on the darkroom table between the trays, put a lit lamp on the table, then lifted a heavy hooded cloth and set it over the lamp.

Total darkness closed us in; I heard her light breathing, and the shift of cloth as she moved. "Look," she whispered. "Into the prism."

I looked down, seeing nothing. Of course there would be nothing—there was no light for the prism to reflect. But as my eyes adjusted, glints and glitters—shards of light no bigger than fingernail clippings—dappled the prism. The effect was like light on water, except in colors across the spectrum.

There was no possible way that thing could be reflecting light. The lamp was completely hidden. I could not make out anything of Tania's form, though she stood within arm's reach.

I shut my eyes, then opened them. This time I caught after-images, no more than a second in duration. Rectangles that seemed to stack, a little like mirrors facing mirrors.

I described it all to Tania, then finished, "What am I seeing?"

"Light from the Nasdrafus. That much I know," she whispered back.

"If I take this prism to, say, France, will I see the lights?"

"If there is a place where the border is thin."

"How about other places in the world. Same thing? Where the border is thin?"

"That is what we are taught."

The glinting shapes were curiously compelling, like windows, and within each, colors flashed, sparkling and shifting like light on water, opening gradually into bits of images: a diamond ring on a woman's finger, a portion of the back of someone's head; a shoe; the smiling stone face of a faun from the shepherdess statue. I stared harder, trying to see the entire image, but there was this giddy sense of falling down, and down, and down . . .

Tania drew in a short breath and yanked the cover off the lamp. I lurched back, violently dizzy. I'd thought I was falling, but I hadn't actually moved.

I steadied myself against the table. The lamplight seemed quite bright. In its light the prism lay on the table, cold glass.

Tania's expression was thoughtful. "I am told one should not stare into the lights for long."

"You said *into*, not *at*. Because?"

"If you've the Sight, your mind can fall Between, is what they say."

"That sounds creepy enough. How would someone with the Sight go about learning? I guess I should ask Salfmatta Sarolta herself for that sort of thing."

"Salfmatta Sarolta oversees the charms of health and protection," Tania said as she replaced the lamp and the prism. "She and Sister Franciska."

You have the Sight . . .

"Grandmother Ziglieri," I said, remembering the day of Anna's wedding. "She said something about the Sight."

Tania pursed her lips. "She is very well known."

"Can I find her?"

"Taaania!" The shrill voice penetrated the thick door. "Taaaania!"

"I will send a message." As Madam came barging in, Tania's face smoothed into professional politeness. "Here I am, Madam Petrov." And to me, "Do you still wish to buy a prism?"

"I do. Let me think about which one I want." And in whispered French, "Thanks for the lesson, Tania."

Her employer shooed Tania over to wait on the old fellow, who was still poring over the cheap frames. Then Madam Petrov retreated to the back room, shoulders twitching with indignation, as I let myself out the front door.

The temperature had dropped, and the sky pressed low with strands of heavy gray cloud. At the bottom of the street, a group of little kids zoomed about, skidding on the ice and laughing, as I made my way toward the inn.

There, I found Anna and her mother serving supper.

Frustrated, tired, achy, I let myself into my room. It was chilly, though I smelled a faint trace of cleaning stuff. Maybe the room had been aired.

I opened the wardrobe door . . . nothing. Remembering what Tania had told me, I widened the door in increments, so that the reflection, and refraction, altered by degree as I muttered, "Ruli, you called for my help. Come out. Come on. Talk to me. Tell me how to help you."

A flicker—but it was Grandfather Armandros. Another couple of degrees, and he was gone again.

Moving the mirror a millimeter at a time, I caught Armandros again, and froze. He was clear, yet obviously a reflection, more like a reflection of a reflection. The highlights and shadows had flattened toward uniformity, as if seen through several layers of glass. His body was still, his gaze direct, and yet I wasn't certain he saw *me*. The slow drift of smoke from his eternally burning cigarette belied the impression of a still life.

I moved the mirror minutely, and he winked out.

I shifted in a slow circle, fighting the urge to kick the mirror into shards.

Questions everywhere, and instead of answers, just more hints, mysteries, and . . . questions.

I really needed to talk to Alec. How I wished cell phones worked! Where would he be, at the palace or Ysvorod House? Or was it possible he'd go out? How could I check without causing gossip? Maybe by looking for someone who might know where he was.

I could begin my search somewhere public—like Zorfal. No one would have to know I was looking for him.

The weather had gotten so nasty that most of the inkri drivers had raised canopies. It was cold and stuffy inside the passenger compartment, reminding me of tents at summer camp. I wondered if this was what old-fashioned coaches had been like.

Zorfal was all lit up, music drifting out each time the door opened. I walked into brightness, good smells, and a kind of folk-rock beat that reminded me of some German and Swedish bands. Again there were a lot of Vigilzhi uniforms around. This had to be one of their hangouts.

A waiter appeared. "Are you meeting anyone?"

When I shook my head, he led me up the stairs to the first gallery. A tiny table had been tucked between a rail and a wooden support that looked like the entire trunk of a fir. The table was perfect for one.

I had a good view of about 300 degrees of the lower gallery, as well as the rail tables opposite me on the upper. There, a large group had gathered, at least half of them in blue uniforms. A sudden gust of laughter rose. In in their midst stood a tall, elegant blonde, a sleek chignon flattering her well-shaped head.

Phaedra Danilov must have felt my gaze, or else she, too, was checking out the scene. Our eyes met briefly across the intervening space as the band below played a resounding finish. She looked away, I looked away.

No sign of Alec. All right, then, I'd have dinner and listen to music, then nerve myself to try Ysvorod House. Maybe if I pulled my scarf entirely over my head, the entire world wouldn't be gossiping about my visit within seconds of my arrival. They don't *need* cell phones, I thought sourly, then I was distracted by a flicker at the edge of my vision. Instead of the expected waiter, I found Phaedra leaning against the wooden support.

I said, "I'm in really bad mood, so if you're about to accuse me of trying to murder Honoré and set fire to his house, don't."

"Eliska and Boris."

"Huh?"

"You went inside to save Eliska and Boris. The cats. They were in the secret room."

"Yeah, well, wouldn't you?"

She made an impatient gesture. "No one trying to murder someone would save their cats. Or drag him and his papers out on a rug to safety." She looked across the space at her party, as the band began the intro to another song. "You're here for a reason?"

She wasn't friendly, but the outright hostility was gone.

So I didn't lie. "I was hoping to see Alec."

The band launched into the chorus with a rattling of tambours, strumming guitars, and someone playing wild cadenzas in counterpoint on a violin. Phaedra leaned toward me. "Beka took him to the Hanging Gardens first."

"First?"

She lifted a shoulder. "At eight, a small party, given by Hans for him, and Cerisette, and the others."

She turned away before I could ask who Hans was. Not that it mattered.

A minute later, I said to the first inkri driver I saw, "Hanging Gardens."

She gave me a look that became an eye-widened double take, then she hastily faced front. Easy enough to interpret: *Ghost of Madam Statthalter—no, it's the imposter—none of my business.* The longer I stayed, the more I was going to see that, I thought as she whistled to her reindeer. It did not improve my mood any.

Back up the hill. By the time we reached the posh streets again, my hands were sweating inside my gloves, making those scabs itch.

The inkri eased down St. Ladislas Street. There was a row of fancy-fronted shops across from an enormous baroque building that I later found out was the museum and library, that had once been the royal riding school.

Above a marble-fronted shop selling imported rugs was the Hanging Gardens, and stepping inside was a male figure. I saw no more than a shoulder in a long coat and curling locks of pale hair escaping from under a black Russian-style hat, but I recognized Tony instantly.

I paid the driver and walked inside the restaurant, where a wash of herbal-scented air greeted me, followed by sensory overload.

Somebody had gone to an enormous amount of trouble to create an indoor garden filled with secluded dining nooks that overlooked a waterfall fountain surrounded by terraced bonsai gardens and lit by tiny lanterns. Discernable above the plash of fountains was Jewish folk music from North Africa, the acoustics carrying as subtly as the warm, scented breeze. As I looked around in amazement, I felt that sense of being watched, and so I did a slower scan, but the complication of hanging plants and tiny lanterns effectively screened me from seeing into the nooks.

No Tony in sight. And no Alec.

A somberly dressed older woman approached me, wearing an elaborate sashed robe that was embroidered with peacocks and parrots. I said, "I'm trying to find a friend."

Like the inkri driver, she glanced at me, then did a furtive double-take, her gaze shifting from feature to feature. "At the top of this stair," she murmured with an air of shared privacy, though I couldn't see anyone listening.

She indicated one of two narrow tiled stairs curving off to either side. Each vanished beyond a wall of hanging orchids in graded shades of gold, yellow, and white.

The lighting was dim, so I stepped slowly. The tiled stairway worked its way up along the wall, with the dining nooks discreetly curtained off at intervals by fantastic embroidered silk hangings.

I'd just reached the third nook when I heard Tony's soft laugh from the other side of the hanging. I froze, one foot on the next step as he said in that warm, intimate drawl, "*Draska mea*. I hoped you would change your mind."

"I have not!" Beka whispered fiercely. "Why are you here?"

"I couldn't resist. And neither can you, I see."

"I am before you," she whispered, "because I am so angry. I promised him a quiet dinner. And you are supposed to be with Honoré!"

"I had to escape from Gilles and his pack of French wankers."

"Gilles is in Riev? He brought people with him?"

"Seems to think he can turn this farce into a film."

"No!"

Tony laughed. "And speaking of alone, it looks like you are as well. Shall we be alone together? A holiday truce. For tonight. . . ."

I had absolutely no excuse to be eavesdropping, and I didn't know which would be worse, to be caught at it by him or by her. Or both.

So I propelled myself up the stairs. When I reached the top landing—the stairs started their descent beyond it—I stepped into the alcove, which looked out over the fountain. The only person was a young guy busy bussing dirty dishes.

When I stepped out, there was the woman again, who said in that low, confidential voice that she was sorry, but I'd missed the Statthalter by mere moments. She indicated the stairway going down the other way.

Tears stung my eyes as I stared down at the half-eaten supper, the full glasses of mulled wine. The inescapable truth was before me: Yes, Alec could socialize the day of his wife's funeral, and yes, he was in the mood to go out for dinner.

With Beka. Not with me.

If he'd really wanted to see me, he could have.

In fact he had, he'd seen me come in.

And then he left.

NINETEEN

*O*KAY. *I CAN TAKE A HINT.*

As I climbed wearily into another inkri, aching all over from the adventures at Honoré's, I tried to be a grownup. Yeah, Alec had said, *I don't want you dragged into this,* and it sounded noble. Put less nobly, it could be rephrased, *Don't make things any worse than they already are.*

Because he obviously didn't want my help. Okay. So we were pretty good together during summer, but people change their minds. Happens every day.

If so, why did he invite me to Zorfal, and why did we connect that evening? Surely that was real, not just me wanting it to be real.

Wasn't it?

There was no time to crawl into a hole for a good self-pity wallow, because the moment I walked into the inn, Theresa darted toward me from where she'd been lurking between the counter and the stairs, obviously waiting for me.

There were customers gathered in the dining area. From the sound of their tuneless singing, they'd downed a few gallons of the mulled wine, and they paid us no attention. Nevertheless, Theresa fingered her long braids as she looked around carefully, then whispered, "Grandmother Ziglieri postponed her journey home. For you! To test." She held her fingers before one eye, and blinked.

Huh? Oh—the Sight. More fooling around with prisms. "Great." I tried to summon up some enthusiasm. "Does she come here or do I go there?"

"Oh, you must go to her, it would be much better." Theresa's eyes widened. "Tania will take you, as soon you have breakfasted. Madam Petrov thinks she will be making the deliveries of spectacles and lenses," Theresa added with somber satisfaction. "I will make them."

I trudged upstairs, fully expecting another dismal night of little sleep . . . and I woke up with clear wintry light streaming in the window.

An hour later, Tania and I toiled up the steep street north of the inn, where I'd never been before, Tania clutching a large covered basket against her side. At least I could find out more about how to contact Ruli's ghost, I thought. But when I expressed that to Tania, she gave her head a shake.

"No. This test is for the Sight—that is, catching glimpses of events in a specific location. None of them see ghosts, so far as I am aware. The Salfmattas asked me many questions when Sister Franciska first brought me before them. Most people do not see ghosts."

I sighed. "Why did I suddenly start seeing ghosts when I came to Europe?"

"You probably always saw them but mistook them for other people." Tania hugged her basket tighter against her side, one hand reaching protectively under the red-and-white checked cloth covering it.

"About that," I said. "I have the vaguest memory. Maybe it's not even memory, but anyway. When I was real little. I do remember being scolded for pretending someone was there. My grandmother was adamant about pretense. That's all I remember, her being mad at me for the first time."

Tania said soberly, "She had denied everything, had she not?"

We both knew the answer to that and fell into silence.

I brooded as we climbed, first inventing excuses for Alec's avoiding me at the Hanging Gardens and when none of those were convincing, totting up reasons for leaving Dobrenica. Meantime, Tania and I zigzagged up streets that switch-backed up the steep mountainside. Here and there I glimpsed older houses and an occasional round, tile-roofed cottage set among ancient trees. Toward the end we had to bend forward, feeling for purchase on the slippery ground. I wished we'd taken a sleigh, though that icy steepness might have been challenging even for reindeer.

Finally Tania led the way up a stone footpath past a fiercely tangled hedge of holly and hawthorn. We ducked through an arbor and emerged onto a small plateau that overlooked Riev.

The city was a beautiful sight, sloping gently below the peak of Mt. Adeliad, and divided by the shallow valley made by the River Ejya. On the cliff above the river, I could make out Beka's house, which was much larger than I'd thought. It, too, was mostly hidden among very old trees, but I was able to make out the dome of a glass cupola, below which Prime Minister Ridotski had to be keeping his famous orchid collection, which he'd described at the masquerade during summer.

To the far right, at the highest point, the palace was like a crown, its snow-topped complication of roofs gleaming in the sun.

Below the palace, were more modest, modified mansards along the finer business streets, and everywhere else, slanted gables and a forest of chimneys. "Someone told me you used to sit on ridgepoles," I said to Tania. "I think that's awesome. Was that for cats?"

Tania looked down at the path. "It was to watch the dance of the mist ghosts, when the moon was full and the sky clear. Also, during the sun's eclipse, though that only happened once, when I was eight or nine."

"What are mist ghosts?"

She lifted her shoulders. "I do not know what else to call them. Not like the ghosts we see when we are close. These are silvery, as if made of vapor, coming and going like this." She wiggled the fingers of her free hand. "It is as if they are almost visible and yet not."

Chill ran through me. "I saw those. During the funeral mass."

Tania gave me a startled look, then a slow nod. "You are the first to ever tell me you have seen them! We must go inside. They are waiting."

I followed her up a swept stone pathway, bordered by the stumps of severely trimmed rose bushes poking out. Behind the house, on a smaller, higher cliff dotted with linden trees, inside a holly and hawthorn border, I made out rows of beehives that were blocked from view as we stepped onto a broad porch.

The house was small, no more than two or three rooms under an attic loft, the furnishings so old they brought Tante Mina's cottage to mind—where my grandmother's governess had lived since World War II. Inside, enthroned on a very old chair, sat little Grandmother Ziglieri, who I'd met at Anna's wedding, wearing widow's black. She had to be near her century mark. Her eyes were narrow, framed by countless lines, but her gaze was alert.

A young wife—recognizable as a married woman because she wore her hair tied up in a kerchief, and an apron over her skirt and tunic blouse— came forward to greet Tania, who set her basket down and lifted the checkered cloth. The two seemed about the same age. The wife had slanted eyes and red-glinting dark hair curling out from under the embroidered kerchief. She watched as Tania lifted out a kitten with a bandaged paw.

She and Tania vanished with the kitten into an adjacent room, followed by a junior-high-aged girl with honey gold braids. Then Grandmother Ziglieri said, "Come forward, please."

Small as she was, she dominated the room. "Welcome, child."

Seated across from her were three older women. One looked like she might be a nun. She wore a pince-nez, and her mouth looked like it smiled a lot, though she was serious now. Another, a tiny old woman with curly salt-and-pepper hair, was familiar. She wore expensive clothes with that distinctive French air.

"Have we met?" I asked.

She smiled. "At a party during summer. We spoke briefly about ballet, which was my passion when I was young. And more recently a day or two ago, you visited my brother's home after you rescued the Baron de Vauban."

Honoré. I remembered the smell of smoke, and my scratched up hands more than I remembered her. "You are Beka's Great-Aunt Sarolta?"

"Yes."

Next to her sat an old man, and in the background, near the tiny kitchen, hovered the kid with the braids; she wore a long knitted sweater, dyed a kind of streaky blue, over a skirt embroidered with flowers and leaves and birds.

Grandmother Ziglieri addressed me in Dobreni, "Do you yet speak our tongue?"

"I'm still learning, Grandmother."

"Come forward. It is well enough for a test."

She motioned me to the table, on which sat an honest-to-circus cliché crystal ball.

"Look. Tell me what you see."

I sat on a hassock embroidered with entwined whitethorn leaves and red berries, and stared down into the crystal ball. Wham! Images flitted like crazed bats through my head, too quick and too splintered to catch. They spun away, leaving the twinkle of distant stars, drawing me down and down. . . .

Do not fall. I don't know where the voice came from, or even if I imagined it instead of hearing it. I shut my eyes, and caught myself as I was about to tip off the hassock to the floor. I straightened, wrenching all those bruises down my side.

Someone exclaimed softly behind me. Grandmother Ziglieri said, "Not the sphere, Margit."

The young wife, Margit, picked up the ball with both hands, and carried it away. Then she returned with a pyramid prism similar to the one Tania had showed me, but smaller.

The images in it were like splinters of mirror: half a baby's face; rushes; smoke billowing from the fireplace; a woman's watchful eye. Mine?

Another muffled exclamation, and Grandmother Ziglieri said, "It is not in balance."

Margit looked up. "Tania?"

"I brought several," Tania said.

A five-sided pyramid was set before me. When I bent over it, red lightning flashed in its depths, corresponding with sharp pangs in my head.

"You are angry," the Grandmother said imperturbably. "Take a moment. Breathe out your anger. It will not serve you. It distorts what you see."

I sighed sharply, then did some tai chi breathing as everyone waited. Another peek made me squinch my eyes shut—it was like a steadicam on speed, jittering through a smear of images too blurred and too quick to decipher. I turned away, dizzy and nauseated, restraining the urge to fling that prism through the nearest window.

"This place is a wellspring of Vrajhus," Grandmother Ziglieri murmured.

"Wellspring?" I repeated.

The old widow turned her head. "Baroness, will you explain?"

Beka's Great-Aunt Sarolta said, "The wellspring is a place that makes it easier for you to see but is more difficult to control when you have the ability and no training. Do not attempt to see all times and all places. It is very dangerous if you attempt that and succeed."

"Dangerous, like vampires will get me?"

A frisson went through them, a quick exchange of glances and shift-ings of posture, then she said, "The danger is what some have called madness. It might become difficult to regain, and to keep, your mind in the here and now."

Okay, *that* was really creepy.

"We exhort ourselves to learn control as we experiment. We start simply, and learn to control the small things. Then venture beyond. Does that ease your mind?"

"Control." I swallowed. That made sense. From ballet to fencing to just about everything, you're taught control of the easy stuff before you get to the hard stuff.

She said, "Now give yourself a simple goal. Try to see this room."

The next prism Margit set before me was six-sided, the faces rect-angles instead of triangles.

I braced myself, looked into one of the long rectangular faces . . . and felt the inward sense of pressure ease. No splintered bits of image or flashing lights. Framed like a widescreen TV was the room I sat in, the furnishings in slightly different places. The room was blurred by smoke haze as a wimpled woman in a long, ragged-hemmed, woolen dress tended a cauldron over the fire . . . two men sat before the fire, working with wood, one young, one old and bearded, their smocks and leathern trousers dark-hued.

Instinctively I reached past that time, and my perception shifted. Though again I saw the same room, the curtains were a different color, drawn back and tied in old-fashioned swags. A dog trotted in, the plume of his tail catching the light; I blinked, and there was a stocky, fair-haired young man in a rumpled German uniform sitting at the table, his chin stubbled, and pink from a razor scrape. He was reading a wrinkled newspaper. When I tried to focus on the newspaper's date, the scene slid smearily—

Blink.

White curtains framed the window, and four children sat around the table, all wearing Soviet Young Pioneer kerchiefs. One was bent over a dog-eared comic—a forbidden comic during the days of foreign control. I could see the cover image in purple ink, depicting the mythical half-boy, half-faun Fyadar about whom Gran had told me stories when I was very small.

The children looked up as one, then swept the comic into a basket, a girl dumping balls of wool on top as the boy flung battered schoolbooks with Cyrillic print onto the table.

Blink.

Now I saw the room from an odd angle. It was us! It began to smear and slide, making me dizzy.

"Hold it still," Grandmother Ziglieri said.

"I see the top of my head, as I look into the—ugh." I shut my eyes, then opened them. "When I tried to look into the crystal inside the crystal—well, it was a mistake." My entire body was clenched, my toes crunched up inside my boots. My scalp began prickling with sweat under my hat until I grabbed my hat off and stuffed it into the pocket of my open coat.

Nobody moved, so I bent over the prism again. This time I tried it with tai chi breathing, keeping my eyes open. One point . . . not the crystal in the middle. Grandmother Ziglieri's intent face. Yes. I could hold that.

I tried to see what was next to her. The only thing I can compare it to is learning to ice skate—you hold the rail, venture out a step, let go, and immediately begin to skid. So you grab the rail again. Then you put your foot out once more, tentative and slow, your hand poised above the rail.

By keeping Grandmother Ziglieri at the center of the image—and seeing her as a portrait—I could sneak furtive stabs at other details: the nun's folded hands, the Russian-style wool coat the old man wore, the wooden buttons, Tania seated on an old milking stool, watching intently. Margit hovered directly behind me, ready to move at the slightest flick of the Grandmother's eyes.

The kid with the braids stood directly behind her, watching us all, the light from the window caught in the wisps of hair escaping from her braids and surrounding her with golden light.

I tried to widen my mental camera lens, but as soon as I saw myself it all began to slide away and then to dissolve.

Grandmother Ziglieri said, "That is enough."

I sat back and discovered my entire body was damp with sweat, as if I'd done a couple of hours of hard fencing or danced an entire ballet.

Margit handed the prisms to Tania, who wrapped them in cloth and stowed them in her bag.

Grandmother Ziglieri said, "Do you have questions for us, child?"

"No." I tried to get my soggy brain back online. "Yes. Amaranth. I keep seeing it everywhere, worked into stone and wood and weavings. Is it a real flower?"

The baroness said, "It is very common, with many types. Some are called weeds. Our amaranth, with the distinct heart-shaped petals around the diamond-shaped leaves, is the ever-blooming flower of Nas-drafus. We use the shape for very powerful charms."

"There's a door with it worked into the hinge," I said. "At the fountain, oh, and there is one of those rowan trees, I think, only it looked . . ."

As soon as I mentioned the door, the nun stirred, and the man looked at the others. When I got to the rowan, they reacted again, and not happily. In the background, the teenager stepped back. The light limned her body, a gold-framed silhouette, head bowed.

Grandmother Ziglieri said slowly, "That tree is dead. Someone salted it."

"Is this related to the rumors of protections being destroyed?" I hesitated, then got it out. "And vampires coming around?" I asked.

They didn't laugh, or scoff. I found myself wishing that they would—where's the safety of good old everyday reality when you need it?

Baroness Sarolta said, "We have discovered within recent days that many of the old protections—most untouched for generations—have been systematically demolished or defaced, over the past couple of weeks. If they were living protections, such as the hawthorn and rowan trees, the roots have been salted with hot water."

"But people wear those protection things, don't they? I see them in windows, too."

The baroness touched the necklace glinting at the neck of her beautiful sweater. "Some no longer wear the protections. They believe that Vrajhus has faded, or they do not believe it exists at all. Some of this can be explained away by the teachings of the Soviets, but only in part. Vrajhus itself has its . . ." She looked to the side.

"Tides," said the old man. "A useful metaphor, even if not correct."

"Tides, yes. Though we talk of patterns."

"And we of seasons." The nun's eyes crinkled behind the pince-nez.

"We have no measure for its waxing and waning, though many factors contribute, such as light and the flow of water," the baroness said. "And there are elements we cannot explain. Around 1950, many of us thought that Vrajhus was fading from the world, for there was so little sign of it here. Yet we kept faith with the protections anyway."

"Some regard them as traditional rituals," the nun said. "A comfort, you could say."

"As perhaps you yourself have found, it is difficult to prove these things when one person's perceptions are not those of her neighbor." The baroness spread her hands.

"Have you more questions?" Grandmother Ziglieri said. "I must return to my village before the weather worsens."

Obviously I wasn't going to learn everything in one visit. "Thank you," I said to them all.

The grandmother gave me a dignified nod, and the nun uttered the

Dobreni blessing. The baroness said, "When you experiment, remember: control small things first. You can always ask my grandniece Rebekah for clarification. Though she has much to learn—we all do, so very many things were lost when I was young—she studies diligently."

"Thanks." I pulled myself together and got to my feet. They were all still sitting—probably to talk about me, as soon as we were gone.

The kid walked out behind Margit, who addressed Tania in a low voice, one hand patting Tania's basket.

The dizziness dissipated as I headed down the stone path. My senses were sharpened, almost to a painful degree: the sight of the city below, glinting in the slanting winter light; the sounds of the rising wind soughing through the evergreens above the plateau; the smell of mud and fireplace smoke; the taste of cold air. With my heightened senses, I caught the gist of Tania's and Margit's conversation:

". . . we keep the windows tight."

"Unlock the windows, Tania. The animals have learnt to be wary. If they smell the Shadow Ones, they will not go out."

Margit stepped back and gave the old-fashioned farewell, but she spoke all the words instead of the abbreviated version: "Go with God's blessing."

She vanished inside, and Tania joined me, clutching her basket. The kid stood a yard or two away on Tania's other side, and all three of us gazed out over the city below the massing clouds, underslung like hammocks of gray wool. The top of Mt. Adeliad, up the white-coated slopes behind the palace, was already obscured.

"The city is older in the middle, isn't it?" I asked, peering directly below, at Natalie's neighborhood. "The palace isn't the center. That fountain of St. Xanpia seems to be the center of the old part."

Tania inclined her head. "The fountain was the center until the eighteenth century, when the city expanded across the river southward, joining some of the old castles that became manors. Finally their grounds were broken up, and the streets laid for the great houses along the ridge."

I gazed over the city, thinking about how there were always layers that one didn't know about, even if they were right under your nose. In this case, the protections.

I said, peering down at the St. Xanpia circle, "Vampires have magic, that's what I understand."

Tania touched her wrist, where her crystal bracelet was hidden by her coat sleeve. "They are from the Nasdrafus, and though we are taught they do not have the powers here that they do beyond the border, it is bad enough."

I remembered Tony's words. "Powers like glamour, that's what I was told. What exactly does that mean?"

Tania said soberly, "What does it mean, to be attracted to one person but not to another?"

"You mean they've got magical pheromones?"

Her brow wrinkled. "Pheromones. . . . Sister Franciska says that is a very inexact science, for even if we identify our pheromones, why do they work for one person, but not for the next? She says that the glamour operates on a sense we are not conscious of; not as we are conscious of scent, sight, sound, taste, and touch."

"They're night-biters, right? Or can they cruise the daylight?"

"They say the younger ones, the new ones, or the ones who have recently fed off of fresh blood, can bear a measure of indirect sunlight without turning to stone. But not the direct touch of the sun. Yet they are all drawn to the warmth of the sun's touch." She gestured toward the distant peaks. "I am told that there are many stone vampires in the gardens of the Eyrie castle, up on Devil's Mountain. That is how the von Mecklundburgs used to execute them, bind them in the sunlight."

My nerves chilled, icier than the air. "I thought those were statues."

She spread her mittened hands. "They would be statues now."

"But not carved statues. Those were once . . . people?"

"They were once people made into *inimasang*. They are also apparently drawn to the scents of rose and hawthorn, yet those plants are deadly to them."

She turned abruptly and plunged down the path, through the arbor, and to the street. I followed, buttoning up my coat again, but I left my hat off. It felt good to cool off after the sweaty exercise I'd gotten working with the prisms inside the cottage.

As we began to slush our way down the steep street, I glanced back, and caught sight of those round hives. "Is Margit a beekeeper?"

"She is the beekeeper's wife," Tania said. "The beekeeper is Josip's brother Mateo."

"Who were the others?" When she hesitated, I raised a hand. "No, I get that they are important Salfmattas and a Salfpatra. I also get it that they have all kinds of secret levels and so forth." I was on the verge of asking, *What I really want to know is, why did all the important people feel it necessary to tramp up here on a winter's day to watch me nauseate myself over prisms?* "Except maybe the kid."

"Kid?"

"The schoolgirl with the blue sweater. . . . You didn't see her, did you."

Tania's dark eyes flashed wide. "A ghost invisible to me. Curious!"

"May I buy that hexagonal prism?"

Tania's rare smile lit her face briefly. She dug in her bag, then handed me a narrow box carved of rowan wood in intricately interwoven patterns of oak, ash, and hawthorn leaves. I slid it into my pocket, where it thumped against me, an unfamiliar weight.

"I don't have that much cash on me," I told her when she named the price. "I only brought enough to take an inkri if we needed it."

"You can bring it to the shop later. I must return now. Theresa will have long finished my deliveries."

As we slid down a patch of ice under the sheltering boughs of twisted fir, I said,"You never used a prism to talk to ghosts, right?"

"Never. Has your ghost spoken to you?"

"Not the smallest hint of a screech, a groan, or a clanking chain, and I can only see him in the mirror, for some reason. The only one who has spoken to me was Ruli, or Madam Statthalter. But that was just once. Not since." And when Tania's eyes widened, I told her what had happened. At the end, she shook her head.

"I do not know why she would fade so fast or how you can speak to her again. As I told you on Christmas Eve, it is seldom that I hear them anymore. It is strange, how there seem to be no rules for ghosts."

"Well, I think she saw me. I am sure she was talking to me. But I don't know if Armandros sees me. The only thing that moves is the smoke on his cigarette."

Tania accepted that without surprise. "Those I saw did not always speak, as I said. The older ones, I couldn't understand them. The easiest to speak to, the one who heard me, was the little girl."

"The little girl?"

Color stained Tania's cheeks.

I grimaced. "Hey, was she a friend of yours who died? I'm sorry."

"No, no! No friends died. She was an ancient ghost. *Very.*" Tania looked away, then added firmly, "I am not sure of her identity."

Oh yes she was, but she didn't want to fess up. She cast a furtive glance around us. The street had begun to broaden, and a sleigh whizzed by, carrying a group of kids singing a round in Russian to a skipping, minor key melody.

It was clearly time to drop the topic of ghosts, even in French. Besides, I wanted to get to more urgent things. "When they talk about madness. Do people really go mad, or are they accused of being mad, because they see things no one else sees?" I kicked at muddy slush. "It's fairly recent that I learned to accept that I can sometimes see other times. Now I'm told that that's dangerous. Or maybe I already am mad, because when you really think about it, it should be impossible to see other times."

Tania sent me a narrow, considering glance. "You have studied the mathematics, I think you said."

"Well, some. I wasn't all that great at it."

"You know what they teach about how we move about freely in three dimensions, but the fourth is time. That is, the past is still there, but we cannot move back to it. We can only move forward."

"Theory of relativity, replacing Newton's idea that time is immovable and absolute."

"Now we are taught that, in some places, the border is thinner, so that yes, some people can look backward," Tania said. "The Seers find it easier with the prisms, though some use the sphere."

"Okay. Practice with the prism. Got that. But Tania, sometimes I see the past and there isn't any prism, or diamond, or anything."

"Yes," she said, casting another of those wary glances around as we tramped through the slush toward the inn. "That is why you must learn control."

I stopped in the middle of the street and faced her. "They're worried about me. Aren't they? Grandmother Ziglieri postponed her trip, all the others were there, not because of my grandmother and the Dsaret name, but because they think I'm either crazy, or going to go crazy with this Sight thing?"

Tania's gaze dropped, then she squared herself to face me. "Yes. This is why they advise you to learn control."

I whooshed out my breath. "Okay. Thank you for telling me," I said, struggling mightily for a cheery tone, while my inner chicken was going *bucka-buck-buuuck!* in a mad cackle.

A few yards farther was the intersection with the inn's upper street. People stood in knots talking and gesticulating. The energy reminded me of crowds right after witnessing a fender bender, or when some big sports event was going on.

A few buildings short of the inn, I got that crawly sensation of being stared at. I thought immediately of Ruli's picture and wished I'd put my hat on. Yep, there were weather-ruddy faces staring my way. Then they looked away quickly.

Tania picked up the pace. I stumbled beside her, studying those cobblestones under the slush as if reading my future there.

When we reached the entrance to the inn, she said, "I must go to work."

"Okay. Thanks for everything, Tania."

She scurried on, and I stepped inside.

Natalie Miller sat at the table nearest the door, coffee and a slice of Anna's date bread before her.

She swallowed her coffee and hefted a canvas bag. "Laundry delivery! You can buy my lunch—"

A roar outside the dining room windows sent splats of snow flying up to rattle the glass so hard the holly wreaths jumped and the glass amaranth pendants swung and glittered.

Everyone faced the window, where a screaming red Maserati hulked, engine growling.

A slim figure in a drop-dead black duster and spike heeled boots ran up to the door and thrust her way inside.

Phaedra Danilov yanked off her bug-eyed glasses and said into my gawping face, "Get into something good. Fast."

"What?"

"I think you'd better be at this Council meeting," she yanked back her sleeve, glared at her wrist, cursed softly, then said, "in five minutes. But they always begin with a reading of old business."

Nat flicked me a wave. "Catch ya later, okay?"

I grabbed the canvas bag and jetted up to my room, where I flung the clean clothes. Years of fast costume changes for ballet got me into the periwinkle dress and downstairs at mach ten, where I found Phaedra checking her watch again.

She gave me a chin-lift of approval, and we climbed into her fuel-injected rocket car. She took off with a roar, zipping in and out of traffic with skill and far too much speed. I contemplated advising her never to visit L.A. unless she wanted to spend her entire stay in traffic court, but suddenly there we were, whizzing under the triumphal arch. She skidded sharply right—no cars allowed in Sobieski Square—and pulled up behind the imposing building on the north side of the square. I'd sat in front of the same building on my first day in Dobrenica, wondering how to get at my grandmother's (nonexistent) marriage records.

A pleasant half-hour's walk was a streetcar ride of about fifteen minutes. Phaedra got us there in six.

She released the wheel and let out a sigh.

"Why am I here?" I asked as we got out.

"Cerisette showed up at Zorfal right after you did, on her way to the party. She was a little too smug about this Council meeting."

"Smug? What about?"

"There's something going on. Danilov and I both thought you should be here." Phaedra's voice sounded like a gull's cry. She was furious.

We bent into the rising wind, Phaedra leading the way toward the middle of the row of four Palladian buildings, all connected at the second story and above by windowed arches.

The inside lobby was steamy-warm. It had a surprisingly martial air that I attributed to crossed cavalry sabers and rapiers mounted on the walls between gold-framed black and white photographs, along with older lithographs, of Riev a hundred years ago.

At a coat room inset midway along one wall, a Vigilzhi attendant gestured for a cadet of around eighteen to take our wraps, which he did with such scrupulous care I would have been amused any other time. The Vigilzhi gave us a pat-down—the Dobreni version of a modern-day weapons scan. But modern day took sharp turn when he picked up little silk bags from a basket. "Any diamonds or crystals?" Phaedra asked me.

"Don't own any," I said, as she displayed her hands for the Vigilzhi with fingers spread. The diamond she usually wore was gone.

We stepped away to find ourselves face to shirtfront with Count Robert, Tony's uncle. He stood there with one foot on the slate-tiled floor, the other on the first step, blocking our way. He was imposing in a handsome suit, massive studs of white gold (or platinum, more likely) winking at his cuffs as he gestured toward me. "She has no business here."

"Oh, I think she does, Uncle Robert." Phaedra sounded like Shirley Temple in her most sugary movie.

The Vigilzhi addressed me. "Mademoiselle Kim Moor-r-r-ee?"

Consciously not looking at Robert's glower, I said blandly, "*Aurelia Kim Murray.*"

The Vigilzhi turned apologetically to Count Robert. "She is on the Prime Minister's list."

Robert looked affronted, then he smiled broadly, with a crimp in the upper lip that suggested smugness to me. "Perhaps as well."

He turned his back and started upstairs, but the cadet cleared his throat, and Robert remembered what he'd been sent down for, glowering as he began to unfix his cuff links.

"What's his problem?" I muttered, glancing around Phaedra's answer surprised me.

"Old sore point, made worse because you're on the list."

"Sore point?"

"Uncle Jerzy was banned ages ago."

"Him again. Why didn't I meet him last summer?"

She laughed softly, then her brows rose. "He's your uncle more than he is mine. He's your mother's half-brother." She laughed again as we started up the stairs. "How odd that sounds! He and Tante Sisi have always been close."

"So he doesn't live in Dobrenica, I take it?"

"Tante Sisi gave him the Paris flat, on the understanding we would always have a place to stay when we visit the city. The older people say he's a horrid flirt—they either love him or hate him." She laughed again.

"Gave him? How come he didn't inherit?"

"He is like your mother. How to put it delicately? Grandfather Armandros's son without benefit of marriage. He has lived in Paris for the past forty years. Tante Sisi asked him to come back with her, Tony told us. In support."

We reached the top of the stairway, which gave onto a broad flagged landing with two sets of high double doors. They were open, revealing an auditorium-sized room set like theater in the round, the tiered circles of chairs looking down at a central table. The walls were paneled in dark wood, and hung with kingly portraits plus some ancient flags.

I turned to Phaedra. I wanted to ask if this Uncle Jerzy's mother had also been scammed with a fake wedding, like my Gran, but the Council was already in session.

If I ever get you face to face, I said mentally to Armandros's ghost, *we are going to have a little talk.*

A young guy wearing a pince-nez read minutes in a deliberate monotone. He perched at a high desk, like a pulpit or podium, behind Baron Ridotski. The Prime Minister had an old-fashioned bell, rather like a smaller ship's bell, before him, as well as the customary papers and pens.

Alec sat at opposite the Prime Minister, slim in his Saville Row suit, his expression shuttered. On our entry his eyelashes lifted, and our eyes met. His reaction was subtle, no more than a slight lift of his chin, a scant tightening of the corners of his mouth, but I knew with sickening certainty that he did not expect to see me there. He did not want to see me there.

Phaedra found seats where we could see everything.

The other Council members listened, or shuffled papers, or stared into space as the secretary droned out his flatly delivered summation of the minutes. Midway down the other side of the circle sat Tony, unfamiliar in a black suit with a tunic collar, no tie, his hair combed back into a ponytail, his ears bare of diamonds.

Honoré sat sideways to accommodate his leg. His shoulders were tight, his profile taut with the discomfort he obviously felt, and his silky black hair covered the knot on his skull where he'd been attacked.

There was only one woman on the Council, an older nun. She had to be the Councilor for Education I'd heard mentioned once or twice. The rest were well over sixty, some the age of the Prime Minister.

The first row of spectators was at least half women, promising, I hoped, change in the next generation. Central was the duchess, wearing elegant mourning black including a velvet hat with a sheer veil. Her hands were folded, one holding her gloves. For the first time she was not wearing her diamond ring. Next to her sat Cerisette, fashionably skeletal, her mourning black somewhat mitigated by the low neckline revealing the knobs of her sternum. Do guys find that attractive? I wondered, as the droning secretary shifted without fanfare from minutes to old business.

He cleared his throat, looked at the Prime Minister, then in that droning voice that was so flat it took on a kind of singsong quality, he summarized the findings of committees or witnesses, pausing when the Prime Minister touched his bell. After each touch, the secretary called for votes.

The only times the Council members spoke was "Ja," "Nen," or the Dobreni words for "second" and "third"—although twice, others spoke actual sentences, but that was after they raised their hands. The Prime

Minister touched the bell, which silenced the secretary, after which the Prime Minister would say, "State your question," or "State your comment."

"Don't they make speeches?" I whispered to Phaedra, under cover of a long report of a committee on findings about resurfacing a street.

"Cannot," she breathed. "Used to cause duels. Arguments made in hearings only."

The votes were not simply a show of hands. That is, the hands went up, but an old man, nearly hidden by the huge pulpit, read each name aloud as he counted, then noted the vote in a ledger.

"Who's he?" I asked.

"Judicial. He's a seer. All testimony goes before him first, no diamonds."

When old business was concluded, causing a susurrus of shuffling papers, I whispered to Phaedra, "Does that secretary guy read everything?"

"The Interlocutor. Tradition, dating from the days of Baron Stavraska of the Golden Tongue." As the Council members murmured to one another, and the secretary consulted the elderly gent in an earnest, low conversation, she added, "The Soviets hated it."

"New business," the Interlocutor stated.

"Is it always like this, no one but him allowed to talk?"

"The rule's only for public sessions." She added in a breath of a whisper, "Honoré says there hasn't been a Council bloodbath since 1714. Though in 1939 they came very close."

I could feel the tension building as the Interlocutor set aside his old papers and picked up the new. "Guild messengers from the three eastern mountains report an outbreak of illnesses in the past week," he droned, then rattled his papers and said even more dryly, "In five villages, people insist that these are vampire attacks."

The Council and attendees stirred, some making scoffing noises, others shushing the whisperers.

Someone was permitted to ask a question, which I only partially heard because of the rustling and whispering, but it sounded like he was asking for a precise report on the illness in question, and whether or not it was an epidemic.

"As always, the weather has prevented us from hearing from the more remote villages," said the Prime Minister. "But the Vigilzhi are sending investigative teams."

Everyone accepted that.

Wind vanes, street lights for Habsburg Street, the dam—each item had to have three Council hands before it was either put to a vote or else remanded to committee for investigation. The only time the three hands were not required were when either Alec or Baron Ridotski seconded it.

The secretary then cleared his throat and held up his next item of business. His fingers trembled, and the paper rattled.

Phaedra stiffened.

Cerisette lifted her chin, her little smile totally I'm-all-that.

The secretary read out, "Introduced through Lord Karl-Anton von Mecklundburg on behalf of his mother, the Duchess of von Mecklundburg, on behalf of the people of Riev Dhiavilyi, and on behalf of the population of Dobrenica, a petition for the indictment of Statthalter Marius Alexander Ysvorod for criminal negligence that resulted in the death of Madam Statthalter Ysvorod, Aurelia von Mecklundburg by birth."

Tony was staring straight ahead, his mouth grim. Several of the Council members looked at one another, some of them uneasily; one shuffled, and cleared his throat.

"What are they waiting for?" I breathed, my entire body shivering with horror.

"They're all waiting to see who will be the first to—"

Alec raised his right arm, and the room stilled.

"I second it," Alec said.

The silence after that was like a pistol shot.

Yeah, I know pistols aren't silent, but it felt like I'd been drilled right in the heart.

He got his memory back, I thought. *He drove while drunk, and he hates himself for it.*

Cerisette tittered softly, and the Duchess hushed her with a twitch of her elegant head. Robert smiled, nodding in evident satisfaction.

Baron Ridotski made a sign and the Interlocutor droned, "The

Prime Minister observes that the Statthalter's second abrogates the necessity for the reading of preliminary testimony made by the witnesses gathered on behalf of Lord Karl-Anton."

"You find your own witnesses?" I whispered in disbelief.

"They all will be examined. Sh!"

The Interlocutor droned in a flat-tire tone, "An investigative committee will be appointed, to which committee may be submitted said testimony in hearing. Should the committee recommend, the question will go to trial before the Grand Council."

There was more stirring and whispering, until the Prime Minister tapped his bell and the secretary called loudly for the next item.

My skull rang with shock. As usual, all I could deal with were the inconsequentials. "Tony is a duke, right?"

"Not sworn yet," Phaedra whispered.

The next item was something about the budget. People seemed unable to stop whispering as the Interlocutor bored on, reading a list of numbers, but I didn't hear a word.

My gaze stayed on the three of them: Alec, who had completely masked himself. Beka, who stared into space, stricken. No, it was a lot worse than that. She looked like someone who'd had her heart ripped out by the roots. And Tony, whose expression was the same cold, intent anger I glimpsed briefly just before he killed Reithermann with a knife and when he came at me, sword in hand.

TWENTY

ASSOON AS THE SESSION was over, Phaedra jumped up and dodged deftly between people. I caught sight of her again as she bent over Honoré in earnest conversation.

I tried to spot Alec, but he was completely surrounded.

Now I understood why he'd been avoiding me. He'd already condemned himself. It was just a matter of the legal world catching up, and until then, the only thing holding him together was work. I stood there, unable to move, my head buzzing with sorrow, regret, helpless rage, and a bit of residual headache from that prism experiment.

People moved about urgently, determined to talk, question, exclaim. A shoulder brushed my back, an elbow caught me in the side, after which the old man begged my pardon profusely, then went back to his conversation. Everyone seemed to have something to say to someone, but not to me.

So I ducked, dodged, and ran down the stairs.

Fifteen minutes later, I was at Nat's. She was in the middle of eating lunch, so she had no patients.

I told her everything. Halfway through she began pounding her fist into her palm.

At the end, she jerked her head up. Gone were the laugh lines I had thought intrinsic to her face. There was no humor at all; I did not recognize this Natalie.

"Do you know what this means?" she asked.

"It's just sinking in. This isn't a hearing for manslaughter."

"Right."

"Or whatever the Dobreni call an accident."

"Right."

"He's going on trial for *murder.*"

"Right."

"Natalie, he *wouldn't* have driven her to her death on purpose. But he seconded that horrible motion of Tony's. Alec's already condemned himself."

Natalie sighed. "Neither of us know what kind of political B.S. is going on, but there's something." Nat smacked her fist into her hand a couple more times, then said, "So what are you going to do?"

I flapped my hands. "What *can* I do?"

Nat pursed her lips.

I said, "To tell the truth, I'm half ready to get on the train and go back to London. It's too late to help Ruli. I get the distinct impression I'm a complication in Alec's life. And I'm sure as hell worse than that to the rest of them. Well, at least to my relatives. Most. The duchess and—"

"Kim. You're gibbering. What are you going to do?"

"I don't know."

"Want Auntie Nat's advice?"

I folded my forearms across my middle. "Go for it."

"Look, I don't know how you feel about Dobrenica, and life here. Maybe it's not fair to ask because you've been here what, barely a week? And last summer, a month? But . . . well, it's kinda like the wounded dog thing."

"Wounded dog thing?"

"You know. You can have a tidal wave that kills millions, or talk about the ongoing suffering in African countries, and people throw up their hands, feeling guilty and depressed and helpless to do anything about it. But let some scumbag hurt a dog, which someone else vids and puts on YouTube, and everybody gets bent out of shape, demanding justice, because here's a situation where justice can actually be done."

"Who is the wounded dog here? Alec?"

"No! The wounded dog is anyone, or any *thing*, that people feel can be rescued. That can get justice. And you're the one they're gonna turn to. Last summer, to a lot of people outside the nosebleed league, you were a hero."

"Shouldn't a hero feel heroic? I don't."

"You were. Ask that kid Theresa and her posse. Ask the Vigilzhi. Ask half the city, last summer when you opened a can of whoop-ass on those thugs of Reithermann's with your handy-dandy sword. And on your return? You not only saved a baron, but you saved his cats. Never underestimate the P.R. power of animal rescue."

I had to laugh. "Cat rescue aside, for the duchess and her crowd, I'm still the conniving gold digger who lies like a rug."

Nat grinned. "I think they want to believe it. I think they want you to believe it. I think they want the city to believe it. But at least some of them have to know, on some level, that that's a load of cow patties."

"Yeah. I'm beginning to think that a lot of their attitude is because I stumbled in the way of their getting their pretty paws on the Dsaret inheritance. Money trumps even animal rescue—if you think that money should be yours. But all that can wait. Do you know what a trial means for Alec? I mean, the political side."

"From what I understand, he carries on as usual while the committee does its thing. But if he's called to trial, then the Prime Minister takes over, and Alec's suspended from his position."

My throat was so tight that for a second or two I couldn't speak. I forced out the words, "So what do you think I can do so heroically?"

"If I knew what to do, *I'd* be the hero."

"I can't think past my nose. But I know who can. Nat, can you get me to the palace, to use the phone? I mean, without us causing a major photo op?"

Nat's eyes flashed wide, then she shrugged and grinned briefly. "Alec gave me a key long ago. I've been careful never to abuse the privilege. Somehow I don't think this is abuse."

She got up, then dropped back onto her old couch, slapping her hands onto her knees. "No. I've got a patient right after lunch—wow, that's in four minutes! And also, if we take a cab to the palace, people will see us. Maybe not such a good idea right now. I think the best time to go is after the sun drops. The weather's turning nasty. We'll use it as cover. So meet me here at six."

Back at the inn, I looked around at the delivered clothes and the half-spilled canvas bag of my clean laundry. I could deal with trying to get all that into the wardrobe later. What I needed most was to find out what was going on, not just politically but also with the weird world of Vrajhus.

The prism was sitting on the night table where I'd put it. I opened its box, which released a faint sharp scent. I lifted the prism out and set it down on the night table. Then I sat on top of my clean laundry in lotus position, hands on my knees to steady me.

Practice. And control.

I glared into the prism. "Okay, Ruli. I know this isn't supposed to be able to talk to ghosts, but glass and mirrors seem to be my vector to the ghost-phone. Come on. Pop out and talk to me."

Nothing.

I leaned closer. Tipped the prism this way, that way. Colors flashed— glimpses of unfamiliar faces, none staying long enough for me to catch and hold.

One thing I knew: none of them were Ruli.

So I got up, opened the wardrobe door, and experimented with that. No ghost appeared, not even Armandros. Next I tried balancing the prism so that I could see the mirror reflected in it. Finally I stood by the wardrobe with the prism in hand and tried staring into the prism via the mirror.

All I got for my pains was the faint pangs of a headache.

So I tucked the prism back into its case and left it on the nightstand. To clear my head I tackled the clothing problem. That, too, reminded me of poor Ruli and her mega-wardrobe up at the Eyrie. I couldn't get all those new things into the wardrobe and still fit my old stuff, so I hauled out my suitcase and stuck my old stuff in that.

I slammed the wardrobe door, then put myself through a full work-out. At first my body twinged and the bruises ached, but the twinges faded as I warmed up.

When I was done, I sat down with the prism again, and this time tried the Zen approach, emptying my mind.

Lights swarmed and twinkled as before, sometimes shifting through images too quick to catch. Nothing held, nothing made sense, though once I thought I saw myself at the window, wearing one of the Ruli dresses from summer.

I put the prism away then discovered that I was hungry.

Downstairs, I found Theresa and Tania near the counter. The way they looked up at me made me wonder if I'd been the subject of their talk.

Tania's expression was wretched. "I beg pardon, Mademoiselle," she said almost inaudible, her gaze downward. "Madam Petrov sent me to collect for the prism."

Theresa's indignant expression was more revealing.

I said, "Did she think I was going to grab it and run off?"

"Domnu Petrov would never make such a demand," Theresa whispered angrily. "It's *her.*"

"She is his wife. The lens store is half hers," Tania said.

"Tchah!" Theresa said fiercely. "She would not have said that this morning. She is so stupid—" A quick, revealing glance my way.

The truth hit me like a punch in the gut. "It's this murder trial. Right? She thinks I'm implicated."

"She is stupid," Theresa hissed. "Those who talk so are stupid. They have forgotten all about this summer, and how you rescued the baron days ago. And so the smart people tell them!"

Madam Waleska came out then to ask if I wanted the goulash or the pörkölts with bean soup for dinner. Even she seemed subdued, her voice almost quiet.

I returned to my room to count out the heavy stamped coins, which I brought back to Tania. I saw the evidence of tears as she pulled on her coat and left.

I was glad I got that meal into me by time I'd been outside for five minutes. An icy wind had kicked up, special delivery straight from the North Pole.

It seemed to take forever to get to Nat's, but I finally stamped down her narrow hall, which smelled like chicken paprika and olive oil.

She'd made fresh tea. It was still hot enough to scald my tongue. I gulped it down, then she said, "Let's beat feet. The wind is rising. It's only going to get nastier."

Nat had borrowed an ancient V.W. "No cab," she called over the roar of a very old engine. "We don't need the driver blabbing from here to Moscow. Everybody in town is talking about that freakin' trial."

As the flying snow beat against the windshield in clumps, making the wipers struggle, Nat crouched over the wheel in exactly the same way I had on that horrible drive with Honoré, which seemed a thousand years ago. We bumped along slower than a snail.

There were two cars in the lot at the far side of the palace. Nat peered at them and grunted. "Both belong to the Vigilzhi. Good. Their windows face that way, so even if this storm miraculously lifts, we won't see them, and they won't see us. I counted on Alec sending his aides home ahead of the weather. Nobody will be in the government wing."

I hid the pang of hurt at the mention of Alec's name. He had way more serious things to deal with than me. I wouldn't pester him and add to his burden.

So maybe it's time to give up and go home.

Every instinct cried out against it, but emotional logic isn't real logic, I thought grimly, as Nat pulled in close to the building and cut the lights. Though it can hurt just as much.

There was one last thing to try, and I was here to try it. If nothing came of it, I'd find out when the next train was leaving.

Nat had brought a powerful flashlight, which splashed the blizzard with a silvery beam. We bent into the wind and began to wade. She knew her way. I kept my eye on her back. We reached a wall, the wind whistling mercilessly along it. It seemed a thousand years later when she finally unlocked a door.

We almost fell inside. The silence was peculiarly loud, after the moaning, hissing wind and snow. As Nat had predicted, nobody was there.

The air was almost as cold as outside. Nat lit our way with the flash. We moved through a couple of rooms fitted with somewhat battered nineteenth-century furnishings, then reached Alec's office. I felt his presence. I saw him in the fountain pen on the desk, the neat stacks of papers, the illuminated manuscripts on one wall, and a framed print of the Beatles' *Revolver* album cover opposite, as Nat played the flashlight around the room.

"There you go." Nat opened her mittened hand toward the phone, which was an old-fashioned, thirties'-style desk phone with a rotary dial. "Want this to be private?"

"Why? I'd tell you everything afterward. May as well save the effort."

"Good. This thing is at least tepid." She dragged a visitor's chair over so she could lean against the ceramic stove and kept the flash steady on the desk for me.

The phone. What was Mom's London cell number? Her voice whispered in memory, *Your dad's birthday and the license to your junker.*

"You are seriously hardcore, Mom," I muttered as I pulled my gloves off long enough to dial.

The phone sounds were so unfamiliar I didn't know if it was ringing, or busy. Holding my breath, I waited. . . .

And my mother's voice came through. "Marie, here."

"Mom?"

She whispered, "Darling! Hang on."

Then came those fumbling, squishy noises that you get when someone is walking around, muffling the phone with a hand. Some garbled whispers, and then Mom's normal voice, "Okay, we're outside on the porch, where no one can hear us. It's freezing!"

"We?" I said.

"Your dad and I."

"Are you back with Milo, then?"

"We never left. Milo and your grandmother decided . . . never mind that now. Listen, sweetie, Milo likes to eat early, and Emilio said we'll be sitting down soon."

"Do you know what's going on? What happened to Ruli? And to Alec this morning?"

Sound was garbled as she and Dad whispered. Then Mom said, "Yeah." And in the background, Dad's voice: "We got caught up the night you left, and we got another report this afternoon."

"What do you think I should do? Mom, I want to help but I think I'm only in Alec's way. And as for poor Ruli—"

"Hey, dude," Nat whispered.

I motioned for her to wait.

"Tell us your side of things. Here, your dad is standing next to me, and I'm pressing speaker. Go ahead."

The phone made noises, and I could hear their breathing.

"Kim?" Nat whispered.

I glanced up as she pointed to the hallway, then killed the flashlight. "I think I heard something," she whispered into the sudden darkness. "Besides the storm, I mean."

Darkness made it easier to talk, somehow. I gave my parents a fast rundown, telling them everything except the dire warning of possible madness for those with the Sight.

When I finished up with the Council meeting I said, "So what do you think I should do?"

There was whispering, then Dad took the phone. "Rapunzel, what does she want?"

"The duchess?"

"Yep."

"No idea. And there's no way she's going to tell *me* the truth. Power? Revenge?"

Mom came on next. "Hon, it sounds like she—and Tony—have either wigged out or they're after something. What do they want?"

"Really, Mom. I have *no* idea. I've only seen the duchess once. She didn't even invite me to the private part of the funeral. Not that I was all that hot about going. But I would have. She's avoided me otherwise, and at the wreath party, the only thing she talked about besides why did I dare to show up was how much she wanted her chef Pedro back. Tony talks, but he only says what he wants you to hear."

There was more muffled mumbling, then Dad said quickly, "Mom's filling your grandmother in, and—fewmets! Emilio just gave us the high sign. Hon, if you can figure out what they want, you should be able to make sense of what they're doing to get there. What's that?"

Squish, bobble, fumble. Mom said, "Gran wants you to stay there. Help Alec."

"I can sure try," I said. "If he wants me. But I'm not really sure I haven't become just another hassle for him to deal with. Isn't Milo coming? If anyone can convince the von Mecklundburgs that Alec didn't crash that car on purpose, it's Milo."

Mom said, "You can imagine what a bummer this is for him. But Milo can't show up for the same reason you want him to. He can't pull the king shtick over them, not if they want their laws to work. He's got to park it here and wait for justice to follow its course."

"Yeah, I guess you're right, but you'd think . . . never mind. How's Gran?"

"She's fine. She says—"

The lights came on in the room, startling me. I closed my eyes against the glare and bent over the desk, concentrating as Dad said, "Emilio is waving, food's going to get cold. Look, do your best. If you need to come back, then do it. If there's something you can do there, then go for it. You've got good judgment. We'll do what we can at this end."

My throat tightened, and I couldn't speak.

"Love ya," Mom breathed.

The phone went dead.

I looked up, straight into Alec's eyes.

TWENTY-ONE

NAT GAVE A HELPLESS SHRUG. "It's his office. Couldn't lock
him out."

I don't think Alec even heard her.

"My parents." I pointed witlessly at the phone.

"Got that," he said.

Nat's wide gaze shifted between the two of us in a way that would
have been funny another time, another place, then she said loudly, "I
gotta see a dog about a man." She mouthed some words that looked like
Full Monty! and the door clicked shut behind her.

As if released from a frozen spell, Alec moved to the desk, laid a
stack of papers down, then crossed to the Louis XV cabinet in the corner. There he stilled, head bent.

I began to babble. "I'm so sorry about what happened. Nat and I
were trying to think of ways to help, so I thought I'd call the folks."

As I repeated disjointedly everything he'd obviously already heard,
his hand stretched out toward the cabinet—then he pulled it back as if
he'd burned his fingers.

Finally I said to the floor and the desk and the ceiling, "Alec, I see
that it was a mistake to come to Dobrenica. I only wanted to help Ruli.
She appeared to me, like I said, but I didn't tell you that she said, *Help
me.* Twice, in French and English." Afraid I'd try his patience, and he'd
stop listening any second, I talked quicker. "And so I came, but after
Nat told me what happened to Ruli, well, the truth is, the *real* truth, is I

wanted to see you. One more time. Even from across a room. And yeah, I totally understand that you don't want to see me—"

He turned around so fast I took a step back. "Kim, the worst part of being a murderer is that I don't remember getting in that car."

Bam! The world exploded.

No, it was just my brain. Then stuff started trickling back in, first thought being, *This isn't about you at all.* "You *didn't* get your memory back?"

"No." He said bitterly, "Out of three blackouts, the only one I remember is the first."

Blackouts? "I don't believe . . ." My voice trembled. "It was an accident. Not murder."

"If I'm out and drink heavily, I always get Kilber to drive. Always. Always?" Alec pressed his fingertips to his eyes, every line of his body taut with stress. "It's no use saying I can't believe I got behind the wheel stinking drunk, because I obviously did. The burnt wreck with her in it is proof. Because *she* would not have driven that car, drunk or sober. She hated driving in the snow."

We were standing across the room from one another, him by the chiffonier, me leaning against the desk, my heartbeat slam-dancing. *You said you were going to deal with this peanut butter knife. So deal.* "You haven't recovered your memory."

"No. That's just it." He dropped his hands and then faced me squarely. "Here is the truth. I couldn't face you and admit that I blacked out from drinking that day. I've successfully avoided facing the fact that I've been drunk for three months. Before September, I prided myself on stopping when I willed and relying on Kilber or Emilio if I passed the limit."

Remorse hit me, sickening in its intensity. Three months meant he'd been drinking hard since the wedding. He hadn't changed his mind about me. Put it another way, he'd been drinking hard ever since I took off without so much as a *See ya. And your wedding? Good luck with that.*

I knew it wasn't my fault that he'd been hurt. He knew why I'd gone. But there was no triumph in me to realize that yes, he did care, because what hurt him hurt me.

He went on, "When I was with Ruli, cocktail hour began at noon. It was the only thing we shared. It's been two, or three, or four, to get me through the day, and if I had no business to keep me occupied at night, then I'd get serious." He shook his head.

He stopped, looking down. In the back of my mind, lines of the poem I'd studied so earnestly came to me, chanted in a childish voice: *Fame is the spur that the clear spirit doth raise/(That last infirmity of Noble mind)* . . .

I still did not understand how Milton's "Lycidas" had anything to do with Alec's life, but those words about the cost of fame? Oh yes, right here before me was the evidence of the cost of living your private life in public space.

"You blacked out?" I asked stupidly.

The low quick voice went on, dropping to a whisper of self-hatred. "It wasn't the first time. It happened twice before. The first one was a week after the wedding. That time I sat down to—" he paused, looked away, then said, "to get obliterated. I don't remember getting into bed, but I do remember trying to get there. Impressions before."

He paused again, and I waited.

"I woke up sick. Had to sit through meetings with a head like death. Swore I would cut back. Thought I did, but I blacked out again around the first of December. Could have sworn I hadn't drunk much. That scared me. I made a conscious effort to limit myself. Thought I had." He walked on a few steps, then back.

I was trying to catch up. "What exactly do you remember from the twentieth?"

"The last thing I recollect is offering Ruli a drink in *pax*, after we agreed she could skip the holiday here and take di Peretti to Paris. I remember pouring the zhoumnyar into coffee the way she likes it. We hit our glasses together. I remember that. The next clear memory is waking up on that hillside with a Vigilzhi tying a rope under my armpits."

I was going to say, *So you drank a toast. That doesn't mean you got drunk.*

He'd been watching me, because he said, "Kim, I drank enough to black out. And then I got in the car and drove. I may as well have shot her."

Wayward strands of hair fell onto his forehead. With a quick gesture he wiped them back, apparently oblivious to the cold. Or too distraught to notice.

He'd begun to prowl the perimeter of the office.

I stopped near the cabinet with the crystal decanter inside—the one he poured from when I first arrived.

He'd had to down a drink after seeing me for the first time since summer . . . days after poor Ruli's death.

I frowned at the decanter, a desperate hope blooming. "Isn't that lead crystal? Could it be the blackout was due to lead poisoning?"

"The whisky isn't in this thing long enough to be poisonous," he retorted, without any anger. "Kim, I'm grateful for the support. One of the worst nightmares has been the thought of your condemnation. Justified condemnation. This is partly why I've avoided you, except on Christmas, when we were safely in public. I was too much of a coward to look into your eyes and see the judgment that I deserve. And the other part is—"

"I know. You said you didn't want to drag me into the gossip."

"I don't give a damn about gossip," he said roughly. "That's just talk. When judgment is passed, I didn't want to drag you down with me."

He stood there staring at the cabinet like it was his lifeline, and I thought, *You do care. Too much.*

I took a step toward him. "Alec, I'm not saying that this isn't serious, and that you shouldn't feel the way you do about Ruli's death, but when's the last time you slept?"

He made an impatient movement. "I catch a nap whenever—"

Another step. "Alec. When is the last time you slept?"

"I can't sleep." He turned away. "There is too much to be done, and every time I close my eyes I'm sitting on that cliff watching the smoke rise from the wreck below."

But that two-handed engine at the door/Stands ready to smite once, and smite no more. The poem again.

The tension in his hands, the pained blue gaze, brought back that dead, flat voice: *I second it.*

He made an effort and faced me again. "Until the trial I can keep myself busy making things ready for whoever replaces me, because the most important thing, more important than individual concerns, is a peaceful transition to a government all can accept."

His mouth was white with pain. The blood-sport spectacle of a trial didn't matter to him. The important thing was that in his own mind, he was already tried and convicted.

He was waiting for judgment not from the Council—to him that was foreordained—but from me.

"Let's go somewhere warm and talk." I crossed the last of the space between us and slid my hand around his arm. "There was steam on some of those upstairs windows, so I know you've got some heating somewhere."

His muscles tightened, but he did not pull away. "Can't go there. Not her rooms."

"We don't have to be in her space," I said. "This is a palace. You've got a zillion rooms."

"The only warm ones are our suite. I'm being a fool. We'll go there."

"Good. If I stand here any longer, my California blood will freeze me into a corpsicle." I slid both arms around him and hugged him tightly against me, which I'd been wanting to do for an eternity in the time measure of the heart.

Swift thoughts streamed through my mind, carried by sarcastic laughter at the idea of myself being so proud of accepting him and his baggage of imminent crown princedom. Now, with it all on the verge of being stripped away, there was a steadying sense of balance. We were two human beings. And I loved him.

With that came the clarity of a paradigm shift. I'd spent all that time trying to decode "Lycidas," looking for hidden clues, when all along it was the poem *itself* that was the clue. Until this past three months, poetry had been his emotional safety valve, just as it was Milo's.

"Lycidas" was not just Alec's favorite poem, it was also his father's. Alec's furniture was his father's, his job was his father's. His *name* was his father's, as was his fame. Though Alec loved what he did—he was passionate about Dobrenica, he'd told me during our last argument along the Adriatic coast—what was the cost of having your entire life decided for you from birth, as you strove to follow in the footsteps of a hero?

I hugged him tight, breathing when he breathed. "Think you'd like the endless summer of L.A.?"

"Kim," he whispered, and rested his brow against the top of my head.

But time cannot be suspended, even in happiness.

"Let's go."

I took his hand, and his fingers gripped mine as we left the office. The inner door led to a nicely furnished waiting room with a plug-in heater, now shut off, as well as one of those big ceramic stoves that someone had obviously let go cold.

Beyond that was a hall and a stairway. Alec hit a switch that killed all the lights in that suite. There was a single light at the top of the landing; the shadows were sharp-edged and long, making me wonder what it had been like for my ancestors, lighting their way up with a candelabra. Except that they were royalty, and someone would have gone before them to carry the candles.

Upstairs was marginally warmer, the old-fashioned radiator set on low. Alec touched the light control and looked around. His manner was wary, not at all that of a man coming home.

There was a museum feel to the rooms. I recognized modern settings in the way the furnishings were placed, that is, in squares or circles, rather than along the perimeter in order to accommodate a crowd of courtiers. Other than that, the only modern touches were electric wall sconces. The furniture was all simple, elegant antiques of the Sheraton sort, exquisitely carved, with rosewood inlay and satin upholstery.

This was obviously the Statthalter private suite, though a less homelike atmosphere would be tough to find.

Alec stopped then looked around, clearly in pain. "I haven't set foot in here for days."

"We can go away if you don't want to deal."

"No. I'll have to . . ." He made a gesture that could have meant anything. "Want coffee?"

"Sure."

"I had an annex put in."

He led me past two more salons. The biggest one reminded me of Wedgwood dishes, all blue and white, beautiful but killingly formal.

The last room gave onto a short hall with a small kitchen off it. "We put this in for Magda," he said. "The palace kitchens are downstairs, and Magda complained bitterly about the long walk. Ruli hated the food arriving cold."

As he spoke, he set about filling the kettle and lit the stove, which seemed to be hooked up to a butane container. He took out a small ceramic jar that, when he opened it, filled the room with the heavenly aroma of ground coffee—though I don't like to drink the stuff, I love the smell.

He gazed at it, brow furrowed, then said, "You prefer tea, don't you?"

"I can drink coffee. If you have milk."

"Plenty. Though I don't know if it's still good."

The very homeliness of the task seemed surreal, as we stood there in the little kitchen in the center of a palace, snow falling so heavily outside that there was nothing visible but white framed by the long palace double window.

The milk was good enough for coffee. Soon we each had a mug, and I followed him through the kitchen into another room, which was a kind of den, with a big screen TV and DVD/VCR player, and a solid wall of DVDs.

Beyond that, to a bookcase-lined study, where he stopped short. I nearly bumped into him. My coffee sloshed.

His head lifted. "Someone's been in here."

He walked past the desk to an old-fashioned wooden file cabinet. The middle drawer was not shut all the way. He opened the file drawer. Then another.

He looked up, his expression bleak. "Someone's gone through everything."

"Servants doing some cleaning, maybe?"

"I had these rooms shut up right after the accident. Nobody has been in here but me."

"What could a searcher be looking for?"

"I don't know. There's nothing private here. That is, everything here has carbons in both my offices."

"Carbons. Wow."

He smiled. "We do have a few computers, but as yet, they're only networked between offices in the same building. Cables running everywhere." He indicated the file. "That middle drawer has a broken latch. You have to lift the drawer and depress the latch to make the catch hold. Milo taught me the trick. It was his father's cabinet."

He demonstrated, and the drawer clicked into place. Then he stepped back and looked around again.

"Let's go," I said. "That gives me the creeps, the idea someone's been sneaking around. Though I'm sure they're long gone. Whoa. That reminds me. I was told that vampires are like shadows. Did you know that?"

"I've never seen one." Next was his bedroom—a beautifully decorated space, with nineteenth-century antique bedstead and matching wardrobe and bureau. It was as impersonal as a hotel room.

"How much time have you spent in here?" I asked as we crossed it.

"Probably a week all told. If that."

"This suite is enormous. How long a hike from one end to the other?"

"It's actually not that large. That is, it's built in a square. See?" He unlocked a door on the opposite side of the bedroom, which opened onto a short hall with a guest bath, and beyond that was the big formal salon. "Ruli's rooms are there." He indicated another closed door. "On the other side of the den with the television. Through that door there is the formal entry, leading down into the state chambers. We came up the back way."

"Where in the palace is this suite located?" I asked as we entered an informal salon he'd pointed out when we began the tour.

"We're in the residence wing—the central bar, if you see the building as an E with a bent spine. We're directly above the old royal suite."

On the far side of the informal salon was a couch, covered in smooth raw silk the color of dull gold. I tugged him to that. "Ever sat on this thing?"

"Once. Ruli preferred to hold entertainments in the state chambers downstairs." His smile was rueful. Bitter. "Those huge marble fireplaces were actually pretty good at heating the rooms. At least during autumn."

I plopped down and pulled him next to me, still almost delirious with happiness, though I knew I shouldn't be. There was too much wrong, too many mysteries, but oh, to find ourselves in rhythm again! "Too nice a piece of furniture to be so neglected."

I turned his way. He sat there, the untouched coffee cradled in his hands, his profile tense. Some of my joy diminished.

I said, "Where is home for you, anyway?"

"Not here." He cut a glance around the quiet, tastefully decorated room, then lifted his chin. "Home was . . . here." The same word, but his tone had changed, a higher note, reflective, and I knew before he said it, that he meant his homeland. "Dobrenica." He stared down into the cup. "It sounds facile, I suspect. But it was true, from the first time my father brought me."

Lycidas. "Go on."

"You know Ysvorod House was occupied in those days? My father and I shared a room—a cell, really—with the Dominicans."

"A cell?"

"Not a dungeon cell, if that's what you're thinking. The Dominicans are an active order, and so they're not often in their rooms. A bed, a trunk, a plain table. Small, austere, but comfortable. I had a sleeping bag on the floor. But my father and I spent our happiest hours ranging about the country, then talking our day over in the long summer evenings. The Germans had left the Dominicans alone, and after a few rough years the Soviet commander, and the MGB, considered the Dominicans too boring to cause trouble, and so never bothered them with searches. Later, when I began coming to Dobrenica alone, or with Tony and Honoré and some of the others, we sometimes camped out in our cell, eating food we'd smuggled up, the lighting a single candle, as we gassed on about how we were going to chuck the Soviets out of the country." He stopped and shrugged.

"Go on."

"Not much more to say. By the time I got my house back, it felt like just another stopping place. When I became Statthalter I had three offices, two official and one unofficial—a cubby in the Council building, which was so old and badly heated the Soviets only used it for storage. They ignored that part of the city except for gatherings in Sobieski Square, or as they called it then, the People's Square. Not that the people ever used that name, except derisively."

"Oh, yes, that huge hammer and sickle. Not very well painted out."

His smile flickered. "It was quite thoroughly obliterated after the Soviets left the city, but the paint has gradually worn away. That's an ongoing debate in Council, actually—those who want to reflag the entire square, and those who want to leave it as is, as a memorial to our eventual triumph." He paused, staring sightlessly into his cooling coffee. "Here's the funny thing. After I'm chucked out as a murderer, I'll miss those debates."

He said it lightly, as if it really was funny, and not heartbreaking.

I blurted, "You did not murder her."

"Driving drunk is the same as picking up a weapon, if someone dies as a result. That means murder," he said to the coffee, as snow thudded against the glass and the wind screamed.

I wanted to argue, to defend him, but I could tell from his tone that he'd already had this argument before, over and over, inside his own head.

"What will happen if they decide against you?"

"Ridotski is determined that it will be exile, though I am willing to sit in prison if that's for the best. But I don't know what's best. Except that everything go according to law. The problem is, which law? We are in the middle of so much change."

"You have prisons, right?"

"Yes. That is, historically, common people convicted of crimes were put to work. We didn't have an underclass to force into the work no one else wanted to do, so our convicts built the railroad. Certain capital crimes put you on the chain gangs to do tunnel blast work, and everyone knew it. But aristocrats were exempt from those laws. They were subject to the king."

"So they got away with murder?"

"The king's cronies might. You know how human nature is. Otherwise, you might find yourself assigned to border duty at one of the mountain castles for twenty years, or for life. Exile. Sometimes firing squad, if the crime was deemed to fall under the military code. That's what some anonymous letter writer has been demanding for me, by the way."

"What?"

"Anonymous letters sent to the Council and to the paper. But the editor won't print unsigned letters, so whoever is trying to stir up trouble for me—so far—has been muzzled, at least as of the latest edition."

"Oh, Alec, that's—"

He looked into my face. "Kim, I *killed* her. If the country decides I should stand against the wall, then I will do it. The law should extend to everyone." He stared down into his cup again, in bleak isolation, though we were scarcely two inches apart.

I would not insult him with the fatuity of, *It will turn out all right because I love you.* Though that was the way I felt. So I said, "Do you remember when I asked you to kiss me, after I got drunk that night when we were running around the Dalmatian coast?"

"I haven't forgotten." His voice lightened.

"I kind of wish you had. Kissed me, I mean." I made a horrible face, winning a hint of smile. "That was painfully embarrassing, but I will say this, at least you rejected me kindly."

The smile was gone. "Kim, you were the right person in the wrong circumstances, and drunk as I was, I knew that I should be thinking that you were the wrong person in the wrong circumstances. I wanted very badly to kiss you."

In answer, I did the thing I had longed to do ever since I left Dobrenica, believing that I was making the honorable choice for him and for his country.

I set aside the coffee and lifted my palm to his face. "So, kiss me now."

My touch seemed to go through him like a shudder; his eyes closed, then he laid his hand over mine. I took the coffee from his other hand, set it beside mine, and closed both hands around his face. And then I kissed him.

It was tentative, at least it was meant to be. But my inarticulate question, my offer of solace and comfort and tenderness ignited a response in him, desperate in its intensity. And so, there we were, lip-locked like a couple of teenagers on the living room couch as a shock wave of intense desire obliterated the past, and the future, and even the now.

Rap rap. I didn't hear it at first, then I didn't want to hear it.

Rap-rap-rap!

We broke for air, and he uttered a breathless laugh, then clawed his hair out of his eyes. "Should we answer that?"

I knew who it was, just because my life wasn't complicated enough. "No," I said, a second before the rapping started more insistently.

Then Beka's voice came through from beyond formal entry, muffled but audible, "Alec, if you are in there, you must this instant unlock the door!"

TWENTY-TWO

ALEC TURNED TO ME, dismay verging on laughter. It was so good to see that smile, though it was almost immediately quenched.

"Do you want to be here?" he asked.

"It's either that or hide behind the couch, and I really don't want to do that. For one thing, it's too cold."

He opened the far door. As he crossed into the marble entry way, he twitched his clothes straight, and I took a swipe at my chignon, which had been knocked askew.

There were two grand carved doors. He opened one and Beka stamped in, snow dusting her from her blue fuzzy hat to her neat boots. Her gaze shifted from him to me, her brow puckered in question, then cleared. "*Alors*, here you are, Kim! *Bon*. You were next." And back to Alec, "Honoré is in the car. I've been all over the city looking for you. We've got to find a place to hide him."

"What happened?" Alec and I asked at the same time.

Beka stopped short, took a breath, then said, "You know the Danilovs took Honoré straight back to Mecklundburg House after the funeral."

"Yes," he said. Then asked, "Something happened at Mecklundburg House?"

"Poison," Beka said bluntly.

Flash! In every single surface that could reflect, Grandfather Armandros appeared: windows, the polished black table top, the oval mirrors behind the wall sconces.

I yelped.

Alec and Beka started. "What is it?" Alec asked, leaping to his feet, hands up and ready. Beka pressed her hands to her heart.

"Didn't you see that?" I squeaked, flailing my arms in every direction.

"No," he said.

"See what?" she said.

"Grandfather Armandros—oh, never mind." I rubbed my eyes, and peeked. No ghost. "Poison? Someone tried to poison Honoré?"

Beka had recovered her customary poise, except for the strain around her eyes. "The only reason he isn't dead is because he went to the bathroom to wash his hands. Shurisko got at his tray." Her lips trembled as she added, "An innocent dog! The darling."

"Where's Honoré now?" Alec asked as he delved into his pocket and jangled keys.

"In my car, right outside your Vigilzhi command station," she said. "There's a guard stationed around it."

"What did the von Mecklundburgs do?" Alec asked.

"This is via my mother. I haven't spoken with any of them. She said that the family arrived home to find the poor dog, and a note from Honoré saying that he was leaving, and not to look for him. They went wild. The temporary cook they'd hired for the holidays was sacked the very first thing, though he swore to the Komandant that the food was fine when he fixed the tray—and that he even ate some of it himself. That from Danilov, who left with the cook howling that he would heave up his lunch to prove it."

"Who took the food in?"

"Danilov says that the cook claims he handed the tray off to Luc. Who insisted he took the tray straight to Honoré's room."

"Who is Luc?" I asked.

"Been with the family since before I was born." Alec's gaze was distracted. "I'd be very surprised if he's turned poisoner."

"Shurisko is dead? That beautiful dog?"

Beka gave a short nod, her lips tight. "Honoré got back in time to hold his head as the poor thing died. Then he wrote his note, picked up his coat and cane, and went straight out, down the back way through the garden. He came to my house. My mother brought him over to me at school. I left the faculty meeting and have been driving around with him in my car ever since. I tried the Danilovs, which is where I got the report I just told you. They were willing to take him—Phaedra said she knew she could get some of her Vigilzhi friends to guard him off-duty as well as on—but Honoré said no. That's too much trouble for too many people, and you know how many doors that old house has."

"It's true," Alec said, adding to me, "the Danilovs' house was the Soviets' MDV HQ for a while, until they figured out how easy it was for our people to get in and out and read their communiqués at leisure. Beka, why don't you take him to Anijka?"

"He won't. He's afraid the poisoner would go to her next and maybe attack her family."

"I don't get why Honoré is a target, unless someone knows about his aura thing," I said.

Beka crossed her arms. "I think we can assume that it is exactly that. But why? Who is to be exposed?"

"Maybe the duchess?" I offered doubtfully. "No, I guess that doesn't make any sense."

"Especially as she and Tony and Robert were at the Council meeting, arguing with Baron Ridotski about who was going to be chosen as the investigators when this must have happened," Beka said.

"Unless that's her alibi," I said, but if she went to all the trouble to be away when someone tried to kill Honoré, why did she invite him to her home in the first place? The duchess was a lot of things, but stupid wasn't one of them.

Alec asked, "Did Honoré say anything about the Council meeting itself?"

"He said that at least eighteen people had no auras." Beka then turned to me. "Old Domnu Chandos was never as gifted as Honoré. He is able to perceive the intent to mislead but little else. Honoré sees auras reflecting all emotion. So eighteen people with no aura were either dead, and they were too lively for that, or they were masked by hidden charms."

"We don't know that this poisoner is connected to the investigation of Ruli's death. If anyone does suspect a connection," Alec said drily, "suspicion will turn my way."

"I hate this," I muttered.

"Yes." Beka's voice was quiet.

Alec frowned at the floor, then lifted his head. "Does Honoré suspect me?"

"No," Beka said. "He asked me to find you. And ask for your help."

Alec took a deep breath. It was clear that this small sign of trust heartened him. "I know where to take him."

"Then you do that, and don't tell me." Beka raised a hand, palm out—the same gesture Tony used. "Honoré might have been followed to my place. You know how bad I am at lying, and if this killer is someone I know, I want to be ignorant of Honoré's whereabouts."

"Let's leave no sign we were here," Alec said to me. "Why make it easy for someone to follow?"

"I'll wash the cups, you check around," I said.

That's what we did. He was back by the time I'd washed and stashed the coffee mugs. I also poured the rest of the coffee down the drain and rinsed out the pot, placing it where I'd seen it originally.

Then the three of us left, Alec having doused the lights one by one. He picked up a flashlight from the closet off the main salon and led the way through a confusion of doors, sometimes opening onto plain white-plastered walls, other times carpeted or parquetry hallways, the flash glinting on gilding and crystals, catching on the warm colors of ancestors in their silks and lace in the wall portraits. The last hall was one of the plain ones, leading to the Vigilzhi guard station, where we found bulky figures stationed around Beka's car, two with bayonets fixed. Next to her car sat a Jeep, engine running.

When we neared, a flicker in the whirling snow resolved into a leaping dog ghost. Shurisko bounded frantically around the car, passing in and out of its steel casing. His fur flew, glimmering with ethereal light. I pointed, but since no one was reacting, I dropped my hand.

Commander Trasyemova came out of the station, bending into the wind. He spoke briefly to Alec as Beka opened the car door. A Vigilzhi and Alec helped Honoré out. He looked wretched. And though he could see auras, he obviously didn't see his pet leaping around him, trying to catch his attention.

As soon as Honoré was settled into the shotgun seat of battered Jeep, Beka turned to me. "Let's go. We've work to do."

I watched Alec settle into the driver's seat of the Jeep. Before the windows clouded he cast a glance through at me. We exchanged smiles—I knew what he was thinking, as I was thinking it, *Interrupted again.*

He backed the Jeep, and I climbed into Beka's car. She fired up the engine as I wrestled the seatbelt over my coat. "Work?" I asked.

She crouched over the wheel much as Nat had, intent on the two feet of visibility, most of it taken up by wildly gyrating clumps of white. "Great-Aunt Sarolta passed on a report of your session with the prism."

"You mean my total and complete lack of any control whatsoever?"

She shook her head. "Of course you did not master the use of the prism on the first try. Does a sculptor make a statue when she first takes chisel in hand?"

"I know," I said. "It's just frustration. Besides the useless ghost thing, I find I have this other talent that doesn't seem to do anything besides make me get motion sickness while sitting down."

"The work I have in mind is actually concerned with your ability to communicate with ghosts."

"Jury's out on that, too." I told her about Ruli, in detail. She listened in silence as she drove slowly in the whirling snow. I finished up, saying, "I've been trying to contact Ruli in every way I can imagine, to ask her what she meant, what she needs. No luck. Armandros, same thing. Did I mention I also see him? Ghosts don't talk to me."

She gave a small sigh of disappointment as she navigated uphill. "Very well. Then the only thing I can think of is to try Tania Waleska's skills. I am told she has had commerce with ghosts all her life. But you will have to extricate her without Madam Petrov making trouble for her."

"Tania? She says she has trouble talking to them now that she's not a little kid. But I know she'd be willing to try, if it was important. Why?"

"Because I believe the only way we're going to have any success is if we go out to the site of the crash to talk to Ruli's ghost."

"Whoa," I said, trying to get my head around *that*. "Okay. I guess I can see it. And yes, Tania would definitely be better than I, as she does hear them, and so far, outside of Ruli's single *Help me*, I've got zip on Ghost Audio."

"*Bon*," she said, and sighed. "What a diabolical day."

She stopped the car and shut off the engine. Peering through the steam-smeared window, I discovered Nat's building looming above the drifts of snow.

Nat was alone. Her dinner— a meat-stuffed sandwich and a fruit tart—sat on the jumbled coffee table, half eaten. She'd been watching a DVD on her laptop. As we shed our coats, she shut it down with a swipe and set it aside, then threw a pile of magazines off her chair onto the floor. "Where did you two meet up?"

"At the palace," I said. "She came to Alec's."

"Ooo-kay."

Beka was too intent on getting her gloves off to notice Nat's pursed lips and rolled eyes.

I mouthed, *It's okay*. And out loud, "Somebody tried to poison Honoré de Vauban, and got his dog instead. I wish ghosts could bite," I added.

Beka flicked a fast look at me. "You saw the ghost of Shurisko?"

"Running around Honoré, in and out of your car."

"Day-amm! I don't know if that's sad or spooky." Nat grimaced, shaking her head.

"Both," I said. "It looked to me like he's trying to guard Honoré."

"That's a dog for you."

Beka sank down onto the sofa. From that I took my cue to sit in the chair, and there we were in our accustomed spots. Weird, how humans do that.

Beka flexed her fingers, which had to be as cold as mine. "Natalie, I must beg you to bring tea, or even your so-terrible coffee, or I shall perish. It's been an evil day, and a long one."

"So come on back, and give me a sitrep. I've always wanted to say that," she added as she led the way back to her jury-rigged kettle system. "Situation report! Sitrep! Makes me feel part of the action."

Beka gave her a fast summary of events from her point of view, ending with, "And so I had to find Alec, and Kim as well, because I thought she could talk to Ruli's ghost. When I found both together, I saved an hour of more driving in this storm. It is the first good thing of a terrible day."

Hidden from Beka's line of sight by the complicated water heating structure over the bathtub, Nat snapped a look my way and wiggled her brows.

". . . but if she cannot hear ghosts, she suggests we approach Tania Waleska. That must be our next step," Beka finished.

At that moment the pot began to whistle. Nat pulled the chain, and boiling water cascaded into the teapot she held out.

With her free hand she unhooked some waiting mugs from a shelf, and the three of us shuffled down the narrow hall again, to the living space. "I'm going to have to get me a house," Nat said, as she set the teapot on her cluttered table. "But only if I find someone to clean up, or I'd fill a house with junk. I already know that junk expands infinitely, no matter how many rooms you have. So, tell me this. How many ghost speakers do you have, out of interest? Dude, if there is a maniac murderer on the loose, it seems harsh to be using Tania. I mean, she's just a kid."

Nat poured out the tea. Beka took her cup and cradled it in her hands to warm them. "Technically," she said, "Tania is no longer a kid, having reached twenty, but yes, her youth disturbs me as well. There are only three besides Tania and Kim, that we know of. One is very old and infirm, another seems to only see family ghosts. The best one lives on Devil's Mountain. In the circumstances, I think it better not to put anyone into a possible position of divided loyalties."

"In other words," Nat leaned forward to pass me the creamer, "you don't trust those von M gangsters as far as you can throw 'em. Makes sense to me!"

"I do not *dis*trust Ruli's family," Beka said, staring down into her coffee, a revealing flush along her cheekbones. She looked up, her expression bleak. "We don't know if Ruli's death and the attacks on Honoré are connected. It makes little sense to assume that they were, other than our private dislike of the duchess, and perhaps Count Robert."

Nobody mentioned Tony—out loud.

"Then there's this: Honoré was attacked in their house, yes, but he was also attacked in mine."

"True. But I want to see the duchess blamed because she's a total wanker," Nat said cheerfully.

Beka smiled, then gave that little French shrug. "I hope that Gilles and his group finished with their filming today. We will have to postpone if we see them at the crash site tomorrow."

Nat thumped her elbows on her knees. "Filming? What for?"

"They are making a documentary about Dobrenica they hope to sell to French television. Tchah! I am so angry with Gilles! I know that he took Honoré home from the Council meeting. If he'd stayed with his brother . . ."

". . . then this murderer would have found another way to off him. Why murder him, anyway? Has he got the skinny on somebody?" Nat asked.

"We are going to find that out," Beka promised, neatly evading the aura question while still telling the truth. "Will you help us if you are needed?"

"Count on it." Nat smacked her fist into her palm. "You count on it."

We finished up our tea and then left Nat to her meal. The snow was thicker than ever. Not ten paces away I could barely make out Nat's building. Beka and I hustled into the car, shutting out the howling world of white. My lips still buzzed from Alec's kiss.

Beka started the car, then eased it out, peering through the windshield as before. She kept the pace down to a crawl, then said, "Will you tell me exactly what happened with the ghost after my arrival at Alec's?"

"Grandfather Armandros?"

"It was he?"

"Yes. For the zillionth time. He zapped out right after you said 'poison.' It was like a photographer's flash going off, or lightning. Except instead of a bright light there he was, reflected in every surface that could reflect. For a second. Then he was gone."

"No sound?"

"None. Oh. I was wrong, what I said before. Except for Ruli's *Help me,* I did hear ghosts once before. It was last summer, up at the Roman church. I'm pretty sure it was ghosts. Children singing."

"That place," she said, "is haunted. More people have seen and heard ghosts there than anywhere else."

"There were also a zillion of them at the cathedral the day of the funeral. Was that really only yesterday? It feels like a month ago." I fought against a sudden, violent yawn.

"Are you sure you were not seeing displaced time?" She shot me a narrow glance. "Today, did you . . ." She paused.

When it was clear she was not going to continue her thought, I said, "I'm having trouble telling the difference between ghosts and ghostly times."

She considered that, her gaze searching intently in the hypnotizing mass. Once, the wheels jolted, and she yanked the steering wheel to the left. Every so often the outline of a building, a statue, would emerge from the morass only to slide away again.

The pause stretched into a silence, then she said, "Ghosts are distinct. Time, though . . . When you see a past moment, you see the people in that moment. They are not ghosts, even if they seem ghostly. You are the one who is out of place and time."

"I don't get how the prism comes in."

"It can aid, or help you control, the Sight. There is much about light, specifically the bending of light, or light in conjunction with what some are calling *aether.*"

"Why not Vrajhus, or is that a different thing?"

"Same thing." She gave a quick shrug, the angle of her head expressing irony. "'Vrajhus' means magic, and some seem to feel that more precise terms are needed. I think that the veneer of science is more respectable than magic. Whatever we call it, we lost so much knowledge during those long years of occupation! There's much that we do not understand, in particular because Vrajhus behaves differently in various locations."

"I'm definitely getting the idea that it's not consistent. Or if it is, we're not seeing how. So you can't clue me in about how to see in the past without my brains leaking out?"

Beka said carefully, "This is what I have been told. To see into another moment, you either have to have proximity to the person whose past you wish to see, or some other kind of connection. An object. A place. You also need your medium, the prism, which, when charmed, seems to separate the strands of light. Then the Vrajhus reforms them in such a way as to give glimpses into other times, and some say, even into the Nasdrafus."

"You mean, like the old stories about crystal balls?"

"Exactly. Well, not completely. The limits are to a person or a location, from what I understand."

"Okay, that makes sense. Every time I've flashed on the past, I'm pretty sure I saw different times at that same spot. Okay. So, what else about time? I get the sense you're holding something back. I already know about the dangers. They made that, um, crystal clear."

Her eyelashes lifted—they were even longer than Alec's—her expression tense. "I wasn't thinking about that. . . . You know mathematics?"

"I was a history major, mostly."

"As was I. Well, then, I believe there is a mathematical concept that warns, or maybe hints, that the act of observation can affect the thing observed."

"I may have heard of that and didn't understand any of it."

"Well, then, it could be, that there are . . . things that, once explained, may change."

I struggled with that, and then got an idea. "You're talking about time travel?"

"I do not know about travel," she answered cautiously. "But you know about theories having to do with time?"

"I've seen the *Back the Future* movies."

It was a crack, but she surprised me. "I remember, in the second film, how the danger of changing events in the past could lead to a changed present. Do you recall that?"

I shuddered. "Except for those movies, I really hate time travel conundrums. All right, if telling me more is going to pitchfork me into a weird timeline, I don't want to know. Tell me instead what I should say about Tania."

"Yes. I was coming to that. You know that she is twenty. Customarily that is the age the apprenticeship ends. Tania is excellent at making lenses, and she has also been trained in the faceting of crystals, though she has not worked with diamonds. But last September there was more than one marriage made that—"

Beka squinted out the windshield and jerked the wheel. A street lamp slid by very close to the car.

"For Tania, Domnu Petrov's marriage was not a good thing. Madam is known for being stingy and would like nothing better than another year or two or three of unpaid labor from Tania, who should have received her certificate of training completion several months ago. You must understand that these certificates are like a graduation degree elsewhere. To the artisans they are more important than their school certificates. They can get jobs and join the guild."

"So where do I come in?"

"You could hire her."

"Me?"

"Yes."

"For what?"

We thumped over something, and Beka grimaced and yanked the wheel. "That was the rain gutter at the St. Marcos crossing. Just a few more streets. Hire her for anything. You do not need to say for what. The Petrovs would not ask. He would be glad to see her placed, I think. He knows that the two other lens makers in the city already have their apprentices, or she would have been hired out after her birthday. His wife would not dare to question a Dsaret, once it is brought home to her who you are."

"Making me feel like a total poser again," I said. "But I can deal with that if it'll help Tania. Am I supposed to pay her a salary to sit around, or what? Would Tania even want that?"

Beka said, "There is something else." She slowed even more. "The day you came to the palace. You walked into Alec's office, and what did you see?"

Alec's arms around you. "Alec said later that you were demonstrating something."

She addressed the windshield. "What you saw was . . . two things. One was a demonstration. The other was the shared comfort of conversation."

"Okay. You're talking about comforting him because of how I complicated his life, and he comforted you, what, because of Tony?"

She gripped the wheel, the knuckles of her gloves pulled against the seams to the straining point. "Tony is . . . never serious."

"He sure was at the Council meeting," I said. When she winced, I added quickly, "I know what you mean. His radar is definitely stuck in broadcast mode. So Alec needed comfort because I turned up in Dobrenica?"

"He was glad," Beka said quickly. "He was very glad to hear that you were here, and yet your arrival, I think, sharpened the sense of guilt that has troubled him since the day of the accident."

"And there was also all the gossip. I get it. So what were you demonstrating?"

"Something that I have been working on, with some of the other Salfmattas and Salfpatras. You must understand this is very secret. As yet." She took a breath. "In the past, there was no electricity."

"Right," I said.

"You know that we make the crystal charms during sunlight hours, do you not? Diamonds are charmed only at noon."

"Tania told me that," I said.

"What we are doing is trapping electricity in stones in the form of sunlight. Only a few of the Salfmattas and Salfpatras are able to do this effectively, but a well-made charm can run small things that require very little electricity."

"Whoa."

"So when you walked in I was showing Alec how to run my Palm Pilot off a charm, and he was attempting it."

A flaw in the wind revealed the inn's familiar door, not fifteen feet away.

"How this works, why this works, we do not yet know. It is too new. But Tania would be the very person to hire to experiment, do you see?"

"That's a cool idea. So why don't I call her my . . . what did they call that Magda? Personal assistant. I gather that is not merely a fancy name for maid."

Beka was amused. "Ruli had at least a dozen domestic servants. Her wardrobe was substantial."

"Oh, I remember."

"Good. Are we agreed, then?"

"Sure. I'll take care of Tania, but hey, aren't the roads going to be impassable? I mean, if this storm ever ends?"

"This storm is supposed to be gone by midnight. See? It is already breaking, over the north. I see stars. I'll come by after an early breakfast, and we shall have to stop by Madame Celine for your fitting. I would be very, very surprised if the Vigilzhi do not see to it that the south road is cleared by mid-morning."

TWENTY-THREE

AT BREAKFAST THE NEXT DAY, I found Tania and Theresa together, setting the tables. Because I knew the sisters shared everything, I broached my offer.

"Oh, I would like that so very much," Tania said longingly. "But—"

"So you *shall*," Theresa said with a ferocious grin. "I shall come with you to see you take leave!"

We left at once, Theresa holding her sister's hand tightly.

Halfway down the steep street behind the inn, Tania pulled away from us and stooped. A skinny cat emerged from a crack between the inn wall and the foundation of the stone house next to it. It sniffed Tania's hand, and its tail lifted high. Tania took something out of her pocket, gave it to the cat, who chomped on what looked like a bit of dried fish, and with a twitch of the tail, vanished.

We continued on to the shop. As soon as we got in the door, Madam Petrov began scolding in that high, shrill voice, "Taaania! Why have you brought company? Do you expect them to watch you sweeping?"

"We have come to inform you that Tania has been offered a paying position," I said.

"Who is this?" Madam asked, flicking her fingers in my direction, though she looked back uncertainly when she saw me without a smothering hat or scarf. For the first time ever, I reveled in my resemblance to Ruli.

"This," Theresa said in a portentous voice, with a relishing grin, "is the granddaughter of the Princess Royal, Aurelia Dsaret, daughter of the last king!"

Madam's mouth opened, round as her eyes. But as she took me in from top to toe, her forehead wrinkles altered from annoyance to perplexity. I felt an unexpected spurt of sympathy, irritating as she was. Here was yet another change in a lifetime of sudden changes.

"I would like to hire Tania," I said politely, then turned to the lens maker. "Domnu Petrov. I hope that you will declare her apprenticeship finished."

Domnu Petrov gave me a dignified nod, almost a bow, then turned to Tania. "Tania, you will have your certificate by day's end. In fact, I will walk it to the guild myself, if you are required by your new employer to begin your duties now."

"But I—the sweeping! The windows! The snow!" Madam's voice got more shrill with each word. "Can it not wait a day?"

"Thank you, Domnu Petrov. Here is my key," Tania said with her pensive smile, and laid the key down on the counter. "God be with you."

Her gentle voice was drowned out by Theresa's crisp, "God with you!" And she closed the door with a snap. "I would kick the snow, except that I think Madam must sweep it, and I would not help her a bit." Theresa stamped down the enormous drifts, saying to me, "I never liked her when she was at the bakery, and she would scold her brother if he gave us day-old buns when we walked to school. She would rather throw them to the pigs. Tchah!"

On the walk back up the steep street, even while we were slipping and sliding in the enormous drifts, Tania seemed to expand inwardly. By the time we reached the inn, Wednesday Addams had vanished, leaving a tall, grave young woman with her head up.

Beka was there at the inn, drinking coffee. Madam Waleska hovered. Beka was saying in a patient tone that made me wonder how many times she'd had to repeat it, "No, thank you. I really did eat breakfast right before I set out."

"But you could say my rolls are kosher. I know your laws! No meat touches my good rolls, and you must know we buy our meats from your own butchers!"

"Thank you, thank you, but I am truly not hungry. I am only waiting for—ah. Here they are."

"Mama," Tania said, her chin up. "I am now employed. I am to be Mademoiselle's assistant."

Madam W. threw her hands up, then turned to me. "You need the spectacles?" She made circles of her thumbs and forefingers, holding them before her eyes.

"Tania will have many duties," I said. "Beginning with accompanying me on my shopping expedition today."

Madam went off to the kitchens to share the news. I said to Beka, "What first? The fittings for my ball gown?" Listen to me, I thought, laughing inside.

Beka obviously didn't find anything amusing in that. She had been studying Tania's usual shirtwaist dress. This one was a dull dun, instead of gray, or murky blue. "We might have to climb," she said slowly. "There is a shop around the corner from Madame Celine's. Very comfortable, Persian-style loose clothes."

"Lead on!"

Beka drove, bumping slowly over the streets that hadn't been cleared yet, as sleighs jingled by us. The fitting went fast, as I wanted to get in and out. I found the other two in the shop Beka had mentioned, Tania having been drawn to linsey-woolsey outfits of loose trousers under a long belted tunic.

"Must I wear a certain color?" she asked me, as soon as I appeared.

I felt weird about this invisible money. My instincts kept sending off alarm bells. From everything I'd ever heard or read, big money always comes with big trouble. No one is able to be neutral about it. But for now? Why not enjoy the Lady Bountiful role! "Get what you want."

With a little of her younger sister's ferocity, Tania said, "Then I shall have violet."

Within a short time we were on the street again, Tania with the ugly dun shirtwaist in a bag, wearing a warm outfit of deep violet that turned her slightly sallow complexion golden. It was embroidered with patterns of leafed rowan berries. She'd chosen another of deep midnight blue, embroidered with tiny blood roses.

"One more stop," Beka said. "Any questions before we do? Phaedra

Danilov is going to drive—she is much better behind the wheel than I am. She can be trusted to keep silent, whether we are successful or not."

Phaedra? That was a surprise. "Oh. Maybe I shouldn't have brought this," I said, patting my pocket where I'd tucked my prism.

"You don't have to take it out," Beka said.

"True. So tell me. Who is this Jerzy guy? Phaedra called him uncle, but said something about my mother. Is he a von Mecklundburg, or not?"

"Heh." Beka's mouth twisted. "Not so easy to answer."

"Well, what's his background?"

"That much I can tell you. His mother was the stonemason's daughter up on the Devil's Mountain, and when Count Armandros . . . no, he was the duke then, briefly, because his brother had already been killed. Anyway, he was wounded after an encounter with some Germans. Hid up in her village as he dared not go to the Eyrie, which they held. She took care of him, and . . . well, along came a son. Gossip was evenly divided about who seduced whom. A year or so after Armandros died, she came to the city and first tried to blackmail the family, but by then everyone knew about Princess Aurelia and her daughter Marie, so this new little scandal hardly raised a brow. So she sold him outright to the family and vanished."

"That sounds kind of harsh."

"Your Aunt Sisi took to this little red-haired baby her own age, and they have always been close. He always traveled with the family. When they came here in the fifties, he began getting into trouble. During the sixties and the early seventies, the trouble escalated, especially with women."

"Just like his dad, eh? I don't remember any mention of Jerzy in Milo's diary."

"Milo was very discreet about certain kinds of trouble."

"Yes, as in didn't mention at all."

Beka gave that French shrug. "Jerzy was also implicated in a series of thefts, though he always seemed to have an alibi—usually corroborated by women. When one of those thefts ended up with a death they all insisted was accidental, his friends went to the prison work force for a time, and Milo and Grandfather prevailed on the Council to ban Jerzy from the country."

"But he's here now."

"This ban was forty years ago. Because of Ruli, and for the duchess's sake, you understand, no one has said anything about his reappearance. Anyway, we all called him Uncle Jerzy when we stayed at the von Mecklundburg flat in Paris."

"I take it this flat is not a small apartment."

Beka threw me an amused glance. "Your Tante Sisi have something small? It is the upper floor of a very fine address. Four suites altogether. We all called it Uncle Jerzy's place. I do not know if he actually owns it, as I do not know how legal is his use of the family name, but he acted as host as the family and their guests came and went. Here we are." She pulled into the palace parking lot.

I felt Tania's gaze and said, "Uncle Jerzy seems to have been over at the inn asking questions about me."

Beka pulled up and parked. "He must have been as surprised as everyone that the mysterious Marie's daughter was back."

I laughed at the idea of Mom being mysterious as Phaedra Danilov came striding out of the Vigilzhi command post, looking elegant and athletic in a black and white ski outfit.

She beckoned impatiently.

"Ah. All ready for us," Beka said in a brisk voice.

We got out, and Phaedra pulled off her sunglasses. "I want you to know I think going to the crash site is a stupid idea. I'm only here because I don't want to hear about *you* driving off a cliff." She waved the sunglasses dismissively at Tania. "Who's that?"

"We will talk in the car," Beka said.

Phaedra shrugged sharply. We climbed into a four-wheel drive vehicle with huge snow tires, and began bumping up the steep road behind the palace, Phaedra handling the wheel like an expert.

"Tania speaks to ghosts," Beka said over the rim noise.

Phaedra shot a fast look in the rear view mirror. She drove like a maniac in the city, but I was relieved to discover that she was more cir-cumspect in her mountain driving—still fast, but not crazy. "So you re-ally think you'll find Ruli's ghost at the crash site?"

"It hasn't been seen by anyone else except Kim. When she died, yes?" Beka turned to regard me.

"Actually, Tuesday morning, if we figured right," I answered. "I don't know if that makes a difference."

Phaedra shrugged sharply. Clearly it made no difference to her. Beka gave me a perplexed glance.

"Ruli would go back to Paris if she was going to haunt anything," Phaedra stated with conviction.

"Perhaps. Perhaps there is no choosing," Beka replied. "All I know is what the Salfmattas say, that sites of violent death will most often have a revenant, at least for a while."

Phaedra did not respond, and we fell into silence.

The mountain roads were beautiful, but bumpy with snow that had drifted down after the plowing, and had turned icy in the shadowy can-yons and turnings. Tania rode beside me in the back, eyes closed. I won-dered how many times she had ever been in a car.

The dramatic slopes had been smoothed into blue-white folds, punctuated here and there by stands of evergreen and weather-worn rock. Once I saw a grayish goat-like creature bounding like a deer high on a peak and realized I'd seen my first chamois.

Then Phaedra let out a "Hah," and pulled up to a stop.

A flag had been planted on the roadside. Phaedra got out, slammed the door, and walked to the snow piled along the edge of the cliff. The rest of us got out more slowly. Tania rubbed her temples with her mit-tened fingertips, rewrapped her scarf, then took a deep breath.

"Go ahead, whenever you're ready," I said, disappointed that I couldn't see any ghosts.

Tania turned to me, I shrugged, then she said quietly, "No one here."

"Let's look over the ledge, shall we?" Beka asked.

The crash site was below a hairpin turn. We walked carefully along the piled snow at the verge, but we couldn't see directly down. I was hesitant to climb on that pile—it was fresh, loose, and I couldn't see how close to the edge it was.

The trunk slammed, and footsteps crunched up. Phaedra reappeared with coiled rope over one shoulder and a broad shovel balanced on the other.

She attacked the plowed snow, flinging shovelfuls over her shoulder. She soon created a gap. We edged into it, and peered down at the smooth expanse of white. To the left was a ledge. Below that, a steep drop. Here and there snow-dappled trees reached skyward. One was broken off. The other trees showed pale bark where branches had been violently torn away. At the bottom were two blackened tree skeletons sticking up from the fresh snowfall.

I saw no ghost. Tania's gaze was fixed, and I felt a surge of hope.

"Ready for a climb?" Phaedra snapped an end of the rope free of the coil, and began fashioning a knot. "Or is there nothing to see?" she addressed Tania.

"I think . . . I think there is something," Tania said to me.

"Okay," I said in my most encouraging tone.

By that time Phaedra had anchored her ropes to a strong young pine, and had tested them. "You know anything about rappelling?" she asked Tania, who shook her head.

Phaedra had only a single harness, which she worked over Tania's coat, and checked it. "Let's go."

"Do you need a harness?" Beka asked.

"This is like a stepladder," Phaedra waved dismissively at the treacherous climb. "I only need harness on cliff faces."

With that she wrapped her own line around her hips, took it in hand, leaped over the edge, causing Beka and me to gasp. She ran, bounced, then jumped again, landing solidly on the small plateau twenty feet below, sending snow flying.

"That's where Alec was found," Beka murmured to me.

"I'm surprised he didn't break his neck!"

"He was, too." Her tone was subdued.

Phaedra held out her arms, encouraging Tania over. With Beka and me guarding the rope from above, and Phaedra from below, Tania inched her way down the chasm. Once or twice the two caused small avalanches that covered them with sprays of white powder.

"What's Phaedra's issue? Is she mad at me on Ruli's behalf, or mad at you?"

Beka laughed softly, sending a cloud of vapor into the still air. "She dislikes me for something unforgivable that I did in childhood, and again when we were teens. And yes, that time, it was about Alec."

Tania said sharply, "Here." Her voice echoed up the rocky crags.

Tania balanced on a rock near a broken tree, staring in that fixed way that reminded me of cats. Phaedra had also stilled, her head shifting in quick, minute flicks. Clearly she didn't see anything out of the ordinary.

"Something about Alec?" I asked, prepared to be shut down. Or ignored.

Beka sighed. "I said she was stupid. Because she doesn't read. I was a horridly arrogant teen. Arrogant and jealous."

"Smug or miserable, all part of the teen package," I said. "She's still angry?"

Voices echoed from below as Tania said something, and Phaedra answered. Then Phaedra lifted her head, her hands curving around her mouth to amplify the sound as she yelled, "He won't talk."

Beka and I looked at each other. "He?"

"Is this the wrong accident site?" I asked.

Beka peered downward. "There is where the trees burned. The wounds in the higher trees are still fresh. We're in the right place. But the ghost might be old. Perhaps others have crashed here. It is a treacherous turn."

We had to contain our impatience as the two labored their way back up. Phaedra guided Tania's every step, frequently catching her when Tania slid or got panicky.

Tania never made a sound. Her face was crimson, especially where she'd bitten her lips, but when she regained the roadside, she said, "There is a man. He is dark of hair and eyes. He wears a coat of smooth leather and very fine shoes."

"Old fashioned clothes? New?"

Tania touched her chest. "New. His trousers, they zip here." She patted her waist in front. "Many of the old ghosts, they have buttons."

"That ghost could be from last summer, or seventy years ago," I said. "Zippers in men's pants became standard around the time of World War two."

"I *still* think Ruli would haunt Paris," Phaedra called as she freed her ropes. "Probably at Hermès."

I'd been fingering the prism in my pocket. "Look," I said to Beka in an under-voice. "It's probably a waste of time, but like Phaedra said, we're here. We should try everything."

Beka looked puzzled, then her eyes widened. "I agree."

Phaedra had stowed the rope in the back of the car. She paused, one slim hand on her perfect hip, the other jamming those intimidating glasses on her nose. "What now?" Her voice changed. "What's that for?"

I had the prism on my hand. It winked and glittered, catching shards from the sun riding above the northern mountains. The sparkles were so intense I closed my eyes.

"Experiment," I said. "Beka, what do I do to find that day?"

"I don't know how seers find a specific time. Perhaps look for Ruli's face? Maybe you will see her in the car?" She spread her hands, a quick, graceful gesture even with fuzzy mittens. "I am out of my realm."

I drew in a deep breath, reaching for my one clear memory of Ruli, when we first saw one another up at the Eyrie. I recalled her features as I shifted the prism a millimeter at a time.

Something flashed, too quick to catch.

"It's like a single frame of a film, but I know it's there," I said, frustrated.

Tania came to my side and peered doubtfully at the prism. "Are you perhaps seeing her in a moment of motion?"

"*Alors!*" Beka exclaimed. "That must be it. She is passing in and out of the space where you stand."

Phaedra plucked off her glasses, then her brows arched skeptically.

"Or you are imagining her? I don't understand this. Is it something like Honoré's auras?"

"No, it's different . . ." I shook my head. "It's fast, but I get enough of an impression to see different colors—she's wearing different clothes. Weird."

"You are seeing her at different times," Beka stated. "You need to isolate that day, if you can."

"How?" I looked around. "Oh. I'm in the middle of the road. So, if those are different times, then I'm seeing her being driven along. I need to catch her going off the cliff. Which means . . ." I didn't know much about prisms and Second Sight, but I knew plenty about how traffic and cars worked. I stamped along the slushy ground to the side of the road. "If they began to skid off there, they probably started right about here." I faced the road and moved the prism, trying to see the green Daimler that I'd ridden in for so many days.

This time the blur was less smeary and the image more clear, enough for me to recognize the Daimler coming at me head on. I jumped back, then steadied myself. No car was going to hit me.

When I tried again, it was easier—and the blurring, sliding image lasted long enough for me to see that there were two people in the front seat.

And I didn't know either of them.

TWENTY-FOUR

"IT'S THE SAME CAR?" Phaedra asked for the third time.

"I know that car. I rode in it for days. It's definitely the same car."

Beka shook her head slowly. "Perhaps a similar car, from another year? I do not understand how it is possible that two people you have never seen could be in a car that no one drove besides Alec or Klaus Kilber. You didn't see Kilber?"

"A woman is driving. She has a pointy face." I motioned to my chin. My head panged. "Narrow here." I touched my cheeks. "Dark hair, very short, escaping under a red cap."

Phaedra made a stifled noise and waved for me to go on.

So I finished, "She's wearing a brown coat."

"The man?" Phaedra asked, arms crossed. But her tone was interested, not derisive.

"He's asleep, or leaning his head back, so all I could see was dark hair and a sort of smeary gleam here." I touched my shoulders. "Light along a smooth thing. Not fabric. Maybe a leather jacket."

Tania's words *coat of leather* reverberated in my head. Beka's eyes widened, and Phaedra tipped her head.

"You imagined it," Phaedra said emphatically, jerking a thumb Tania's way. "Because she said her ghost is wearing a leather coat."

Instantly doubt hit me. "Maybe I saw what I expected to see," I said. "Except why would I see that woman? I don't know her."

Beka's lips were a tight line. "Wait. Kim, is the car sliding, like it's out of control, or is it coming to a stop?"

"I don't know. Could be either. It's moving slowly through my space, with a sense of movement like this." I pushed my hand toward the side of the road.

"*Vache!*" Beka's sharp exclamation snapped our attention her way. She made a visible effort and spoke in that neutrally flat teacher's tone. "Kim. Would you try one more thing for me? To be thorough."

"Name it."

"Come back to this point, here, where the car might have either stopped, or gone off the road. This time, instead of trying to see the Daimler, try to see Alec."

"Oh, good thinking." I paused to breathe and sloshed a few paces closer to the verge of the road. It had given me a bit of a headache, concentrating on the two strangers. But try to see Alec? That should be easy. I gazed down into the prism, turning it minutely, then shifting from left to right—

There. Gone in a blink, as usual, but now I was getting better at the tiny adjustments I needed to make to bring the vision back into focus, even if only for a second or two.

There.

I recognized the back of Alec's head. Below that one shoulder, and his arm, utterly inert, his hand loose, hanging off the back seat. He lay on his side.

I moved a yard diagonally and turned slowly to look back. I stood in the space where the front seat had been. I looked down into the prism— and there he was, not two feet away, hair spilling across his forehead, the rest of him sprawled in unconsciousness. Caught in time. I looked so long and hard that dizziness frazzled the edges of my vision.

I looked up, blinking rapidly until I regained focus on the trio of waiting faces. "He's asleep in the back seat."

Beka was pale as death. She said carefully, "Good. Now look again at the man in the front seat, if you can."

He would be in the same space I was standing, so I edged to my right, then turned again, so I stood in the driver's space, and I stared down through the prism at where the shotgun seat would be.

There was the man a few inches away.

You move as if inspired, sweet Ruli, a voice whispered.

Cold poured through my nerves as if someone had shoved a bucket of snow inside my skin.

"I know that guy," I said numbly. "I mean I recognize him. It's the guy I danced with in the Split nightclub."

"Marzio di Peretti?" Phaedra squeaked. "Marzio? And Alec, in the Daimler? But everyone said . . ."

My throat was tight. I swallowed, instinct forcing me to be exact, as if every move, every word was important. "It is the same man I danced with. I never heard his name. He—he thought I was Ruli, you see. That day in Split."

Phaedra gazed over the ledge. "I don't get it. How could Marzio become a ghost?"

"If it's the same man," I said. I think *I* was squeaking. My voice sure didn't sound like mine.

Beka rubbed her cheeks fiercely. "I think the first question is, why was Magda Stos driving the Daimler with two sleeping men inside it?"

Phaedra jerked around. "You thought that, too? Magda wears a red cap. She has short hair, and that chin—" She said to me, "We used to call her *Barbe*, when Aunt Sisi first put her to spy on Ruli. You know, for that pointed beard of the musketeer days." Phaedra's words came in a quick rush. "She drove Marzio to the border that day, we know that. But Alec in the back seat? Are you sure?"

"That is what I saw," I said, hoping so hard that I tried to squash hope down.

Beka looked my way, her gaze stark. "There was one body found," she said softly. "I could see Alec sliding out of the back seat if the door somehow opened . . ."

"But how would Magda call from Paris on Stefan-Zarbat, if she was driving this car, which ended up down there?" Phaedra pointed downward.

"She called?" Beka asked.

"You remember," Phaedra said to me. "We stopped the fencing practice.

She told the family that she drove Marzio to the border, as he requested. But I'd swear someone said she used one of the palace cars. And she wouldn't take the Daimler. Nobody drove it but Alec, and Kilber, and maybe Emilio. The clutch was temperamental. Stalled out if you breathed wrong."

Tania had gone pale and still. Beka rubbed her hands slowly, then stuck them in her armpits. "Kim, one last request. Can you see any other cars around?"

"I'll try."

My head was pounding by then, but I trod through the slush to the place where I'd seen the car head on and shifted the prism. Nothing. But when I concentrated on the Daimler, I got the blur-images like before. "I guess for this to work I have to look for something specific, either a car, or a person."

"It was a good try. I think we are done." Beka gazed into space, her brow troubled.

"No, we're not." Phaedra put her hands on her hips. "All we've got are more questions."

"Let's talk about it on the way back," Beka looked around at us. "I'm freezing. You must be, too."

"I'm fine." Phaedra shrugged.

I was rubbing my achy fingers, and Tania shivered. Phaedra threw her hands wide and started for the car.

As soon as we were in, Phaedra swung the car in a neck-twisting tight U, but when we skidded, she slowed, her voice revealing her frustration as she said, "Marzio has never been in Dobrenica before, so it couldn't be any other day. So where was Ruli?"

Beka stared through the windshield, her expression tense, even nervous.

Tania said softly, "Might she have gone in another car?"

Phaedra said, "Then where's the wreck of that one, whatever car it is? In Paris we were told that Ruli was in Alec's green Daimler when it went over the cliff. It's Milo's old car. Nobody else has one like it. Alec said he had her purse, so she had to be with him. She would never go anywhere without her purse."

I said, "But what if it's not Ruli in the wreckage in spite of the purse?"

Phaedra retorted, "So who is in that coffin?"

I said, "Who identified the body?"

Phaedra shot an exasperated glance over her shoulder at me. "I was in Paris—" The car drifted, and she snapped her gaze back to the road. "But I heard Uncle Jerzy breaking the news to Tante Sisi. Dr. Kandras reported that she was burned beyond recognition." Phaedra braked and slewed around in her seat to frown at me. "Are you saying he mistook a man's body for Ruli's?"

"If it was burned beyond recognition. . . ." Beka began. She shook her head. "I do not know enough about such things."

I said, "This I've learned from lots of television crime shows: male and female skeletons are instantly recognizable to medical guys. Even if everything else is ash. And it takes a really hot fire to incinerate bones. I wonder how hot that fire got, considering that the car landed in snow."

Phaedra made a scoffing noise, then started driving again. After a while, she spoke in her old drawl. "Then what you're saying is, there's a conspiracy? Among the servants and Dr. Kandras? What would they get out of falsifying Ruli's death?"

"Alec being shot by a firing squad," Beka said in a flat voice.

"What?" Phaedra slammed on the brakes.

"You didn't know? My grandfather showed me the letters. Typed on one of the old Soviet typewriters—there are still many left— and written in Russian, which everyone had to learn until not so long ago. And unsigned. But someone wants Alec convicted of murder and shot."

After another silence, Phaedra muttered, "I am going to *kill* Tony."

Beka's chin snapped up. "Why do you say that?"

"Who else would benefit?" Phaedra sighed. "Don't get me wrong. I adore Tony. I was kissing him before *you* ever did, Beka. But you know how wild he is."

"Wild, yes. But murder?"

Phaedra lifted an elegant hand toward the towering peaks on the other side of the valley, gray and silver and white against the wintry sky. "Tony despised Marzio. I can see him throwing Marzio off a cliff. Especially if he'd found out how much Marzio was bleeding Ruli for money."

"Do you really think he'd set Alec up like that?" Beka said slowly, eyes still narrowed. "And send anonymous letters?"

Phaedra gripped the wheel with both hands again. "*Merde!* No. The coup, like in summer, yes. No one gets hurt, and no one looks bad, except—" She paused.

"Me," I said cordially. "And yes, I know you all thought I was a gold-digger. But who got you to believe that?"

A pause while we all considered the duchess.

"Tony would despise anonymous letters. However, humiliating Alec would give Tante Sisi exquisite pleasure." Phaedra downshifted, sending the engine into a roar as the vehicle started up an incline. "I can't see her writing them, but maybe she'd get someone else to. She was *very* angry after summer. And Magda has always taken orders from her first. That's why Ruli and I used to ditch her to go nightclubbing."

"Someone needs to talk to Magda face to face," Beka said.

I said, "So . . . about Ruli." I thought of Ron Huber, whose heart had stopped then restarted. "Is it possible that she's still alive?"

That caused a real firestorm of emotions—relief, regret, dread, determination, and above all fury. Why would anyone fake her death? Not for any good reason, that was the only thing I was sure of.

"I could see her running away with some boyfriend," Phaedra said. "If not Marzio, someone else, with money. She and Percy threatened to run away together when we were all just out of school. Hah!" She gave a crack of laughter. "They would have gone, but they hadn't a penny between them. Ruli wouldn't stir a step without access to cash."

"How could she run off without a car, and if there was another boyfriend besides Marzio, how did no one see him?" I asked. "I think it more likely the duchess locked her up again. Maybe we should check out the Eyrie. Only this time I want a pack of armed Vigilzhi at my back before we go for round two."

"Let us stop speculating on such scanty evidence," Beka said. "Even the ghost is not admissible before our judicial system, because it cannot be proved if not all can see it."

Phaedra made an extravagant shrug, then said, "I'm still angry with

Tony. Not because I think he's a murderer, but because he has to know something, yet he's not telling us and worse, playing games with us again. Tchah! He can find his own partner for the tango."

She shot a triumphant glance Beka's way.

Beka's cheeks reddened. After a long moment she said in that flat teacher voice, "There will be the tango played at the gala? In such a large crowd?"

"I drove Cerisette to her appointment with the conductor to go over the music." Phaedra made a miffed noise. "Enough! I'll wear my Balenciaga. I can barely waltz in it, so he will have to give up his exhibition. How he loves to show off!" Phaedra's gaze met mine in the rear view mirror. "Have you ever seen the past before?"

"Yes. I think I was seeing a past Christmas in someone's diamond at the Christmas Eve Mass. It was my grandmother, Princess Lily, and her sister Rose. I also saw Milo as a young cadet."

Phaedra puckered her lips in an *ooo*, her eyes wide.

"Was the vision sustained that time?" Beka asked.

"For a few seconds, long enough for me to get a good look at them all. There was another time, when I was a kid, in California. It was in the window of the bus. I saw a girl my own age, outside a kiicha hut. She was on a palisade looking out over the ocean. She wore Acjachemen dress. I could see her hair lifting in the wind. Last summer I was lost in the countryside east of Austria. I saw farm workers in the past, and then the modern farm overlaid it. But not before I got a drink of water."

Beka looked sharply at me over her shoulder, mittened hand before her mouth.

"What is it?" I said, instantly suspicious.

"Nothing. A surprise to hear. Such things are . . . rare." Beka was staring through the windshield, so all I could see was the back of her head.

Phaedra glanced at me in the rear view mirror. "I take it you know about Honoré's auras."

"He gave me permission to tell her," Beka said. "A couple of days ago."

Phaedra chewed her under lip, and then met my eyes in the mirror again. "There is definitely a conspiracy, and Tony has to be at the center of it. I will strangle him."

"Did you remember something?" Beka asked, neutral again.

"Only that I thought something was strange from before December twenty-first," Phaedra said. "It was so strange that Tony had to go to England over the Solstice, instead of going up to the Eyrie as he has ever since we were teens."

"I thought that was a traditional family party," Beka said, still in that flat, careful voice.

Phaedra was too angry to be careful. "Party! A bloody sort of party, as the English say."

I leaned forward. "Tony was with me in London the night of the twenty-first, that I can definitely tell you."

"Yes, so I said. Tony went to London because of some legality over his father's estate. Tante Sisi insisted he see to it before the holidays, and she told us that Uncle Robert would take over the tradition at the Eyrie, now that he was Count, and Ruli had agreed to go as well. Once. Because of her new position. That was a surprise, because Ruli had repeatedly said that nothing would get her to the Eyrie, ever, after her summer as a prisoner. She didn't even want to be in Riev over Christmas."

"She never mentioned going to the Eyrie." Beka tapped the dashboard. "When Ruli and I went to Madame Celine to order gowns, Ruli said she and Alec were arguing about Christmas and Paris. He wanted her first Christmas as Madam Statthalter to be spent in Riev."

"She probably lost her nerve and wanted to run." Phaedra shrugged. "Then Marzio showed up. Cerisette said that the morning of the twentieth, Ruli asked her to host a party to introduce Marzio around, since Ruli couldn't give one at the palace for him."

"She didn't mention the Eyrie, then?" Beka asked.

"Not according to Cerisette." Phaedra cursed in Russian, then said, "She wanted an out. That's it. No vampires. No Night of the Thorn treaty."

"Night of the Thorn?" Beka said.

"Vampires?" That was me.

Phaedra ignored Beka, and glanced at me in the rear view mirror.

"Didn't Tony tell you any of this last summer, when you were with him at the Eyrie?"

"No. His exact words were 'a tenuous truce.' He also told me he's *seen* vampires. But nothing about any thorns, night or day."

"Damn their secrets." Phaedra smacked her hand on the steering wheel. "Here is the truth. Once a year, on the longest night, at least one of the family must meet the vampires up at the Eyrie. And give them blood. In return, the vampires caught on this side of the Nasdrafus are supposed to leave the mountain people alone. Tony's father wouldn't do it, so Tony took over when Robert's father died. Danilov often went with him. Felt obliged. Tony had treated him like a brother after the duchess took us in."

"I didn't know that," I said, but as soon as the words were out, I remembered Ruli saying, *I cannot tell you how much I hate the Eyrie*, and: *My brother talks to the undead*. She'd all but told me. If I'd asked the right question, would the rest have come spilling out?

"Is the eclipse part of that, by the way?"

"Oh, yes. That is, according to the old stories, the increase in darkness is said to increase the Shadow Ones' power, or if not that, their ability to move around."

Beka's lips were compressed in that way I'd seen whenever Tony was mentioned, and I wondered how much of this was new to her.

"Tony lets vampires chow down on him?" I was so grossed out.

"He won't let them touch him," Phaedra said. "He cuts a vein open with this very old hunting knife, the handle made of rosewood. Called Thorn. Fills this small golden bowl carved over with flower patterns, called the Rose. Equally old. Probably both charmed. The bowl felt that way, the one time I touched it. Everyone adds blood to it, then it's handed off to the Shadow Ones. It's an old ritual. I did it once. Thought it would be a thrill."

"A thrill? To cut your arm open?" I hugged my arms against me. "That's way too kinky for me."

Phaedra flashed an ironic grin into the rear view mirror. "They say there's a sexual kick, when they glamour you. Your blood is supposed to taste better if you are in love or in fear."

"Adrenaline or pheromones. Maybe they can taste the difference. Ick."

Phaedra said, "There was no glamour for me. No kick. Tony was angry, and I was puking scared. Anyway, it's a family secret." Phaedra gave a sarcastic laugh. "Kim, you are supposed to be part of the family, yes? While you're up at the Eyrie looking for Ruli, why don't you go introduce yourself to them?"

"While I'm all for expanding my social networking, that does not include vampires," I stated. "And Tony didn't tell me any of that."

"If Tony's hiding Ruli again . . ." Phaedra began.

I thought of Tony sitting there in that council chamber and accusing Alec of murder.

And Alec saying *I second it*, because he believed he had been driving that car while drunk. Fury burned through me.

Phaedra smacked the wheel. "*Percy* will strangle Tony! He's hardly stepped from his room. He won't even touch his paints. They have been arguing so much, he and Robert, over how the opera house is not finished, I never want to go to Mecklundburg House again."

"Percy is a *painter?*"

"He says he's not." Beka glanced back at me. "He claims only that he is merely a restorer of the old work."

Phaedra grimaced. "Mixes his paints the old ways. Grinds them. The stink! I stopped him talking about it when he mentioned earwax for touching up waters and skies."

Beka said, "He's extraordinarily good. But he does prefer the old masters to more contemporary art styles. Is he still restoring the interior of the opera house?"

"He stopped for a time, right after the news about Ruli, but Uncle Robert was wild, saying it won't be ready in time for the ball. Danilov says, maybe Uncle Robert should offer to pay him." Phaedra's drawl was back; the subject of vampires and Tony had ended.

"Kim, did you know that Percy's great grandmother was the royal portrait painter? They called her the Baroness of the Brushes. Most famous painter of the century. Her last portrait was of the twin princesses. But the Gestapo killed her not long after because she was mixed up with the Salfmattas somehow. Beka knows all those secrets." The irony was definitely back.

"I wish I knew all those secrets." Beka's tone was neutral, peace-making after Phaedra's sarcasm. "Great-Aunt Sarolta was only a girl then. She heard rumors that the baroness put charms in her paintings, but if that was true I don't know what they were."

As if Beka's admission of ignorance improved Phaedra's mood, the talk shifted to famous paintings and painters among the Dobreni, and secrets captured in paint, and where famous portraits were hidden during the years of occupation until we spotted Riev between mountain peaks and started descending toward the upper reaches of the city.

When Phaedra parked at the Vigilzhi command station, she said in challenge, "So who tells Alec?"

"No one," Beka stated, and when Phaedra zapped a laser glare her way, Beka said, "Look. Have you considered why Alec is not under arrest? Not even guarded?"

"I know what you'll say." Phaedra scowled. "If he thought it just, he'd follow the Regulus road, and everyone knows it. He made that clear before the Council."

Regulus? I was about to ask, then I remembered the story about the Roman general who was imprisoned by the Carthaginians, given parole by them to negotiate a peace with Rome, went to Rome and argued against peace for the good of Rome, then went back to Carthage to honor his parole, knowing he was going to be executed. Maybe Phaedra wasn't much of a reader, but she was far from ignorant.

Phaedra went on. "It would be cruel to give Alec hope, only to take it away if Kim is imagining things." She hit the steering wheel again."So, not until we have proof." She flung the door open. "But I *am* going to tell Dmitros." She slammed the door and strode away.

Nobody spoke as we got out and trooped to Beka's car. As soon as we were inside, I turned to Beka. "Is telling Commander Trasyemova all right? Because I have a feeling he's getting an earful right now."

Beka started the engine and jammed the heater to high, looking tired and dispirited. "Dmitros is as discreet as he is loyal to Dobrenica. I am almost certain he will say nothing to anyone; the Vigilzhi never meddle with matters of Vrajhus." She made a fist and leaned her forehead on her hand. "I am not certain what to do next."

"I think we should find someone who can test out what I saw in the prism. On the other tentacle, as my dad says, I'd rather not be spreading it around. Maybe *we* should. Is there a way for us to check Ruli's tomb, horrible as that sounds?"

Beka looked doubtfully at me. "Nothing can be done without the family's permission. Do *you* want to ask the duchess or Tony if we can open that tomb?"

"Um, that would be a no."

Beka's mouth flattened into a line. "I don't, either." Her expression changed. "But there is another way. The bishop could give permission. He would have to be convinced of the necessity, though. And then there is the problem of Dr. Kandras, who should have recognized that he had the wrong bones. *If* that is the case. You know he is their family physician."

Doh! "Speaking of doctors. Why can't we ask Nat to check?"

"Natalie." Beka breathed her name, and threw the car into gear. "A *very* good idea. I will consult my grandfather at once."

While we were gone, most of the upper level streets had been cleared. A short time later we parked behind Sobieski Square. Beka shut off the engine. "It should only take a moment." Her smile was slightly mocking. "That's all the time he ever has to spare for interruptions."

She slammed the door shut and walked briskly into the Council building. I looked over my shoulder at Tania in the back seat. "I didn't know that this job was going to involve vampires and politics," I said. "Any time you want to quit and return to what you were doing, I will completely understand."

Tania's wide gaze shifted to me. "The vampires I learned about when I first joined the Salfmattas. It is not as secret as the Devil's Mountain people think."

"Well, it was a big surprise to me."

The corners of her mouth lifted briefly, a flicker of a smile. "I think that you bring surprises to Dobrenica, but it has surprises for you."

"Got that right." The words came out oddly in Dobreni. "Very true."

"For the rest," she added in a low voice, "when I think that otherwise today I would have had to sweep the store, then polish all the brilliants, and then tend those customers Madam Petrov did not want to talk to. . . ." She shrugged. "I only miss grinding lenses."

"You can go back to working with lenses, but we'll talk about that plan later." I studied the Council building. Beka was nowhere in sight. "Sure is a long moment, if the Prime Minister is even there."

I fought the urge to get out of the car and go poke around inside. My head had that achy, on-the-verge-of-dizzy sense, and I was still getting after-images of Alec lying unconscious on the back seat of his own car and a totally unwanted imaginary image of Tony cutting open a vein with an ancient knife.

I glanced back at Tania. "Do you see any ghosts hanging around me?"

"No," she replied.

Time to experiment, since Beka was still not out yet. I took the prism from my pocket and balanced it on my hand so the weak light coming in the windshield shone through it. Rainbow colors spilled and glittered with the intensity of sun-splashes on water, but I couldn't make out anything in them.

My eyes teared up. I put the thing away and blinked after-image spots from my vision for several minutes.

They were still dappling my sight when Beka came marching out, her face tense. She got in the car, started the engine, then locked the doors.

"Thank you for waiting," she began. Her voice trembled. She pressed her fingertips together, like someone bracing up inwardly. "I did not see my grandfather yesterday evening. You know that I was with Honoré, then searching for you and Alec. Because of the storm, Grandfather spent the night with my uncle and aunt."

"Okay," I said, wondering why she was giving us all this backfill.

"So he was not able to tell me what was in those witness testimonies until now," she said. "In one, Dr. Kandras testifies that Magda Stos confessed to him that, during October, she overheard Alec on the phone, with you, planning your family's visit to Milo as the first stage of a conspiracy."

"What?"

"And once Ruli was dead, you would all come to Dobrenica together, with Milo, to heal the grieving nation."

I gritted my teeth on an explosion of wrath. "That's a freaking *lie*."

Beka's eyes were angry. "I know. First of all, if Alec was stupid enough to form a conspiracy while talking on the palace line, with half a dozen assistants in earshot, he would deserve to be discovered. But he would do such a thing. No, there is definitely a conspiracy, and Magda must be deeply in it, or why would she lie?"

"So what do we do now?"

"My grandfather said to wait. He will recommend that the investigative committee compel Magda's actual presence here, so that she can be questioned by the Council. He also said that he would talk to the bishop."

I sagged back in the seat. Then burst out, "What is the point of all those lies? Surely they'll be proved wrong. They *can't* believe Milo would assent to any plan to off Ruli. Not with *his* record."

She made a quick gesture, as if pushing something aside. "To drag Milo's name in is to taint everyone. Everyone." She shut her eyes.

"What I'd like to do," I muttered, "is find Tony, tie him to a chair, and pour boiling oil onto his head until he tells the truth."

"I would drive you to his house right now and personally boil the oil," Beka said. "But Grandfather also told me that Tony flew out directly after the Council meeting yesterday, ahead of the storm. To Paris. *He says*, to interview cooks."

"Then he can bring that Magda Stos back along with this hypothetical new cook, if someone calls him."

"Oh, that is being done. My grandfather himself has been trying to call the von Mecklundburgs' Paris flat." Beka flushed angrily.

Nobody spoke again as Beka drove us back to the inn, and Tania and

I climbed wearily out of the car. Beka took off with a roar that reminded me of Phaedra, as my new personal assistant and I trooped inside. I longed to eat something, take a long bath—hopefully it was early enough for hot water—and pour my exhausted body into bed.

The prism thumped against my side as I shut the door behind me.

The first thing I heard was Madam Waleska's bullhorn squawk. "No! Everyone knows that Americans spit upon the floors. She has very clean habits, as she is *French!*"

As I stepped into the dining room, this is what met my eyes:

Honoré with short platinum hair, jeans, and a leather bomber jacket.

A tall, smiling, red-haired Armandros.

A bunch of punk and Goth guys fooling around with camera stuff, and—

Shurisko's ghost.

All except the ghost dog stopped what they were doing to turn my way. Shurisko bounded around and through the table where Armandros and the blond Honoré sat, making me dizzy enough to stumble against the counter. I stopped, shut my eyes, and tried to banish the dog.

When I opened my eyes, he was gone. Good. Luckless as I was at seeing ghosts when I wanted them, maybe I could at least un-see them.

"Ah, here is Mademoiselle Dsaret herself," Madam Waleska announced, emphasizing the "Mademoiselle." And to me, "I shall fetch your tea at once."

As she bustled away, she muttered loudly, "No American drinks tea. They threw it into the ocean, everyone knows that!"

The door to the kitchen shut crisply.

I forced myself into the dining area. The locals had given the newcomers a wide berth, I noticed—especially one of the Goths, a huge guy with three-inch spikes dyed black at the roots and orange at the tips. His nose, lip, and ears sported piercings, and he was dressed completely in black. He was arguing with a skinny punk guy dressed in black, red, and green, with short blue hair. They spoke fast, highly idiomatic French as they argued about light filters.

I forced my gaze away from them and back to Honoré, only it

couldn't be Honoré, not only because of that short platinum hair and the long dangling earring, but because of that manic smile.

"Gilles?" I said.

I'd thought it impossible that such a grin could widen, but it did. He leaped from his chair, arms out as if to hug me. "You know me, you! Hear! I speak him, the perfect English. I am a filmmaker. How many you know the stars?"

Out of metro L.A.'s population of nearly twenty million, so far no stars, I was tempted to retort. But I wasn't going to go there. Yet.

"None," I said in French, taking in the guy who resembled my grandfather's ghost. He had to be the mysterious Uncle Jerzy. There was the lopsided smile so many of Armandros's descendants—and ancestors shared—with Tony's charm and Tony's slanted gaze, though his eyes were light brown. His hair was red with silver on the sides, and silver also spangled the front. Like the duchess and my mom, he was very good-looking for his age. His face was broader than Tony's. Age had deepened the laugh lines at the corners of his eyes and around his mouth.

"I hope you do not mind that I came along with Gilles," he said in French, hands out in greeting. "To listen to him interview you. It was time we met."

I remembered being told about the friendly man who'd asked questions about me. "You were here once before, right?" I asked.

"Jerzy von Mecklundburg. Enchanté." He lifted his shoulders. "I missed you that morning." He clasped one of my hands in both of his. My fingers were cold. I only realized it when I felt how warm his hands were. "The lady of the house was full of stories about you, Mademoiselle Dsaret."

"Call me Kim. Kim Murray," I managed.

"So you do not claim Dsaret?" Gilles asked.

"They insist on calling me that. Probably easier to say than Murray."

"Mau-r-r-r-ayyy. It is simple!" Gilles back-throated the R sound, French-style.

"We have heard much about you." Jerzy laughed silently.

Gilled leaned forward. "Tell us your version. It is for a film, you see.

Perhaps it will not sell, but eh, the family will enjoy it." He waved at his guys and their film equipment.

Guaranteed your family won't enjoy it with me in it, I thought. But the idea of annoying the duchess was tempting. Especially if she was plotting to smear Milo and Alec! Anger burned through me, banishing the tiredness.

Jerzy said, "So you are a formidable fighter, eh?"

I smiled. "Is someone planning to challenge me to a duel?"

Jerzy shook with inward laughter. "None that I am aware. However, I would like to ask if you are coming to the gala tomorrow."

"Wouldn't miss it," I said, my smile so wide my teeth felt cold.

The film guys were still fiddling around. Madam Waleska appeared, set a tray down before me, and when Spiked Hair said something in extremely idiomatic French to Blue Hair, Madam crossed herself and backed away hastily.

Gilles said, "What I'm told is, up on the mountain, they think you are somewhere between Brunhild and the French heroine Jeanne Hachette."

"That's because they didn't actually see me running from two sets of fighting men, until I got shot." I rubbed my shoulder. "Haven't fought a single duel since." *Actually, I have* . . . but oh, I was *so* not mentioning Tony.

Gilles said, "So you came back to Riev to see Alec Ysvorod?"

"No." I couldn't help a blush at the mention of Alec's name, which really annoyed me. "I did not. I came to see Ruli, but I was too late."

Gilles leaned forward expectantly. "You came to see her about?"

"How she was doing," I added firmly. "Because I hadn't spoken to anyone from here or had any news at all, since summer."

"But your parents did?" Gilles asked.

"I don't know who spoke to whom," I stated. "I was in another state, busy with my teaching job."

"There is no telephone at your teaching job? No e-mail?" Gilles asked.

The camera was rolling now. The second I became aware of it, it was like my skin developed a case of the hives, and I itched all over. Clenching my hands to keep them from scratching my nose, my scalp, my ears, I poured out more tea and busied myself stirring in milk. "Yes, and yes, but I didn't use them to contact home."

"And then—though you did not speak to anyone—you decided that you must speak to Ruli? Though the holiday was coming and, as you said, you wished to join your family?" Gilles nodded in a *Verrry interesting, but I don't believe a word of it* manner, as his film guys pointed their cameras in my face.

"I wish you could have met her again," Jerzy said softly. "She needed a friend, poor Ruli."

Most of my hostility leaked out as I met his sympathetic smile. "I know."

Gilles leaned forward. "So you knew the marriage was . . . not happy?"

Bang. The hostility was back, full force. "I *told* you, I did not have any communication *whatsoever* with anyone here. But I was not impressed by the way her family talked about her last summer. And treated her. Since you were in Paris, did anyone tell you that she spent the *entire summer* as her brother's prisoner, and her mother knew it? Alec spent the whole spring trying to find her."

Jerzy was still smiling sympathetically. I thought, *How much do you know about your beloved half-sister's evil plots?*

One of the film guys dropped a piece of equipment with a crash. Another argument broke out, and Jerzy gave a gentle sigh and murmured in Dobreni, "These are the only workers you could find?"

"The only ones willing to come here and on little pay," Gilles returned in the same language. Then he got up and started yelling at his minions in rapid, idiomatic French.

I decided that this would be the perfect moment to get out of there. I got up. My chair scraped. Gilles turned to me expectantly.

"Excuse me," I said. "Bathroom break." I ran upstairs, carefully shut my door instead of kicking it to splinters, and threw myself on my bed.

The familiar ghost chill roughed the skin on my arms and the back of my neck. I sat up, dug the prism out of my pocket, set it down on the nightstand, and reached for the wardrobe door.

There was Grandfather Armandros, cigarette burning, his gaze boring straight through me.

"Esplumoir," he said, the voice going straight inside my skull without benefit of ears. "Esplumoir. *Esplumoir.*"

TWENTY-FIVE

MY DAD TOLD ME, when I hit those angsty early teens, that going to bed angry only guarantees a lousy day before you even wake up.

I kept telling myself that I wasn't angry. Yet I was. And frustrated. Not to mention hungry, having stayed in my room to avoid any more encounters. Every day seemed to get longer, wilder, raise more questions, without ever giving me enough answers.

Esplumoir? What was *that?* The maddening thing was, I knew I'd heard it before. But there was no handy Google Search to plug the word into—assuming I heard it correctly enough to guess at the spelling.

After long series of nightmares full of car crashes, Buffy-style vamp blood fests and a general sensation of being watched, I rolled out of bed at the first hint of dawn, hungry as I was, and did a hundred pushups. Then I put myself through a full workout until my muscles went stringy.

But when I went to take a bath my brain still felt like it was going to explode. I needed one quiet day. Just one. But I knew I wasn't going to get it. There was that gala ball to go to. I could skip it. On the other hand, I hate missing a chance to dance. On the third hand, who would care if I didn't show up? Alec would. The memory of that kiss helped banish at least half of the irritation.

But then came the questions. There he was, ready to march up to a firing squad, and I was convinced that he hadn't even been in the front seat of his car. Except that in my prism vision, Ruli wasn't in the car at all, yet it was Alec's Daimler at the bottom of the gulch. How to explain any of that?

I got out of the tub, dressed, and sidled past the row of bags, boxes, and suitcases lined up along the wall. Looked like all the Waleskas' mountain relatives and patrons were preparing to return home from their holiday.

I peered around the bend in the stair to make sure no Gilles, Goths, or von Mecklundburgs of any make or model lurked among the breakfast guests.

What I saw was a complete breakfast, waiting. Theresa sat nearby, wearing a burgundy velvet dress with lace at collar and sleeves. Next to her sat a thin, familiar teen with long, dark red braids, her coke-bottle glasses flashing as she laughed at something Theresa whispered. She was wearing a pretty dress made of robin's egg blue wool, edged with ribbon, and embroidered with darker blue amaranth flowers.

"Is that breakfast for me?" I said, summoning up a smile.

"I heard you in the bath," Theresa said, beaming at me. "It is right above the kitchen."

"Thank you. Is that Miriam?" I said, recognizing one of Theresa's two best friends from my summer stay. I offered a heartfelt smile and the girl's face flooded with delight.

"Mademoiselle Dsaret," she whispered, and after a nudge from Theresa, she asked faintly, "You said to Theresa you are coming to the concert."

Theresa said, "Everyone is going. My grandfather says you may ride with us to the temple if you wish. He and Father have gone to get the wagon."

I had completely forgotten the New Year's concert including Nat's sweetie, the tenor. Ordinarily I'd jump at the chance to hear good music, but I really, really wanted a quiet day. Half a quiet day. I glanced at the window, cravenly hoping to be saved by a blizzard, but the low winter sunrays slanting up the street, highlighting the snow piles and the windows of the opposite houses, made it clear that the weather was not going to rescue me.

So I said the only thing possible. "Thank you. Looking forward to it." And attacked the breakfast Theresa had brought out for me.

While I ate, the girls traded off telling me about the concert program, then Miriam and Theresa exchanged looks.

As I poured tea, Miriam whispered, "Now?"

Theresa breathed, "Wait for Katrin."

Tall, dark-haired Katrin, Theresa's other best friend, showed up five minutes later, self-consciously smoothing a dark green dress accented with gold lace. As I greeted her, the girls looked at me expectantly, and I said, "Right. Back in a flash—" And at their uncomprehending looks, translated that into, "I will return shortly."

I ran upstairs and put on one of the new dresses, made of autumnal rust colored, super-soft wool. Wool! Not a Los Angeles fabric, but it felt good.

When I got downstairs, one of the grandfathers appeared at the door, causing a general exodus.

I grabbed my new coat, which was hanging on its hook, but my scarf wasn't there. Yet another annoyance. After a useless hunt through the coat racks, I debated running upstairs to get the new one, then decided the heck with it. Didn't look that cold out, for once, so I slipped into my coat and followed the others out.

In the weak, watery sun the air seemed almost warm. As I clambered into the big holly-decorated wagon with the rest of the family and guests, Theresa, Miriam, and Katrin exchanged what I think they thought were subtle nudges and glances.

The wagon jolted, and the huge, shaggy horses began clopping forward. The unspoken consensus seemed to be that Theresa had to speak. To keep from embarrassing them I pretended to be looking up at the carved owls on the corbels of the next building up the street until Theresa said, "Mademoiselle." She shifted to French, and whispered, "You will save the Statthalter, will you not?"

I gawked at the girls—three serious faces waiting for my answer.

Miriam leaned forward, hands clasped. "We will help. Tell us what to do."

"Girls, there's . . ." I was going to say, *There's nothing* I *can do*. But I was, in fact, trying to do something. I just didn't know how successful it was going to be.

"You saved Baron de Vauban from the fire," Miriam whispered fiercely. "And his cats. We know it. We had it straight from the butcher, whose sister is married to the father of Anijka—"

"Shhh!" Theresa patted the air, as a couple of the adults glanced our way. "Not so loud!"

Wedged next to me, Katrin scowled. "We know that for truth. And not the rumor that came after."

I leaned toward them. "Rumors about me trying to kill him?"

Three nods.

"And I suppose there are rumors about the Statthalter and I forming a conspiracy?" I stopped.

They did not look surprised, or bewildered, but knowing.

Theresa put her mittened finger to her lips. "We do not believe such."

"There's one way you could help. A lot," I murmured. "Find out who is passing those rumors. Don't do anything dangerous—just listen and pay attention."

Theresa grinned, Katrin's small mouth crimped with ill-concealed pride, and Miriam whispered, "Madeuffween, madeuffween." I was surprised she still remembered from summer my accidental exclamation in English, *You are made of win.*

"We will," Theresa promised.

We got to the temple not long after. Two steps inside, and I rocked back on my heels, my eyes trying to take in the intricate, gloriously colored art that covered every bit of wall and ceiling space.

The family filed into a couple of pews. Already the place was nearly packed, and the concert wasn't supposed to begin until noon. But there was a gallery, I saw, and people were filing in there, too, under elaborate paintings of lions blowing horns, twined flowers of all kinds, including the deep blue of the amaranth. There was an onion-domed, walled city done in stylized perspective, with doves flocking skyward toward stars and clouds encircled by more interwoven decorations.

Miriam had disappeared. Theresa said, "She is singing today."

"Do you know what this art represents?" I asked.

Katrin said, "The Tower of Babel. The Babylonian Captivity. Zion. Jerusalem of olden times."

"Music." Theresa pointed to representations of cymbals, horns, lyres, and other instruments worked in. But easily the most beautiful was that depiction of a Jerusalem that probably never was nearly so grand, making me wonder what Jerusalem would be like in the Nasdrafus, and would Jews, Muslims, and Christians get along there? Or was some other kind of religious expression ruling there? I'd have to ask Beka—and there she was, sitting near the front with her entire family.

The von Mecklundburgs were sitting across the aisle from them—all, that is, except Tony.

And Honoré.

A rustle and a clearing of throats from up above, in the gallery behind us, indicated the music was about to begin. There was a tap on my shoulder, and a "Squeeze up."

Nat plopped next to me just as a single male voice began a wordless melody, poignantly minor key. One by one, other voices joined, young and old, male and female, rising to a crescendo of emotional power, and then fading as the voices dropped out. Never a word spoken, yet the effect was as strong as if Wordsworth or Hopkins had been set to music.

"That's the Fifth Day *nigun*," Nat whispered. "Also, for Ruli."

"I need to talk to you about that," I whispered back.

"Not here."

The program began. Nat nudged me once to say, "My Stavros," when a tall guy, built like a fullback, rose to sing a solo. He had a Heldentenor voice, powerful enough to launch rockets, well up to the demands of "*Mes amis, écoutez l'histoire*," a terrific opera aria that ends on a soaring note that nearly blew the roof off.

The climax was introduced as a new composition. It was that poignant song with the tritones and diminished fifths, played by that boy I'd first heard in summer, and again at Zorfal on Christmas Day: Misha. As the entire choir, children and adults responded antiphonally, the clarinet wound around the voices like liquid gold.

"I want that on iTunes," I breathed after the thunderous applause began to die away. "What is it about, besides Xanpia?"

"Xanpia's Wreath." Nat chuckled. "Some say Xanpia's Halo. History is mixed on it, my sweetie told me. Some think it was only a love song, then it was gussied up with religious context, as often happened to popular songs during the Middle Ages. But when the country got whacked last century, it got politicized—called the *Song of Freedom*, they changed the verse to 'open the door to freedom' instead of 'open the door to my heart' and so it was forbidden. Anyway, this is a new arrangement, and some people are trying to get that kid to a recording studio," Nat said. "I hope those guys got it on tape."

She pointed with her chin to the other side of the gallery, where Gilles's film crew were busy with their lights, cameras, and other equipment. I looked away, not wanting to spoil the after-music exhilaration by remembering how annoying Gilles had been the day before.

As people got up and began retrieving coats and pulling on wraps, I said, "Coming to the gala tonight?"

Nat grinned. "Got a gig. But you should go. Rock out." Her smile faded. "Better, get Alec to rock out. I saw him last night on a bit of city business, and he looked like death warmed over."

"If I dance with him, then all those conspiracy jerks will be yapping."

"Do it anyway." She bopped me on the shoulder. "They're gonna yap whatever you do. Gotta run. Chill!"

"Wait! There's something—"

She glanced back, half obscured by the people crowding out. She mouthed something in which I made out the word *Beka*, and then she vanished.

I'd taken two steps before I was nearly mowed down by Beka, who barreled up to me like a guided missile—a short one. "Come," she said over her shoulder.

She drew me through a side door, where it was quiet. A lamp burned on a small table, and farther along the hall I heard laughing voices, and someone sang a snatch of song: the choir members were getting ready to leave.

Beka looked both ways, then whispered in English, "You know where Gilles and his fools were yesterday?"

"Yes, they were at the inn, harassing me."

She made an impatient gesture. "I know about that. Before—while we were at the crash site. They were at the cathedral, doing their best to talk the bishop around to letting them open Ruli's tomb."

"Why?"

"For their film, they said. Gilles wouldn't give up. He followed the bishop around and kept begging, pleading, even tried to bribe him."

"That doesn't make any sense. What possible use is showing pictures of a burned corpse, no matter whose it is?"

"I do not know." Beka looked both ways again. "Here is what's important: my grandfather received a message late last night. Very disturbing. The bishop himself, after receiving my grandfather's request, checked the vault and sent to say that there were signs it had been tampered with. Probably at the very moment Gilles was pestering the bishop."

"Dude!"

Beka drew in a breath. "I don't know how many conspiracies there are, at this point. Outside of our own, which at least I know is not intended to harm anyone. So I wished to warn you, be careful this evening."

"You'll be there, right?"

"I will be there trying to guard Honoré, who insists on going."

"What about the Vigilzhi, don't they usually do guard duty?"

She gave a quick nod. "Dmitros Trasyemova has seen to that. My job is to guard against—"

A door opened, Beka linked arms with me, and walked me back into the temple, which was mostly empty. "*Au revoir,*" she said, letting me go.

"*Au revoir,*" I repeated and hustled out, hoping I hadn't kept the Waleska contingent waiting. No, everyone was standing around chatting with friends as a snarl of wagons and sleighs slowly sorted itself out.

"You will get ready for the ball tonight?" Theresa asked and, on my nod, she sighed. "I would so like to go to a ball."

"Not I." Katrin wrinkled her nose. "Not if you cannot dance the round dances but must be partnered with a boy."

"Don't like boys?" I asked.

"Most of them seem to be like my brothers." Katrin made a gag face. "They would put spiders in my hair, or step on my hem, or belch tunes, and think it funny. I like the grand balls Miriam writes in her st—"

Theresa shushed her, and launched into a description of the perfect ball gown, reaching flights of fancy that Katrin, who apparently was an experienced seamstress, would shoot down as impractical or impossible.

"Theresa, a gown with a thousand diamonds and rubies would weigh so much the neckline would reach your knees the first time you tried standing up"—which caused a friendly argument, Miriam joining in once she had recovered from the horror of nearly being outed as a secret novelist.

Anna, who had stayed behind to start the supper, had taken delivery of my ball dress. The girls promptly insisted on seeing it. Tania followed us, but her expression was unreadable. I waited for her on the stairs. "Tania, what's the problem?"

She gave me a quick smile. "Nothing!"

"Want to go to the ball?"

She gave her head a shake. "I have nothing to wear, and the girls . . ." She clammed up.

We'd reached my room, where the two sixteen-year-olds were waiting for me to open my door. When I did, they went in and stood looking in awe at the gown hanging over the edge of the wardrobe door.

"Look but don't touch," I said. "It's got to stay fresh, at least until I get there."

I shut the door on them and pulled Tania out into the hall. "Tania, there's a problem. I can see it."

Tania opened her thin hands. "I think I need a better place for experiments than my room," she admitted.

I was about to exclaim *Why didn't you say so in the first place?* But I knew it would hurt her. She was scrupulously honest as well as careful. I had a responsibility for another person, for the first time in my life.

"What we really need is an office of our own, where we can experiment, and meet," I said. "Or a classroom! Listen, if you don't know of a convenient room to rent, then go talk to Beka Ridotski. She might be able to set you up in a classroom over at the temple school, where nobody will ask nosy questions. Tell her that I sent you."

Every word that established a possible line of communication had a visible effect, and I thought about how much we depend on knowing whether we're doing the right thing. In Tania's view, going to Beka on her own was wrong, but my asking her to go to Beka was right. Weird, that.

We went back into my room, to find Katrin bent all the way over so she could examine the stitchwork on the gown. She'd begun to lecture Theresa on satin stitches versus chain when Madam's voice boomed from below, "Theresa?"

Theresa's hands flew to her mouth. "The apples! I am supposed to peel and core the apples for the *gibanica!*"

"I'll help," Katrin said as they started out. "We have to get it done, or we'll never get a good place in the crowd."

"Miriam promised to save space. . . ."

I shut the door on their chatter. "Tania, I just thought of something else. Something small."

I held my breath as an intense, visceral memory seized me: the brush of Alec's fingers, the scent of his soap, and the fabric of his Vigilzhi formal tunic as he set his mother's diamond necklace around my neck.

I wondered how many charms that thing had on it.

"I didn't bring any jewelry, and I'm about to go to this ball in a few hours. I would like you to take my cash and get me something that will go with this dress. You choose. I like your taste—I saw that when you were dealing with customers in the lens shop. Bring me something I can wear, and put your best charms on it. I have a feeling that I'm going to need it."

She whisked herself out, her body language full of purpose. I shut the door and slumped onto the bed, whooshing my breath out.

Then I thought in disgust, I still didn't know what "Esplumoir" was.

TWENTY-SIX

HERE'S THE THING about long hair. Yeah, it's a hassle to wash, dry, and comb out, but if you want an elegant do in about two minutes flat, all you need is to pull it on top of your head, coil the locks around in twists, and skewer them with a pretty hairclip. Instant elaborate hair style.

Then I dug out the makeup my mom had bought for me in London. Usually I only wore it when dancing on stage. Well, I thought, as I painted in the eyeliner, this is a dance, and I am going on stage.

As I slithered at last into the dress, I thought about going alone. I'm so not Party Girl. That is, I like parties, but nobody thinks of me when they count up those charismatic personalities that turn a disparate gathering into a good time for all.

When I stepped back, my spirits lifted. Maybe Madame Celine was about as Parisian as I was, but one thing for sure, she and her team were awesome dressmakers. The gown was as dramatic as the one Ginger wore while waltzing with Fred up and down that fantastic staircase in *Swing Time*.

I studied my reflection, turning this way and that. Decked out like this I could totally take my place among those grand portraits of my ancestors and their relatives. I tried my smile—the crooked smile with the single dimple that was so rakish on Tony, whimsical and rare on Honoré, cool and sophisticated on Phaedra, and supercilious on the duchess. On my mother, it was utterly charming, which was interesting, because Mom and the duchess were doppelgangers, same as Ruli and me. Yet you couldn't find two women who were more different in all other ways.

I wondered what would happen if the two of them were ever to meet.

Then I took a last look from my pale hair down to the perfect black shoes. All that was needed was something sparkly.

Tania returned as I sat down in the dining room to a cup of soup and a piece of bread, with a tablecloth swathed around me in case I slopped. She sat across from me with a decided air of triumph as she handed me a handkerchief-wrapped item.

The necklace was very simple—a crystal pendant on a thin silver chain—but the pendant had been exquisitely shaped and faceted so that it shone like a diamond. In the center glimmered a five-petaled star. Looking into it caused sparkles to glimmer at the edges of my vision, and I rocked unsteadily, fighting that sense of being drawn down into it. I caught images of an old woman's hand closing around it, a carved box with marquetry done in Old Norse knotwork, an intent gaze from a pair of black eyes in the face of a child.

Dizziness threatened to overwhelm me, and I shut my eyes to steady myself.

"The charm on it is very old," Tania said. "Renewed by a Salfmatta every time it comes to a new person."

"Where did you get it?"

She handed me the money I'd given her. "Domnu Petrov gave it to me. He would not take money. It was his mother's."

"I'll have to thank him in person," I said. "But right now I'd better get going. Everyone going to that ball will be wanting an inkri, and I don't want to walk in this outfit."

Tania smiled. "People are lining the streets to watch the arrivals. That is why the girls wanted to leave early, to gain a good place."

I bent my head, fixed the necklace on, and watched the sparkling crystal drop against my breastbone, framed by the V neck of my gown.

"Thank you, Tania. It's perfect."

She flushed with pleasure. "You look beautiful, Mam'zelle."

"Kim," I said. "We're co-workers now." I almost said co-conspirators. She gave me a quick, shy grin. Wednesday Addams triumphant.

I got up to fetch my long black velvet cloak but froze when everyone in the dining room turned toward the street windows, where golden lights shimmered and swung. The young Waleska cousin with the wannabe mustache called, "You must see this!"

The family and patrons stopped what they were doing and crowded around the window. I peered over shoulders at the fantastic sleigh that waited out in the street. It must have been designed by someone like Lalique, with art nouveau ironwork runners that curved up in the front like swans. The body was a combination of steam-era cool and Cinderella, with a canopy hung with fairy lamps made of glassed-in candles with mirror insets that reflected and refracted the light.

The driver looked just as fantastic, wearing a white wig à la the eighteenth century and a black livery complete to a skirted coat, knee pants, white stockings, and diamond shoe buckles.

He walked to the door and called into the total silence, "Mademoiselle Dsaret?"

Zip! You could practically hear the swivel of every head turning my way. "Me?"

I recognized that driver. It was Jerzy von Mecklundburg. He bowed suavely, his lopsided smile almost a grin. "Count Robert promised to provide the appropriate carriage, and I volunteered," he began in French, then shifted back to Dobreni, in an appropriately grand manner. "Shall we depart, my lady?"

A minute later he was settling an enormous, brocaded carriage rug around me—kind of like a down-filled quilt. There was a footrest that must have had hot coals inside, because it was nice and warm. So even though the sleigh was open to the air, between the carriage rug, the heated footrest, and my beautiful new silk-lined cloak, I was toasty, except for my face. But the ride wouldn't be long.

"Comfortable?" Jerzy asked as he climbed onto the driver's seat, and took up the reins.

Up front was a matched pair of huge horses, their manes decorated with black and white ribbons.

"Very," I said, feeling a tad silly sitting all alone at the back of a sleigh large enough to comfortably seat ten. "This was a very nice gesture, but I can take an inkri if the family needs this sleigh."

Jerzy glanced back over his shoulder as the horses pulled us into the middle of the street, harnesses jingling. "The family is already there. Some have been all day, busy at their tasks. Mine is to serve as chauffeur tonight." He sounded like a Frenchman, unlike the rest of the family, who had the faintest trace of Dobreni accent.

"You're not attending the gala?"

He laughed. "I'm not supposed to be in the country at all. I was wild as a youth, and they banned me. I'm content to play roles now. Behold me, am I not fine?" He flicked his wig with an insouciant air that brought Tony to mind.

"Very fine. And so is this sleigh."

"It's been in the family for six generations. I'm surprised the Russians didn't break it up for firewood."

"That would have been a shame. It's lovely." I leaned forward. "Shall I come sit beside you? I feel silly, sitting back here all by myself."

"No, no. We must play our roles. The crowd expects it. I can hear you, and I shall turn my head, so, and you will hear me."

I raised my hand to block the halo around the swinging lights, and discovered people standing in the remains of the most recent snowfall, watching as we glided by. Some wore elaborate masks, others didn't. Many were talking, laughing, and drinking.

"Tell me about your mother," he asked. His half-sister. Weird.

"What do you want to know?"

"Has she ever been to Dobrenica?"

"No."

"Has she plans to visit? Perhaps she might wish to stop in Paris on her way here."

"Here?" I said witlessly.

"You sound surprised. Will she not want to visit the land of her mother's birth? Parents' births?"

"She never said so. But you have to remember, she didn't know where her mother came from until four months ago."

"So she is not curious? I was." He flashed that smile over his shoulder.

"All my mother knew was that her father was shot down during the war, which was a very distant sort of thing in Los Angeles. She was more interested in the present, like becoming a pastry chef, than in the past."

"Perhaps we can lure her to Paris," he said cheerfully. "What a crowd!"

We? I thought. Who's included in that *we?* If he meant the duchess and Robert, yeah *right.* A safe bet they wanted to meet my mom about as much as they wanted to catch a dose of pink-eye. Time to change the subject. But I didn't have to. The crowd had swelled. The street streamed with decorated sleighs a-jingle and alight with colored lanterns swaying merrily.

The city showed another of its many lovely faces that night, framed by softly glowing snow on street and rooftop, the lanterns on every balcony and post and pilaster throwing into dramatic relief the medieval carvings: amaranth and acanthus, rowan and rose, extravagant creatures of every degree—winged, fanged, pop-eyed, grinning, claws outstretched or curved protectively. Figures medieval and Renaissance, and here and there, age-smoothed classical, given a semblance of life in the beating light.

Jerzy slowed the animals as we neared St. Xanpia's fountain. Up on balconies of all the grand buildings, people waved lanterns and shouted "Urra! Urra!" as decorated conveyances hissed by, ringing and jingling. I smiled, feeling self-conscious as our magnificent sleigh jostled into the stream moving slowly around the circle. Someone had decorated the statues and trees with ribbons and tiny lights, which emphasized the shocking gap where the murdered tree had been dug up—no doubt to prevent salt from leaching into the ground and poisoning the rest of the trees. And how hard had it been to break that iron ground?

Voices swelled in song, the melody rising and falling around the once-forbidden tritones. More voices joined in the love song turned anthem, until the St. Xanpia song seemed to come from everywhere at once. And here I was at her fountain as the stone creatures shifted. No. It wasn't the stone creatures. They were ghost animals—fifty, a hundred, more. Dogs, cats, badgers, rats, ferrets, foxes, even a few wolves, all manner of small mammals, swarming, leaping, chasing about, flicking in and out of view, their shapes silver and gray, amorphous as smoke.

From them, Shurisko leaped out at me, a vaporous glow. Glints of starlight gathered in his eye sockets as he barked noiselessly, galloping around the sleigh. Around and around he raced, then he vanished beyond the sleigh in front of me, the crowd of people in it unaware. From the spicy aroma carried on the cold air, they were sharing out mulled wine as they talked and laughed, and I caught the clink of glasses above the ring of tiny bells.

I sat up straight, hands in my lap. I felt very much on stage, which was an odd sensation without ballet shoes on my feet, and a clearly choreographed dance to follow.

Some children raced between the sleighs in a line, chasing and laughing, until one of the mounted Vigilzhi shooed them back behind an invisible line. I caught a few admonishing words about horse and reindeer hooves. Most of the children wore masks of beasts, birds, and a couple that looked like Fyadar, the mythic boy faun who'd befriended St. Xanpia in centuries-old Dobreni children's stories.

Shurisko raced out again and leaped across my sleigh. Then he was gone like a puff of smoke, as in the distance, the singing receded until it was subsumed under the closer noise of merrymakers.

"Monsieur von Mecklundburg," I began.

"Call me Uncle Jerzy. All your cousins do."

"Uncle Jerzy, what's the story behind the masks? Not everyone wears one."

"That's because the custom fell out of habit during the Soviet years. Superstition of any kind was frowned upon. When the Soviets left, some promptly went back to the old ways because they could, but many didn't."

"So masks on New Year's Eve was a tradition?"

"For centuries. To hide from the ghosts of the old year, it was said. And from other mythological figures. There was a practical aspect— hiding one's identity, so whatever you did that night, you would not begin the new year with regrets. Ideally, anyway." He laughed. "Rules were relaxed on New Year's Eve, like the Twelfth Night celebrations in some countries west of us."

Ghosts of the old year. I was tempted to ask if he saw Shurisko but was reluctant to talk about ghosts. Besides, what would I learn if he saw the dog? Zip.

We jingled down one of the many short streets that spoked off St. Xanpia Circle. On either side of the street were three grand Palladian buildings, with Greek statuary along the edges of the roofs. The shops on the first floor were all lit, though closed to custom. Richly hued rugs hanging in one window complemented marquetry furniture across the way. Antique clocks on my right reminded me of Dad, and I wondered what my parents were doing—if they were having fun in London.

Of course they were. They'd always believed in creating your own fun. But this was the first time ever that the four of us were not celebrating in our small kitchen in Santa Monica.

Homesickness washed through me. Not for place but for people. A vivid image of Mom and Dad laughing around the kitchen table seized me, followed by Gran's quiet smile, her silver head held high. The images vanished, restoring me to the here and now as the sleigh jolted past a row of four conveyances that seemed to be in one party.

What was the hurry? But then we slowed again as we emerged onto a smaller traffic circle with a Renaissance era fountain at the center. The buildings around this square were all Italianate. To the right was the start of the grand St. Ladislas Street, and to the left Ysroel ben Elizier Street, which curved back toward the temple.

The crowd on both sides had thickened. Jerzy stood once or twice, peering ahead, then sent the team into a trot as he wove between sleighs, trying to avoid the traffic jam.

"Oh, for the days when the bluebloods could send out minions to clear the streets," I said facetiously.

"They still can." Jerzy flashed a grin back at me. "Or could. Milo forbade such things, I'm told, unless there is dire emergency."

"I guess a dance doesn't rank as an emergency," I said. "Why would Milo forbid it? Can't afford the minions?"

"I'm told that the saintly Milo felt that such actions caused resentment. I must say, I understand. Would it not be annoying to be cleared to the sides of the road in pouring-down rain because some baron was in a hurry to go to lunch?"

He was so right, and I laughed as I looked around. We'd lurched forward a bit and had reached the area of the exclusive shops I'd visited with Beka. We'd soon reach the place where St. Ladislas Street widened and became tree lined. The cathedral complex lay on one side, and what had once been the royal riding school on the other. It had since been divided into the museum, library, Vigilzhi headquarters, and now—the new opera house.

Jerzy pulled us back into line as the crowd surged, making way for four mounted Vigilzhi on horseback, wearing full uniform right down to epaulettes. They surrounded a handsome fiacre, in which rode: Alec, alone, wearing a fine tux that reminded me of an Edwardian frock coat. Over open top coat, he wore a long, beautiful silk scarf.

As his *fiacre* slowed, someone in the back of the huge crowd bellowed, "Murderer!" And again, "*Mur*-der-er, *mur*-der-er, *mur*-der-er," in a cadence meant to start a chant.

My mood snapped from enjoyment to anxiety, and from there to anger as a few people took up the cry.

The mounted Vigilzhi pulled their swords (not ornamental, either) but Alec gestured impatiently toward the guy at his right—Dmitros Trasyemova—and stood up in his fiacre.

He said something, lifted his voice, and said it again. I couldn't hear him over those hissing, "Silence!" at the chanters behind.

"Murderer!" the unseen man yelled again, as the crowd noise diminished. "Murdered your wife to marry your French trollop!"

"Come out and face me," Alec said as he jumped down from the fiacre, his fine formal shoes sinking in the layer of slush. I'd never heard Alec lift his voice. He had been trained in public speaking, of course, and he pitched it to be heard but without yelling. "I am visible to you as well as answerable. But I have the right to see my accuser."

"That's right," someone called, and a woman yelled, "Show yourself!"

That same voice bellowed, "You killed your wife!" And tried to begin a chant, "MURderer! MURderer! MURderer!"

One or two joined him, but mostly the crowd noise escalated to arguments and questions and unheeded cries of "Be quiet!" and "Don't shove!"

Alec walked directly into the crowd, as people moved back to give him space. Others surged at the back, and I heard fierce hissing, but not what anyone was actually saying. Alec said again: "You have a right to accuse me, but I have a right to see my accuser. Come out and talk to me."

The roiling in the back of the crowd radiated outward as people tried to move and to see. Dmitros gestured to his people to dismount and walk among the crowd. "No weapons," I heard him say.

They were waiting for the accuser to appear. The mood could go either way. I knew enough about crowds to be scared, my toes cramped in my shoes, my hands gripped.

"I will answer all your questions truthfully," Alec said. "You have only to ask. But face me first."

Then that same voice bellowed hoarsely, from farther back, "Maybe we should ask your doxy! She's right there!"

People looked around—I looked around—until I discovered everyone looking at me. Sick with embarrassment and anger (and a bubble of hilarity—*doxy?*) I sat there, exposed to view.

The crowd stirred restlessly—then a girl's high voice shrilled, "That's Mam'zelle Dsaret, who saved the Baron de Vauban from the fire!"

Another girl yelled, "Urra, Mam'zelle Dsaret, Urra!"

The shrill one screeched, "She fought the villains on Devil's Mountain!"

"Murder . . . conspiracy . . ." The shouter was moving farther away. Other voices rose angrily, for and against, but that shrill girl's voice cut through them all: "She saved our city!"

"Urra! Urra! Urra!" A ragged cheer went up. It sounded like kids.

Then a boy yelled, "Mam'zelle Dsaret, urra, urra, urra!"

More people took up the cry.

As the crowd surged, focus shifting, I caught a glimpse of teenage girls standing in a line holding hands, as other teens joined them. At the center was a scrawny figure with long red braids: Miriam.

"Urra! Urra! Urra!" the teens chanted. "Urra, Urra, Urra, Dsaret!"

"URRA!" The crowd took up the cry. "DSARET!"

The Vigilzhi walked slowly among them, but by then there was no need to break up a mob, because everyone had taken up the cry, as the teens clapped their hands to the beat. "Urra, urra, urra, Dsaret!"

TWENTY-SEVEN

I LOOKED AROUND, amazed, gratified, and embarrassed, too, as Jerzy clucked to the animals, and we caught up quickly with the line in front of the opera house. There, with somewhat more haste than order, guests were climbing out and going inside.

Alec was somewhere behind me. Would it make things better or worse for him if I walked over and joined him?

Urra, urra, urra, Dsaret! The crowd chanted.

Jerzy had tied the reins. I tried to peer past the heads. If I saw Alec, I could take my cue from him.

But Jerzy's hand closed firmly on my arm. "Quite a claque you have there," he said, flashing that slanting, jaunty smile. "Careful with the step. It's slippery on the pavement."

Firmly he helped me down, guiding me toward the entrance steps as the chant dissolved into a general roar of approval, then talking and laughing. The moment was passing, and I still couldn't see Alec, so I walked up the steps next to Jerzy and then said, "Thank you for the ride."

"It would be my pleasure to escort you inside," he said gallantly, "but I must be off to fetch my aunt, the baroness." He left me at the door and started down the steps. "Also, I mustn't leave the animals standing about."

A wigged footman came forward to take my wraps. Another came forward with towels to wipe the slush off my shoes.

The wind was turning icy, teasing at my skirts and hair. I was already shivering. Then I passed through the next set of doors into a vast chamber filled with gold light, whose vaulted ceiling was starred by thousands of candles. The stage was framed by magnificent swagged curtains of deep burgundy, very much in the grand old style. On the stage an orchestra was busy tuning as guests walked around admiring one another, talking, laughing, or cruising the food-filled tables on the opposite side of the room. The refreshments were dominated by ice sculptures of musical instruments wielded by mythological figures.

"There you are." That was Cerisette von Mecklundburg in a retro Chanel flapper dress, the one look that is seriously chill on scrawny women. It had two layers of very long fringe, one overlapping the other at hip length. The dress itself was black silk damask, the fringes black at the top and slowly shading down to silver at the ends. Over her elaborate chignon she wore an art deco headband decorated with diamonds and a single ruby brooch pinning a white feather that curled up and back over her head. Her necklace was a single, very long strand of jet, with ruby rosettes every foot or so.

Thinking that if I complimented her she'd probably go straight home and change, I said only, "As you see."

"Where is Uncle Jerzy?" She peered past me. When she wasn't glaring at me, she looked stressed. But then she was running this entire party.

"He went to fetch his aunt. A baroness," I said, feeling an unexpected spurt of sympathy for Cerisette.

She sighed. "That can only mean Grandmother Romeşçu, who's so shortsighted she wouldn't know if a bear had the reins. Damn it! He's got Tante Sisi's pills. . . ." She spoke under her breath, sounding like someone pushed to the limits. "This way," she said, and as I fell in step beside her, she added, "My father invites you to sit at the high table."

Instantly suspicious, I stopped walking. "Why?" No matter the reason, Robert von M was the last person I wanted to share this evening with.

She stopped as well. "Why what?" For the first time she looked right at me, not past my shoulder, or raking her gaze dismissively down my body, no doubt in search of fashion flaws. Her gaze met mine for about a heartbeat, her eyes a shade darker than my own. There were subtle silver sparkles in her eye shadow, and she was close enough that the acrid scent of cigarette smoke wafted from her clothes and hair, mixing with her expensive perfume.

"Why this invitation to the high table?" Red flags were waving wildly, as the inner Kim insisted, *I'm being set up.*

Tic-tic-tic. One of Cerisette's elegant long fingers tapped against a ruby rosette in her necklace, reminding me more than ever of a cat's tail twitching. Or the rhythmic flicker of antennae.

"Look, I know what your family thinks of me. So you'll forgive me if I don't want to ruin my evening by walking into some kind of bad scene."

"My father wants to speak to you—" she began.

I was choking off the words, *No chance!* when the Danilovs swooped down on either side of us; he, looking like Prince Charming in period frock coat with a hint of lace at the cuffs and a diamond stick pin in his silver-patterned silk cravat. Phaedra wore a tight black sheath that only a perfect figure could carry off, and super high heels.

"There's Alec. Right on time," Phaedra said, nodding just past my shoulder. "Shall I give the signal?"

Cerisette's head twitched, almost a flinch. She was definitely stressed to the max. "Yes."

Phaedra walked away and lifted her hand in a gesture. A row of black-suited musicians stood up on the stage and pealed out a trumpet fanfare, the stirring chords echoing in triplets.

Everyone turned, and there was Alec, walking in alone. Phaedra and Cerisette headed toward him with intent as Danilov said to me, "Phaedra thought you might want company."

"I did. I do," I said. "Thanks. Unless you're in on their plot."

"Plot?" Danilov's blond brows lifted.

"Cerisette said her dad wants me at the high table. This can only be bad."

Danilov looked elegant and amused as the fanfares died away and the orchestra struck up a waltz. Out in the middle of the room, Cerisette and Alec were waltzing expertly, her fringes rippling gracefully, rubies winking in the brilliant candlelight from those iron chandeliers.

Robert and his wife had also begun waltzing. "Is Alec doing his part as Statthalter or as Ysvorod?" I asked.

"Both." Danilov lifted a hand.

"So is Cerisette now the ranking single girl, or is he dancing with her because her dad is host?"

"Interesting, how you phrase that. Cerisette's status has been a subject of much debate among those who care about such things. It is not so clear that she is the highest ranking unmarried woman."

"Oh. You mean me. I keep forgetting." As the corner of his mouth twitched in irony, I said, "You have to remember I didn't grow up knowing any of this stuff. It still doesn't seem to connect to me. Besides, how could I rank above a count's daughter if my mother's birth was illegitimate? Is it because Gran was a princess?"

"Yes. And so the debate. No one pays the least attention to your mother's marriage. She, and you, are Dsarets in the public eye."

"By that reasoning, so should Ruli and Tony be Dsarets, as their grandmother was Gran's twin." When Danilov shrugged, I said, "Oh I get it. Marriage only counts when it comes with a title."

"You could say," he responded. "But you know it's not so simple."

"I know. Alec told me that once Rose married Armandros, nobody regarded her as a Dsaret anymore. As if all her DNA had magically shifted to his family. Then she died young, and Tante Sisi, of course, was born a von Mecklundburg."

Danilov looked away at the mention of Rose's name, and I thought, Okay, this subject has been thoroughly thrashed. So I looked around, too.

We'd been strolling along the perimeter of the vast room. I glanced up at the enormous, vivid paintings of various martial scenes from mythology. Solomonic pilasters added at intervals around the walls divided the paintings, and these pilasters were decorated with stylized Dobreni motifs: amaranth first, then lilies, laurel leaves, roses, and rowan berries and leaves. Once I'd thought these mere decorations, but when are decorations "mere"? We choose things that have meaning to us. I wondered if those lilies and roses and cobalt blue amaranth flowers were loaded with Vrajhus charms.

My gaze dropped to the rows of chairs along the walls—chairs in several styles from over a century and a half. The crystal on my necklace threw glittering refractions outward, and there, on a hazy summer day long ago, teenage boys rode, prancing horses in circles, their slash-sleeved doublets stippled with dust, some waving basket-hilted swords inexpertly as they practiced hand to hand combat on horseback. . . .

I stumbled, blinked. The vision was gone.

Danilov lifted a lazy hand. Diamonds glittered in the cuff of his shirt sleeve. I shut my eyes to avoid another dizzying flashback. "We had to raid all our houses," he drawled. "You'll see half the families' plate under the refreshments. Want to dance, after they do their obligatory circle?"

Alec and Cerisette looked fabulous dancing together. As they passed by the people pressed along the perimeter, I saw her gaze flicker past us at the refreshments tables, at the waiters circulating with trays to collect empty cups and glasses, and checking the late arrivals still streaming in.

They passed out of sight, and her parents waltzed into view. Now that I did not have to dance with Robert, I could admire how so big a man could move so lightly on his feet. Last summer I'd been too busy trying to avoid his wandering hands and the accompanying cloud of alcohol fumes.

What had his wife thought about those wandering hands last summer? She had to have seen. I'd never spared her a thought, other than trying to avoid her obvious hostility. Nearly as skinny as Cerisette, too much sun had aged her so it was impossible to guess her true age. The tight lines in her face, the thin, compressed lips, however expertly made up, also aged her, in spite of the exquisite gown—a thirties' Mainbocher, with layers of alternating black and white ruffles, and two long white streamers hanging from her bony shoulders to her spiked heels.

As soon as she and Robert finished their round, she glided back to the high table—set off to one side of the stage, out of the path of the steady stream of servants tending the refreshments—and lit up a cigarette in a holder.

Robert, still on the dance floor, lifted his hands in invitation, and people began to join him. He turned to an elderly baroness, bowed, and held out an arm.

"Shall we?" Danilov asked me.

"I am always up for a dance," I said.

Danilov was as good on the ballroom floor as he was in the fencing *salle*. Two or three steps, and we found one another's rhythm and whirled around, in and out of the slower couples, until so many people began dancing that we were forced to slow.

"Okay," I said, once we were safely in the center of the floor, strangers all around us. "Why does Robert von Mecklundburg want me to sit at that table? Is there a poisoned dish waiting especially for me, 'Ooopsie! She must have choked on a canapé, oh well!'"

"Poison!" Danilov repeated sinisterly, causing a sedate couple dancing nearby to give us wondering looks. Then both pairs of eyes widened, and looked away.

"I can't get used to that," I said as Danilov expertly guided us past a stiff pair of teenagers counting their steps. "At home I'm nobody. Here, my face is . . . notorious?" I paused a second. "Well," I said, "certainly known. Though it's not really my face that's known, it's Ruli's. Is that why they want to lure me over there, to get rid of me once and for all?" I was joking, but I wasn't.

Danilov's well-shaped upper lip curled. "Do you really think they are that stupid?"

"I don't know what constitutes stupid, but somebody tried to poison Honoré in their house, so why not me at their table? They hate me much worse than they do him, right?"

"*Merde!*" Danilov's smile vanished. "I don't know who did that, or why, but I would be very surprised if it was anyone in the family."

"Because?"

"They have been working so very hard to match Cerisette with Honoré."

"I thought Cerisette was after Alec," I said.

Danilov twirled me under his arm, sidestepping neatly out of the way of an oblivious pair. "For her? Higher the rank the better. And it would have been sweeter to shut out Ruli. But the family? They are more practical."

"I thought Cerisette and Ruli were friends."

"Sometimes a truce, sometimes allies." Danilov shrugged and handed me into another twirl. "Hated each other from childhood, those two."

"Frenemies, then. Allies against whom?"

Danilov was a handsome guy, and he danced like a dream, but he gave off a cold, detached vibe. "That? Ah, too fatiguing to explain. But you can see, it was always irresistible to bunk into the hills whenever we could."

"Bringing me to Tony," I said. "Are you going to tell me he's not plotting?"

Danilov's expression hardened. "When he returns, we'll converse."

"Where did he really go, do you know?"

There went the curled lip again as we spun away from the orchestra's side of the room and straight down the middle, which had briefly opened up. "To Paris, I believe."

"To hire a *cook?* The same day that his family accuses Alec of murder, and me of conspiracy? Yeah, right."

Danilov gave me a rueful smile and another of those airy shrugs. "Aunt Sisi was assured by Magda that you and Alec were telephoning between London and the palace all autumn long."

"But I wasn't *in* London!"

"No one knows that."

"Milo does. He is not known for being a liar. Oh! *Tony* knows," I snapped. "He visited several times. He met my mother. And he would have heard her say that I was teaching German and French in Oklahoma. If he'd really wanted to get in touch to see if I was there, I'm sure Mom would have given him my email. I might even have answered it." Then I remembered. "Have you talked to that Doctor Kandras about identifying Ruli's body in the wreckage?"

"We learned yesterday that he returned to his home village for the holiday." He tipped his beautifully sculpted chin slightly, and as we whirled, I saw Honoré acknowledge him. Honoré was sitting with the Ridotski family. A cane leaned against his chair.

So, he wasn't sitting with the von Mecklundburg party at the high table. In-teresting. I turned back to Danilov. "You really think Tony went to Paris? I don't believe for a nanosecond that he spent all that money for a private plane in order to hire a cook. I bet anything he's out there somewhere interviewing Reithermann Junior."

Danilov's lips twitched. "What a catastrophe that was."

And yet you were in on at least part of the plot. "Because Tony didn't win?"

Danilov matched my tone. "Because Dieter Reithermann was hired to reorganize the Vigilzhi along modern lines and, incidentally, gain their allegiance. But Dmitros Trasyemova threw him out of the city after an hour's conversation. We all wished we could have been present," he added. "It must have been memorable."

"No, it would have been boring. Reithermann couldn't open his mouth without tripping over every X-rated word in the dictionary. So Tony used him anyway. It figures."

"But he had to. The man had been paid. Quite an extortionate sum. And after the Devil's Mountain people were trained, Tony was sure he would win in spite of Reithermann's try for leadership. Tony usually wins."

I was going to argue but an all-too-vivid recollection of Reithermann's violent end made me say, "I guess he did. But I'm here to tell you that it was a *very* close call."

The dance ended, and couples began to part, to reform, and some to walk off the floor. I grabbed his wrist. "Oh, no, you don't. I am finally getting some answers, so we'll have to dance again. And if local custom condemns me for being fast, well, it's not like I have a reputation to lose."

"I think 'fast' went out of mode fifty years ago." His lazy smile mocked me. "There is little more I can tell you, but eh? You dance well. Many do not."

"There is plenty you can tell me. Like the reason why Robert and his gang want me at the high table. The way I see it, it has to be extra nasty because they sent that sleigh to pick me up."

That actually made him laugh, or utter a short huff that was probably as close as he ever came to such a wild display of emotion. "Nothing more sinister than a desperate need for money. You can see this place is unfinished." The new dance was a fox trot. As we parted to step outward, his hands arced to include the room. "Until last summer, they were all but certain the Council would vote the income from the Dsaret holdings toward this opera house, among other projects. Then . . . you showed up, with the news that Princess Lily is very much alive."

"That's right, Tony said they didn't have much money." Someone jostled me, and I nearly tripped. "Right before he tried to kidnap me."

Danilov shrugged slightly. "The rest of us were convinced that the so-called Dsaret Treasure was an old war rumor, but Tony was so sure that your grandmother ran off with the king's treasure—either that or his grandfather, Count Armandros, got his hands on it when he ran off with her—"

"No doubt because that's what he would have done?"

"—that we went along with his plan to get you alone and find out where it was."

"I can assure you, my grandmother didn't have any treasure. Or she wouldn't have had to teach piano for years and years. Ow!" A sharp elbow hit me right in the ribs.

A flushed older man wearing a baldric with genuine medals apologized before he and his partner were swallowed in the crowd.

I jerked back—and a broad back thumped mine, nearly knocking me into Danilov, who winced and hopped as a teenage girl exclaimed, "I beg pardon, I beg pardon," and was whisked away by her partner.

I looked around. The floor was so crowded there was scarcely an inch between one couple and the next. "We're not dancing," I said, "we're bobbing and weaving. Let's get something to drink, and you can tell me more about vampires."

He gave me a startled, wary glance. "You want to find them?"

"There are two things I want to know: how to avoid them, and if I do meet one, how to defend myself. 'Shadow ones' or 'wild folk' may be poetic, but it doesn't tell me anything, unless they really look like walking shadows."

The crowd of dancers was scarcely moving, and I was glad of my lightweight gown, for the air was nearly stifling. Danilov's forehead was damp. It was a relief to get out of the press and reach the tables.

The ice sculptures were beginning to soften slightly at the edges. A young girl dressed in white and black carefully poured us some punch. We each took a cup, then Danilov said under his breath, "Ah, Gilles! That stupid film! Smile and look at the dancers, unless you want him pestering you for an interview later, on what it was we found so engrossing in our conversation."

My face tightened into the bland smile I always wore on stage. I scanned the crowd then lifted my head to take in the iron chandeliers, the more martial gods of Olympus looking down from the clouds in the main dome, and, below that, the gallery running all the way around, that I'd missed before. It was filled with observers, except for one of the round royal boxes at either side, which furnished a splendid view of the stage. One of them was cordoned off, and Gilles and his film crew were there, looking vastly out of place in their punk rock attire as they operated their film equipment.

Danilov lifted his cup to someone in the crowd as he said under his breath, "Vampires. You will not see the older ones. The longer they survive, the more powerful they get. They can bend the weak light of night around them—moonlight, starlight, artificial light. At most you might perceive a deeper shadow. Or a sharp chill."

"Cold? I thought the cold was the presence of a ghost."

Danilov moved along the table, sipping at the punch, which was a fruit and citrus concoction with the bite of zhoumnyar mixed in. I resolved to make this cup last all night; zhoumnyar was potent stuff.

"Both." Danilov brushed something from an elegant shoulder. "My experience with ghosts is confined to the Bloody Duke up at the Eyrie. We used to stand on the landing outside the Weapons Room, which is where he always walks out. Usually after midnight. When he walked through me I felt a chill. But the cold of a vampire in proximity reaches your bones, and sends out a current that stirs the hairs on your arms. If they pass you while you are asleep, they give you nightmares."

"I thought it was ghosts who handed off the nightmares," I said.

"Ghosts don't have any influence on the living, waking or sleeping, not that I've ever heard." He shot me a fast, narrow look. "If you've been getting vampire nightmares at that inn of yours, then they are on the watch. I'd get out."

"It's got protections all over it. Those work, don't they?"

"Yes, but you have to leave sometimes, right?"

"Why would they be staking *me* out? Whoa, is that a pun or what?"

"Good question." He drank off the punch, then grimaced slightly as he put it down. "Another question is, why are they in the city at all? But there are others who can answer that. Not I. To your question about the efficacy of protections, my understanding is that, as long as they have not recently fed, the younger they are, the easier to defeat. They must be caused to bleed faster than they can repair themselves. Pistols only work at high caliber—you blow them apart—but these weapons can be untrustworthy. Vampires use Vrajhus to interfere with the firing mechanism, if they have the time and the strength to do whatever it is they do. But they cannot interfere with steel."

I'd heard about a mysterious force that could keep guns from firing, but this was the first time anyone had related it to vampiric powers. Though he wasn't saying that this ability was exclusive to vampires. "How about the wooden stake thing?"

"If you stab a vampire in the heart with rowan, hawthorn, or especially yew, it poisons them into immobility. At which time whatever it is in them that keeps them alive, and enables them to heal from small wounds, causes the stake to send out roots. It's not an easy sight—"

"Okay. Stop right there. I've got the picture."

"What picture would that be?"

I whipped around as we were joined by Niklos, Tony's handsome second in command. He had on a kind of Zorro mask but I recognized him instantly.

His gaze shifted past me to Danilov and lingered long enough for me to register it as a Look. I didn't have to turn around to see that the Look was two way. I blushed when the cluebat hit me that Niklos was running a rescue from the grabby foreigner—me.

I wanted to yell, "It's not like that!" but a woman about my age, wearing an ice-white damask ball gown complete with bustle, slipped her hand (in armpit-length gloves) through Danilov's and cooed, "You promised me a waltz." And off they went, leaving me alone with a bunch of beautifully dressed people I didn't know. I was not about to dance with the guy who'd shot me, and the way he watched Danilov and Bustle Princess whirl their way into the crowd, he wasn't in any tearing hurry to dance with me, either.

So I looked into that expectant, slightly wary face and said, "Ever seen a vampire?"

Niklos's brows shot up. Then his face smoothed into bland wariness. "Yes."

I could tell he was going to be as easy to question as a rock, so I gave him the Mick Jagger point-and-shoot with my forefingers, and walked away.

I think I heard him laugh.

On the other side of the room, Alec was dancing with Beka. Her gown was white on top, with a black floaty skirt. It moved like a dream, or rather, she moved well in it.

"Care to waltz?" asked a guy.

He was around thirty, maybe older, a thickset fellow whose broad chest looked splendid in his wide-lapel box tux and black bow tie. He and three of the others in their group wore extravagant Punchinello masks—jaguar, lion, bird. My partner was the jaguar.

I thanked him, and he swung me so energetically out onto the floor that my skirt flagged behind me. "I'm Carol Madaksos. You are Mademoiselle . . . Dsaret?"

"For tonight that will do," I said. "It's actually my grandmother's name."

"Your grandmother really lives?"

"Yes, she does."

"Is she coming home?"

"That I don't know." And when his eyes widened behind the jaguar mask, I said, "I've been traveling for several months, so I haven't spoken with her."

"Ah," he said. "You have such a look of her. A Dsaret, alive! We thought they were all gone."

I wanted to point out that there were plenty of descendants of Princess Rose around, who would technically be as much "Dsaret" as I was, but decided it was better not to get into it. What was it Danilov had said? "Too fatiguing to explain"? I just wanted to have a good time.

So did he. When I asked what he did, I got a stream of information, not only about his family's business in floor restoration, but about how his tux had been his father's, remade by his cousin the tailor, about how the food for the party was divided between the Vigilzhi kitchen and the pastry shop across the alley from Cuzco's Pies ("Everyone knows their pies, the best in the city") and how those who had donated skills and or materials to the opera house got bumped up the list of businesses used by the palace, arranged by Mam'zelle Cerisette herself.

He was a nice guy, and apparently he was popular, because as soon as our dance finished, a swarm of his friends descended.

And so I spent the next several hours dancing. I noticed that the crowd had, in typical fashion, separated into two groups. The VIPs migrated to the area near the orchestra and the refreshments around the high table, at the center of which, the duchess sat in a fancy, throne-like chair (the only one in the room, as far as I could tell). She didn't even seem to talk to anyone. A couple of times I danced near her, and I couldn't tell if she was watching me or staring through me in an old-fashioned cut direct. The other group was everywhere else.

Twice I spotted Robert heading in my direction, but there was always another partner for me to turn to and make my escape. Once, when I was between partners and I saw him trying to zero in, I tried my summer move—a beeline for the rest room. I was saved by teenaged Sergei Trasyemova, who had scraped up the courage to ask me to dance. We fumbled stiffly through a cha-cha.

Then there was a new partner, one whose red hair and huge chin I recognized. In slacks and pullovers, or in that stupid pirate costume last summer, Percy von Mecklundburg had looked dorky, but in a Brioni tuxedo, he came on with an old-style movie hero vibe.

"Will you dance with me?" he asked shyly.

Thirsty, my feet protesting after avoiding being smashed by nervous young Sergei, I even so, said yes. He was so shy, and his eyes were so unhappy I felt like turning him down would be puppy-kicking, even though he was at least my age.

Percy's dancing was more absentminded than enthusiastic. It was clear within a few steps he mainly wanted to talk. "I don't care what they say," he began. "I believe it, that you came to see Ruli."

Unlike the rest of your family? I thought, wincing inside.

"She liked you," he went on.

Help me, I remembered. "She didn't know me," I protested, feeling the weight of guilt.

Percy's lips shaped words, and one hand twitched in my grip, a gesture subdued, as if he struggled to give voice to images. "Beka says you were for Ruli a symbol of freedom. I think that is right. Like my pirates were for me." He smiled, and I remembered his pirate costume at the masquerade.

Tony'd had the exact same costume, which he'd worn with a piratical air, so he could kidnap me right off the ballroom floor. But that was never Percy's fault.

He went on, "Only my pirate drawings were more, oh, more freedom of—of choice, of imagination. Pirates were free of family, of obligation. I love Dobrenica," he said quickly, earnestly. "I could never be happy anywhere else."

"Not even Paris?"

"I could have loved the old Paris of candles and artists. The Paris of today, with neon and diesel fumes, no." He lifted his gaze up at the martial figures of the baroque era. "Ruli, she wanted Paris, she wanted freedom. You were free. She had Magda always watching and reporting to Tante Sisi."

"Why didn't she just leave?"

"Her mother would cut her off." He lifted his shoulders. "Unless she went to the north of England to be mired up with her father, and that would make her just as unhappy. How should she survive?"

I was going to retort, "She gets a job, like anyone else," but I clamped down on that. What seems so easy to one person can be impossible to another. While I don't have much (well, any) sympathy for the rich who suddenly find themselves having to struggle like everyone else in the world, I could understand how Ruli, raised all her life to the job of princess, would feel lost if she ran from that to the unknown. And face it, who would hire her? She wasn't trained to do anything except wear expensive clothes and act like a princess.

Percy went on. "Ruli helped me here, did you know that?"

He flashed a glance up at Jupiter gazing sternly down at us from beyond the wheel chandeliers. "See over there? Ruli got Honoré to help her find the portrait of Alexander II for me. All that was left was the outline of his battle tunic and his feet. He built the first riding school here, on the site of the old medieval castle. Took six of us to shore up the fresco, which was crumbling at the touch. Moss had grown where the walls weren't filled with bullet holes from the Soviets. Or maybe it was the Germans. Did you know that the Soviets used this hall as a car park for their trucks and transports?"

Image flash: the mossy, bullet-pocked walls, a smell of mildew and gasoline, the hulking shapes of mud-splattered old vehicles. I blinked it away, amazed. In all the times I'd seen Percy the summer before, I had never heard so much talk from him. He was like a dam released at last as he told me the history of the riding school and what he and his team of painters had to do to restore the old frescos—with mostly volunteer labor, from the sound of it. Huh, I thought as the dance came to a close. Robert might be short on cash, but he'd sure scored by getting Percy to do the restoration as a freebie.

When the dance music wound down, Percy smiled. "Thank you. Oh, there's Phaedra. She seems to want me, or maybe it's you?"

We slipped through the crowd forming up for the next number, and made our way toward Phaedra, who leaned against a chair midway along the wall, well away from her family, cool and elegant as a knife.

When we joined her, she greeted Percy, asked him if he was having a good time, and listened to him go on about the last-minute rush to get the south wall done—"Nobody knows it but the paint under the gallery is still wet," he said, pointing to the martial scene directly below Gilles and his film crew.

Phaedra made social noises, but I sensed she was waiting. When a couple of twenty-year-old girls pounced on Percy, drawing him into the crowd, she leaned toward me. "Tony is back." Her smile was angry. "And he's here."

"He flew in about four hours ago," came a familiar voice.

We whirled around: there was Alec.

TWENTY-EIGHT

A LEC SAID TO ME, "Dance with a dead man?"

"As long as he's not a zombie," I said, holding out my hand.

"Bra-i-i-i-ns," Alec murmured in my ear as his arms closed around me and every nerve shimmered like a carillon of bells. This was where I belonged, in his arms.

His grip tightened as I looked into his face.

"No," he whispered. "I am not drunk." His body shook. He was laughing silently. "If they put me against the wall, will you bring me a last shot of whiskey? Make it a fifth."

"Don't." I shivered as we twirled into the middle of the floor. "Don't say that. Even as a joke." And though I'd meant to keep the secret—I knew how horrible it would be to raise his hopes only to smash them if I was wrong, and it was so very, very easy for me to be wrong, but: "You didn't do it, Alec."

His smile was almost manic. His blue eyes were wide, the marks of tiredness revealing how little rest he'd had since I last saw him. "Didn't do what?"

"You were not driving that car."

His grip tightened almost painfully as the blue gaze intensified. No, it was that his pupils had snapped to pinpoints. "What?"

An older man looked our way, his expression intent, as if he wanted to speak to Alec.

But Alec twirled me under his arm, and with an expert sidestep and another, he guided me between two couples to relative safety. As we whirled, I caught sight of Tony and Beka framed between two amaranth-crowned pilasters, she with arms crossed, he with that smiling, proprietary air I so distrusted. They were quite a contrast, he so tall, she petite, his long hair pale against his shoulders in the black coat, and her dark curls against the white bodice of her gown.

I finished the spin, facing Alec once again. He gazed down at me, not even breathing for a long moment.

Beka and Phaedra had been convinced that it would be cruel to give Alec hope without proof, and I'd agreed. But that was before I saw him, and got hit with that overwhelming sense that keeping secrets from him was like shutting off access to half my brain and senses. He needed hope, and it was maybe crueler to keep it from him.

So I said in English, "We weren't going to tell you until we proved it."

We barely moved in a taut little circle, our bodies fit together hip to hip, as I gave a fast description of the accident site journey. It not only felt good to tell him, it felt *right*.

Alec's grip was as intense as his breathing. Then, "How do you know it was that day?" He whispered the words into my hair.

"I don't. There's no helpful LED date thingie running at the bottom of Prismview. So tell me this. Has Magda Stos ever driven your green Daimler with you in the back seat?"

"Not to my knowledge. And I haven't been in the back seat since I was a boy." On the last word his hand tightened on mine, but when I wriggled my fingers he instantly loosened his. "Sorry. I'm sorry. I just remembered something."

"From that day?" I looked up in hope—and a bit of trepidation.

"I don't know. I thought it was some kind of nightmare, because it didn't make sense, but I recollect a hand pushing my head down. Then cold leather under my cheek. Dizziness. Thirst, even."

The cluebat whapped me. "Alec, is it possible that blackout was caused by your being roofied? Drugged?"

His mouth thinned into a pale line. "I never thought of that. But who? There was no one in the palace that day but staff. Far more likely I lost track of how much I was drinking, than some mysterious person was lurking around with potions."

"What you described, those unconnected physical impressions? Well, that's what it was like when you put Kilber's sleepy-powder in my wine in Vienna."

We were moving in a such tight, tiny circle that we were clinging to one another, barely dancing. His eyelids came down for a brief, painful second, then his expression changed, rueful and mildly ironic. "If it's true, would you call that payback?"

"Don't joke about that," I whispered fiercely. "Yes, you did a stupid thing that day, but you didn't mean me, or Ruli, any harm. If it's true you got roofied, it sure as *hell* wasn't for any good reason."

"No, but I'm beginning to see that no reason is good. How can anyone trust me if they cannot trust a drink from my hands, or food from my house?"

I looked up into his face. His gaze had shifted to that distant look he got when his mind was running, and he said quickly, "Is that not the essence of civilization, that we can trust something so fundamental from each other as food and drink?"

"Kilber used it during the war. He said so he wouldn't have to kill anyone."

"Yes, but he used it against those he didn't trust, who didn't trust us. Don't you see? When we do such things to those we want trust from . . ." He looked away.

"You did it exactly once. You haven't again," I said. "And you won't." He had that slightly pained, inward expression that I knew meant that, once again, he'd been judge and jury, and he'd found himself guilty. "Speaking of evil and rotten, do you know what Tony's up to?"

"Dmitros has von Mecklundburg House under constant surveillance," Alec murmured. "I sent someone to Paris to find out what Tony did there."

"And? Did he come back with that Magda person?"

"No. Dmitros went himself to the airstrip to intercept Tony, who told him that Magda had already left Paris by the time he arrived."

There we were, back in the rhythm of our former exchanges. Alec's hand drifted up my back and down again, causing me to shiver with pleasure, as he said, "She's returning to Dobrenica by train, which would be her usual habit unless she was accompanying a family member. She left her mobile in Paris—which is typical, since, as you know, they don't work up here."

"What about Tony's excuse for going to Paris to hire a cook?"

"Apparently Tony has actually returned with a cordon bleu chef." He chuckled. "Dmitros accompanied them to Mecklundburg House himself. He said Madame Tullée hit that household like a bomb. Redhead, designer glasses tinted green, wearing clothes straight off the Champs-Élysées. I've never believed that about redheads and temper, but apparently she arrived with her own food—bales of it. Threw a fit when the Vigilzhi insisted on inspecting her crates, but there were no racks of guns, just fresh vegetables and the like. When she got to Mecklundburg House she chucked the family out of the kitchen and proceeded to sort them all to her liking, while Tony stood by, laughing. When Dmitros left, the duchess was standing in the middle of the kitchen in silk and diamonds, surrendering to *force majeure.*"

I loved the idea of a cook menacing the Evil Family of Doom. "Why don't you arrest Tony? It would make my day to see him dragged off the ballroom floor in chains."

"Because there is no evidence that he's done anything to warrant the chains."

"All right, though personally I think there should be more *off with his head!* to your job. Okay. Instead of what-iffing each other to death, tell me this: Do you by any chance know what the word 'Esplumoir' means?"

"No. Yes." He frowned. "Dmitros and Honoré are both signaling," he said quickly, as the orchestra began bringing that dance to an end. "Strange how memory sometimes gives you the context before you remember the actual words. When I was around twelve, and we first came to visit Dobrenica, and we were staying with the Dominicans, my father read me medieval French grail stories when we holed up during bad weather. You haven't read those?"

"My early Arthurian familiarity is pretty much limited to Chrétien de Troyes and Wolfram von Eschenbach."

Alec's eyes narrowed pensively as he navigated us between two pairs of young dancers who were trying to speed-waltz. "Esplumoir. All I recall was that Esplumoir was Merlin's prison, or his secret retreat. At twelve, the idea of a secret retreat has instant appeal, though the rest of the romance is pretty much rot. Ah. Another stray fact: it was the magical place where falcons went to molt. Why?"

"Because Armandros's ghost said it to me."

"What did Armandros say to you?" Tony asked.

The jolt was physical, like a shock of cold water. The music had stopped—and Tony was right behind me.

Alec gave me one of those looks—his hidden laughter revealed only in the slight lift to his lower eyelids. He left the question to me to answer. Some old legend about Merlin didn't sound important, but why would a ghost say it?

At any rate, I didn't trust Tony enough to say so out loud.

"Pistols at twenty paces?" Tony said to Alec in English.

Alec cocked his head, brows raised interrogatively as he asked me, "How are you with a pistol?"

Our eyes met, and there was that flash that obliterates everything but the other. Of course he knew that I would hate someone fighting over me, that I would fight my own duels. He knew it, and I rejoiced in the knowing. But the intimacy of that moment demanded privacy, and we did not have that. So I turned away.

"I can learn." I glanced at Tony then back to Alec. "If the target will stand still."

Tony laughed. The next dance hadn't begun yet. I could hear some shuffling up on stage. Tony held out his hands, and said, coaxing, "If I promise to stay strictly in the room?"

Alec flicked his fingers up in a wave, squeezed my left hand, and then left me alone with The Enemy.

I longed to zap him with a snide, *So where is Ruli this time?* but what if I was wrong, and he really didn't know that his sister had not been burned up in the Daimler? His chin lifted and there was a musical *thrump!* followed by the reedy wail of a concertina in a fretful minor key note, which was punctuated with another drumming, guitar-strumming *thrump*, in the nervy syncopation of the tango.

Tango is a seduction without words.

"No way," I said.

He flashed a grin. "Chicken?"

"Buck-a buck!"

"Come on. They're all watching."

I looked around. The floor had mostly emptied, except for a few brave souls. Cerisette stood near the high table, smoking through a long holder and eying me scornfully. The duchess stared, stone-faced. I didn't see Robert, but his wife looked utterly disgusted. So, the duchess and her allies hated the idea of seeing me dance with Tony?

Phaedra drifted like an elegant shadow behind Honoré, on the other side of the room. Catching my eye, she curled her lip and gave me a surreptitious thumbs up. Honoré smiled faintly, then sent a challenging glance at the head table.

"Righto," I said, and took his hand. Time for another duel. But it wasn't going to be seduction.

One by one, traditional instruments joined, playing lonely airs in counterpoint to one another and to the beat, as the orchestra hummed beneath, like the ocean pounding the shore. Step, step, step. For the first time I was really aware of the excellent fit of those bespoke shoes, the heels high and tight. The beginning of the tango is always exploratory, the figures meant to be a stylized flirtation as one steps forward and the other retreats, then spin and counter, feet touching in the sweep of the *barrida*.

This wasn't traditional but a *tango fantasia*, in which anything can happen. The lissome, airy gestures punctuated in sexy counterpoint with the tight geometry of the steps, in and out, in and out. He pulled me in but I kept my distance with the quick complications of the *ochos, saccadas, adornos*, the cat-like stroke of the *caricias*, and when the tension slowly increased, the sharp *gancho*, where I hooked a leg around his, followed by a *cortes*—the suggestive pause—just long enough for him to register my heel's proximity to horrible pain. "This is not a seduction," I whispered. "It's a duel." I left him to decide if I meant his family—or him.

He smiled, and snapped me into a spin so tight that my hair shook free and tumbled down to my hips. He whirled me back again into a *carpa*, shifting expertly so I leaned down him, my hair cascading to touch the floor. "Duels *are* seduction, *draska mea*," Tony whispered. "Haven't you figured that out? Tell me what Grandfather Armandros said. I have a right to know."

"The only right I'll give you is to go jump off a bridge."

On the word *bridge* I whirled a fan kick high in the air, my skirt whooshing in a perfect arc, and rolled my shoulder out of his reach.

Duel was mere rhetorical flourish. There was no seduction, or maybe I might have felt it if all my muscles were not remembering the fire of that last slow dance locked in Alec's arms. But Tony wasn't completely wrong, either, for tango is always communication—conversation—whatever the intent.

Tony's emotional communication was never done in words, at least not with me. His words were all deflection, a smoke screen. His real communication was all physical, in somewhat the same way that Alec expressed emotion through the safety and deflection of poetry. Tony kept offering me the lift, over and over because he was saying *trust me*.

So with all my twirls and kicks and arabesques, I pushed him away: *no chance.*

Ocho, salida, the wicked snap of the *gancho*, inside, outside, side-step inside, outside. He grinned and flung his damp hair back, as the diamond swung and glittered in his ear and I felt the invitation through the lean of the *carpa*.

A look shot over his shoulder, half of challenge, but his eyebrows lifted in question. Even—if it were anyone else—I would say, appeal.

Why was he asking for my trust in this non-verbal way? I was not going to find out unless I answered.

I always loved lifts and leaps because they were like flying. I surrendered to the *valida* at last. His hand slid to my hip, the other hand gripped mine and up I went over his head, one foot kicking high in a split. He whirled—I felt his balance shift, and stiffened—and he rolled me down his body, my hair slithering over both our hands.

There was a gasp and an *oooh* from the watchers.

"Grandfather Armandros?" He murmured in my ear as he pulled me easily to my feet.

"Who?" I breathed into his ear, then I leaned into the *carpa*, using my free foot to describe an extravagant arc in embellishment, then kicked all the way up behind me in a grand arabesque, coming out of it with my balance my own, but there was his hand at my hip, ready for a lift.

In other words, *truce, not trust.* And that momentary. *Of course* Tony would choose to communicate through the danger-fraught complexity of tango. That would be part of his games. He was strong, fast, coordinated, and used to winning. To that kind of guy, everything was a game.

If he wanted to talk, he would have to use words. In the meantime? I would change the game.

Draska mea. I slowed a spin enough to look around . . . ah.

Front and center, a small, curvy figure in a knockout gown with a white velvet bodice drawn up at a slant across the hips, and then the other way to one shoulder, where it was pinned with a fine golden leaf of hawthorn with a single diamond glinting. The wide chiffon skirt was pure black, counterpoint to her curling hair, and everything dominated by wide, intelligent brown eyes: Beka.

That straight-shouldered stance, the line of her thighs in that form-molding skirt, I would bet anything she'd studied ballet at least as long as I had.

And so I finished my turn, gave her a look—come on!

Her eyelids flashed up. I stamped my foot, held out my hand—and she ran lightly forward, the black skirt foaming around her toes. I took her hand, and snapped her into spins back to Tony. The black skirt whirled around her knees, revealing balletic legs in silver silk stockings—and perfect balance on her toes, as the watchers gave a collective "Ahhhh."

Oh yes, she was a dancer. Other than a laughing glance of surprise my way, followed by a sardonic twist to his grin, Tony took this move as if we'd planned it.

As I prowled in a circle around them, Beka took up the tango by mirroring the exact sequence of figures and embellishments that I had used, only she danced a challenge through the steely precision of her tiny steps, the whip-like *boleros*; she arched her back, her chin up, and I swear there was an electric charge between the two of them as they prowled slowly, then flourished back and forth in *al reve*, me moving counterpoint to them in a larger circle.

Hand to hand and hip to hip, chest to chest, foot to foot they dueled, for this time it was a duel—even their gazes locked.

The tension between them was all the more sexy for the precision of their control; I could feel the audience drawn into the battle of wit and skill. When Tony shifted and threw her into the air, there was a gasp that seemed to draw every molecule of air from the room.

Aerial, hands out like the wings of a bird, she balanced on his hand, and then kicked up in a flip over his head, to land lightly, her skirts swinging.

Whish! The air was back in a collective sigh. The music reached a crescendo. The dance was ending. Time for a flourish! I began to twirl on one leg in lazy *fouettés en tournant,* my hair and skirts flaring and fluttering around me. The music crashed—I whipped into a triple pirouette—and Tony grabbed Beka, whirled her once, and let her sink into a split.

A beat of silence, and then the audience broke into thunderous applause. As the two recovered, their attention on one another, I picked up my hairclip and backed away, looking around for Alec, who was nowhere in sight.

TWENTY-NINE

I WAS DISAPPOINTED to discover he was gone. But I hugged the memory of that silent signal with the eyes, the unspoken promise that we would meet again, as I moved away, looping up my hair by feel, and clipping it securely.

There was the refreshment table. I picked up a glass of punch. As I tipped my head back to drink, I caught sight of the forgotten royal box, where Gilles and the Punks were busy tracking me with their cameras. Oh, great.

"*Dayyyyy*-amm! I am *so* glad I was here for that."

I turned. "Nat?"

Natalie sauntered up, looking like *day-amm* herself in a killer black corset that made the most of her curves. A loose off-the-shoulders peasant blouse with big poofy sleeves, a flounced skirt in layers of black and white, and a frilly cap set on her brown curls finished her outfit.

"That dance ought to be R-rated. Weird, when you consider all clothes are on, and half the time there was air between you." She wiggled her brows. "Not much air. Between those two especially. Woo-ee!"

Noise and color filtered back in. The ballroom had seemed less crowded, but behind Nat had come a group of noisy people, all obviously pretty well lit. Shouting back and forth and laughing, they looked around, commenting loudly as the orchestra struck up a cha-cha and people moved out onto the floor to dance.

Because of my proximity to the high table (and probably because she intended us to hear) Cerisette's thin voice managed to float above the music, the shuffle of feet on the floor, and the woo-hoo, party-hearty noise of the newcomers as she observed, commenting on how they should have shut the door, something *de mal en pis.*

Nat chuckled deep in her chest. "What did she call us?"

"She told them to shut the door, because the crowd has gone from bad to worse."

Nat laughed. "I think she means me."

I glanced past Nat, to meet Cerisette's angry gaze. "Actually, I think that was aimed at me."

Nat shook her head. "Come on, let me have my share. I don't want to have to fight over which of us is trashier."

"What do you two argue about?" Beka was there, the only evidence of that wild tango a few strands of curling hair loose on her neck, and her color high.

"Lady Snotnose over there. That's got to be Cerisette, right? I think you pointed her out to me a year or so ago, but she was a blonde then," Nat said. "I hoped you'd show up. That was one hot tango, and as I was just telling Kim, I was sooo glad I saw that."

Beka flushed to the ears and gave a quick nod. "Thank you."

"Is it supposed to have three people?" Nat asked. "Not that I'm complaining. That made it about ten times hotter."

"No," I said, as Beka looked down. "But it seemed like a good idea at the time."

Nat's grin faded. "I got news, peeps." She beckoned us close. "I told you both I had a gig, but I didn't tell you what, so you wouldn't have to be hiding anything in case anyone on the villains' list asked. Bek, Anijka put me with her cousin Yaschka, and one of his Vigilzhi pals. I got my Stav and his buds from the choir to come along as cover, though they think it was a New Year's Eve bet, whether or not I could sneak all the way through the monks' space without getting busted. They decoyed the cathedral people—got everyone singing—while we snuck down to the crypt. I wore this, and Yaschka and his sidekick are dressed up, too, so we could claim to be lost party animals if we got nabbed."

Beka pressed her hands together.

"Find anything?" I asked.

"Oh yeah." Nat rolled her eyes. "The guys wrestled the lid off that sarcophagus, but they wouldn't touch the coffin inside, so I had to climb in and do the honors. Reminded me of med school, the time we—" She paused, shrugging. "Later. I got the lid up and zapped my trusty flash inside. I won't bother you with the names of the bones. You wouldn't know them anyway. But I can tell you that the entire city gave a royal sendoff to some guy."

"Guy?"

"Then where . . . ?"

Nat raised a hand. "I won't say that Ruli's ashes aren't there as well, as I didn't see the accident site, or supervise the retrieval, but I can tell you the pubic inset in those pelvic bones, and the skull with the brow ridge, were not grown by any female."

"It *is* a conspiracy," Beka breathed, her pupils black.

Nat shrugged. "I've been sure of that ever since I thought about what happened to Honoré. Somebody definitely gave him a whack, but didn't hit hard enough to kill."

"That would be left to the fire," Beka said grimly.

"*Why*, is what I still can't get," Nat said, throwing her arms out wide. "Nothing adds up. Isn't the hearing on Tuesday? Surely the liars have to know that Alec's people haven't exactly been sitting on their hands—that someone's bound to have proof of at least one of their lies. What's the *point*?"

Beka shook her head. "All I can think is that someone has gone mad."

All three of us sidled covert looks at the high table, where the duchess sat, watching the dancers like a queen on her throne, and showing about as much expression as a stuffed effigy.

"Or someone wants everybody mad at each other," I said. "And that's sure been a wild success. Did you find Alec, and tell him what you found?" I asked Nat.

"I didn't see him when I came in. But I'll bet you anything that Yaschka and Friend have him corralled right now." She grinned. "We all walked over with Stav and the choir, one big party. By the time we left the cathedral, they'd passed the zhoumnyar around so many times we didn't need anything but a suggestion: Hey, let's hit the opera ball! Which, by the way, will be the last thing any of us do tonight, the way that wind is rising."

Beka said, "I heard there was a northern storm coming."

"I think that baby is already here—"

"Mademoiselle Dsaret."

All three of us whirled around. There, looming behind us as large as a dinosaur, was Robert von Mecklundburg—a *quiet* dino. I hoped he didn't speak English.

"If you will honor me with a moment of your time," he said grandly, in a rehearsed voice. "I should like to show you what is being done."

Relief ballooned inside me. He was obviously so intent on his own errand, the three of us women may as well have been cackling in Urdu. If Urdu cackles.

"Sure," I said, far more cordially than I would have ordinarily and sent Nat a *that was close* grimace before Robert extended a hand in an invitation to accompany him.

He promptly began to speechify.

I guess that's unfair, but that's what it felt like—a sales come-on, given by a guy who hated my guts as much as I hated his. But as we strolled along the perimeter of the walls, I could see him making the supreme effort to be pleasant as he told me the story behind the enormous martial murals, and who had donated the red velvet for the stage curtains and swags ("The layer at the very top is left from the royal palace throne room, hidden by the servants two days before the Germans rolled over the border"), the four-hundred-year-old steel wheel chandeliers that had dripped candle wax onto cadets-in-training, how they were converting the warren of medieval jail cells that had been partly converted to storage in the sixteenth century, and so on, practically to every squarehead nail on the stage, which used to be the gallery where the royal family and principle nobles sat to watch the martial and equestrian exercises.

I found myself interested enough to wish, for the first time, that I'd get those weird glimpses of what might have been the past, but I was too wary, or we were moving too fast.

So involved I got with imagining the history of the building, I was only vaguely aware of the deep, clammy chill as we passed through a door to the side of the stage and into a low corridor, still smelling of wet plaster, toward the backstage area. The wiring still wasn't in. There were honest-to-medieval torches stuck in sconces on the walls, outlining our jumpy shadows in fitful ruddy light as we entered the big space directly behind the stage.

The orchestra finished an old-fashioned minuet, and after a creaking of chairs, a few muffled coughs and whispers, struck up another waltz as Robert preceded me.

We were alone. Well, not completely alone. The orchestra was thirty feet away, behind a movable flat and a sturdy curtain. If Robert tried to strangle or poison me, I could spring through the curtain and burst into the middle of the musicians, and with my luck fall into a tuba or get tangled in harp strings.

Still, I looked around for a possible defensive weapon as he went on talking about his grand plans. The space was inadequately lit by two lanterns on a pair of mismatched tables, throwing the ceiling and most of the perimeter into shadow. A closer glance revealed corridors leading off at either side, and there were two padlocked doors behind boxes of stuff.

I walked around with what I hoped looked like aimlessness, keeping the biggest table between him and me as I studied stacks of boxes and baskets.

". . . and so we are arrived at the backstage," Robert said, hands out, a huge diamond on one hand glinting with candlelight. "*Helas!* This ends the tour. Last spring we had hoped to witness the first opera performance tonight, but. . . ." He paused, frowning fixedly at the lantern on a table.

Waiting for what? For a good moment to attack? I pretended interest in the old costumes and props in the boxes, tawdry half-rotted fabrics and battered, dull steel enriched by the forgiving candlelight. Ah! A sword?

"I humble myself," Robert said finally, through all but gritted teeth. "You must know that the Dsaret holdings were as good as promised to us for this opera house. And other projects. For the good of the city."

I looked up as I reached for the prop sword, complete to basket hilt.

"But no matter," he went on. "*C'est fini, tout cela.* I only ask that, in your generosity, you consider a donation to finish this project. The Dsaret name, I need hardly mention, would feature prominently."

I closed my hand on the hilt just in case, as I said politely, "I would love to donate money, but you have to remember that it all belongs to my grandmother. Who is very much alive, I am glad to say. You've got to ask her."

He breathed out through his nose. Then smiled—I could feel the effort across the width of the space. "If you will give me an address to which I can write," he began.

I was about to remind him that she was staying with Milo when he scowled, the lantern light from the table making his brow look furrowed and ferocious. He took a step toward me—no, he was glaring at something behind me!

I whirled around, the blade coming up hard in a defensive block as a black-shrouded someone, or some*thing*, raised a crossbow. Not aimed at me, but past me. My blade hit its arm—it grunted as the crossbow twanged.

A bolt hissed past my head.

I jerked around. For a split second the world stilled. Robert stood there eyes and mouth round in horror, hands out, fingers spread like massive starfish, then the side of his head flowered with blood.

I swept the blade around in a haymaker. The figure leaped back, as Robert thudded to the floor. I glanced his way, then back as something clattered in the box by my hand. I stared witlessly down at the crossbow.

A rapid flurry of steps, and the figure was gone. A vampire? No, not unless they grunted like normal human men.

I flung myself down by Robert. He lay motionless, blood running into his eye and down his face.

As the orchestra heedlessly went on with the waltz, not thirty feet away, I looked back and forth, wondering what to do—chase the villain? Do something for Robert? Only what?

Staunch wound. I leaped up and grabbed some of the costume cloth. It was horribly dusty, and old—would it cause an infection? I stood there uncertainly as footsteps clattered, and Nat appeared.

"Oh, I got lost," she began in a loud, fake voice. But then her face changed, and she ran forward. "What the hell happened here?"

"Someone shot him. From behind me." I pointed. "Then threw the crossbow right here in this box and ran off. Why are you here? Did you hear it?"

"No. Beka sent me to rescue you—she was sure that guy was going to shake you down for cash." Nat looked from the prop box down to Robert, and then back at me. She knelt down beside Robert, keeping her skirt well away from him as she tested his pulse under his jaw, and then lifted an eyelid. "It's bad but not fatal. One inch farther in, and he would have lost an eye at the least."

"Not fatal? It looks like a thousand gallons of blood!"

"Head wounds are always bloody—"

From the side hall came voices, led by a faint, acid drawl. ". . . wants me, he could have come to get me himself. I have quite enough to do, trying to watch those wretched people from the lower city . . . Ro-*bair-r-r-r?*"

"The countess!" I whispered.

Nat and I looked at each other in horror, then she smacked the side of my leg. "Get out of here."

"What?"

"Don't you see? Alone with the murder weapon? I saw this on way too many Perry Mason reruns when I was a kid. It's got to be a setup. I can take care of him. You get out."

I got to my feet. "But what if they blame you?"

Nat grinned. "So they arrest me. I bet anything you care to name Bek will get me off, once they get a load of what I have to tell 'em. Worst case scenario, my rep can stand being hauled out of here in cuffs, but yours can't. So vamoose."

I grabbed up the prop sword again. "In that case, I think I am going to go hunting," I said grimly. I grabbed up a lantern with my free hand and started down the corridor that Robert's shrouded attacker had taken.

Yeah, I know—really smooth, Murray. Hunting a would-be murderer while wearing a ball gown and high heeled shoes, armed with a prop sword that would probably break if I blocked a serious blow, and carrying a lantern which—anybody who has ever seen a horror movie knows—will go out, guaranteed, as soon as the person is alone with the killer.

But nothing happened beyond my managing to get myself thoroughly lost in the tangle of narrow corridors, many of which had been closed off and boarded up, or led nowhere due to the reconstruction. It was quiet, deserted, yet the more I walked, the colder I felt, until my teeth ached, and the hairs along the edge of my scalp stiffened.

Then I reached an intersection where four ways looked equally uninviting. I held up the lantern, desperate for a clue. The crystal necklace picked up the light somehow, sending rainbow shards sparkling down one hallway, where the uncertain light caught on the pale fold of a gown.

A person!

"Hey! Wait up!" I yelled, hastily following it up in Dobreni, French, and German. I walked fast, the lantern swinging, which made the light dance crazily, shadows leaping and flickering. At the other end of a turning a flash of splintered light revealed the outline of a teenage girl, her marcelled hair pale below a graceful tiara. Shadows closed her away, but not before I saw her turn a corner.

I ran after her, yelling, "Wait, wait!"

My footsteps echoed, the light swung so much I had to squint against the dizzying effect. Once again I caught sight of her back, in a dress that I recognized: the delicate black and white striped, full-sleeved gypsy dress Chanel introduced in 1939, before she closed her shop for fifteen years.

Copy or vintage? The light, the gown. The profile. Not quite Gran's, and then I remembered that Christmas Eve vision. Gran's twin sister, Rose—once Gran's rival for Armandros.

I am seeing Rose's ghost.

The light was so splintery that my head panged as I tried to see past the winks and shards of distorted light as I ran after her. The lantern jiggled and shook in my hand, worsening the effect; the closer I got, the more difficult it was to see the ghost, but then I heard party noise. Another turn led me to the other side of the stage. Not twenty feet away was the Ridotski table.

I caught Honoré's gaze. He said something to someone behind him, and from the jumble of people talking, laughing, and drinking, Beka emerged, her expression anxious as she rushed up to me. "I sent Nat to rescue you from . . . Kim. What's wrong?"

"First, where is Tony?" I asked.

She didn't have to look. "Over at the head table, bookended between Cerisette and the duchess."

"How long has he been there?"

"Since he stopped dancing with Cerisette," Beka said.

"So he hasn't left the ballroom?"

"No. He's been dancing the entire—what happened?"

I told her in a few fast words. Her mouth pressed into a line, then she said, "No wonder Natalie never came back. Neither has the countess. But there's been no sign of any trouble out here."

A loud *wham!* caused people to jump. A girl shrieked, triggering the nasal, braying laughter of a bunch of teenage boys. The orchestra faltered as a cold wind surged around the room from the door that had slammed open.

"A bad storm is coming in. I think it might be time to go home." Beka added, "I hope you and Natalie will come to my house tomorrow. We can talk about all these things, while these people will be busy at their traditional New Year's dinner." She indicated the von Mecklundburg table.

I thanked her as I looked around for Alec. I had to see him—talk to him! So did all Dobrenica, apparently. There were more Vigilzhi than I'd noticed before, moving efficiently through the crowd. Above, Gilles and his crew had finished their filming and vanished. Reluctantly I joined the general exodus.

I got my wrap and made it outside, where the wind nearly knocked me off my feet. It blew with icy force, flagging my cloak and skirts like banners. I looked around, but of course there was no luxury sleigh waiting. So I bundled into a crowded cab with several other people I didn't know. It smelled of long-ago eaten dinners, and it did not keep out the bitter cold, but it did give some protection from the biting wind. Shivering in my corner, I endured until at last the cab reached the inn.

A hot bath, some tea, and I dropped into bed, too tired even to consider the fresh mushrooming of unanswered questions.

I slid gratefully into sleep . . .

And then came the nightmares.

THIRTY

FOR TWO DAYS the entire city was locked down by smothering shrouds of blizzard white. The lack of street noise was so profound that for the first time I could hear the distant cathedral bells faintly ringing the hours.

That sound was reassuring during the day, but at night they only rang once, at midnight. Otherwise there was the howling wind, and a spectacular series of nightmares that kept waking me up during those interminable hours of darkness.

I couldn't help remembering what Danilov had said about vampires and nightmares. I tried not to imagine fanged blood-suckers prowling around the inn. There were enough weird things going on without my imagination creating more. *How could anything, even a vampire, even see out there?* I kept thinking as I walked from window to window, hoping for any sign of a letup so I could slip out and try to find Alec.

At least there was Tania to mull some of the mysteries with. We met downstairs late on New Year's Day. The last of the fresh vegetables had been consumed, so hearty stews and meat pies were now the main dishes. As Tania and I sat over our pepper stew, we could hear Madam Waleska's irritable voice fog-horning from the kitchen as she scolded generally everyone.

Tania admitted that she was having nightmares as well. I asked what they were about, wondering if they were somehow broadcast into our brains like personalized television from hell, but as soon as she mentioned lost, hurt, and sickened animals whom she couldn't help, I abandoned that notion with gratitude: mine pretty much centered around car crashes.

"But that reminds me," I said, leaning forward out of habit, though we were alone in the dining room. The last of the local patrons and relatives had departed on New Year's Eve. I hoped everyone had gotten safely home before that storm hit. "I was so busy telling you about Count Robert and the crossbow that I forgot to say that on the ride to the ball I saw Shurisko again, this time around St. Xanpia's fountain. A lot of other animal ghosts were with him. That's the second time I've seen that."

Tania's thin fingers paused in breaking open a rye biscuit. "Yes, they seem to meet there. I have seen them, many times. I used to go there at lunchtime on school days to watch them, when I was small."

"Shurisko didn't stay at the fountain, but started jumping around the sleigh I was in. This is like the third or fourth time I've seen him doing that. Do you think it means anything? Of course it doesn't mean anything. I'm beginning to think that ghosts are all crazy, either that or the ghost world doesn't make any kind of sense to the living."

"Shurisko is a dog," Tania said slowly. "Dogs are so very loyal to those they love. There must be meaning in his actions. I will ask."

"And here's another question. I finally heard that ghost. He said only one word, 'Esplumoir.' I'm told that this is an old Arthurian legend. Do you know how it relates to Dobrenica?"

Tania spread her hands. "I think I have heard it mentioned once, as a medieval legend. We have many of those." She gave me her quick smile, her manner apologetic.

I smiled determinedly back, hiding my exasperation. It would be nice to have an answer to *something* that didn't bring on another ten questions, but I kept that whine to myself and, after the meal, I went upstairs to get in a hundred pushups, then do a full set of barre stretches. Now that the other rooms were empty, I could do ballet combinations up and down the hall, followed by some lunges and fencing moves. Using the fireplace poker from downstairs helped keep my arms in shape .

Next morning, I did the same, only this time I used the entire dining room as my gym while the rest of the family slogged through the snow to Mass. When I say that they left twenty minutes early for a church two blocks away, you get an idea how nasty the weather was.

When Tania got back, she came up to my room. "I overheard one of the teachers reminding Theresa that there will be a partial solar eclipse at dawn Tuesday morning. The students are supposed to observe it for school."

I snapped my fingers. "If eclipses are supposed to have influence on Vrajhus, how about we experiment with looking for ghosts? Except," I jerked my thumb at the window. "Would we see anything besides snow?"

"Everyone insists that this storm will be gone by tomorrow night," Tania said. "If you can trust the older folks' predictions."

"Do you trust them?" I asked.

Her cheeks colored. "We always go by Grandfather Kezh's bones. Every time they ache, we get a storm, and when the ache eases, it passes."

"Bones and barometric pressure. If Grandfather Kezh recovers his spryness tomorrow, shall we make a date for Tuesday morning on the roof?" *Then later in that day, see if I don't make my way to Alec . . . or he to me.*

Tania flashed a grin. "Theresa would love an excuse to climb on the roof."

The snow was still falling on Monday, but when we looked out, we all told each other that it wasn't coming down quite as hard as it had been.

By mid-morning, I actually began to believe it, because—faint, but there—were the houses across the street. Grayish and indistinct, but there.

Not half an hour after I made that observation a white-dusted figure labored up the street, which was waist-high in snow, to drop off the newspaper delivery.

Everyone pounced on a copy. Usually the family shared a single copy, leaving the rest out for the patrons. But I was the only patron, and Madam didn't even expect any. The household vanished into the back, and I sat down by the window, alone in the dining room, and opened the paper.

So what's the first thing that met my eyes?

Statthalter Seconds Motion to Investigate Own Complicity in Death of Lady Ruli

I flung the paper away as if it had bitten me, but then I picked it up again. I had to know the worst. More, I had to figure out the agenda behind the articles, if I could.

There was an article about the accident site. The most often quoted source was Dr. Kandras's report describing the remains of a young woman around age thirty, with strands of pale hair caught in the broken branches of a tree.

"Gotcha," I thought, hot triumph burning through me. There is no sweeter sight than a view from the pinnacle of moral superiority. Liar— caught in the act!

Except . . . the quotations were from the twenty-second. Nobody had spoken with him recently. What if the bones he found really were a female's, but someone got to them after he saw them, and they were swapped for Marzio's?

What if . . . what if.

Impatiently, I shut down the eternal grind of questions, and turned to the rest of the front page. There was Dr. Kandras's report, another from the Vigilzhi who climbed down to the accident site. They were so circumspect that every other word was the Dobreni equivalent of "alleged," whenever there wasn't a more straightforward "we do not have that information at this time." The von Mecklundburgs had been interviewed ("Is not a second to our motion an admission of guilt? We only ask for justice," Robert trumpeted from *his* pinnacle) as had the Bishop ("We will investigate every witness, corroborate every fact"). The article ended, perhaps intentionally, with no comment from Alec, but following that were his office's plans for the forwarding of various projects.

The news shifted to local stuff, reports of the previous week's festivities and a strictly formal, respectful report on Ruli's funeral. I was scanning rapidly through that when another snow-dappled figure lumbered through the door, pausing in the vestibule to shed the worst of the white. What emerged was a worn Vigilzhi greatcoat, with no collar tabs or shoulder markings, meaning a low rank. His hat was pulled down over his ears and his muffler wrapped up nearly to the hat brim.

I began to refold the paper, remembering that the locals often read the paper when they came in for meals or a drink. The Vigilzhi messenger had already slipped from my notice until he paused by the counter and looked around. Something in the line of that coat, the way he moved. . . .

I dropped the paper—he raised a gloved hand and yanked down the muffler to reveal a familiar square-cut chin, and the curve of mouth that had first entranced me six months before.

"Alec?" I breathed.

He pushed the hat up slightly, his eyes rueful with laughter. "I didn't think I could get away with it. But I had to try."

"Uh." *Think!* "Come on up to my room. Nobody's out here. Yet."

Here we were, two adults—one of them the most powerful person in the country—sneaking upstairs like teenagers when Mom and Dad aren't looking. I certainly felt that way, and from the quick look he cast behind the counter before we headed up the stairs, he was feeling the same.

I shut us into my room, and let out my breath with a sigh. Alec looked around, and I said, feeling self-consciously warm, "Um, want to take off that coat?"

He set the hat on the little table and slowly began to unwind the muffler. Desire beat between us, intense and vital. "I had to see you," he said, then gave a small, breathless laugh. "This is probably a bad idea."

"No. It's a *good* idea. I was sitting here feeling every jab in today's paper, and trying to figure out how to cross the city to find you." I hesitated, my longing to throw my arms around him so strong it had become a physical emptiness that hurt. But his stance, the slight question in his eyes, the hand half-raised in mute appeal, and I remembered: *Ruli is probably alive.*

The guy was still married. When last we'd been alone together, he was a widower, ready to face heavy time as a murderer. Now?

I wrenched my gaze away, hooked my foot around the little chair, and plopped down. "Have a seat," I said, striving for casual, though it hurt not to touch him.

"The paper," he repeated, as if trying to remember what a paper was. He looked around again, this time apparently seeing the room, and sat on the edge of the bed, elbows on his knees. "I haven't seen the paper yet. I was over at HQ early, and . . ." He lifted a shoulder. "Bad?"

"Yes. No. Could have been worse. I get the sense that the journalists are definitely not in anyone's pocket. What news do you have?"

"Robert von Mecklundburg is recovering. When he woke up he corroborated what you told Nat."

"So he doesn't blame me?"

"No. Said you tried to defend him with a prop sword. That's the good news."

"That reminds me, if you get a suspect, check his arm, and it definitely was a he. Tall. And I smelled guy sweat. He'll have a bruise right here." I smacked my arm just above my elbow. Then the last part of what he said sank in. "There's bad news?"

"There was an attempt on the Ridotskis."

"What happened?"

"Someone iced their driveway the night of the ball."

"How do you do that? Oh, put water over it when the temperature is dropping?"

"Correct. That storm was just moving in, or they might have seen the danger. Whoever did it iced the top half of their drive, so the sleigh lost friction, slid all the way down, and turned over."

"Was anyone hurt?"

"Beka. She broke three ribs cushioning her mother's fall. The Prime Minister is badly bruised. The animals were unhurt, at least."

"That is so creepy."

"I've got the Vigilzhi spread far too thin, guarding them and everyone else. We're going to have to redesign the patrol routes. That's where I—"

"Should be," I finished, and though I knew it was wrong, I could not resist the pull from chair to the bed to sit beside him. "Thanks for coming to see me."

"I've watched the windows for three days."

"Me, too. I don't know anything about snow, but I figured that if I couldn't see the buildings across the street, going out might be a bad idea."

He nodded. "The entire city shuts down during blizzards, by law. Too often the weather clears, and we find someone frozen twenty feet from their door." His weight shifted, and we were touching, shoulder to shoulder as he glanced around. "You like staying here? It can't be convenient. Or is it the company? You are comfortable among them?"

I was about to say, *I'm used to ordinary citizens.* Which was true. My end of Santa Monica was only a bike ride from Beverly Hills, but it may as well have been on another continent. But before I could claim to be Ms. Everywoman, I thought about that bathroom reserved just for me, and the "Mademoiselle Dsaret" attention, and I made a face. "They make me comfortable, and I really like them."

His arm drifted up my back to close around my shoulders; his voice was low, warmed by a smile that I felt and heard more than saw. I shivered, and leaned into him as he murmured, "I had to tell you in person how much it meant to me, the things you said at the opera house ball."

"That you're not a murderer? Is anyone going to listen to any of it at that hearing on Tuesday?"

"There's only one piece of evidence that we can introduce, because it can be proved: those bones in Ruli's sarcophagus."

"Right." I sighed. "Alec, I want so badly to kiss you, but . . . when Ruli gets back—if she gets back, and I hope she does—if she's okay with us hooking up, because I get it about the political stuff . . ."

"When Ruli gets back, the three of us will have a chance to talk." He drew in a deep breath. "I was going to say 'the four of us,' but Marzio . . ." He shook his head. "I wish I knew where Ruli was. I hope she's alive. There are going to be a lot of questions asked at Tuesday's hearing. Honoré is going to be there, and no one will be wearing charms if we have to strip them down. People are very angry. Not just with me, anymore."

"Have you told anyone about the bones?"

"I've left that to Dmitros. He's doing his best to investigate, but as

I said, the Vigilzhi are stretched to the max. There are more rumors about vampires around. Missing animals. So far no missing people, but the reports have increased, and they have a lot in common: old charms smashed or missing, shadows crossing windows, shadowy places on streets, and local animals going wild."

"Okay, that's really creepy."

"And did I mention someone's been searching my things? Not just at the Palace. Ysvorod House as well. Even the cubby over at the council building, though anyone who knows anything about how our government works would know there is nothing remotely personal or secret kept there."

"Are you being guarded?"

"No. Better those men be used for other purposes. My mood is so vile I might even welcome a confrontation." He shifted slightly, using his free hand to dig into one of the pockets of his long coat. He pulled out a pistol.

"Ick," I exclaimed, jumping to my feet in instinctive recoil. "But if it keeps you safe . . ."

He slid it back into his pocket, and I was going to sit down again, but he got slowly to his feet. "Dmitros is probably waiting for me. And I took the street car. One nice thing about this weather is the anonymity."

"That goes for the killer, too, unfortunately," I said as I rubbed my damp palms down the sides of my jeans. "Um. Can we do something together, like a normal date, or is that a bad idea?"

"We'll do something tomorrow," he promised. "After the hearing. It feels so good to talk to you, and . . ." He left it hanging, and looked at the window.

I knew exactly what that self-control cost him. As I debated the risks of grabbing him and kissing him, he lifted his thumb and caressed the single dimple in my cheek. I leaned into his touch, without meaning to. He leaned down, and his lips replaced his thumb, so softly, and I couldn't bear it any more. My lips met his, and we twisted together in a long, devouring kiss, and there was the heat and the fire, and I wanted nothing more than to fall on the bed and *burn*.

Somewhere remained a spark of sanity. We both broke it off at the same time. "I'd better get out of here." His voice was gravelly. He cleared his throat.

Silently I handed him the muffler, which he flung around his neck and lower face. He jammed on the hat.

"I'll see if the coast is clear," I said, moving to the door.

"We've got to find you another place to live," he muttered as I peered out.

No one was in the hallway—of course, as mine was the only room occupied at the moment. But downstairs, Madam was bustling around the dining area, putting out fresh tablecloths in hopes of walk-in custom.

Alec and I exchanged looks; the laughter was back. I ran downstairs and asked Madam about the evening's menu, positioning myself so that she faced me, with her back to the stairway.

I could see Tania and Teresa behind the counter, stacking dishes, but that couldn't be helped. Alec flipped a hand at them and walked out with a quiet step as Madam talked on. I nodded at everything without hearing any of it, and breathed with relief when the door shut on Alec.

When Madam turned away, the girls looked at me. I mouthed the word "Messenger." I hated lying to them, but it seemed necessary.

As I went back upstairs, I thought: If I stay in Dobrenica any longer, maybe it's time to see about finding a place.

This time, the nightmares set in about midnight. Car crashes, being burned alive—oh, that was only the start. After an eternity of gasping, clammy wake-ups, I gave up trying to sleep. I took a hot bath, which relaxed my body but left me wide awake. So I dug through my clothes for something that would be practical for climbing out on the roof. Some tights, my boots, my jeans, and three layers of cotton shirt with one of the new soft wool sweater-tops over it should make an okay roof-sitting outfit.

When I was done, I looked out the window. The sky was brilliant with stars, promising a good view of the solar eclipse in a few hours, if weather didn't come boiling over the mountains. I spotted a faint rectangle of golden light painted on the snow-blanketed terrace below: Someone else was up.

I let myself out of the room, moving noiselessly to the head of the stairs, in case the wakeful one was a senior member of the family, maybe in their p.j.s and expecting privacy.

Tania emerged from the kitchen, carrying a tray of hot chocolate cups. Theresa appeared a moment later, her silky black hair loose down her skinny back instead of in the ubiquitous braids. She was followed by her friend Miriam. All three wore chenille bathrobes of the sort I vaguely remembered Gran having worn ages ago. I'd loved rubbing my fingers up and down her sleeve.

I ran downstairs, to be greeted with twin expressions of welcome by the sisters, and beaming delight by Miriam.

"I saw the reflection of your light," Tania said, pointing outside. "The nightmares?"

"You too, I take it."

"I haven't slept," Tania admitted. "All the cats are here. No one roaming. They are troubled."

Theresa briskly passed out cups. "I heard Mama and Papa saying a rosary in their room. I said mine while Miriam sang her prayer of protection of the home. It calls on extra angels," she added.

"Extra?" Tania asked. "Will you sing it? I think we can use the extra help."

Miriam shivered, and everyone cast an anxious glance at the holly wreaths in the windows as she sang the ancient Hebrew words in a small, light voice. Then she said, "If I translate, it goes something like this:

In the name of Adonai
the God of Israel:
May the angel Michael be at my right
and the angel Gabriel be at my left;
and in front of me the angel Uriel,
and behind me the angel Raphael,
and above my head
the Sh'khinah."

"Sheh-khin-ahhh," Theresa repeated, drawing the word out. "Does that not sound like the perfect word for Divine Presence?"

Miriam tipped her head in the thoughtful way I remembered from summer, her forehead puzzled. "We agree not to tell the other her way is wrong, but if Theresa believes the way to heaven is as the priests teach, and Katrin's third cousin up on the mountain thinks the Orthodox is the way to heaven, and Sister Maria's pen friend in Kosovo, who is Muslim, thinks her way is right, and Katrin's father says that there is no heaven, when we die we snap out like the electrical lights, then how do you decide who is right?"

Three pairs of eyes turned my way.

"Maybe they all have pieces of truth, like my prism? Every day I keep learning how much I don't know about how the universe works. But here's something I do know. Miriam, I think that was you and your school friends defending me in front of the opera house, am I right?"

Theresa grinned in triumph. "That was our class. And everyone joined us, did you hear?"

Miriam made a sour face. "My grandfather says, that man must have been a hireling."

"How's that?" I asked.

She shrugged her skinny shoulders. "I don't know. Grandpapa said, it was in the way this man spoke. Everyone says Lady Ruli, or Madam Statthalter. This man said, 'your wife.' But mother says Grandpapa wants to think that everybody in Riev believes the Statthalter innocent, because King Milo's son would not do such a thing."

Now two pairs of eyes studied me, and Tania looked down at her hands.

"He *is* innocent," I said. "I can't prove it yet, but I know he is."

"Hah." Miriam drank her hot chocolate with a defiant air. "I knew that. Like Grandpapa said, King Milo's son wouldn't. If they do not like each other, they would have a divorce. Mother says that nobody has changed *that* law from the Soviets."

"But they were married in church," Theresa said, looking unhappy. "In church law, there is no divorce."

"There can be annulments," Tania murmured, then reverted to her imitation of a fence post.

Miriam spread her hands. "Mother says, King Milo's son or no King Milo's son, it takes more effort to throw somebody over a cliff, and burn a good automobile as well, than to go to your bishop for an annulment. What I hate is how such rumors make everyone look horrid, especially the Statthalter, who is so handsome, and who everyone knows paid out of his own pocket for the street lamps down in Old Market, when the Council said the taxes must go to the drain treatment plant yet again." She folded her arms with an air of defiance, then added: "He would have married Lady Rebekah if he did not have to sacrifice their love for the alliance with the Devil's Mountain people."

Theresa stole a look my way, and when she saw me doing my own fence post, she said in a long-suffering voice, "You know it isn't true. Your own second-cousin, whose aunt lives right at Ridotski House, said they weren't in love. It was only flirtation." She flickered another look my way. "Besides, how could he be in love with *two* people?"

Miriam glared into her hot chocolate, then fixed me with her wide stare. "That's true. But Hannah at the dairy said that her cousin at Mecklundburg House heard the family saying that he threw Lady Ruli over the cliff so he could marry you. Yet Tomas Bogdan said that his uncle, who drives an inkri, said that the Statthalter was angry because Lady Ruli had another man in secret."

Whoa. Where to start? There was no use in slamdunking the girls for gossiping when it's human nature to gossip. I gossiped with Nat every chance I could get. We all like speculating about hidden motives and intentions, and so if I harshed all over the girls for gossiping, they would merely stop talking to me.

But one thing I could try was damage control.

"I know that the Statthalter was not angry with her. They decided she was to go to Paris to spend Christmas with her family," I said, then explained my reasons for coming.

After I got done describing Ruli's ghost—or apparition, or communiqué—Miriam let out a dramatic sigh. "Of course she would call to you in spirit across the waters! Everyone knows the two of you decided which one was to marry him, for you were seen together in Temple Square. Besides, Lady Rebekah would not befriend an untrust-worthy person, everybody knows that." Miriam nodded so vigorously her glasses bounced on her nose. Fiercely, she said to me, "You will stand up at the trial and smite the false accusers. I wish to be there!"

Theresa shook her head. "Anna says that it could be months and *months* before there is any trial. And Grandfather Kezh thinks they will solve everything behind closed doors. Like the hearing today, everyone knows only the very important people will be let in. No one else."

"I will be at the trial if I have to sneak in through the rafters," Miriam stated, her glasses flashing as she lifted her chin. "I shall see justice done."

Theresa sighed, as if long accustomed to Miriam's fervent vows, and shifted the conversation to who among Tania's pets had stayed in during the storm, and who had shown up safely since. Judging from the many nicknames, Tania had a lot of pets.

By the time we'd finished up the hot chocolate and the slices of de-licious rolled walnut and date bread called *petitsa*, dawn was only an hour off. Theresa bounced up, piled everything on one of the trays, and bounded off toward the kitchen, Miriam in tow.

Tania said, "Would you like to come up to my room? The roof is easily reached from there."

Everybody fetched coats, scarves, and mittens, then trooped to the attic. We squeezed past a jumble of old furnishings to a neat little door, which opened onto a lovely little room with two dormer windows, under the slanting roof.

Tania twitched curtains, straightened an already ruler-aligned rug, and fussed around the scrupulously tidy living space. It was cramped and had the musty aroma of many pets, but it wasn't the nasty smell of untended cages. Fitting under one of the roof slants was a chicken-wire screened off area with a kind of basketwork city built for rats. The rest of the room had cats everywhere—at least six curled on the narrow quilt-covered bed, a row of cats in meatloaf shape on the wardrobe, and several on jury-rigged cat scratching posts, with carpet nailed to wood. There were a couple of little houses, with glowing eyes appearing briefly, and I glimpsed a cat tail through a little shuttered window.

"I hope you do not object to cats," Tania said, her hands gesturing nervously the way some do when someone else first enters their private space.

"What a great rat-town you made! And I love the colors in your quilt. It's so cozy here," I said, to ease her tension.

The younger girls appeared, Theresa still drying her hands on her sturdy bathrobe before she wrestled into her coat. "Did you see the cat doors?" She pointed to little slatted doors set below each dormer. "And this one for the rats. We can't do anything about what happens outside. They *will* fight, you know, the cats and rats."

"I wish they wouldn't," Tania whispered.

"You wish nobody would fight, not people or beast," Theresa said, patting her sister's thin shoulder. Then to me, "Which is why she will not eat meat."

Tania fought a yawn, saying, "I just wish they would go out. The wind is not up. Maybe weather is on the way again."

"I hope it doesn't come until after the eclipse." Theresa pushed open a little door on the other side of the room, directly beneath one of the pointed eaves. She and Miriam pushed their way out, chattering about cats versus rats, and how much noise they made, and was any of it play, or did they always fight to the death?

I followed the teens out through the roof door, dropping to my hands and knees when I saw that the ridgepole was about the width of a ladder. Tania sauntered with the ease of years of habit, and Theresa and Miriam scrambled about comfortably, exclaiming as they kicked and smacked snow from the ridgepole. In the light from Tania's room, the snow glittered white on their slippers and mittens.

I looked around, trying to get used to my perch. The roof was a complication of angles, with a thick, smooth blanket of white where the girls hadn't marred it.

As the view cleared, Theresa and Miriam settled themselves where they could not only see the eastern mountains, solid black against the deep midnight blue of the sky, but also the southern end of the city. They leaned out to examine the street below. Tiny golden glows from lanterns, no larger than fireflies at this distance, appeared here and there on the visible streets immediately below us. As the girls discussed who lived where, and who they thought might be outside doing the assignment, Tania was turning in a slow circle, her face serious.

The scene was peaceful to look at, but wow, was it cold. A few clouds drifted slowly across the sky, stars still glowing. I turned my attention to the streets. No sign of any ghosts, either glowing, smoky, vaporous, or anything else. The back of my neck tightened, however, when I peered into the dark shadows between buildings. The absence of light seemed . . . *intense.*

"That's weird," I muttered, my breath clouding.

Tania leaned out so far my stomach dropped and the muscles in the backs of my legs twitched. "Tania?"

"There. What do you see?"

She pointed below, at the intersection near the shop where she'd once worked.

"I just noticed that," I said. "How the light isn't getting between that building with the brick decoration and the one with the frog gargoyles, though it gets between all the others."

"I see," Tania said. "And there. Oh! Did that shadow . . ." She swallowed. I heard it. "Move?"

She didn't wait for me to answer, but called, low-voiced, "Theresa."

The teens were peering at the eastern mountains, impatient for any sign of the sun, and muttering dire predictions as the graying shapes of clouds silently blotted the northern stars. Both turned.

Tania said, "I think you said you know someone who sees . . . shadows."

The way her voice dropped to a whisper on the last word carried such a freight of meaning that Theresa's jaw dropped, and Miriam gasped, both hands pressed over her mouth.

Theresa said doubtfully, "Horrible Haru *says* he does, but . . ."

"Can we fetch him?" Tania asked.

Theresa said, "Katrin thinks he's making it up as one of his horrid jokes. Maybe it would be a good test, eh?"

I peered over Tania's shoulder at the girls. "Theresa, show us where Katrin lives, would you? It could be important."

That was all it took. The four of us scrambled back into Tania's room, then Tania uttered a terse order, "Meet at the counter in one minute."

They left, Theresa muttering, "But the eclipse hasn't even begun yet!"

Since I was already dressed, I stopped by my room to grab that crystal necklace, then I ran downstairs, where I found Theresa lighting three glass-sided lanterns. The girls appeared, tugging and tucking and buttoning various pieces of clothing, Miriam squirming impatiently as she braided her thick red hair. Theresa let hers hang loose, a glossy, straight, black cloak as long as my own hair. Their round faces were solemn in the warm glow from the lanterns; as the flames inside leapt and flickered, our crystals answered with red and blue and yellow glints and winks and glitters.

"I could only find these three," Tania said in an apologetic voice. "The summer lanterns are locked in the storeroom, and my father has the key. Shall I rouse him?"

I felt way out of my depth. "I think we need to hurry. How about I go without, but we stick together and avoid any really dark shadowy places, okay?"

"I know every step of the short cut," Theresa said. "If there is a new shadow, I will know it." She fingered the crystal on a cord around her neck

'Then let's go."

We dashed out of the empty inn, and Theresa led the way between the houses across the street, the lanterns making three swinging, jiggling pools of light.

In an effort to avoid looking at the lanterns, which would give me light blindness, I peered up and around. On a little balcony overhead, I glimpsed several school children with an adult who lectured about how the moon and the sun interacted to create eclipses. A kid said mournfully, "I see the clouds over the mountain. Will teacher see them, too?"

We passed too quickly for me to hear the answer.

"I hope Haru is telling the truth," Miriam muttered as we waded across a street no wider than an alley. "He put a slug in Katrin's shoe one day."

"Her middle brother Ladi sends him to do it. Ladi thinks the jokes up." Theresa puffed as we trudged on, the heavy snowfall squeaking underfoot.

We burst into a small cul-de-sac with a well at the center, an angel carved into the housing above it. Reflections from the gold-lit windows gleamed along its mossy, carved edges and its upturned face. Children's voices came from somewhere nearby, though no one was in sight on the freshly swept flagstones. Then I spotted the wild swing of lanterns in what had to be a pocket park behind the two biggest houses, as a teenage boy said, "Put out that lamp. You'll never see anything with that light."

The houses were two-story with a narrow attic floor under slanted roofs, cornices and gables with fanciful carvings worn by a century of weathering; Theresa raced to the third house in, banged twice on the door, then opened it.

Inside was noise, the colorful clutter of a small home inhabited by a lot of people, and a smell of cabbage and pepper and coffee. We set our lanterns on a tiny table just inside the door, then went down a narrow hall lined with galoshes and boots, into a long, narrow kitchen hung with pots and dried herbs and garlic.

A harried woman in a bathrobe was saying to a couple of lanky teenage boys, "Eat later. You must go outside, too."

The tallest boy protested, "We'll only see a corner of it because of the mountain, and the clouds are sure to come."

"The clouds are building now. Nobody is going to see any eclipse," a newcomer—another teenage boy—said as he stamped in, shedding snow.

"So I said," the tall boy said triumphantly as his mother exclaimed about the snow all over the kitchen.

"I have to talk to Haru," Theresa said over them. "Please?"

"What's he done now?" The mother gave us a distracted glance that turned into quick surprise when she saw me. Then she threw up her hands. "He's probably in his room."

We streamed past the table, on which several steaming bowls of the spiced cornmeal *mammaglia* sat, one boy drowning his with tablespoons of jam.

Theresa pounded up two flights of stairs, then paused and said over her shoulder to Miriam, "Get Katrin. She has to be over at the garden."

Miriam gave a firm nod, and pushed past us down the stairs as Theresa banged on a narrow door at the top of the stair. "Harulam! I have to talk to you!"

"What's the password?" came a boy's voice. It sounded like he was about eleven.

Tania pushed past, tried the latch, found it locked, and said, "*My password is, I am doing the work of Sanctus Xanpia.*"

A second later there was a metallic cling, and the door opened to reveal a stout boy with bottle-thick glasses who scowled up at us. The scowl eased to doubt. "Tania Waleska?" Then the scowl was back, even more fierce. "Did my teacher send you? This won't be a good eclipse. The mountain will hide most of it, and you watch, up will come the clouds."

Miriam whispered, "Katrin told us you can see the Shadow Ones. Is that true?"

Haru opened his door wide. The room was no larger than a closet, stuffed with a bed, a trunk, a tiny desk, and shelves. Every surface seemed to be covered with cardboard castles, forest, and paper warriors representing at least six centuries, judging by the armory and weapons.

"Yes," the boy said, and then, after a good look at me, more uncertainly, "I see their shadows."

I addressed him. "We need you to come and tell us what you see."

"I will get my coat."

"Don't you want to get dressed first?" Theresa asked, while I tried not to squirm with anxious impatience.

The boy jerked up a shoulder. "Who cares?" He pointed in triumph to his pajama bottoms, which were sturdy wool not unlike sweatpants.

"Been wearing these for four days. I'm trying to go without changing all the way until school next week."

Theresa rolled her eyes, and the four of us pounded down through the house—to fetch up against a tall, lantern-jawed man with thick glasses. "What's this?" His gaze ranged the row, stopping at me.

"They want me to see if the Shadow Ones are coming," Haru stated, his voice shrill with triumph. "*Some* people believe me!"

Whatever the dad thought about vampires wasn't clear. The problem, I realized with a sinking sensation, was with me.

"I know who you are," Katrin's dad said flatly, his gaze narrow and suspicious, his mouth crimped with contempt. "I know who you are. Isn't there anyone else you can put into danger besides my son? If you ask me, someone should sweep away the whole crooked lot of you, driving each other off cliffs and burning down one another's houses, like there isn't real work to do."

"Whoa, whoa, whoa," I said in English, thinking furiously. Dad had always said that you can cut a lot of arguments short by addressing what appears to be the other's assumptions, rather than loudly defending your own. Saying things like, *I know in my heart that Marius Alexander Ysvorod is innocent of wrongdoing,* only works in situations where there's a beautiful soundtrack playing in the background.

I said, "'The whole crooked lot of you'? 'You' as in me, or 'you' collectively? Because if your objection is to me as a person—"

His mouth twisted. "Those of you with venerable, ancient names of *honor* who run the rest of us." A volcanic layer of anger heated up every adjective and noun. He swept a hand out toward the darkness. "Is it not your privilege to lead the way?"

Haru jounced and jiggled in an agony of impatience. "The *inimasang,*" he whispered over and over.

The girls also looked agonized, but the dad was planted squarely in the doorway. I gazed back at him, thinking fast. Mom had always been live and let live. Dad and Gran shared a slightly different view, that every man and woman was king or queen of her own demesne, whether that be a ticket kiosk, a cab, or a kingdom. A notion that had taken on especial poignancy when I'd discovered Gran's past.

So here I was in this guy's house—his castle—and from his perspective, I wanted to sweep his son along on my quest. How could I acknowledge his demesne but *hurry up?*

By addressing the assumptions under the most corrosive of those adjectives. "The way I define honor," I said, "is choosing the right thing to do for the good of all. Even if no one's looking. Even if it hurts. Anybody can do that, whatever family they are born to." Haru rolled his eyes, but his dad was at least listening. I said quickly, "I can't do anything about the rumors, and I can't prove that I didn't burn down the baron's house, but I have two pieces of evidence that the Statthalter is not complicit in the death of his wife, and I am only waiting for irrefutable proof before taking it to the investigative committee."

The dad gave a nod at the words *Irrefutable proof.* "Ah, then. What do you want my son for?" Now he was a wary parent.

Haru hopped up and down. "I *told* you, Papa. I *told* you. They *believe* me about the—"

Haru's dad snapped his fingers, and the boy clammed up.

"We saw suspicious shadows from the Waleskas' roof. I want to see if Haru can corroborate them. Or not. Nothing more."

"Then I shall go with you," he said in challenge.

"Excellent. But we need to leave right now."

"Get your charm," Miriam said.

"Tchah." The father waved a dismissive hand. "Anyone who trusts mumbled words over a piece of glass is a fool. I'll get my own protection." The dad lunged through another door in the kitchen and came back ten seconds later with a coat, an old rifle with a rusty bayonet attached, and a cricket bat. He held them both out to me. After hesitation, I took the rifle, figuring I would be better with a blade, any blade—and judging from the size of his shoulders, he could make a cricket bat into a lethal weapon.

Katrin and Miriam dashed up. Katrin was wearing a necklace, I noticed.

"Where?" the father asked me.

I turned to Tania. "We're not very far from the beekeeper's, right? Could we go there? We could see over the city."

No use in describing the next stressful few minutes of toiling and shoving our way up the steep mountainside, lanterns jiggling and jostling over our wrists. I tried not to look at those lanterns, but I kept getting distracted by the zings and glitters of cobalt blue, emerald green, sun-bright yellow, plus orange and purple and ruby as the lanterns and the crystals shot sparkles back and forth.

Twice we had to make a chain of hands, but we did it, and at last dashed through the holly arch onto the beekeepers' terrace. Their cottage was lit. Through the uncurtained windows we could see Margit busy in the tiny kitchen.

"Don't look at the lights," I warned belatedly.

The lights. I remembered Tania's voice from the day she'd first tested me with the prism. *Light from the Nasdrafus . . .*

Haru did a violent about-face, his small body stiff. I had an idea he was torn between the glory of responsibility and a deadly fear of failing, as he took his dad's hand.

The girls hid the lanterns behind them and backed up to keep their light from worrying at the edges of Haru's vision.

Above the eastern mountains, the thickening clouds faintly glowed with the promise of morning. I whispered to Tania, "Even though the clouds have hidden the eclipse, will it still have whatever effect it's supposed to?"

"I do not know," she whispered back. "It is one of the things we have yet to learn about."

As we spoke, Haru moved to the edge of the garden terrace and peered intently at the city below. Then he dropped his dad's hand, snatched off his glasses and wiped them on his pajama shirt under his coat. He replaced them and leaned forward, as if those extra few inches would afford a clearer vista.

I shifted my attention to the city barely emerging from darkness into three dimensions, studded by golden or silvery lights where there was electricity.

"They're walking," Haru said at last, unhappily. "The man-shaped shadows are walking."

"Are you sure you're not seeing what you want to see, son?" His dad's voice was gentle.

"There's too many of them." Haru's voice was high with tension. "They're *moving*."

A small sigh behind us, and Katrin whispered in a disgruntled voice to Theresa, "Why isn't it me? *I'd* know what to do."

I stepped up on Haru's other side and strained to see what he was seeing. Was that shadow on the street above the inn flickering? Maybe it was my eyes. "Can you tell where they're going?"

Haru wiped his glasses again, snorting through his nose as he jerked his head back and forth. His curly dark hair flopped over his ears like his dad's.

"There." A short, sturdy finger pointed . . . at Sobieski Square.

Theresa's practical voice echoed from earlier, *All the important people will be there.*

The Council building, right on Sobieski Square. Where all the important government leaders would be soon be meeting.

THIRTY-ONE

"I 'VE GOT TO WARN THEM," I said, and tossed the rifle to Tania. "Haru, you are awesome."

"Mam'zelle?" Theresa gasped, as Miriam cried, "You can't go alone in the dark!"

Two things at once. Nasdrafus, vampires . . . I smacked my hand over my eyes, and tried to clear my thoughts, but all I saw were the glittering lights—

Oh. "Tania," I exclaimed. "Our experiment. Let's try something right now. Hold your charms next to the lanterns."

Tania's eyes widened. She thrust Haru's lantern into her sister's free hand, and brought hers forward. Her charms were on a bracelet, so she held out the lantern with her wrist next to it, the biggest crystal dangling. It seemed to fill with light, twinkling and gleaming. Rays shot out, not behaving like the light we were used to, that is, the rays did not create a circle of light on nearby surfaces, or cast shadows, but they did form a nimbus around the charm.

"Vrajhus," Tania and I said together, as Miriam began to squee, "I see it! I see it!"

Katrin sighed. "It just looks like a crystal with a bit of reflection from the lantern flame. *Why* can't I see what you see? It's not fair." It was clear that her dad didn't see it either, but he was listening, his expression wary and puzzled.

I said to Katrin, "Maybe it functions like color blindness, I don't know. But here's what I think is going on. The sunlight caught in these crystals is interacting somehow with the candles in the lanterns, and I believe this keeps vampires at bay. We know that sunlight is poison to them. Spread the word, all right? Get everybody to put their charms and lights together, in every single shadowy place." Hearing an echo of Danilov's drawl as we waltzed, I added, "And take swords and hawthorn or yew stakes as protection. I've got to get to that Council building!"

"You should take a lantern," Tania called to me as I ducked through the holly arch.

I paused, peering over the steep street, down at the city below. It wasn't that far to the Council building, and I saw window lights glowing. I could zigzag between those. Fear prickled at the back of my neck, but stronger was my reluctance to lumber along with a clumsy lantern jiggling and banging against me—and probably going out.

"I'll be fine," I said, holding up my crystal necklace. "I'm faster without, and I will feel better if all of you keep those lanterns."

I ducked the rest of the way through before anyone could protest, and began sludging my way down the street as fast as I could, my legs sinking to the thigh at every step.

The streets at the north end of town were terraced into the mountain slope. Scanning ahead for shadows I couldn't see into, I plunged and skidded and a couple of times rolled downward, my crystal sparkling reassuringly. Much tougher to deal with was lumbering through snow. It seemed forever before I finally reached a cleared street. I oriented myself fast, discovering that I was somewhat north of Nat's neighborhood.

And then I heard something pacing me.

I ran forward a few steps and paused. Yes, those were definitely slushy foot falls, and I definitely had that crawling sensation I get when I'm being watched.

My charm sent rainbow patterns of glittering light in an aura around me. But every time I looked back, all I saw was Stygian darkness.

When I reached the open street, the footsteps were on both sides, and getting closer. That's when I heard the hisses and faint skreeling cries, like distant bats. *Sinister* bats.

I whirled—and there, etched against the plaster wall of a building, was a flickering shadow in vaguely human shape.

Ever stuck your finger in an electrical socket? That's what the zap through my nerves felt like.

That thing is a vampire.

I halted, staring. The shadow shifted and flickered, making it difficult to see. It was like trying to make out shapes at the bottom of a pool after everyone's stirred up the water, only in photographic image reverse—where you'd see light gleaming, you saw darkness, the facets making the shadow ripple and shift.

Didn't take a user's manual to figure that I was going to be surrounded pretty soon, and all I had was a glittering necklace for defense. At least it caught every slightest reflection from golden windows around me, strengthening the aura to a halo.

I looked around wildly, ready to bang on the door of the first lit house I could get to, then I heard the muffled, rhythmic thud of horse hooves in the snow.

And riding around the corner came a pair of Vigilzhi on horseback, armed with swords as well as pistols.

"Hey!" I yelled. "Here!" Argh—I'd yelled in English. I switched gears and called out in Dobreni, "I need aid!"

The guys were around my age. They wheeled their horses. I pounded up, my legs caked with snow to the knee. "Council building. Emergency!"

The one with curly dark hair and slanted eyes looked around warily as the fair-haired guy said, "Trouble?"

"Oh yes. Oh yes," I gabbled. "Vampires! They are all *over* the city."

Say that in L.A., and people will laugh—or look for someone with a camera trying for YouTube fame. In Dobrenica? They both scanned grimly, then the dark-haired one pulled his sword.

"Take me to the Council Building?" I asked.

"Where'd you get that crystal?" the dark-haired one asked. "It's alight."

"This is what the charms do," I said, "when vampires are around. And vampires don't like this light."

The other guy extended his gauntleted hand, I put my foot on top of his boot in the stirrup, and up I went. I had enough time to register that horses' backs are about fifteen yards off the ground before a nine point three on the Richter scale nearly sent me hurtling off the other side.

"Hold on," the guy said.

I flung my arms around his waist in a death-lock, and the horses began bucking and leaping, or that's what it felt like. My disjointed explanation of how the crystals worked turned into "Oog!" and "Argh!" as we jolted a thousand miles an hour down the road.

By the time I registered that no, we weren't going to be flung onto our heads, the animals slowed, and there was the parking lot behind the Council building. I scrambled gracelessly down, trying to hide how shaky my legs were.

"Thanks," I managed. "Tell anyone you see to put crystals to their lamps and hang them outside!" I said, and bolted for the Council building door without waiting for an answer.

I was mentally preparing my report for Alec or Dmitros or even Beka, who I figured wouldn't be kept away by mere broken ribs, when I yanked the door open, lunged into the lobby . . . and stopped dead.

"Hello Kim," said Tony.

My wits flapped out my ears as I stood there staring.

Standing in two tight groups behind him were the Council people. In the center of the first group was the duchess, her gaze glassy as she clutched an exquisite shawl around her fine mauve suit. Robert stood nearby, disgruntled as usual, wearing a bandage over one eye. Near him, hands in twin muffs, were his wife and Cerisette, looking confused.

The second group was made up of Honoré and the Danilovs, Beka, and her brother and grandfather. In their center stood Alec, immaculate as always, wearing a fine suit under a long camel overcoat.

And circling these two groups, pistols cocked and ready, stood Tony's mustachioed mountain riders, most in Russian-style belted coats and trousers stuffed into boots, some wearing furry conical caps.

As Tony strolled toward me, my distracted senses took in stray facts, like how the frigid lobby smelled of stale wine, old laundry, and vinegar-soaked cabbage, as though people had been camping out for days. Tony was the only one smiling. "Kim! A surprise, but you're most welcome."

Almost at the same moment, Cerisette shoved past Phaedra and said nastily, "Who invited *you?*" Her put-upon drawl was such a contrast to Tony's suavity that it would have been funny if the situation hadn't been so very unfunny.

The best answer I could give her was nothing, so I looked past her to Alec, and Beka right behind him, white with fury. "What's going on?"

Tony was still smiling, though he wasn't looking at me. "Why are you here, Kim?"

"I just—" I began.

"Danilov," Tony said. "Let's keep a pretense of friendliness, shall we? Step away from Alec. Kim, I beg pardon for interrupting."

"I have—" I tried again.

"But I detest pretense," Danilov retorted, a flush along his elegant cheekbones. And he added a pungent Russian curse.

Phaedra glared at Tony. "You wouldn't have got away with it if the Vigilzhi weren't stretched to the limits, guarding every house in the city, including *yours.*"

I was beginning to get the picture: as everyone, council members and privileged attendees, arrived for the Council meeting, they walked straight into Tony's trap.

Tony usually wins . . . who had said that?

Didn't matter. The important thing was, though it seemed that most of his cousins had turned against him, it looked like Tony's second try at hijacking a government had worked.

THIRTY-TWO

A LEC HAD GONE INTO heavy-duty Statthalter mode. "Your game, Tony. You scored. Have you thought out the consequences?"

Tony retorted with superficial ease, "I've thought out the consequences if you—"

Honoré muttered something. Whatever it was, Tony recognized it because his cheekbones reddened and his eyelids flashed up, betraying his own anger.

Tony said, "Will it sting less if you think of this as preventive intervention? It really was heroic, my boys getting here during that storm in order to hold the building." He tipped his head toward the neat line of sleeping bags and rucksacks stashed in front of the coat room, where a Vigilzhi guy stood with his hands up, a pair of goons at either side. "I apologize for the cold in here. It's a mystery how the furnace could go out midway through the first still night in three days, but we were too preoccupied to deal with it—"

"Hey!" I stepped forward. Furious as I was with Tony, I had to get my news out, but just as I spoke, the doors at the far end of the lobby rattled, then someone pounded loudly. That was followed by a sharp whistle.

The guard at that end was curly-haired Niklos, lounging with one foot propped against the wall behind him, a twelve-gauge shotgun loose under his arm, barrel down. He straightened up. "Vigilzhi, probably from the perimeter check."

"Let him join the party." Tony made an expansive gesture. "We're nearly ready to begin—missing only one guest."

"Listen," I said, but Tony had turned to Beka, who stood with both arms folded across her middle.

"Would you like to sit down, Beka?" he asked in a low voice.

"I can stand up until your firing squad gets here," she said.

"Beka!" Tony protested.

"What else are you going to do with us?" she retorted fiercely. "Stick us in the dungeon up at the Eyrie? Because you know the *second* any of us get free—"

Her words were drowned by the door opening for the Vigilzhi. Everyone stared as Commander Trasyemova dashed in, tall and handsome in full uniform, complete to shiny boots and saber at his side. He was supporting another Vigilzhi.

Up came the pistols. The commander ignored them and spoke across the lobby to Alec. "Geslin started the perimeter patrol to relieve the night guards. He and his partner were attacked."

"Beniamin?" Alec asked sharply.

"Covered me so I could report." Geslin spoke up from the commander's side, his voice hoarse with pain. "There were three or four . . . things coming at him when I ran." He swallowed, staggered, and Trasyemova propped him up. "We found both night guards dead. Drained of blood."

A moment of stunned silence. I'd never get a better cue.

"*Excuse* me! I've been *trying* to tell you something!" I faced Alec, because one's instinct is always to talk to the one you trust and who trusts you, because then you have only to speak, without having to explain and justify every word. "We got up to watch the eclipse. Saw shadows. Hundreds of them, converging here. *This* building. *Right now.*"

"That's impossible," the duchess stated, as if her disbelief could undo fact.

The old nun on the Council said, "There has been no outbreak for generations."

"The eighteenth century," the Prime Minister said.

"If your people never saw them," Alec said to Tony, "Then they must have come in through the basement."

"They couldn't have," Niklos began, startled out of his Casual Tough Guy cool. "We've been camped here for two and a half days." His gesture took in the lobby where we all stood.

Tony and Niklos exchanged a look. "Did you do a sweep through the basement today?" Tony asked.

"No—we stayed put so the outside guards wouldn't detect us."

"There's your explanation for the furnace having gone out," Danilov drawled as he sauntered a couple steps toward the wall. "They probably came in through the old fire tunnel. Did you think to check that?"

"Nobody checks the old fire tunnel," Niklos protested. "Not even the Vigilzhi."

"Not since the Soviets left," another guy said. "You can't even find the other end, it's got to be buried under snow—"

"*They* obviously found it!" Niklos retorted.

Everyone began talking at once, Cerisette shrill as she clutched at the commander's tunic. A few paces away, the duchess said, "What is that, *chérie?* What is he talking about now?"

"Sisi, how many of those pills did you swallow?" Robert's wife asked, for once not whining.

Alec had drifted a few steps, his expression mild. His brows rose, and he looked past the Council members to Tony. "Will you get the Council to safety?"

"Me?" Tony put his hand on his chest in a mocking gesture. "How?"

"*Nunquam est fidelis potente societas,*" Honoré intoned, regarding Tony with half-shut eyes. He stood, as if by accident, directly under one of the crossed pairs of weapons mounted on the lobby wall, his hands crossed over the head of the cane he leaned on.

Alec turned to face the Prime Minister. Beka, her older brother Shimon, and their grandfather had been whispering. Baron Ridotski gave Alec a short nod.

"Grandfather, the keys?" Shimon murmured.

"There's a tunnel," Alec said to Tony, who laughed, one hand flashing up in the fencer's acknowledgment of a hit.

"Why didn't I guess that?" Tony asked as he watched Beka's brother unlock the door on the other side of the coat room. "And why didn't I find that?"

"Because you never looked behind the old files," Beka said. "Honest work of any kind being much too dull to examine."

As Tony's smile tightened, Beka turned her back on him. The door that had been unlocked opened on a dark space. Beka stepped in. A scritching sound, a flare, and a lantern lit, throwing yellowish light over shelves stuffed with files and old ledgers.

She was joined by Shimon, who did something that I couldn't see, and out swung a hidden door behind a bookcase stuffed with moldering files, opening onto a narrow passage that sent cold, dank air flowing in.

"Better make sure they haven't discovered this tunnel, too," Danilov said.

"I'll go," said Shimon.

He reached for one of the mounted swords. The two of Tony's guys nearest him stirred, but Tony didn't say anything, so the guys didn't react as Shimon pulled a sword off the wall. It had not been bolted down. So there was an unspoken truce, at least long enough to escape the vampires. But Tony's guys still held all the weapons.

"If you've got a diamond or a crystal," I said to Shimon, "hold them near your light."

Shimon gave me a short nod, then tucked the sword under his arm. He yanked his shirt cuff below the hem of his coat. The diamond cufflink caught the light brilliantly, glittering through the full range of colors as he took sword in one hand and lantern in the other, then started down the tunnel.

A door slammed from behind and above us.

Everyone jumped, then did an about-face, toward the shadowy stairway to the Council Chamber. Gilles and the Punk Brothers came thundering down the stairs and leaped to the floor. Instead of camera equipment their hands held weapons—and their punk hair was gone, their clothes were normal, except for the blood splashes. A couple of them were limping.

"We were going to investigate the basement, but they came up the back stairwell from below. They just swarmed the Council chamber." Gilles jerked his thumb over his shoulder. "We started a fire before we fell back. That should hold them a minute or two. I suggest we get out." He pointed toward the doors.

Commander Trasyemova said curtly, "They'll have the building surrounded now." He started for the stairway to the chamber, pumping the shotgun to chamber a round.

Tony beckoned to a couple of his people and they, too, advanced on the Council stairs, weapons up.

Gilles said in an authoritative voice quite different from the demented *artiste* I'd found so annoying, "Tony, those pistols are worthless. You have to do serious damage to slow them."

Alec pulled down one of the swords from the pair mounted on the wall just behind his head. Danilov got the second sword and whooshed the blade through the air, immaculate blond head at a critical angle. "You've kept them sharp," he said in approval to the commander, eliciting a quick grin.

The commander sent an ironic look Tony's way, and I realized how very close we'd come to bloody battle between Tony's guys and Danilov, Alec, Honoré, and Phaedra—each of whom during the talk had drifted unnoticed to position themselves directly next to a pair of crossed swords.

Hm. From the deeply sardonic expression on Tony's face as he watched Phaedra take down a saber and hand it to Honoré, maybe they hadn't been so unnoticed after all.

Phaedra gave Tony a sour, challenging glare and grabbed a rapier for herself.

"Time to scarper," Tony said, indicating the tunnel Shimon had opened. He turned a narrow glance Alec's way. "We shall resume our conversation later. Escort duty first." He motioned to his guys, who were closing in around the Council. "Politely," he added with a mordant smile.

Gilles stepped up next to Tony and spoke urgently in an undertone as the Prime Minster led the line of old folks down into the tunnel. At the end of the line, the bishop, recognizable by his white cassock and

black shoulder cape, offered the duchess his arm. Their air was deliberate and grave, as if they were being escorted and not herded.

Gilles then stopped Honoré, held a short, whispered exchange, and
jerked his head to summon the Punk Posse. They went over to join
Danilov and Phaedra.

I sensed Tony tracking me as I ran toward the second rapier of the
set that Phaedra had chosen, my crystal winking and gleaming as it
swung. I closed my hand around the sword hilt, lifted the blade—

And that's when the lights went out.

THIRTY-THREE

"**M**OVE! MOVE! MOVE!" I heard someone urge the Council and the older attendees, who fumbled their way down the secret tunnel.

Left in the lobby were Niklos and a few of Tony's guys, the commander's few, the Danilovs, Alec, and me.

From the top of the stairs to the Council Chamber came the beating light of the fire that the Punk Posse had set, which the vampires had obviously gotten around. Fire could burn them, like us, but it took sunlight to poison them.

"Form a line," Alec said to the disparate clumps of defenders. "Don't let any get between you. Now!" he shouted—and led the defensive line.

Ever listened to the soundtrack of a fight with the visuals off? The grunts, smacks, clatters, clangs, and expletives were punctuated by that same hissing and squeaking that I'd heard on my run down the hill. It jolted through me with a thousand volts of fear.

"Come on . . . you can do better than that . . ." Alec muttered to his attackers, every couple of words punctuated by clangs and grunts and weird screeling laughs or screams. Even the vampires' voices were distorted.

The others obviously saw something, but I couldn't see anything but kaleidoscopic splinters of color and Stygian anti-color.

"Kim! On your right," Danilov sang out.

I swung my sword, and it thumped against something. I could not see what I'd hit, but I felt cloth brush my side as I leaped away, and I caught a faint, musty, sweet-sick smell that shocked my nerves. Okay, so maybe the Sight or my GhostVision prevented me from seeing the vampires as well as I could see the others. That meant we needed—

"Fire!" I shouted. "We need fire—no! We need *light!*"

I abandoned fencing finesse and swung the rapier in a vorpal *voom*. The tip caught on something, and ripped free. I kept swinging blindly, the hissing and chittering surrounding me falling back slightly.

From the direction of the file storage closet that held the secret tunnel came some thuds and clatters and a clank, then a triumphant voice, "This ought to sort that lot."

I glanced that way as Dmitros Trasyemova stepped out of the closet and slung one of the lanterns into the lobby bowling-ball style. The glass smashed, sending a long runnel of blue fire down the lobby as the burning oil scattered.

The shadows—normal as well as vampiric—leaped back from the fire. I bent so that my crystal swung over the nearest tongues of flame. The swinging stone sent a scattering of twinkling lights shivering in arcs across the walls.

Phaedra held down her hand so that her enormous diamond ring caught the light. Rainbow patterns of light fluoresced up her arm, radiating out, like the sun on water, over the upper walls and ceiling. The spectrum of flickering light causing a wailing shriek and a susurrus of rustles and hisses from the vampires.

Everyone on our side sprang to join Phaedra and me, aiming diamonds and crystals so that they caught the light and sent out rainbow shards. From the way the vampires withdrew, making those weird noises, the colored light acted on them like poison beams.

Then silence fell. A charged, icy chill, the smell of rot and mustiness indicated the vampires were still there in the shadows.

Dmitros Trasyemova leaped over the line of flames and beckoned to Phaedra and me. "We've got our strategy now. Help guard the Council." He tipped his head toward the tunnel.

"Tony's pinched the lot of them. I won't be part of that," Phaedra stated.

The commander said urgently, "Look, Tony doesn't know any more than you do what you'll find at the far end of the tunnel. Also, you might see a chance to . . . diffuse the situation. I don't think Tony would attack you as readily as he would me."

Phaedra's frown eased. "Right." She turned to me. "Coming?"

I hesitated. I could hear the vampires prowling back and forth just out of the reach of the ruddy glow that limned Alec as he prowled back and forth, as if daring them to attack again.

When I looked his way, he glanced toward me. Our gazes met, and Alec leaped over the border created by Dmitros's oil fire and approached. His mouth curved in tenderness as he slid his free hand around my cheek, the cobalt ring glittering on his hand. It actually seemed to shoot sparks as he said, "Back Phaedra and Beka, would you? I don't think you see these things, right?" So he'd spared a glance for my wild swinging.

"True enough."

"And we don't know what might happen at the other end."

I said, "I'd rather fight by your side."

He kissed me—I kissed him back—we broke apart, and I ducked into the closet in time to catch an ugly glance from Cerisette, who'd come back through the tunnel for some reason. "Alec, the Prime Minister . . ." she began.

Before she could say anything more, the vampires let out another shrieking cry and rushed in at the attack, flinging cushions and things gathered from the Council chamber in an effort to extinguish the flames.

"Shut the door, Kim!" Beka yelled, pushing Cerisette inside the tunnel again. Phaedra followed, her sword at the ready.

My heart hammered as I leaped inside the storage closet and pulled the lobby door shut. I hated leaving Alec out in that horrible lobby, but my presence wasn't going to add anything to the defense, not until I figure out how to see the vamps.

The pain as that door shut was like my heart had been ripped out by the roots and left behind with Alec. But that's how I felt as I ducked through the back door of the musty closet, and stepped down into the tunnel. It was low—I had to duck my head—and it smelled dank. Beka and Phaedra slammed the inner door, Beka with a glance of sympathy, and Phaedra with one brow cocked skeptically. Then we hustled down the tunnel to catch up with the others.

With a massive attempt at normalcy that probably wouldn't fool a newborn kitten, I asked Beka, "What's the story behind this place?"

"There are escape tunnels all over the city. My ancestors had them put in. Beginning in the later 1600s, after the terrible pogroms in the Ukraine."

"Did people use them during the war?"

"Oh yes. Many people lived in the northside tunnels for the duration."

"One of my great-uncles among 'em." Phaedra whipped her rapier point back and forth in front of her, whish, slash. "He was an Orthodox priest."

"Tunnels, I get. Vampires, I don't," I admitted, looking behind me for the fiftieth time in two minutes. No, Alec was not there. "Why are those things all over the place all of a sudden?"

"No one knows," Phaedra said, saluting me with her sword, as she swung the lantern with her other hand. "This is the first time in my life I've ever seen them anywhere but at the Eyrie."

Beka winced. "Please don't do that." She paused, taking a shaky breath. Sweat beaded on her forehead. "This is my first day out of bed, and I was dizzy before you began to jiggle that lantern."

Phaedra started to say something, took a good look at Beka, and shrugged. She carried the lantern with a steadier hand as we descended the last of the stairs and set out at a swift walk in order to catch up with Cerisette, barely visible ahead, her head bowed so she wouldn't clock herself on the low, rough ceiling. Phaedra and I had to duck as well. Only Beka could walk upright, but just barely.

I don't know how long we walked. Time underground, without the sun as guide, alters perception. We went down and down, took a bend to the right, then up and up again. My neck began to ache.

We caught up as the slower old folks reached the end. Shimon led the way, pausing at the top to shoulder open a door that looked like it hadn't been budged for decades.

Tony stood at the head of the line just behind Shimon, sword gripped in one hand. He jerked his chin at Phaedra, who sidestepped around the Council and pushed past her relatives up the stairs, rapier at the ready. I followed in her wake, my palm sweaty as I gripped my sword.

The door opened into brightness—footfalls rustled—and an ancient monk appeared, slippers on his feet. He didn't seem to see the guys with the pistols, or maybe he didn't care.

He gave a cackle, then said in a loud, quavering voice, "That door hasn't opened in seventy years."

The bishop stepped past Tony and Phaedra, and gently drew the old guy aside.

A few of the mustachioed tough guys streamed around the bishop and the monk to do a sweep inspection of the area beyond. When they returned, shaking their heads, Tony stepped out of the way, and the rest of us filed up the narrow stairs past Phaedra and me.

Tony reached to help Honoré, who hissed at each step. "*Nunquam est fidelis potente societas.* What was that?" Tony murmured.

"You don't remember your Latin?" Honoré responded, his voice breathy with effort as he shrugged off Tony's hand.

"You will recall I was chucked out of the two schools that tried to stuff Latin into my head."

"That was Phaedrus." Robert's deep voice rumbled with irony, from behind Honoré. "'Alliance with the powerful is never safe.'"

"Here's another, from Seneca," Honoré's heavy eyelids flickered. "*Ars prima regni est posse invidiam pati.*"

And Robert translated smugly, "The first art of kings is the power to suffer hatred."

"Aimed at me?" Tony said mockingly. "Honoré, you wound me. When I went to all that trouble to get Gilles to dig up Inspector Clouseau and company."

"Who?" Honoré asked.

"My inspectors disguised as punks," Tony began.

"Bugger off, Anton," Robert interrupted, glaring at Tony. "Make yourself useful, for once and find a chair for your mother."

The single-file line had passed into a large, sunny room by then. A couple of sturdy older men from the Council helped the duchess, who seemed unsteady on her feet. Cerisette and her mother walked together, the pair so skinny they reminded me of storks as their heads turned sharply.

The old monk stood there next to the door, wearing a simple, rope-tied white habit. As the last of the train passed, Phaedra and I bringing up the caboose, the ancient monk nodded several times, then asked in a rusty, loud voice, "Shall we sound the alarm, then?"

The bishop, a stout white-haired man about Milo's age, paused by the Prime Minister, addressing him in the low voice of a lifetime of familiarity. "Shimon. How many will know that pattern of bell rings as the alarm about vampires?"

"I believe the children are told in school when taught our history, but I cannot answer for how many retain the knowledge."

The bishop turned to the old monk, who leaned toward him, repeating "Eh, eh?" He cupped one hand around a huge, hairy ear.

The bishop patiently repeated, "It. Is. Time. To. Sound. The. Shadow. Ones. Alarm," pronouncing each word distinctly.

"Ah! Ah!" The old monk cackled. "The alarm against the Shadow Ones has not been rung since 1722." He looked old enough to have personally pulled the bell rope.

The Prime Minister winced as he tottered to a chair. There was an enormous bruise on the side of his head, and another on his jaw. I hated to think what the rest of him looked like.

The bishop held out his hands to the group, Council and Tony's guys alike. "Please make yourselves comfortable. I will see about breakfast."

Tony said, "I'll send someone to accompany you. As guard. You never know what might be waiting."

The bishop gave a short, dignified nod, but returned no answer as he vanished beyond a bookshelf full of centuries-old, hand-bound books. One of Tony's guys followed him, weapon ready, but pointed downward.

The ancient monk shoved the tunnel door shut. It fitted into a wood-paneled wall, and a tapestry depicting St. Dominic fell into place over it.

"I was not expecting this tunnel to come up in monk-space," I muttered as I sank down on the floor next to the tapestry-concealed door, my back against the wall and the rapier at my side. One of the pistol guys wandered by, checking the walls—for more passages I guess—as others scanned out the row of windows, which were blue with the coming daylight. The meeting had been set for eight, just before sunrise this far north. Though it seemed like hours since my arrival, it had been no more than twenty minutes. Twenty very intense minutes.

Phaedra gave a sniff of amusement, then blew out her lantern and began to prowl the room, ignoring Tony's goons.

All the chairs and benches had been claimed by the old folks. Beka winced as she slowly lowered herself down next to me. "During the early Soviet years, most of the religious orders had to take up residence down there, just like during the war."

I said, "All of a sudden a bunch of what I'd thought hazy or innocuous references in Milo's diary have just decoded. Wow. Milo was flashing all around the city, using these tunnels to vanish and reappear, like some kind of superhero."

"He evaded pursuit by using them, yes." Beka gently rubbed her middle over her broken ribs, and winced. "My grandfather showed him the first of the tunnels when Milo was chosen to inherit the throne."

"So all the kings knew?"

"Not all," Beka began, falling silent when Cerisette stalked up to me, and glared down from the empyrean height of self-righteousness.

"I hope you realize," Cerisette said in a venomous tone, "that you can make a fool of yourself all you want but Alec will never stoop to your level. Except as a—"

DONG-dong . . . DONG-dong . . . DONG-dong . . .

Saved by the bell? But I didn't have to hear it to know what she was going to say. A couple of people jumped as the biggest of the cathedral bells began the deliberate toll, in patterns of three.

"Cerisette, this is not the time. Or the place," Beka said as soon as human voices could be heard.

"Shut up, Beka."

During that pleasant exchange, I did a full tai chi breath, consciously trying not to take on the poisonous anger that Cerisette so obviously wanted to share. I said, "'Stoop to my level.' That's a weird way to look at a relationship, or do you mean that what you really want is to be Queen of Dobrenica?" When her face tightened preparatory to an answer, I said quickly, "Never mind. I don't want to hear it. In fact, the worst thing I can think of is to see the world the way you do. But yeah, if I do hook up with Alec, I am completely down with the fact that I will never be more than a mistress, whatever our legal status, because he's married for life to Dobrenica."

"*Ripou*," Cerisette muttered under her breath, then stalked back to her mother's side, where she got the sympathy she wanted, judging from the twin looks of loathing fired my way.

Phaedra sauntered up, her expression cynical. "How much of that do you really believe?"

"Check back in ten hours. Or ten years. Right now I'm making it up as I go along."

Phaedra's fine brows shot up. She gave me a rakish smile, and an unwilling laugh as she flipped up a hand in a fencer's acknowledgement of a hit, then wandered away.

A door opened. Everyone stiffened. But it was only the bishop, to invite everybody to the refectory for breakfast. This was a rectangular room whose line of windows overlooked a secluded garden, now covered with snow. The continuous toll of the vampire alarm was not quite as loud here.

A couple of the white-cassocked Dominicans brought in several loaves of fresh bread, a tureen of *mammaglia*, honey, butter, and scrambled eggs. They set it out for us to serve ourselves, and then departed.

The Prime Minister conducted the duchess to the head of the main table, where she picked up her coffee in both hands, as though the little cup was too heavy to hold. The Council settled themselves along the middle of the table below the von Mecklundburgs. I sat at the end, as far away from the von M.s as I could get, and Beka sank down across from me.

The guards had spread around the perimeter of the room. After a quick glance, Tony made an airy gesture of invitation. "Help yourselves, mates. "

And so our guards swooped down on the platters of food, then decamped to the second table, where they laid their weapons beside their plates and dug in. A distinct atmosphere of vintage laundry plus unwashed male emanated from that side of the room.

I shut them out, and sat there staring at the piece of bread I'd put on my plate. There was nothing wrong with the bread, but I couldn't dispel that picture of Alec, leading the line to attack those horrible *things*.

I looked up at Beka, who was only drinking coffee, as were the rest of her family. I remembered that they keep kosher.

"Do the charms make the vampires difficult to see, or is it their powers?" I asked, touching my necklace.

Beka seemed relieved to have her thoughts interrupted. "I don't know," she said. "Both, maybe?"

"If the charms make us perceive them as confusing splinters of light, is it possible that's how the charms work to protect us—make us into smears of confusing light for the vampires?"

"The prevailing theory is—"

A noise at the outer door brought Tony's guards up and alert. The door opened, and Alec walked in, his coat gaping where steel had sliced it, his hair hanging down in his eyes, smears of drying blood on his ruined suit and on his jaw.

He ignored Tony's guards. "The vampires went to ground as soon as the sun appeared," he said.

"So you didn't destroy them?" Phaedra asked, fierce in her disappointment.

Alec said, "Too many of them, and too difficult to see for some of us, but we think they had trouble seeing us as well. When we set fire to the entire building, and put our charms at every corner, they began their retreat."

Alec looked my way and smiled. "Trasyemova just received a report that Mam'zelle Dsaret gave out an order for everyone in the city to hang charms and lanterns, lamps, candles, every kind of light possible. Before dawn, people were putting them outside the houses, along walls, and in the street on the benches and statues and fountains."

I blushed. "Uh, actually, I asked Tania to spread the word."

Beka flashed a quick smile my way. "Tania was smart. An order from Tania Waleska would be ignored, but not one from the heroic Mademoiselle Dsaret."

"Murray," I muttered under my breath, the old poser prickles making my ears itch. "My last name is Murray."

Alec lifted a hand toward the window. "As you can see, we now have daylight. We have to assume that the vampires will reappear as soon as the sun sets, so Trasyemova is coming up with some kind of strategy while the Vigilzhi lock down the city."

"Was anyone hurt?" the duchess asked. The coffee seemed to have woken her up. "Where is Morvil? Where is Gilles? What was that about Interpol?"

"Gilles brought Interpol agents, Mother," Tony said. "Since everyone's here but Gilles and his people, we might get to the purpose of this gathering. Before we do, I suggest that everyone place their deflections on the table. Honoré, if you would serve as conscience?"

"If you wished to hear the truth, you might have begun by telling it," Beka said.

The silence was . . . really silent. Tony glanced her way, that telltale flush along his cheekbones, but he didn't answer. Instead, he reached up and unhooked his diamond earring and then, at a leisurely pace, divested himself of diamond cufflinks. These he set on the table before him.

He looked around, waiting. The Prime Minister gravely removed a diamond tie clip and laid it gently next to his coffee cup. One by one the others followed suit, some shooting nasty glances at Tony, or Alec, or both.

I took off my necklace, and Beka slowly removed her charm bracelet.

Alec laid his cufflinks down and twisted the cobalt ring off, which had tiny diamonds inset. Then he lifted his hands; his wedding band glinted. He said, "Why, and how, have so many vampires turned up in Riev for the first time in hundreds of years?"

Tony waved that aside. "Where is my sister?"

"Anton!" the duchess snapped, eyes wide in horror.

"*Ubi innocens damnatur, pars patriae exsultat,*" Honoré said in that detached voice.

"If you are going to so rudely interrupt, young man," the duchess said to Honoré, "then you may speak intelligibly."

"I was intelligible, Tante Sisi," Honoré said, completely without heat. "It's from the mime Syrus, once a slave. Roughly translated, it means, *When an innocent man is convicted, part of his homeland is exiled.*"

Alec gazed over Honoré's head at Tony. "So that's what this is about?" A tip of his head toward Tony's guards. "To get me to tell the truth?"

Tony held out his hands. "It seems to be working."

Alec's expression matched Tony's. "Will it comfort or annoy you to be told that I've never lied about what happened that day?"

We waited as everyone swiveled to look at Honoré. "Alec believes what he says," Honoré said in a goading tone, gazing coldly at his cousin Tony.

Alec went on. "As for your question about Ruli's whereabouts. We can begin with where she isn't."

"The sarcophagus," Tony said.

Alec said, "I take it this is not news to you?"

"No." Tony waited as the listeners checked the living lie detector. Honoré sat there like stone.

Alec went on, "You have neglected to share your discovery with your family."

"And that is why I am angry," Honoré said.

The duchess sat back, her face blanched. "Aurelia?" she whispered.

Tony repeated softly, "So where is my sister?"

"What are you talking about?" Cerisette's voice went shrill. "She's dead. And buried! We were all there at her funeral!"

"She is not in that sarcophagus," Tony said, watching Alec. "At my request, Gilles brought a couple of Interpol agents, like I said. One from

Lyon, the other a forensic specialist. Under the guise of filming, they have been investigating everyone and everything they could. Including the crypt in the cathedral. They discovered last week that the bones in Ruli's sarcophagus belong to a male between the ages of 25 and 35."

Alec said, "I found out myself four days ago. There's a strong possibility that those are the remains of Marzio di Peretti. Whom Magda Stos swore she drove to the border. So my question for you is, where is Magda Stos?"

Tony flicked a glance Honoré's way, then sat back down, frowning.

The duchess raised her head. Tears gleamed along her eyelids. She said angrily to Alec, "You were drunk. You drove her off a cliff. You admitted you were drunk!"

"I said the last thing I remembered was that toast, after our agreement that she would go to Paris." Alec said to Tony, "I now believe I was drugged. It would explain why I only remember toasting, and the next thing I knew I was sitting on that mountainside with Ruli's purse. Since Magda brought those drinks, I have some questions for her about that, as well."

"He's lying," the countess's voice trembled with fury. She glared at Honoré. "He's lying, and you're covering for him!"

"He believes it is true," Honoré said. "Every word."

The duchess stiffened when Robert cursed violently, then growled, "I believe *I* was drugged on the twenty-first. Perhaps that is why the vampires are here."

"What?" Tony asked.

"But you told us—" Phaedra began.

"I insist that this discussion be held privately," the duchess stated, sending accusing glances at the rest of the Council.

The Night of the Thorn. She doesn't want it outed, I thought.

"A private discussion can be arranged." The Prime Minister's voice was mild. He pushed himself to his feet with difficulty and tottered past two of the gunmen to address the bishop in a low voice.

And I will bet anything that the Prime Minister has known about the Night of the Thorn all along. Tania had hinted that the Salfmattas knew at least something.

Then the bishop said, "There is an alcove through that door, used by our community for family visits. Please make use of it."

The von Mecklundburgs marched off, leaving their breakfasts half-eaten. Honoré got to his feet to follow, leaning heavily on his cane.

I hesitated, then caught Alec's eye. He twitched his head toward the door, and I got up, making an internal wager on who would try to throw me out first, Cerisette or her mother. Of course there was always the duchess. Why not go for a threefer, I thought as I followed him.

Niklos started to fall in behind me, but Tony waved him back. "Watch the door," he murmured. "If Trasyemova shows up in force, at least give me warning."

The room we entered was a Dobreni-style parlor with cushioned wooden chairs, a low table, and nothing on the walls but a crucifix and a very ancient painting, the saints' haloes glinting gold in the rising light from the single window.

As soon as the door was shut, Cerisette glared my way, ready to start in, but Phaedra cut her off at the pass. "I already told her about the Night of the Thorn. She is related, after all. And so far, *she* hasn't tried to poison anyone, shoot anyone, or run anyone off a road." She pointed at Alec. "As for him, it's about time someone tells some truth, after all the rumors you've been spreading about him being a murderer."

The duchess lifted her head regally. "Magda Stos has always been a truthful servant."

Phaedra rolled her eyes.

"Where is she now?" Alec asked. "Up at the castle?"

Tony lifted his hands. "I thought she was on the train. Did it even get into Riev?"

"Late last night," Alec said. "She wasn't either of the two passengers."

Robert said begrudgingly, "No one has heard from her since she called from Paris and said she was setting out to return."

The countess dismissed that with a quick gesture. "Perhaps she's taken a detour. Gone to Marseilles to visit her married sister. It is the holidays, is it not?"

"Then she would have informed me." The duchess pressed trembling fingers to her forehead. "My head aches." She turned to Robert's wife. "Chérie, are you certain you do not have my pills?"

Tony's voice cut through. "Uncle Robert? What happened on the twenty-first? You swore the treaty was made."

At this semi-public mention of their secret, most of the von Mecklundburgs looked angry or ill at ease. I thought, *Wow, you guys sure don't want anyone to know that you have anything to do with vampires.*

"I thought it was." Robert scowled at Tony, then fingered the bandage over his eye. "But nothing went right, and I was so busy with the opera house . . ."

His own family began stirring at his self-exculpation, which he obviously saw. So he said in an angry voice, "Ruli was supposed to go with us. As future queen." His gaze sidled away from Alec, then he straightened up and said in a more forceful voice, "But on Monday the twentieth, Percy and I waited for her. She was supposed to meet us at the house at one. We waited until three. She didn't come, and no one answered the palace telephone in the Statthalter suite. You know how long it takes to get up to the Eyrie. We had to leave. We got there only a half hour before sunset. We ate dinner and retired early, because we knew we had to rise early to be at . . ." His gaze flickered our way. "We had to be in place before the eclipse began."

The duchess stated, "Ruli did not meet you because Alexander drove her off a cliff."

Everyone ignored that. Tony said to his uncle, "Go on."

Robert crossed his massive arms. "We did not drink. We retired early, as I say. I was up betimes, but Percy was asleep, and I couldn't waken him. Jakov and Boris prepared breakfast. Put my coffee in a thermos, all as always. I carried the . . . implements myself." Another of those looks. "And walked to the site. It was dark, but I knew They were there. As always. Everything as always, though I had begun to feel ill. Groggy. I drank the entire thermos in an effort to wake up."

Robert paused, looked away, then down at his hands. "I don't actually remember anything past taking the Thorn in hand, ready for use. I woke up with the Rose in my lap, encrusted with blood, and a cut on my wrist. I had a headache. I remembered having a headache the first time I had to do the ritual, and I fainted that time, too. I assumed I had carried out the treaty as always, but since I do not remember, I believe that I was drugged. Perhaps it was in the thermos, somehow."

He glanced around, obviously uncomfortable to be exposing a family secret. "Percy was awake when I returned to the ground floor of the castle. He also had a headache. Thought he was coming down sick. Believing that I had done what must be done, I drove us down to the city, and he went straight to the opera house. I arrived at Mecklundburg House to the news that Ysvorod had driven Ruli off a cliff the day before. The staff told me that Dr. Kandras had taken care of retrieving Ruli. I saw no purpose in trying to identify her charred body, so I called Ysvorod, and he agreed to pay Kandras for making the arrangements."

Robert gave Alec a scowling nod, then turned to Tony. "I called Sisi in Paris. And that is everything I know." But in an irritated burst he added, "If I was drugged, I do not understand. Jakov or Boris have never done such a thing in their very long lives."

Tony waved that off. "My guess is that it was someone else."

"Who?" Robert asked loudly. "The place was empty—colder than hell. Everyone had gone home for the holiday."

I suspect everyone there was thinking the same thing that I was: the Eyrie, an enormous castle built in four massive layers and honeycombed with secret passages, would be easy to hide in for anyone who knew the place.

Robert muttered, "I tell you, no one was there. Even the ghosts were gone."

The word *ghosts* did something to my brain. Maybe it was a reminder, or who knows, but a second after he said that, the room was filled with them. Not only this room—the walls were gone, the space entirely different. I was surrounded by barely perceptible ghosts, ephemeral as skeins of smoke caught in sunlight, as their mouths moved in unison. At first I thought they were monks, or maybe it was monks at first, but they blurred and shifted as I gazed down the centuries at people of all ages, chanting in unison. Was that a *nigun* I heard?

Unmoored by vertiginous perceptive layers, I grabbed at the table with both hands to steady myself.

"Kim? Are you all right?" Alec's voice came dimly through the waves of vertigo.

I shut my eyes, willed them away, then peeked . . . and discovered the von Mecklundburgs giving me various versions of the hairy eyeball.

Alec looked intently into my face. "Kim?"

"Ghosts." I swept my hands through the air, causing a couple of people to look around warily. Cerisette was sneaky about it, as if she didn't want to be caught. Another time I would have laughed. "A bazillion of them. Chanting.'"

Grandfather Armandros popped back.

I was too exasperated for laughter, as I pointed at Grandfather Armandros, standing there behind Tony, the eternal cigarette burning.

Esplumoir, he said.

I lifted my voice. "I hate ghosts because they don't make any sense. Esplumoir? Why not—"

"What?" Tony jerked his head up, and for a moment he and our grandfather were curiously blended in the same space.

I rubbed my eyes. When I looked again, Grandfather Armandros was gone. "Esplumoir," I said. "He said it once before. He said it now. You didn't see him? You didn't feel him? He was standing right where you are. You were stepping on his toes."

Tony was staring at me.

"It has a meaning outside of a nearly forgotten medieval text?" I asked.

Tony said slowly, "Its origin is some swill about Merlin, but it's used here as a metaphor for the Dsaret crown." His head turned. "That's what you told me, Mother."

"That's what I was told when I was growing up." The duchess pressed thin, tense fingers to her forehead. "Oh, why did I run out of my pills? My head aches—I cannot think." But she made an effort—you could see it. "Before he died, the king had long given up hope that Lily would return, and he relented. Because of the war. He told my mother a secret that only the king or queen was supposed to know, because Milo was out of reach, leading the defense. My mother told my father." Now she rubbed her eyes. "Her governess, who became mine, heard a part of it from beyond the door. She did not hear everything but when I turned eighteen, she told me what she heard. It was around the same time that Great-Aunt Danilov told me about the Night of the Thorn." The duchess lifted her chin and said to me, "This is what the old king told my mother: that Esplumoir is the Dsaret crown. If these words have another meaning, you should ask your grandmother. If she is who she says she is, she should know."

Ignoring the spite, I said, "She left before her father could tell her. Remember, she left Dobrenica suddenly. And she was just sixteen."

Honoré spoke up. "Here are some facts of which none of you seem to be aware. 'Esplumoir' is the name given to a tapestry in the old Dsaret chapel, right below us now, in the crypt. You've all seen it, though it is so aged it's nearly black."

Alec said, "Would that be the one depicting a kind of mountain, with some kind of shapes in the sky?"

"Those are falcons." Honoré flicked his fingers out briefly. "Like those on the Dsaret device, which became our flag. The interesting part is the Latin tag in gold thread. It is unfortunately so tarnished and old it is barely visible. Some of the words have vanished. But I can tell you approximately what it says."

"I know what it says," Alec said. "Milo told me that tapestry was a representation of the Augustinian city of God and the city of the temporal realm. He thought it was a metaphor for the gateway to heaven, for the Latin says, *Guard the portal well.*"

Honoré muttered something in ancient Greek, then lifted his head. "I believe what we might be talking about is the Portal to the Nasdrafus."

Alec's lips parted. "If it really exists . . ."

". . . it would almost have to be on Dsaret Mountain." Honoré studied each person in the room. "This is the danger of oral traditions. We each seem to have heard a piece of the truth. If we put together everything we've been taught, there is a common thread, which is also supported in so many ancient legends and songs. I've been told by a Salfpatra that they once thought that this portal was a standing archway on the northwest face of Dsaret Mountain. But journeys there to test it have proved fruitless."

I knew that archway. It was next to the hunting lodge called Sedania . . . now owned by the von Mecklundburgs.

"Back to the problem at hand." Alec turned to Tony. "So if your Night of the Thorn is not performed, that is an invitation for vampires to come and go freely?"

"No!" the von Mecklundburgs all said.

Honoré opened his hand in a gesture of appeal. "The ritual was a yearly renewal of a covenant binding those already here from killing anyone, and in turn we promise not to hunt them. We've been taught that covenants are very important to them. Promises, all the legends insist, have power in the Nasdrafus."

"So how many vampires did you see when you observed this ritual?" Alec asked.

"Never more than half a dozen." The duchess shuddered. "In the earliest days, when I was young, it was merely the two."

"*The* two?" I repeated. "You know them by name?"

The duchess gave me a deer-in-the-headlights stare, and Tony said smoothly, "It's a figure of speech. We are not on social terms with those things. My mother is right about the main point, which is that until last year, there were never more than five or six. Usually fewer."

"So where did these hundreds come from?" Alec asked. "*Something* happened. This is the first time the city has been invaded in over two hundred years."

No one had an answer.

Esplumoir, Grandfather Armandros said, this time from the middle of the table, the buttons on his open army jacket glowing crimson through the bowl of jam.

I jumped. "Stop that! Go away unless you mean to help!"

Everyone was staring again.

"Will someone shut *the hero* up?" Cerisette whispered fiercely. "She will *never* get enough attention."

She spoke with such nuclear-powered sarcasm my instinct was to flinch, except I knew that I'd never called myself a hero. Others had.

So why not own it?

I smiled at Cerisette. "The hero is finished here." I headed for the door.

A quick step, and Tony was right behind me, Alec following. Behind us, the remaining von Mecklundburgs, from the sound of rising voices, fell into a full-on quarrel, everyone accusing everyone else of lying or keeping secrets, Phaedra backing Honoré.

I pushed the door open to the refectory, and the three of us walked in. A glance back at Beka, who looked up from where she still sat with her family; at a gesture from Alec, she got up and joined us.

We went through the far door to the library, Tony again waving his guys off. The library was empty except for the old deaf monk, working away at a table with an honest-to-history quill pen.

Tony turned to me. "Kim. Did you get anything else from Grandfather's shade?"

I wanted to tell him to go stuff himself, because I was still mad about the trap. But Alec and Beka were waiting for me to answer, so I said to them, "Just 'Esplumoir.' Listen: When we were up on the beekeeper's terrace, Harulam saw those shadow things converging on the Council Building."

"I believe we know that," Tony retorted pleasantly.

"No, you're not thinking," I shot back. "It was deliberate. A plan."

"They knew about the hearing." Tony shrugged. "So did everyone in the city."

Beka said, "Let's leave the vampires for a moment, and get back to the purpose of the hearing. If you didn't do anything to your sister (and you haven't convinced me yet that you didn't) and Alec didn't do anything to his wife then . . . who did? Who attacked Honoré three times? Who iced my driveway? Who put Marzio in that crashed auto?"

Tony muttered, "Someone is sitting somewhere laughing their sodding ass off at us faffing about chasing one another."

Alec said, "I intend to find out who. But first priority is the threat to the city. We need to figure out where these vampires have come from and shut off their access. I can promise you that Milo never knew about any portal."

Tony leaned against the wall. With the anger gone, he looked tired. "The Thorn ritual mentions a portal, but we thought it was poetic embellishment. One thing for certain, there is no portal anywhere near the Eyrie. The only possibility is that old arch at Sedania, but I have my doubts. People have been running through it all my life without anything happening. If there is a portal somewhere else, I wouldn't know how to find it."

"I think Kim could," Beka said.

"Me?"

Beka brought her chin down. "That ghost seems to follow you around. If you take your prism and concentrate on Armandros von Mecklundburg, perhaps he will show you the way to this Esplumoir."

Tony gave me a distracted glance, then said to Beka, "If it can be found. Is there a way to close it?"

Beka's brows arched. "If there is a portal to the Nasdrafus, everybody in the country knows how to close it."

Alec looked remote. Tony grinned. "Except me."

"Don't you see it?" Beka asked. "You've been singing 'Xanpia's Wreath' since you were little."

"That? It's a song about saints and good behavior." Tony made a dismissive gesture.

"Some of it has changed over the centuries, but there's evidence it's far older, perhaps even older than the Roman Song of the Dawn. It's simple, which makes it easy to remember, and some say that the magic is in the melody as well as the words. Anyway, the heart really is a metaphor. Try substituting the word 'door.'"

"Sing?" Tony repeated skeptically. "We can't just recite it?"

"This is new for me, too." Beka spread her hands. "But everything we hear in every story corroborates how music has power."

She then fell silent, and after a flickering glance at me, studied her hands intently as if something was written on them. Tony watched her just as intently. Alec lifted his head, and took in the view through the long window, though there was nothing to see but the white snow, and the fine gray and gold and white stone of the cathedral as he absently smoothed his hair back. There was a streak of mud or soot or moss along his cheekbone, and a smear of blood on his chin. I had never seen him grubby before. It was unexpectedly endearing.

He didn't look my way . . . because he was waiting. He obviously didn't want to pressure me or exert undue influence.

I sighed. "How do I get to Sedania?"

Tony gave me the old crooked smile. "I'll take you myself."

I pushed out my hands in *No way!*

Alec said, "No need. I'll talk to Dmitros. We should be able to find someone to take Kim up there. You'll want to guard your family."

"My family is already under sufficient guard," Tony returned dryly. "Not just your watchdogs, but Gilles is going to cover us as well, once he talks to Kilber. Is there a preliminary report on how many people those things attacked on their way to the inner city?"

"Surprisingly, no humans. Three missing cows, and several pigs."

Tony said, "Bad sign."

"Yes," Alec agreed.

There was that vibe between them again. It wasn't angry, more wary. To break the impasse, I said, "Why are those low numbers a bad thing?"

Tony gave me a distracted glance. "Because it suggests that someone, somewhere, made a covenant with them, which was to be fulfilled by the attack on the Council." He made a slight, mocking bow toward Alec. "Whether Uncle Robert finished the treaty or not on the twenty-first—and I suspect he lost his bloody nerve, and it wasn't mysterious drugs at all— it will need sorting again. I don't know if the old plonker who customarily comes to the Eyrie is at the top of the vampire hierarchy or even if they *have* a hierarchy. I don't even know if any of them will deign to show up other than on the longest night of the year. But if I can bring them to treaty I will."

Beka said, "Why does it have to be you?" Her tone was odd. There were currents beneath her words that I could not perceive; perhaps of other, private conversations between them.

Tony's tone also hid currents: "Until this year, I've been handling that ritual ever since I turned sixteen." He spoke directly to Alec. "I'll go to Sedania, you handle the vampires already here." His expression was an angry, pained one, and I'd seen it before. Oh yes, right after our sword fight in London, which ended with his caustic words about Ruli's coat: *Keep it. She'll never wear it again.*

One of his motivations for this coup was to find out the truth about his sister, and he seemed to accept that Alec was not involved in her disappearance—or he wouldn't have been standing there, making plans with us. And if we chose to believe Tony (I was sure Alec would ask Gilles some hard questions the second this conversation was over) he had been running an investigation parallel to ours.

Beka's gaze shifted away. So she was determined not to speak. She left the decision to me.

Alec's silence made it clear that he, too, was leaving the decision to me.

Tony turned a questioning gaze my way, his attitude reminding me of the night of the gala, when he stood there and held out his hands for the tango, like he would stand there for an eternity until he got what he wanted.

I didn't care what he wanted. It had very little to do with what any of us wanted and more about what was needed. So though I'd sworn I would never get into any vehicle with him, ever again, things had changed. "When do we leave?" I asked.

Tony's eyebrows lifted. "Niklos will take you back to the inn, Kim. In case any of them are still around. Shall we meet there in an hour?"

THIRTY-FOUR

A MINUTE LATER we'd split off into two pairs. As Tony spoke in an urgent undertone to Beka, punctuated by an occasional *No* from her, Alec faced me. I could feel the apology coming.

"Don't," I said. "As soon as I heard 'Dsaret,' I knew I had been picked out to be the Special Snowflake here. I wish I was better prepped, however, so I wouldn't feel so flaky."

I won a brief smile at the stupid pun, but then he was serious again. "All right. I won't apologize for you being dragged into this."

"I wasn't dragged," I said. "I'm part of it."

His gaze left my face, his lashes shadowing the marks under his eyes, his expression somber.

It didn't take any arcane powers to understand how badly he wanted to be going with me, and I was feeling exactly the same way. The unspoken truce I'd made with Tony at the gala was in force again—tentatively—but I *so* wanted to face this vampire thing with Alec, side by side. Then again, what I'd said to Cerisette was true—he was married to Dobrenica. And yes, Phaedra, I know what that means: Though he wants to be with me, the city and all its uncertainties and dangers are his responsibility.

I gazed into his steady blue eyes, seeing my own emotions mirrored back—two steps, and we locked together in a brief, fierce kiss. No words.

I can't say I felt better when I walked out of there, but the memory of that kiss on my lips made it easier to get my feet moving.

An hour later, I sat beside Tony in a cut down, built-for-speed sleigh, drawn by four pairs of reindeer.

I had the rapier I'd taken from the Council building, which I put in a sword rack on the sleigh, next to Tony's arsenal. Figures there were sword racks. At least I didn't have to wear it. I'd performed a quick experiment in my room, thrusting it pirate-style through my belt. My first step nearly tripped me, so I'd wasted another twenty minutes on various methods, coming to the conclusion that wearing swords as part of your everyday couture is *really annoying*.

As I filled Tania in on everything that had happened ("Did Haru and his dad get back okay?" "Oh, yes. Though they didn't have charms, we did, and they threw a lot of light."), I emptied out my backpack and put in some overnight stuff, with the prism safely housed in the center.

The necklace, I wore.

On the way out, the entire family was gathered to watch me go.

Theresa and both her friends were there, with eager faces. Tania had reverted to Wednesday Addams, worried and clearly wanting to help. She whispered to me that they were making up new lanterns and building the charms directly into the cut glass, which would be readied for sunset.

As Tony and I rode together in silence, I saw that the sky was layered in thin clouds reminiscent of the beach at low tide. I was learning to distinguish between different values of cold. I'd always assumed that the air was coldest during snow, but actually that's not true—the temperature when it's very clear and dry can plunge far below zero until the light seems strange, as if from another world altogether.

When we got to the north road, just past the beekeeper's, from behind trees and hedgerows swooped a bunch of sleighs. They drew up. Each sleigh was filled with several coated and hatted people more or less our age. Not all were men.

Tony stood and lifted his voice. "We will assume that the mountains are full of hungry, pissed-off vampires. Lock and load."

From under blankets, behind seats, and underfoot came shotguns and rifles, and for a short time there was no sound but the clicks and clacks of weapons being loaded. Then swords were tested for ease of grabbing.

When they were all ready, Tony lifted a hand. The drivers clucked or whistled to their animals. The sleighs circled us in formation, except for two riding ahead, far apart, as scouts. The rifles had come out, mostly shotguns and old carbines—the simpler the better. They also had swords.

The terrain appeared altogether different from summer. Distinctive rock formations were snow-shrouded, tree-lines altered by the lack of foliage, smaller waterways white-blanketed, or frozen in a hundred subtle variations of blue, gray, and brown. The white sunlight lit frozen ferns as if they were fragile glass, and turned the few remaining leaves to silver foil.

For a long time the only sound was the muffled thud of hooves and the sluicing of the rails through the snow. The animals kept a steady pace, the rise gradual, with many downward slopes to give the teams a breather. Sometimes one sled would glide near us, then it would swerve this way around a rock or that way to avoid a gnarled tree, while Tony guided his team the other way, so that they all had as wide a field of vision as possible. I hunkered down into my coat and scarf, my hat pulled down well over my ears.

Short on sleep, I drifted into a doze and woke with a snort when the rhythm of movement changed. Rubbing my gritty eyes, I took in the sky, which was covered with white cloud, the quality of the light like watery milk. The sun would set soon, though it couldn't have been much past three. That, I hadn't quite gotten used to yet.

Tony said with satisfaction, "The animals know they're near home."

"Home?" I repeated, surprised. I'd gained the impression during summer that Sedania was next thing to a museum—empty except when the duchess visited for an occasional weekend.

The sled whirred around a rocky outcropping, mica glinting coldly in those fading rays, as we glided between rows of denuded trees, framed by a lacework of familiar conifers.

We passed the last of them and there, sitting austerely in its plateau of snow, was the hunting lodge known as Sedania: a square limestone building whose tall windows had amaranth blossoms carved over them and corbels carved in overlapping hawthorn leaves at each corner.

The reindeer slowed as we pulled around to the back, which was partly screened from the road and the garden by thick hedges. There was a long annex, part garage, part barn, with limestone cottages scattered beyond.

As all the sleds came to a stop, half a dozen teenage boys and girls ran out under the direction of an old man, who carried two lanterns ready to be lit.

"Nobody out after sunset," Tony said. "Make sure the animals are locked up. Lights posted around the barns."

"With charms," I said.

"As she says." Tony gave a nod my way.

The kids hustled to the harnesses in pairs as the people in our cortège of sleighs leapt down. A few of the kids sent anxious looks at the blue shadows gathering under snow-loaded firs as Tony's guys grabbed up baggage and weapons, and trooped inside.

Two more servants appeared to unload our sled, which included an old-fashioned hamper that looked like it had been insulated.

"Arch is over this way," Tony said. "Let's make it fast, shall we? Dark comes quickly."

I slung my backpack over my shoulder and trudged after him through the shin-level snow. My jeans had dried out at the Dominicans', but now they were getting wet again. I made a mental note to tuck them inside my boots, no matter how dorky that might look.

We slogged through the garden until we reached a row of bumps on the snow. The stone wall! I found a good square stone and swung my backpack down so that I could root out my prism.

With that in hand, I worked my way carefully past the wiry tangle of thin young birch and other trees, skeletal in their wintry bareness. I stood a few yards from the stone archway that I'd seen intermittently in dreams. It had once been part of a building. The stones outside the arch, laid in the familiar cross-hatch pattern, were jagged and mossy. Whatever had destroyed the building had happened centuries before.

The tangle of rose branches and brambles winding around this door, or archway, or portal, were also barren of leaves, affording a clear sight of the carvings worked into the framing stone, blurred by time and weather. A Roman cross surmounting a sun, blossoms of amaranth, hawthorn, and rowan were nearly indistinguishable. Here and there were traces of early Gothic lettering, too blurred by time and weather to read.

In the summer, my first glimpse through this doorway had given me faces, inhuman except for two strange eyes—not human, or not completely human.

This time, what did I see? Nothing. Only the snowy slope beyond. Why was this time different? Last time there had been music, played by that talented boy, Misha. Wondering if he'd been making magic—and if it was deliberate or accidental—I cradled the prism in my hands, holding it before the archway.

As I tipped it slowly, I concentrated fiercely on *Esplumoir, Esplumoir, Esplumoir*.

That sense of falling pulled at my mind. I shut my eyes—and toppled headfirst into the snow.

One, two steps, and Tony hauled me to my feet.

"I'm fine. I'm fine. Let me try that again."

"What happened? From here it looked like someone gave you a push."

"It . . ." I gave up trying to find the words, braced myself, and glared down into the prism. My snowy mitten trembled, and my eyes blurred. I did relaxation breathing and began again. This time I got a sense of tunnel, or distance, or corridor, but not right in front of me. It pulled me to one side.

When I tried to force my concentration into the tunnel, that creepy inward freefall made my head spin. I shut my eyes, and my hands dropped in defeat. "This archway is not the portal to Esplumoir, or at least, we're not going to be able to use it. The prism keeps pulling me somewhere that way," I said, flapping a hand. "The Esplumoir has to be there."

"South," Tony said. "At the heart of Dsaret Mountain. I thought this was too easy. We'll get an early start in the morning and find it tomorrow." He looked around. "The sun is just vanishing. We'd better get inside. No telling how many of those damn things are coming through each night."

My neck tightened. "Let's go."

We started toward the house, me blinking to get rid of the blur and slight dizziness as I struggled to keep up with his long strides. He flicked a glance my way. "How much do you trust that prism?"

I fought a sudden yawn, so huge it felt like my jaw would unhinge. "I don't know. If I see something distinct I think I can trust it's real. For certain definitions of 'real.'"

"So what have you seen that you trust?"

I blew out a cloud of vapor as I considered my answer. Tired as I was, I knew the question was not idle. "We went to the crash site. I saw the Daimler just before it went over the cliff. Before you waste your breath saying I saw what I wanted to, Beka and Phaedra tested me as much as they could."

"Beka," he breathed. "She never said anything at all about this."

"Yes, well. I saw Alec asleep in the back, and a woman whose description Phaedra and Beka said fit Magda Stos. They recognized the way I described her chin. They called her *Barbe*." Another yawn hit me on the last word.

"You met Magda last summer."

"No, I didn't. But if you're expecting me to prove a negative, we can drop this subject right now." He lifted a hand in a gesture that I interpreted as *go on, I won't argue*. "In the front seat was that Marzio guy, asleep. Like Alec. I mean, out cold, mouth hanging open."

"Magda was driving, with Alec in the back seat?" Tony's expression had gone grim in the gathering shadows. "How do you know when it was? Oh. Marzio in the car—in Riev only a day, according what Gilles found out from the Vigilzhi."

The last light was fading, and already the stars were popping out, twinkling like diamonds. Several of Tony's guys appeared, each carrying a lantern, and my worry eased. To hide how scared I'd been, I tipped my head back and looked at the sky. "'The types and symbols of eternity,'" I quoted, but got no flash of recognition, only a glance of inquiry. "From Wordsworth's 'Simplon Pass.'" I pointed upward. "These mountains remind me of it."

"I've probably heard it," Tony admitted. "Alec and Honoré used to spout poetry by the yard until the rest of us threatened to chuck them down one of their poetic passes."

"What have you got against poetry?"

"Nothing, as long as I don't have to listen to it when I'm on the watch for Russians, or wild animals. Or it's being declaimed in that bloody moo that schoolboys seem to think appropriate for verse."

An unexpected spurt of sympathy made me laugh. It seemed disloyal to imagine Alec reciting poetry badly, but who is any good at fifteen? He certainly wasn't bad at it now—hoo-ee, *far* from it—but I was not going to discuss Alec with Tony.

We'd reached the door, walking past two guys with shotguns aimed out into the dark as someone hung up lanterns, each with a crystal inside. Tiny glints of rainbow lights twinkled.

Then the door was shut and barred, and I let out a sigh of relief.

We left our wraps in the coat room off the small hall. It smelled like wet wool in there. I leaned against the wall to steady myself. That session with the prism, on top of the long and incredible day, had tired me so much I felt as if I was floating gently at sea as I blinked around in the brightness of electrical light.

People came and went in the fine eighteenth century rooms with a purpose and familiarity that suggested—along with the stacks of ammunition, weapons, horse and reindeer gear, and other stuff—that this place had a whole lot more inhabitants than I'd been led to believe during summer.

"Through that door is the ladies." Tony pointed. "Meet you out here." He pushed a door open through which came men's voices.

There was hot water, I was glad to find. I felt somewhat less sticky and a little more awake after I'd washed my hands and face. The wakefulness came with a measure of uneasiness. Outside, who knew how many vampires there were. And inside? What kind of danger might I be in?

Tony was waiting in the hall, head bent as a familiar figure in a black dress grinned up at him, her prosthetic eye staring beyond him into space. "I shall see to supper myself. Good boy, you brought us one of your Paris surprises!"

"I know how you like your Paris desserts, Nonni."

Madam Coriesçu cackled, rubbed her hands, and wandered off, ducking around guys standing in groups, some armed.

"This is a headquarters," I said.

Tony grinned.

"A military headquarters."

"Think of it as a field camp, if that helps."

"It doesn't matter what I think. What matters are what kind of games you're playing."

"Games?"

I was feeling that stomach-sinking sense of *uh-oh*.

Tony gave me a pained glance. "Our problems with the mining consortium have not conveniently gone away because we're having a spot of trouble with vampires and mystery conspiracies. In fact, the consortiums' continued interest in Dobrenica's mines and minerals in the face of Alec's truly heroic negotiations, as well as our gently diminished quotas, is disturbing. Do they see through Alec's policy of starving their profits? Or do they see something else they want here? But we are not going to solve that now."

The mines—I'd forgotten the mines. Yet these were a huge part of Dobrenica's economy. But as he said, that problem was for later. "I can't help it," I began, "if every new surprise brings my mind right back to the conspiracy. By which I mean *your* conspiracy."

Tony's pained glance this time was far less humorous. "You really think I'd whack my own cousin?"

I was ready to retort *I think you'd whack your grandmother to gain power*, except I knew it wasn't true. Not quite.

Then he said with the old derision, "Perhaps I should rephrase. You really think if I were to whack Cousin Honoré, I'd be that incompetent?"

"I thought that fire at his home was pretty efficient."

"It was efficient at destroying the house. Unless someone wanted Honoré only to suffer, then it was terribly *in*efficient. I think he was supposed to die, and the fire was to destroy the evidence. Only he wasn't hit hard enough."

"So you thought it was me," I said indignantly. "Well, since I thought it was you, I guess we're even on that one."

He laughed as a bell clanged somewhere, echoing slightly. A genial roar of men's voices preceded a stampede.

"This way." Tony opened a tall door carved with wheat sheaves around its edges, and turned an old-fashioned electrical knob on a nearby wall.

Light revealed a small room that I recognized immediately. As my gaze traveled over the darkened windows, the conservatory-grown flowers in pretty vases against walls of pale eggshell blue, and the painted pattern of rowan, holly, and hawthorn a foot or two under the ceiling, I was thrown back to the emotions of summer. How isolated I had felt—an emotion that has its comforts, for there is no responsibility with isolation. Now, as I approached one of the pretty little cabriole-legged chairs and sat down to place my hands on the cozy round table set for two, I felt the weight of my chosen obligations. And loyalties.

And dangers.

"This is the royal breakfast room," I said inanely.

Tony sat across from me. "You and I will get a better dinner than the others. We're to have New Year's leftovers, more than half of our guests having not been able to get to us on New Year's Day."

Nonni herself appeared, wearing an apron of white linen aged to a shade of ivory, the edging a pattern of lace not seen in over a century. With a twitch of shoulder and extra tweaks and pats, she set out dishes of gilt porcelain, edged with deep blues and greens and crimson, the central figures mythological in the neoclassic mode.

She was obviously very proud of these dishes; she'd even decanted the wine into a beautiful porcelain pot and poured it as a last gesture.

In my exhausted, bemused state her hand blurred, and I gazed at another hand, belonging to a much younger arm, charming in its shape. The shade of skin the warm brown associated with the equatorial regions of most of the world. I caught a brief glimpse of a young woman, then I blinked, and there was Nonni putting the decanter on the tray.

"*Bon appetit,*" she said, and left.

Tony lifted his goblet in toast, to which I responded. I took the tiniest sip, but even that much alcohol on top of an empty stomach was a mistake, or maybe I was going to see the ghosts anyway, because this time the vision was longer.

They were about my age: the woman with long-lashed, slanting black eyes and a rakish smile dimpled on one side; the man blond and handsome, his eyes honey-brown. They wore robes of silk and lace, their manner intimate, as morning sunlight streamed from the windows onto the very same set of dishes.

The golden light rippled . . .

A hand gripped my shoulder.

I jumped, and discovered I'd nearly fallen off my chair. I closed my eyes against the sickening swim-jolt of dizziness until it faded, then I cautiously opened my eyes.

Tony moved back to his chair. "I thought you were going to pass out." He frowned into his wine glass. "If it's been doctored, the poison or drug is odorless."

"I think it's just me. Maybe I'd better eat," I said, and to forestall questions, added, "Tell me about these dishes. I know it's an old set."

"It's actually a breakfast service. That decanter is the coffee urn. It was sent by some queen or other, when a mutual ancestor of ours married the crown prince, right after the Dobreni brush with Napoleon. I wonder why Nonni dug it out? I've only seen this particular set once, when I was scouting out something else."

Nonni reappeared, wheeling an elegant cart. With a flourish she uncovered dishes and set them out, then she left.

The dizziness had abated enough to let me help myself to langoustines wrapped in phyllo with mousseline and caviar—a fancy dish I recognized because I'd had it once. "This is delicious," I said grateful both for the food and for an easy subject. "But where did your cook possibly get lobster?"

"My chef?" Tony's lips parted, then he gave a slight shrug. "She brought baskets and boxes of fresh ingredients from Paris. Oversaw the unloading herself, and then put her own locks on the pantry doors." He took another bite. "Though I've had this dish three times since New Year's, it's still good, which is why I brought the last of it up here in the hamper. Anyway, my mother hid all the good porcelain after she asked for this house as a wedding gift. Jakov told me once that Mother was afraid that Milo would remember these old plates and demand their return, as they were a Dsaret heirloom."

"You told me once that this is her lair. When was she here last?"

He grinned conspiratorially. "Maybe five years ago. But she does think of it as hers."

So yeah, he hadn't quite lied. He'd just left crucial information out—as usual. I made a private bet that Alec still thought the duchess came up here to visit "her" vacation house, and that he had no idea that Tony used it as a military outpost.

Or maybe he knew.

I considered that, as we worked through the amazing food. *Reblochon* cheese, *risotto* with *épeautre* accompanied by *girolles* mushrooms, and to remind us that we were not in a five star restaurant, it was all sopped up with plain bread rolls, but they were hot and fresh.

There was little conversation. I was too tired, and too wary of vampires and ghosts and Tony. Too worried about what was happening with Alec, and with Riev, once the sun had set.

"What are you thinking about so solemnly?" Tony asked, raising his wine goblet.

It caught the light, a ruby gleam, and there was the couple again. Ghosts or a glimpse of the past? This time they were silvery, hand in hand. It was the first time I'd ever seen two ghosts together like that. They were not looking at me, but gazing through the south window.

I shut my eyes, determined not to see them. When I opened my eyes, they were gone.

"I'm thinking about how delicious the dinner is," I said, retreating to the safety of food. "I owe it to your chef to savor each bite."

He gave me an odd smile, leaned toward me—then sat back as Nonni came in with the dessert borne triumphantly in a beautiful soup tureen that didn't quite match the breakfast service but had to be two hundred years old—and carried on a heavy-looking solid silver tray, engraved with falcons and other martial symbols of the baroque period.

With the air of a magician she served out *Poires Belle-Hélène*.

The first bite was heavenly. Nonni beamed as I exclaimed, "Delicious!"

Cackling, she bore off the dinner dishes. "Coffee soon," she said. "Coffee soon."

I scarcely heard her. I was too engrossed with the pear dish. Flavor rolled across my tongue to the edges as I savored the undertones of lemon zest and vanilla bean, with which the pears had been poached. The chocolate sauce—the thin almond slivers—the crème Chantilly all brought me back to our battered kitchen table in Santa Monica.

I took another bite. Oh yes. I knew every ingredient. In fact, I could name them, and how much, and the order in which they were added.

I laid my spoon down with absorbing care, as if the slightest motion would cause it to explode. Or the plate. Or me.

This was not weird times, or ghost-vision. This was reality, and all my old anger flared up, hot and bright.

Tony watched me over his wine glass.

"A funny thing," I said. "Though I grew up in a dinky house, and carried my lunch to school in a Disney lunch pail like all the other girls, all my life I've had blue ribbon desserts."

Tony set down the glass.

"After I turned nine, the food I carried was usually five-star French cuisine. Because my mom was sent to Cordon Bleu training by her hotshot Hollywood catering service so she could work on other things besides desserts. She fed us her homework. Dishes like that dinner. Which

in a Russian folk melody, then ended in laughter and a scattering of applause. Tony opened the door onto a warm, lit room, painted in pale yellow, with white scrollwork in arabesques around the ceiling and pilasters. On the side walls were enlightenment-era paintings, and opposite the windows enormous oval mirrors framed with golden scrollwork.

"Misha likes an audience when he practices," Tony said.

The kid had obviously been waiting. He beamed at me, polished his clarinet on his patch-kneed trousers with an absent gesture that seemed more habitual than purposeful, then he raised the clarinet and began to play.

It was like a concert except the listeners sat on the floor, wearing hunting boots and knives at their belts. Niklos lounged in the second window seat as he took apart and cleaned a rifle. The boy began Maurice Ravel's *Pavanne*—and the room began to fill with people.

I was seated on a velvet-covered hassock tucked up against a pilaster. From this vantage it was easier to watch Misha in one of the mirrors. It was amazing that this boy's red, puffed cheeks and stubby fingers were able to produce such heart-rending music. Was there magic in his magic? So intent was my tired focus, I paid no attention to the gathering crowd except to appreciate how quiet they were . . .

Until three barefoot kids stood hand-in-hand in front of the dark window, gazing raptly. Misha faltered. He glanced up, almost eye to eye with a shaggy-haired boy in a ragged, homespun tunic, then he played on.

I could see Misha through all three.

I sat upright and peered around the pilaster. Sure enough, Misha was playing alone. Yet I would swear he'd seen those ghosts.

I turned back to the mirror, and there they were, reflected in the window glass, through Misha.

They were so still that at first I thought the blurring of their outlines no more than the ghostly vapor that Tania had talked about, until I noticed how very shaggy the blond boy was. His hair had thickened to a wild ruff, his hairline arcing down to his nose. His lengthening nose. The backs of his hands ruffled up into fur, and when I glanced back to his face, a jolt ran along my nerves when I saw a wolf's head atop his sloping shoulders.

The boy turned my way, his chatoyant eyes glowing a feral red as he gazed straight at me in the mirror. To his side the smaller boy and the girl had also changed, one into a lynx and the other into a Shepherd dog.

Both looked my way. As the song trilled toward its ending the three gave powerful leaps and bounds directly through the wall to the south, and vanished.

Misha finished, glanced thoughtfully at the wall, then shook his instrument as the listeners clapped and hailed him.

Did *anyone* see that? I took a look, but no one seemed alarmed, surprised, upset. Misha was alone in the center of the room. I did not want to call attention to myself any more than I wanted to interrupt him, so I counseled myself in patience as he performed an arrangement by Debussy that shot me right back to my childhood, dancing as my grandmother played piano. But the memory visit was brief, because my mind was caught in the now. I watched carefully, but the ghosts did not reappear in window, mirror, or in the room.

When the song finished, once again everyone applauded, though there were fewer in the room. Misha began taking his instrument apart to put it away, and as the others got up to go, falling into conversation in a way that suggested that they were accustomed to these practices, I walked up to the boy.

"Did you like it, Mam'zelle?" he asked.

I gave him the compliments he deserved—though it was a struggle to find superlatives powerful enough—then I stepped a little closer and said in a low voice, "Those ghosts. You see them, right?"

"Fyadar?" he asked, and my nerves fired.

"That's Fyadar?" I exclaimed, biting down the *I thought he was just a legend.* My grandmother had told me stories about Fyadar and his child companions when I was small. In fact, it was those half-remembered stories that had prompted my quest to find her relatives, when she sank into the depression that nearly became a coma, the spring before.

And Theresa had shared the forbidden comic books that several generations of Dobreni kids had made during the long decades of occupation.

Fyadar was real?

Misha shrugged. "That's what I call him, when he talks. They don't always talk. But they like my music," he said, flashing a grin. "They come most often when I am alone and play on the hillside near the arch." He pointed. "But nobody believed me. You are the first grownup to see them." He looked enquiringly at me.

"I saw them in the window glass, reflected by the mirror," I said. "They turned into animals and went through the wall that way."

He turned his head to glance at the south wall and gave a short nod. "Usually they go up into the mountain, and sometimes down toward the city. That was very strange." He fought a yawn, his eyes tearing.

"We will be up early," Tony said. "Time for everyone to get their rest. Thank you, Misha. As always, it was excellent."

The boy grabbed up his battered case and scampered off, leaving Tony and me alone.

He stood in the doorway, his coat slung over his shoulder. His clothes were as rumpled as mine, his boots scuffed with a layer of mud on the uppers, his hair tousled, and golden whiskers glinted along his jaw line. "What did you see?"

"Ghost children. They turned into animals and ran south."

"He's talked about ghosts ever since he began using words. We thought he was . . ." Tony touched his head as I followed him down the hall to another stairway, this one leading up to the attic. "Sometimes that goes with talents like his."

"He's completely sane," I said. "No, check that. He's as sane as I am. However sane that might be."

"No argument here. Not after the past few days," Tony said as we reached the top of the attic stairs.

From the rumble of voices at the other end of the long hall, it was clear there was a dorm there, but we didn't turn that way. A sharp right and Tony flicked on the light in a small room with a single window, a bed, and a trunk. It had its own bathroom.

Tony shut the door with a backward thrust, then slung the coat across the trunk. "I don't like sleeping in the museum," he said, turning his thumb below.

"This is your room," I said.

"Yes."

I looked from the coat on the trunk to the window, with the faint glimmer of lights far below in the valley, to the bed. The bed. Up at Tony.

"Do I go or stay?" he asked.

And there it was again, the tingle of attraction. It had gotten past my guard in the doorway of the music room without my notice, or I hadn't wanted to notice, and here we were, and my heart thrummed.

The truth is, sexual attraction is about as solid as a bubble. Which is fine if it goes both ways, because two can live quite happily in that magic bubble. But thinking it's love just because it's strong, or you want it to be . . . well, I knew what love was. Even with my nerves responding to Tony's lazy smile, his reflective gaze, my thoughts returned to Alec, and I could see him patrolling the city streets though he had to be exactly as tired as the rest of us. Guarding Dobrenica. Maybe thinking of me.

"Worried about your rep?" Tony held out his hands. "Everyone in the valley probably thinks we're in the sack right now."

"My rep that your family has already done its best to smear?" I retorted, turning back to him. "All I care about is my own self-respect. Because fun as it would probably be—you're as good a kisser as you are a dancer—you don't respect me any more than I respect you."

"I'm beginning to. And I can't believe you don't respect me."

"I respect your skills. But you? I don't even know you, Duke Karl-Anton von Mecklundburg. I am beginning to wonder if anyone does. I've taken plenty of heat for my lies last summer, but I've been trying to make up for them. You? You seem to exist in a web of lies, half-truths, and misdirections. Like it's all a game, and here you are, but I wonder if it's not about me at all. Just some testosterone antler-dance game with Alec. No. That I can't respect."

Tony had made no step toward me, nor I toward him, but I couldn't look away from those slanted black eyes.

And he knew it. "Deny you feel it."

My mouth had gone dry. "Of course I feel it. And I'm not afraid, either, if that's your next smart remark. I'm sure sex with you would be like a roller coaster without brakes, but like the roller coaster, it has to end, and it's the messiness of the ending I want to avoid. That includes conversations with two people I do respect."

He looked away, and it became easier to breathe. "Sociopaths among narcissists. That's what . . . someone called me and my family recently. What a rep I've got," he mourned.

"And you've earned every bit of it," I stated, betting myself a couple million dollars and a castle or two that his "someone" was Beka. Then I looked at his face, the tell-tale flush, and made a discovery.

"It was!" I exclaimed. "It was Beka—and you care! I can insult you all day long (and I enjoy every second of it) but when *she* does, you care." When he didn't answer, I kicked the trunk. "Yet here you are, putting moves on me! Wow, that is so . . ." I whooshed out my breath while I tried to get my head around just how much I'd managed to miss. "Okay, I'll let that drop. Except for just one thing, considering where we are standing right now, and that is, she *totally* has my sympathy."

"Right, then." Tony took a step toward me, but just to pick up his coat again. "We'll take off at sunup." A casual wave, and he was gone.

I collapsed on top of the bed—his bed—with all my clothes on, folded my arms across my chest, and waited for the nightmares.

THIRTY-SIX

TANIA HAD TOLD ME that Grandfather Armandros (and others) were always with me. "With" I had discovered, is a tricky word when it comes to ghosts. It's not quite like they'd become detachable shadows, it's more like there's ease of access and difficulty of access.

This sank in the next day, when we set out just as the sun topped the northeast peak, spilling weak, milky light down into the valley, touching pale blue on the tiny rooftops of the city far below. It was too far to see how the city had fared during the long night. From a distance it looked peaceful, but that could be deceptive.

The sleigh riders were quiet, weapons ready as we set out.

Tony acted as if our last conversation had never happened, which was a good reality check for me—I was braced for rudeness, coldness, a second-verse-same-as-the-first, but zip. In fact, it was so zip, I strongly suspected that, far from smoldering over his rejection in proper Byronic form, he'd had plenty of offers of comfort or company. But then he'd never been much of a Byronic hero—or villain.

I heaved a private sigh of relief and got the prism out of my pocket. It was time to put my Special Snowflake power to work.

Sedania lay on the lower slope of the Dsaretsenberg, or the Dsaret Mountain. It was the biggest of all the Dobreni mountains. Not the highest—that was Riev Dhiavilyi, the Devil's Mountain, on top of which Tony's castle lay. The Dsaret mountain was more like a wrinkle in the land made up of three interlocking ridges, which I had learned were veined with mineral deposits.

And, if the ancient tapestry was right, somewhere in the middle of these three ridges lay a portal to a different dimension, or whatever the Nasdrafus was.

There was no question anymore about the existence of the Nasdrafus, at least in my mind. Those vampires had to come from somewhere. Even in the relative isolation of this part of Europe, if huge crowds of vampires had been thundering around making noises like snakes and bats, surely someone would have mentioned it on Facebook. Or, in Dobrenica, Madam Waleska's sister would have broadcast it on her gossip network, which was just as fast as the Net.

Misha's concert replayed in my mind as we swooped up ancient valleys, past stands of trees seldom seen by humans, past crags that at first glance looked like castle towers.

The prism lay cradled on my lap. Once I'd figured out how to think "Esplumoir" *at* Armandros, instead of trying to look *for* him, there he was, smoke rising and rising from the cigarette that would never burn down. He only appeared when I held the prism in a specific direction, and if I turned the prism a degree to the right or to the left, he vanished. But if I kept it steady, there he was, like an ectoplasmic homing beacon.

Twice Tony said, "Are you sure?" after I'd point and say, "That way." We were heading into wild country, far from signs of settlement. "I'm sure," I said.

After the third time, I held the prism out. Tony tried to look into it, but all he saw was his thumb on the other side. From then on, he took directions without question.

As we whooshed over the snow, I began to get a visceral understanding of the poem about Santa's flying reindeer—we seemed to fly over those pure white slopes, which were only occasionally marked by animal footprints of various kinds.

The midday sun was sitting atop one of the northern mountains when Tony said, "We might be headed for one of the old mines."

Though he'd warned me of the old political problems at dinner the previous night, I still hadn't counted on another threat besides vampires. "Is that going to get us into trouble with the consortium people?"

"I don't expect much trouble now. The mines mostly shut down over winter. It's spring when things liven up."

Nevertheless, he was watching in all directions, including the sky.

I was watching the sky myself. Everyone was. I discovered by listening to the sleigh riders that there was a Dobreni term for how the winter sun seemed to roll along the mountaintops from east to west. No need to talk about the danger of being caught outside when the sun finally sank beyond St. Xanpia's Romanesque church up above Riev. Because the vampires had to know we were searching for the portal.

Then there the more normal dangers. Twice Tony's head turned sharply. I spotted the twin tracks of snow vehicles, blurred from a light snowfall. At one point he waved his fist in a circle and pointed at a forest road with fresh tracks. One set of our wingmen peeled off and vanished as the rest of us raced down a gully near a huge waterfall so strong it hadn't frozen, though there were blue-ice dragons teeth hanging dramatically down.

An hour or so later, Tony gave me a puzzled frown and said, "Are you sure that thing is still working?"

"No," I said cordially. "But I haven't lost Armandros, for whatever that is worth. Why?"

"It's just that we're running out of mountain. A tricky bit of country with some very deep gorges, then we'll start up the hill to the Eyrie." He glanced upward. "And nightfall comes fast up here."

"All I can tell you is—whoa. Hold on."

I lost my grandfather's ghost. But when I twisted to one side, there he was again. "That way."

"That's some rough country. I wouldn't put it past the old sod to be having us on."

"That's what I see." My sense of conviction faded when I gazed downward into the shadowy ravine that lay between Mt. Dsaret and Devil's Mountain.

Tony put up three fingers, and one of the sleds approached, the reindeer kicking up clods of mud and snow.

"Raise the villages on the Castle Road," he ordered. "We're not going to make it to the Eyrie by nightfall. We'll need reinforcement."

The lanky teenager riding shotgun waved his weapon as the driver—probably his dad—yanked their team in a ninety-degree turn, then raced along the road we'd been traveling until our turnoff into the valley. Tony motioned the next sled into its place, driven by a woman a few years older than me, the Magyar cast to her features handed down from plains riding ancestors a thousand years ago. Niklos's sleigh brought up the rear.

Tony picked up the reins to our sleigh, and off we went again, single file now, into a dangerously steep and narrow valley overshadowed with thick, ancient spruce and fir.

Armandros remained a steady image in the prism. "I can't promise anything," I shouted, without lifting my gaze from the facet. "But I think we might be getting closer."

That's when a ghost wolf dashed across the snow in front of us, the flying feet making no mark in the snow.

Tony had slowed the reindeer, which involved bracing his feet and leaning back as he tugged. When their pace abated, he glanced around.

"Ah." He pointed up at a sheltered little nook with wild roses growing all around in thorny frame. "Now I know where we are."

I peered up at one of the shrines frequently found along roadways. It was mossy with age, crowned with snow. When I squinted, I barely made out the outline of a crowd of ghosts clustered around the shrine. Was that mail and armor glinting in the sun? Helms on heads? When I tried to bring them into focus, they vanished.

"The oldest couple of mines are along here," Tony said, still with that slight frown as he scrutinized the smooth white slope, the silvery glistening firs, the tangle of brambles and old stone. "Abandoned for centuries."

We moved forward again, at a slower pace, and passed a mine. The snow had obscured most of the road carved by years of heavy carts being hauled in and out. Only the too-regular contours of the road indicated that humans had once worked there. Ghosts hovered around the entrance, vaporous as smoke, watching us. Or watching something, maybe eternity.

We passed the second mine a short time later.

Armandros led us steadily farther down the valley, which began to worry me. The shadows were much longer, and bluer.

I think everybody felt the same. The sleigh teams held their weapons ready as they watched warily in all directions.

Then Armandros winked out. I slewed wildly on my bench until I caught him again. "That way!" I pointed without looking up from the prism.

"Kim, we can't go any farther."

I lowered the prism. We'd come to rest on a cliff edge. Beyond was a sheer drop into steep mountain, fir-covered on three sides. I took in Tony's odd frown, an expression I'd never seen before. "You don't believe me."

"We've come this far," he said, and checked the chamber on his weapon. Again.

It was an uncertain gesture—the first I'd ever seen him make, and that opened up a new world of possibilities. "You don't want to believe me. You don't want to believe in the existence of Vrajhus," I said slowly. "You can't beat it in a fight. You can't control it with half-lies and deception."

"Do you really think this is the time to be discussing my shortcomings?" he retorted, his cheeks edged with color. He pointed the barrel of his weapon toward the sun for emphasis.

"No." I turned my gaze back to the prism. And found our grandfather. "Up there. That cliff."

"We'll have to go on foot."

I jumped out—and promptly landed up to my knees in snow. Tony pulled a sword from the rack beside the driver's seat, carrying the rifle in one hand and the sword in the other.

I leaned against the side of the sleigh and yanked my rapier free, wondering how I was going to manage that *and* the prism if we stumbled into danger.

A narrow goat track led up the side of the cliff. I slid several times, and was only saved from falling by the thick clusters of fir growing along the path.

When we reached the top of the cliff, Tony said, "What's that?" in a sharp voice.

Alarm spiked through me as I peered around for what—bears? Vampires? But what had caught his eye neither lived nor moved.

He dropped down beyond a huge boulder and ran about twenty feet along a rain-carved gully between wooded slopes. "Look here." His voice was low, husky with emotion I couldn't define as he flashed the sword point up. "I think you'd better see this."

I was going to need at least one hand for this climb. I tucked the prism into my coat pocket and carefully worked my way down, using Tony's footprints to step in, and the rapier as a bendy sort of cane. When I stopped beside him, I stared in puzzlement at the odd tangle of twisted, corroded metal sticking up from a tangle of holly and trees.

"What is that?"

Tony pointed over our heads to a large rust-spotted apparatus with German World War II insignia partly visible.

"That is half the fuselage and tail of a Junker Ju 88—an early one," Tony said. "I will wager my life that Grandfather Armandros is in that wreck."

"I thought he was shot down. By the Russians," I said in amazement.

"I thought so, too. Maybe he was. Have to get Gilles' friends up here, but in the meantime, I think we can assume that he crashed right here." Tony looked around, then said, "The plane smashed into the side of that cliff, but look—there's the remains of an old stone path. I think the plane crashed into the entrance to a cave. If that was Esplumoir, there's is no getting in."

Conversationally, Armandros said: "*Esplumoir*," from directly behind us.

I jumped, nearly dropping the prism. Tony whirled around.

Armandros lounged against an enormous cracked rock, his military jacket rumpled and open, the cigarette smoke rising from his fingers. He was about thirty feet up the slope.

Tony stared silently at the ghost and then said, "Look." He pointed at the snow around Armandros.

Footprints. Lots of them—old and new, judging from the softened contours of snow in some, and the sharpness of others. Footprints, but no vehicles of any kind.

"Vampires," I whispered. "Who else would hang around here? Look at that crack in the stone behind him. Do you think *that* might be the vampire portal?"

We gazed at the gash in the rock, raw and sharp-edged. It reminded me of the crevasses that would open up after a sizable earthquake. Maybe it was only the its raggedness, implying a violent blast or temblor of some kind, but it seemed to exude evil.

We both looked westward. The sun was slipping dangerously low, a finger's breadth from touching the top of the mountain ridge on the far side of the valley.

Footsteps chuffed on the trail above us. Niklos called, "Anton?"

"We think we found something," Tony called. "Everyone on watch, but ready to bolt."

"*Bon*," Niklos said, squinting westward, rifle under his armpit, sword in his free hand.

"The ghost is gone," I said.

"For you, too?" Tony gestured mockingly at me in invitation. "Then I'd say we've reached the right place. Lead on."

"This is new for me, too." I got a grip on my shivering nerves. "Let's try going into that crevasse as far as we can, and then sing the Wreath Song."

We scrambled up to the cracked rock. I avoided stepping in any of those footprints, though I knew it was stupid. As soon as we reached the cracked rock, which was about twenty feet high, I paused and held up the prism.

There was definitely a cave beyond. We couldn't see anything; we stopped inside the relative safety of the light slanting down to highlight the rough rock near the opening.

I cleared my throat and determinedly began to sing in my non-musical voice, stumbling where I didn't know the words. After a few bars, Tony joined in.

The prism came to light in my hands, an eye-watering radiance of the multi-hued colors fluorescing in its depths.

And so we stood there inside the bone-numbing cold of that fissure, breathing air that smelled of mold and rot, and sang the Wreath

Song. It was a simple song, easy to pick up. I began singing it in round, a counterpoint to Tony's voice. I don't know why. But it seemed to work, because by the third round the prism coruscated in rainbow fulgence, flashes of green, blue, crimson, violet, flame-orange, sun-yellow—

And when I finished the third repetition of the song, the light vanished, like it had been snapped off.

Tony hustled to finish his verse with more speed than art. Then, "The light is gone. What did you do?"

"I didn't do anything." I shook the prism, as if it had moving parts. "It did that on its own. I will bet anything that this thing is now just a cave. I think the portal's shut."

Tony cursed softly under his breath as he scanned the rocks, the snow, the deepening sapphire sky. "Let's get out of here."

"Not that I want to argue, but wouldn't this be the place to make a new treaty with the vampires?" I asked as we bolted out of that crevasse like the vampires were already after us. "Oh. Wait. We need that Rose and Thorn thing, right?"

"Yes," he said over his shoulder. "But even more, we need a good defensive position at our back, because I don't know what's going to happen, not with so many of them around. We're going to ride like hell for the Eyrie."

"We won't make it by sunset."

"Run!" was his answer.

Back up the slope, a horrible journey. I slid and smashed into him twice, the first time knocking him flat into a holly bush, which scratched his face and the gap between his gloves and his sleeve. The second time, I nearly tumbled over a cliff, and I almost lost the rapier when I crashed into a lichen-covered plinth. He caught me, hauled me up. There was no hint of sparkle between us. For the first time it was like being with a cousin.

Was it that easy to cure an unwanted attraction? *No*, came the inevitable inner voice. *It'll be back.*

Yeah, but I knew what to do about it.

When we got halfway up the path, from below us came a thin cry, almost like tears, or mad laughter. It was so creepy that I zoomed back up the rest of the trail, jet-fueled by adrenaline, Tony cursing in Russian behind me.

"Go, go, go!" Tony yelled as we galumphed through the snow to our waiting sled.

Tony slammed the weapons into the rack and vaulted into the seat, me scrambling behind him. He didn't even wipe the trickle of blood off his face from where he'd nearly fallen off the cliff, just took up the reins. The animals were restless, the whites of their eyes visible as they looked around. They didn't need urging to take off at top speed, in spite of the steep hill.

Half an hour later we reached the shrine that marked the crossroad. Tony raised his arm in the halt signal, and the rest of the sleighs pulled up. He stood on the seat, one foot propped on the rein rail, his shotgun resting against his knee. "We're going to run for the Eyrie. Time to mount the torches," he said. "The bloodsuckers know that we shut their portal. We'll expect attack as soon as they have full dark. Load with shot, but fix bayonets and have your swords ready, in case they do something to the gunpowder. Remember, we're unlikely to kill them, so aim low—blast their legs, blast their heads if your aim is good. Slow them down."

He paused, and the sleigh defenders gave him nods or raised hands signifying agreement.

Tony went on. "They'll probably go for the animals first, to crash the sleighs. They want us alive. Our blood is no use to them if we're dead. So I want someone riding each of the lead pairs, torch in one hand, shotgun in the other."

I added, "Make sure it's someone with charms. If you can get your charm near the torch, so the light reflects in it, that might help."

They gave me silent looks, then shifted their attention back to Tony as he used his shotgun to choose the sleighs that would lead the way. "Designate your drivers. Everyone else, load up."

The people joked and laughed, the sharp laugh of impending action. I noticed that Niklos had two shotguns and two rifles—he checked each one of them, making double sure they were loaded as his team traded positions. Again, he was taking the rear. His team all faced backward, clearly expecting attack from behind. I considered that, my scalp crawling. Nobody had ever said the vampires had vehicles of any kind, or weapons, which meant they had to be fast as well as deadly.

Tony turned to me. "All right, my *beau sabreur*." He flashed a challenging grin. "Can you handle a shotgun?"

"I could probably fire one, but I don't know how to aim. Or to load."

"Then you drive, and I'll do the shooting."

I swallowed. "Better give me some pointers."

"Try it now. This is a good team." He explained a few basics as he handed the reins to me.

They were unexpectedly heavy. As the animals began to move, my muscles braced to the max.

"Loosen up, or you'll lose your grip. Keep some tension, but don't pull back unless you want them to stop. It's mostly intuitive."

The biggest trouble I had as we got going was gauging how much pressure was needed for maneuvering. The vectors were not like driving a car, or maybe it was like driving a car that had a twenty-foot hood stretching out in front, and runners instead of wheels.

Once the leader pair of sleighs took the lead, all I had to do was follow them. As the sky turned indigo and began to show stars between the silhouettes of tall trees, the torchlight lit Tony's grim profile from below. The only sounds were the continuous whish of runners over snow and the muffled beat of hooves.

After a time, just as I began to relax incrementally into the rhythm, Tony said abruptly, "What are you going to do if my sister is alive?"

I was so startled I cast him a quick look—and felt the animals shift. The sleigh fishtailed. I steadied the reins, wondering why he asked that now, with the vampire threat hanging somewhere in the darkness ahead. It was difficult to see his face, which was a profile in the uneven torchlight, marked by black lines where the holly had scratched him.

"I don't know," I said. "Why do you ask? Do you think Ruli is at the Eyrie?"

"It makes more sense than anything else. *Something* happened. Marzio ends up at the bottom of the ravine. Ruli runs away. Except if Alec did Marzio, then why did Magda tell us that she drove Marzio to the border?"

"If Ruli ran away from that accident, then she must have had wings, because how else would she get all the way from the western mountains to here—without anyone seeing her, ever? Especially if she won't drive in—"

His hand came up sharply, and I bit off the word *snow*.

For about two heartbeats he was still, then ink-black shapes swarmed out of the darkness, their silence terrifying.

"Keep the reins steady." Tony stood up again, one foot on the seat, the other propped on the rein rail as he fired into the middle of the shapes.

I jumped at the noise, and the sleigh fish-tailed again. I felt the corresponding tension in the animals, but they galloped on and the sleigh straightened out as behind us, flashes of torchlight and gunfire up and down the line caused the shapes to fade back with an eruption of shrieks.

I was just beginning to think we were going to make it when an animal screamed. Riders shouted and cursed, and the vampires rushed forward again, this time with that terrifying hissing and bat-squeal.

Ten, twelve times Tony rapidly reloaded and fired, as did the rest of the sleigh crews. A horrible shriek was followed by a crash—one of the sleighs.

"Niklos!" Tony roared.

"On it!"

I dared one quick glance back, my heart crowding my throat. I was in time to see Niklos's team reach out to clasp the arms of two people and haul them bodily into the last sleigh as the others fired into the blackness that was crowding up around that sleigh. The woman on the lead animal laid about with her torch, fire streaming off in whirling sparks.

One of the rescued people had cut the traces to the fallen sleigh. Three of the animals righted themselves, one of them bleeding from long rake marks down a flank. The blood gleamed, ruby red, as the animal raced after the others into the darkness.

Three of the people from the overturned sleigh were missing. One of the animals had been slain.

We raced on . . . straight into what felt like a fog bank. Only the air was clear. Tony started cussing violently, and flung the rifle into the rack behind us.

All down the line came a sinister silence.

"Weapons won't fire," he said tightly, and swung the sword in a figure eight, loosening his arm. "They've got full dark now. They're going to rush us, and it's going to be hand to hand."

What he didn't say was, *there are too many of them to fight off. And no convenient secret tunnels at hand for a fast escape.*

What could I do? I remembered the prism light from the portal.

I had no idea if it would work, but I was going to try. I wrapped the reins around one forearm and thrust my free hand into my pocket. I pulled up the prism and reached mentally with frantic energy for that amazing light.

And there it was, incandescing, nearly strobing with full-spectrum effulgence.

It hit the vampires like a shock wave. They gave those horrible thin screams and hisses, then faded back to a prudent distance.

"I don't know how you did that." Tony grabbed the reins. "But it was a *very* good idea."

Now I could hold the prism above my head with both hands, my eyes dazzled to blindness. But I didn't need to see. I could hear the things running alongside us, keeping well out of the nimbus; I whiffed that moldy deep-freeze stink that made my shoulder blades crawl.

My arms began to ache as we raced up Devil's Mountain in tight formation. Somewhere, someone began to sing a strange, skipping minor key melody in Russian as we wound our way up toward the Eyrie through the darkness.

I squinted, my eyes tearing. I blinked away the moisture, my cheeks cold, and held the light higher above my head. I began to catch glimpses of things as we passed a shrine, a signpost—Tony scanning ceaselessly—we whizzed over the top of a small rise, and silhouettes converged, torches held high. I gasped, but they were ordinary people, the ones Tony had ordered as reinforcements.

They streamed on either side of us, footsteps churning up snow, and bore down on the cloud of vampires in our wake, roaring in fury.

That is, they rushed the vamps—but though they waved swords, axes, and sharpened farm implements that reflected blood-red in the torchlight, within moments there was nothing to attack. The vamps had scattered.

We rode on, leaving the villagers guarding the road behind us. We glided and bumped through several more hamlets, each enormous with bonfires in the central square, the ruddily lit shapes of burly inhabitants on guard, scythes and hoes and ancient flintlocks or swords or spears at hand. The glitter of crystals in every single window we passed made it clear that the Devil's Mountain people had no trouble with magic, even if their duke did. Or, maybe, once did.

The castle appeared at last, glimpsed between crags, every window lit. Now I understood why they kept the bazillion lights on. We slowed after racing through the mighty gates into a churned-up yard.

I lowered my aching arms and breathed out a sigh as a tall, slim figure loped gracefully toward us, her corn-silk hair a golden halo in the firelight.

"Find the portal?" Phaedra asked.

"Closed." Tony jumped down from the sleigh. "Let's go inside. I haven't been able to feel my toes for hours."

Only then did I realize my feet were numb as well. I climbed out of the sleigh as castle people swarmed about, taking care of the animals. Crunch, crunch—memory added its own whiplash. There was the jeep, and Reithermann died right there . . . Kilber was probably hiding behind that corbel on the rock wall, hidden by the hanging leaves on that now-bare tree, when he threw the knife that buried in Tony's shoulder.

Waves of exhaustion wrung me down, making my head feel like it was floating somewhere above my body. I followed the other two through the same stone archway where Tony had once carried me, a pistol pressed to my temple. We took an abrupt turn into a part of the castle I hadn't seen.

"Phaedra," Tony said. "Battle report?"

"What battle?" Phaedra flung her hands up in disgust. "Wasted the entire day drawing up strategy and tactics—got hundreds of volunteers—just to walk around all night waving weapons at each other under the pretty lights in almost every window and hanging from every arch, tree, and gargoyle. Not a vampire in sight. In Riev this morning, Dmitros passed on the order for everyone to stay in except the Vigilzhi tonight. I couldn't stand another day cooped up indoors without knowing what was going on. I came up here in case they attack the castle."

"About that," Tony said. "No. First, where's Danilov?"

"Disappeared with Honoré and Gilles. Won't set foot in your house until the rest of the family agrees to your plan."

"Plan?" I asked.

Tony shrugged as if it didn't matter, and said to me, "The other day, while you were at the inn getting ready, I went home and proposed that the entire family sit down together with Honoré. No one hiding diamonds or crystals, just some questions and answers. Mother took to her bed, saying that my implied accusation was worse than a vampire attack—Robert roared and stamped—everyone else galloped to the moral high ground. So I asked Jerzy and Percy to guard the house, had Madame Tullée pack up the last of New Year's dinner, and you know the rest."

Phaedra's indifference at the mention of "Madame Tullée" made it clear that that secret was still intact—making me wonder just how many secrets the von Mecklundburgs were keeping from one another.

Phaedra's thoughts paralleled mine. "Now I'm beginning to think that someone wants us at each other's throats."

"We've always been at each other's throats," Tony said tiredly, and to someone down a hall, "Boris! Fetch the Rose and Thorn. Meet us at the garden doors."

"Did you find the Esplumoir?" Phaedra asked.

"Maybe. Those caves are closed, whatever they are. The blood-suckers attacked us on the way back. We lost three people." He named them.

Phaedra flinched at every name, her grief swiftly turning to anger. She cursed as she followed us into the lower part of Tony's castle. This had to be the service entrance with its stone walls and low ceilings cut from stone.

We ran up two flights of worn stairs, and had just reached the massive floor made of yard-wide squares of black and white marble in a checkerboard pattern, when we were met by a tall, gloomy-faced, white-haired man carrying a heavy brass tray with two implements on it. The bowl was made out of solid gold, etched with the Dobreni symbols that had become familiar, twined together with rose vines. Same with the handle of the knife.

The Rose and the Thorn.

"Diamonds off," Tony said, removing his earring. "Crystal, too."

I unfastened my necklace and laid it in a waiting bowl of some translucent material. It looked impossibly old. Tony tossed his diamond earring in without looking. Phaedra took off not only earrings but a necklace.

Niklos turned up, shotgun on his hip and a heavy cavalry sabre in his other hand. A few of the huskier guys, armed with steel as well as shotguns, paced behind us as Tony and Phaedra led the way across the polished checkerboard floor to a pair of grand carved doors that opened onto the garden that I'd last seen in summer, when I ran for my life.

Now the grounds were blanketed in snow, softly glowing from the many lit windows. The sky was covered by a thin haze of clouds. The nice weather was already eroding toward more snow.

Crunch, crunch. We walked past the bare trees. The white statues were easily visible. No, not statues. My heart gave one of those bumps when I remembered that these were vampires—turned to stone.

Yes, there was one I remembered, a mossy, weather-blurred figure in medieval tunic and hose, the shoes elongated, on a carved stand. Its hands were out to the sides—probably bound by ropes. His face lifted skyward.

We paced in the opposite direction from where I'd run during summer, toward the highest end of the castle. There was a secluded garden behind the Sky Suite, which housed the ducal family. This garden was reachable by a long curve of stone steps. One side of the wall had a huge gate, which Niklos and a couple of the guys unbarred and pushed open. Beyond it was forest.

In the center of the garden was a smooth, shallow fountain that reminded me of an ancient Greek kylix—a two-handled cup with a stem. Tony set the tray down in the middle of it, and stepped back.

Then we waited.

And waited.

Nothing came through the gate.

"Don't you have to, like, send a message or something?" I said after what felt like a thousand years. My fingers and toes had begun to go numb again.

"They've got to be around," Phaedra said.

Tony sniffed the air. "They're around."

I sniffed as well. There was a trace of that musty deep freeze smell, charged with a sense of electricity—like the air when the desert winds blow in California, right before the wildfires start. It made the hairs on the back of my neck lift.

There were no ghosts anywhere.

"Damn it," Tony said finally, lifting the tray. "Damn."

"What's the problem?" I asked.

Phaedra said, "Wouldn't it mean that Uncle Robert completed the treaty, if they aren't here?"

Tony headed toward the path, after sending a grim look out into the darkness. "Not that simple. They're out there. They could tell us if he did. I think what this silence means is that there's unfinished business."

He started up the stairs to the castle.

THIRTY-SEVEN

TONY LED THE WAY in angry silence back to a part of the castle I hadn't seen during the summer. This was deep in the lower level, the service area. Past a jumble of baskets and brooms and garage kafuffle, a glance at a huge coat room full of boots and shoes neatly lined up, and coats on hooks, and oh, warmth and light—we walked into an enormous kitchen, with restaurant-sized prep tables and ovens, and glimpses of smaller prep annexes through open doors.

A grizzled old man in a long apron bustled in. "In the boot room, in the boot room." He waved his hands. "You know better, *hertsa'vos*," the man scolded.

"His dukeship" (the closest translation) withdrew to the big closet we'd just passed through, trailing Phaedra and me. We struggled out of our sodden boots and socks. As I hung up my coat, I fished the prism out and stuck it in my pants pocket—then remembered I'd left my backpack full of dirty clothes and toothbrush in the sleigh. Oh, well.

"Leave those wet things there," the man said from the doorway. "Boris will see to them. We will bring you something hot."

He made shooing motions at us as Phaedra led the way through the big kitchen to another smaller one that smelled like cinnamon and nutmeg. Big flour barrels were lined up, and on a vast bread board, pastry dough sat rising.

Through there to a short hall where an odor of chicken paprika lingered, and through yet another door into a small, cozy room with carefully repaired but timeworn French streamline lounge chairs from the thirties. I sank into one with a sigh of relief that came up from my needle-stinging, defrosting toes.

A fire burned in the fireplace. I worked my gloves off my tingling fingers and held out my hands toward the blaze.

"Thanks, Boris," Tony said shortly as the gloomy-faced, white-haired man came in with mugs on a tray. The delicious aroma of mulled wine filled the room, replacing the smell of wet socks that seemed to have followed us in. He served me first.

I looked at the wine, my lips ready to taste it—then I said, "You two drink first."

Phaedra and Tony both gave me startled looks, then their eyes narrowed in exactly the same way.

Tony set aside the mug and went to the door. "Boris?" he called.

The white-haired old man shuffled back in. "*Hertsa'vos?*"

"Do you remember who was here for Thorn night?"

"Thorn," the man repeated. "Jakov and I were alone in preparation. We were going to ride together after, down to . . ." The man rambled on about the servants' Christmas plans, discovered Tony still waiting, then found his way back to the subject." . . . and that was when Count Robert and Baron Parsifal arrived. They were alone."

"Thank you, Boris." As the man shut the door behind him, Tony waved his hand impatiently. "Just as Robert said. We can guess why someone would try to kill Honoré. Who stands to benefit if Robert is dead?"

Cerisette, I thought.

"Cerisette," Phaedra stated. "But if she wanted to organize a family coup, she'd be more efficient about it."

Tony laughed. "At least the planning of it. Though I can't see her whacking Honoré with a poker, much less with Plato."

"If she can lift one of those busts, I'll eat it for dinner," Phaedra said. "Anyway, after her—assuming you're dead—Percy would inherit. Then Danilov. I can't think of two people less likely to do any of these things."

Tony slapped his hands on his knees. "We're not high enough," he said.

"High?" Phaedra glanced at the plaster ceiling.

"High?" I said. "We're on the highest point in the—oh."

"Strategically. I keep coming back to the entire government neatly assembled at the Council Building for that hearing. Obviously I wasn't the only one to think it a convenient way to round up the lot of them."

Ice ran through my bones and nerves. "I think your unfinished business is connected."

Phaedra scowled. "Who stands to gain if the government is all swept away? It's not like vampires would be appointed. Everybody laughed when Honoré dug up the old laws about them, a few years ago. Remember? But laws there are. A vampire is for all legal purposes considered dead."

The cook had kicked the castle staff into high gear. In spite of the fact that they have no microwaves, a hot dinner appeared. It was mainly steamed cabbage, with pickled vegetables and dried venison cooked up in a kind of instant wine sauce, with the remains of the morning's bread.

We hadn't eaten all day. I was ravenous. Tony had to be, too, but he ate about half of his then jumped up and started out, pausing at the door. "No, go off to bed, Boris. I'll put it away." He stepped into the hall. "Ah, there you are, Niklos. Listen, I want you and Teo to go through everyone in the staff. Find out the last time they saw Ruli, and where. Get Anna and Horst to look through every room."

Their voices faded away down the hall.

We'd retrieved our diamonds and crystals on the way back in, but I hadn't put the necklace on yet. It sat there on the table in front of me, tiny lights in it winking.

A few bites in, I said to Phaedra, "I'd be happy to believe she's not as evil as she acts toward me, but why is it so easy to excuse Cerisette from plotting? Seems to me she likes organizing things, and she certainly seems to be ambitious."

"Not Cerisette. Beka Ridotski may be annoying, but she was right in saying once that Cerisette wants to reign at Alec's side, not to rule."

"Is she really that into him?" It might explain the total hate she had going on me.

"Tchah!" Phaedra shrugged. "I think she would be as happy marrying a piece of plaster made in Alec's shape, if it made her queen. Happier." Phaedra grinned and saluted me with her mulled wine. "Then she would never hear the words 'tax' or 'mine,' and would be spared him talking about poetry."

As she spoke, I watched the light shards in my necklace glimmer like light on water from another world. Those lights were clearly hooked in with Vrajhus, and maybe even the Nasdrafus. Would they be clearer if I tried the prism? I set aside my fork and took the prism out of my pocket.

Phaedra leaned forward. "I was just thinking that," she said. "Can you look at the twenty-first? I'll wager anything Uncle Robert passed out and didn't make the treaty. Maybe that's why the vampires are swarming. Nothing else makes sense."

I rubbed the prism on my grubby jeans. "It doesn't work that way. I can't pick a date then look into this thing like it's a video recording. Maybe someone else can, but I'm a beginner at this. I need a person or an object to concentrate on."

"Then think about this room. Everyone uses it in winter. Though I must say, if you think about Uncle Robert, you'll see him a thousand times," Phaedra said dubiously. "Over his lifetime."

"I have to be more specific than that. Objects are better. At least, it was that way with Alec's Daimler. Maybe I should get the Rose and Thorn back," I said, reluctant to have anything to do with those implements.

Boris entered, carrying another tray of mulled wine. As he set it out, I gazed at the mug, an association almost there . . . almost there . . . there! "The thermos," I said, as soon as Boris shut the door again.

"Thermos?" Phaedra sipped wine, eyes closed. "Oh, that tastes good."

"If Robert was roofied, he said it has to have been in that coffee thermos. Maybe if I get the thermos, and look at it in the prism. Even if it tells us nothing about whether or not the treaty was made, if someone puts something in there that isn't coffee, we might have our poisoner, at least."

"If the poisoner is the same person who roofied Alec." Phaedra huffed to her feet. "I will get the thermos. I know where those things are kept."

I was going to sip my mulled wine, then changed my mind and put it down. Not because I thought it was poisoned so much as I wanted to keep my mind clear. Or as clear as it was going to get, considering the wine already in me, and the very, *very* long day. On top of a series of long days.

Phaedra was back in a moment, carrying three thermoses. "Sorry. No one could remember which one they used that night. These three are reserved for the family. The household staff keep theirs in the north pantry."

I bent over the first one, thinking *coffee, ritual,* and a lot of other stuff that was probably useless. The prism flickered between a lot of people I don't know, some drinking from the thermos, others pouring from it, and it was washed a number of times, water splashing toward me in a kind of 3D perspective.

I clenched the prism, trying to narrow the criteria, but the harder I tried, the more splintered the images were. My head began to thump in time to my heartbeat. So I did some breathing, then set aside the first one. If I learned to filter images better, I'd come back to it. I'd try the second one just for a change.

I set the thermos on my tray, put the prism before it, bent over it, and this time I let the images flow. Hands holding the thermos . . . water running in it . . . steam coming up from it as someone poured soup, a wood pile in the distance. Coffee pouring out, held by a feminine hand, then it's set on the dashboard of an old car, right-hand drive. Coffee . . . wash . . . tea. Wash. Another load of soup . . . wash . . . powder—

"What?" Phaedra asked, her high voice going shrill. "You yelped."

"I did?" I sat back, fighting dizziness. "Powder. Someone put powder in it."

"Powder?" She leaned forward, glaring at the thermos and then the prism. "Who?"

"It could be something perfectly innocent," I began.

Phaedra's lip curled.

"Right. Let me try again." I bent over the prism, blinked, concentrated on the hand, the powder, the thermos.

And there he was, facing me with the thermos between us, a tall, elegant man with curly red hair touched with silver at the temples and over the ears. He was still, as if listening, his chin raised. The perspective was strange, as if I held the thermos for him as he measured in a dose of powder from a rolled paper. He dusted the paper to make sure all the powder went into the thermos. Then his hand reached toward me, he picked up the thermos—and it went away.

"It was Uncle Jerzy."

Phaedra burst out laughing. "Uncle Jerzy? Tchah! Some villain! What could he possibly gain? All he cares about is the Paris flat. And whatever Tante Sisi wants. It must be a different day."

"I thought he was forbidden to come to Dobrenica. Until this visit."

She waved a dismissive hand. "He was here all the time, forty years ago."

"His hair is silvery in the prism. Was his hair silvery in the old days? Also, his face was old."

"Then it must be powdered milk." She scowled. "Except he despises powdered milk. He only drinks freshly roasted coffee and nothing to mar the taste."

The door opened, and Tony entered. "No sign of Ruli. I wonder if we should try again tomorrow with the treaty, as Jakov insists there's snow coming through. Maybe scout the records. See if we've ever missed a Night of the Thorn, and what they did about it. If I can find any records. Damn! This is Honoré's business to sort—what is it?"

Phaedra had been waving her hand in a circle to get him to hurry up. "Tell him, Kim." She turned to me.

"I looked in the prism. I don't know when, of course, but I saw your Uncle Jerzy putting powder in this thermos."

"It can't possibly be Jerzy," Tony said, sitting down heavily. "He hasn't left Paris in forty years. Except when he was on the hunt for a chef. In fact, on the twentieth, wasn't he in Chantilly? Or was he in Epernay?"

Phaedra shrugged sharply. "Tante Sisi bored on about it constantly. I remember he was interviewing a man in Chantilly, and a woman in Compiegne. Anyway Uncle Jerzy left the day before I reached Paris, but I was there on the night of the twenty-first, when he returned empty-handed to report that they all refused to leave France."

"But he *was* here," I said. "In Dobrenica, I mean." And when the others looked my way, I added, "That is, an inkri driver at the inn last week said that Jerzy was the same guy he picked up at the train station the week before. He asked a lot of questions about me at the Waleskas'. Is there some way to check the records of arrivals?" I asked, without much hope, considering no one had ever asked for my papers on my arrivals. "Why don't you have passports, or at least I.D. papers?"

Tony leaned back, blinking tiredly. "Honoré says that papers were issued in the bad old days, but they were useless. He's seen MVD re-cords, neatly recording visitors such as Red Baron of Flying Ace, Austria, and N. Buono Parte of St. Helene, France." He flashed a grin. "Honoré showed us an entry a year or so ago, where a man whose papers listed him as A.J. Raffles, of Albanos Village, was flagged with a note: *This is Ysvorod—arrest on sight!* The Soviet guards did not know enough West-ern history to see the jokes."

Phaedra dismissed jokes with an airy wave. "Anyway, there has to be some obvious explanation. Uncle Jerzy? He's just a—"

"Just a steward," Tony said. "Loyal Uncle Jerzy! Everybody loves Uncle Jerzy, who knows how to make Maman happy, who always keeps the Paris house running. Who, we've heard our entire lives, won't inherit anything."

"Who always . . ." Phaedra stared fixedly at the fire. ". . . answers the telephone."

The fire crackled. Tony's chin came up. "Who spoke to Magda Stos last?"

"Jerzy," Phaedra stated, and with an ironic glance Tony's way, added, "Danilov, Honoré, and I have been over it a thousand times, since *you* weren't talking to anyone. It was the night of the twenty-first. He'd just arrived at the Paris house and was telling us the story about the cook in Chantilly and her '*Where* do you want me to go? *What* country? I've never heard of it! Is it in South America?' We were all laughing."

Phaedra gazed into the fire. "When the phone rang, Jerzy got it, as always. He said 'Magda, what's wrong?' And we all crowded around. He kept saying, 'Calm down, calm down, it can't be as bad as you think.' Tante Sisi kept saying 'What is it? What is it? Give me the phone,' then Jerzy started jiggling it, and said either she'd rung off or been cut off. He said she was calling from the road, with Marzio, and the phone box was in the rain. We were in suspense for what seemed like hours, but probably was one or two at most. Then Robert called with the news of Ruli's accident, and that's when Tante Sisi began calling you." She pointed at Tony.

He said, "Uncle Jerzy spoke to her more recently than that. On Stefan-Zarbat, when she called from Paris." He struck his hand on the edge of the table, then went on in a tight voice. "When I got to Paris to interview the new cook, the house was locked up tight. I called home. Jerzy answered and said I'd just missed Magda—she'd called earlier to say she was leaving by train for Riev."

Phaedra's eyes were huge. "If that really was Marzio in that coffin, how could Dr. Kandras have made such an error?"

"We've been trying to talk to him," Tony said. "He's been on holiday. He still has not yet returned. Niklos has checked every day."

Phaedra counted on her fingers. "If something's happened to him, that's four missing people, or three and one set of bones."

While they were talking, I thought back. "I can't claim to have any insight into motivation or intent," I said. "But something's been bothering me for days. You two weren't around when I arrived at the ball, but Jerzy took me in your family sleigh, and we arrived right when Alec did. In fact, when I consider it, he seems to have gone to a lot of trouble to get me there exactly at eight—exactly when Alec was to arrive and kick off the gala. Then someone in the crowd . . ." I described it all, including what Miriam said about her grandfather and hirelings. "Now, maybe those people really were mad at Alec. After all, it did look pretty bad from the outside, I guess I see that. But why would Jerzy say to me that

I had a claque? At the time I didn't notice, but later I thought it odd. A claque would be paid, right? Wouldn't a guy who'd hired someone to stand in that crowd and shout *Murderer* to incite a mob be thinking about claques?"

Phaedra opened her hands in question. "I wasn't there."

Tony was staring at the fire.

"What I can't get," I said, "is how any of this links up with those vampires. It seems impossible that the two things are coincidence."

"The connection *is* the vampires," Tony said, and cursed as he got to his feet. "I think we'd better leave for Riev as soon as the sun is up."

He walked out, slamming the door behind him.

"What connection?" I asked.

Phaedra yawned and headed for the door as quickly as Tony had. "We may as well go to bed. I'll show you the guest wing. You can pick out any bedroom you want."

"Don't you stay in the Sky Suite?"

She shuddered. "Only Tony likes it up there, and that's in spring and summer. It's impossible to heat in winter. That floor is entirely shut up until the thaw really sets in."

I retrieved my backpack and stashed my prism in it. We trod up the grand stairway to the hall lined with suites, on the floor above the ballrooms,. Only a few had bathrooms, though. She pointed out the ones that did, and I picked a room done in shades of lavender and ivory, with beautiful Louis XV furnishings.

Since I didn't have any clean clothes, I wrapped myself in the hand-embroidered quilt, lay down . . . and next thing I knew, Phaedra was shaking my shoulder, her face barely outlined against the indigo window.

Hot *mammaglia* and bread awaited us, with fresh coffee. I forced down the coffee with a lot of milk in it, not wanting to ask for tea. At least I'd been able to brush my teeth, but otherwise I felt frowzy in yesterday's clothes. From the looks of the others, even though they were cleaner, their moods were no better.

"Last night," I addressed Tony, "you said the vampires were the connection," I said, watching them both. "I guess that has to do with Robert and the treaty. I just don't get why Uncle Jerzy would drug Robert. What could he possibly get out of it? And how could it connect with the poison?"

Phaedra's hand paused in the act of buttering toast as Tony said, "Maybe there isn't any connection. How about we wait until we can get back to the city. Jerzy needs to answer these questions."

In silence we set out into a blue-gray world.

Nobody spoke for a long time. Phaedra sat next to me chambering and unloading shells from a rifle, over and over. As we glided over the vast slopes, my brain reverted to the hamster wheel as I tried to argue the world into sanity. Ruli would be home, having run off to Italy; Magda Stos would be with her. Dr. Kandras would be safe and sound after having been snowed in. Marzio di Peretti . . . Jolt. Hamster wheel, around and around.

The sky pressed down on us, a soft cotton quilt of cold. By midmorning light snow began to fall, creating a stipple effect that flattened the forests, crags, and frozen streams into two dimensional pointillism.

The snow increased gently, inexorably. Midway through the afternoon one of the wingmen gave an unintelligible shout, and Tony looked back at us, his eyelashes dotted with snow, his expression the familiar derision, which was actually a relief after that long, grim silence. "That's the third lookout sending a messenger back to Riev. The Vigilzhi should be joining us soon. Wagers on which one of us they are coming for?"

But a short time later, the snow-tired jeep that emerged from the soft curtain of white turned out to have a single driver.

He pulled up, we pulled up, and Alec jumped out.

THIRTY-EIGHT

TONY SHOT A LOOK AT ME. "Looks like your ride is here." And to Alec, "We've some family business that's fairly pressing."

I fumbled out, hauling my backpack. Alec raised a hand in casual salute, a gesture echoed with mocking airiness by Tony, who loosened the reins and they were off. Phaedra sent an inscrutable look back. She was already talking.

Oh yeah, there was definitely something they weren't telling me.

But here I was, alone with Alec.

"You're safe," he said, and I hurled myself into his arms.

When we had to break for breath, I said, "You came alone."

Daylight revealed the exhaustion under his eyes. "I had to see you first." Then a glance toward the road, where Tony's sleigh was vanishing.

That glance revealed a lot, and I stared at him, feeling really weird. Is this how horrible arguments start? You think you've done everything right, then the person who matters most is obsessing about what matters least. No, that's not true. Sex does matter, though it matters differently for different people at different times.

This I did know. He'd been through hell, and though the time was going to come when things would be all about me and my feelings, this wasn't that time. "Tony did want to hook up, but I said no. I also found out who he's really into, I mean more than the rest of his fifty thousand flirts. And that's Beka."

Alec's eyes widened. "Beka?"

So she was as tight-lipped as Tony. "You didn't see it in that tango?"

"I only saw the first few seconds when you were dancing with him. Then I was outside, dealing with . . . doesn't matter. Kim, I don't know what to say. I don't have any right to expect anything of you, but these last couple days, I couldn't think of much else besides you and him up there on the mountain."

Did that make you drink? I wasn't going to ask that, either. We were several conversations away from that kind of question, if that kind of question was ever going to be appropriate.

The bottom line was really all about trust.

"How about if we have the Tony conversation later?" I asked. "We can, with as much or as little detail as you like (and there will be cursing) but before that I have so *much* to tell you. First, what about the vampires?"

"Withdrawn." He made an effort that I could feel and frowned in concentration. I gave in to impulse, stood on my tiptoes and kissed that little fold between his brows as he said, "Somewhere." His breath caught, and I kissed him on the nose. Then on the lips. Then we were lip-locked again. . . .

Eventually we had to stop—there were all the problems, waiting.

Alec shook his head. "Let's take this up later, in more comfortable surroundings than a field. We'd better return. Did you find anything?"

We started back through the snow to his jeep as I said, "Yes. Armandros crashed a plane close to what we think is the Nasdrafus portal. Alec, I think it's real. So what's all that about Merlin? Could there be some powerful Vrajhus mage in Dobrenica's past?"

"Beka and Honoré will go wild with the desire to plunge into research. The vampires are dealt with, then?"

"No. Only the portal. No luck with the treaty. Tony and Phaedra were acting all mysterious about it, but this I can say: they think there is some kind of unfinished business with the vamps."

"Maybe the Salfpatras and Salfmattas will have a solution." Once again he stopped and faced me. "Kim, there is another reason why I wanted to see you first. I have some very good news, though as yet very few people know: my father has returned."

"Milo? Here? But—"

"And your grandmother is with him."

"Gran! In Dobrenica! How are they . . . ?" I looked into his face. "Uh oh."

He shook his head. "Everything's fine on the surface."

"You think." Comprehension hit me. "It's not working, is it?"

Alec put his arms around me. "Milo . . . it's been a long time."

This monumental understatement meant that Milo couldn't easily wave off over half a century of grief any more than Gran could. With that came a cascade of images, including a teenage, poetry-loving Alec trying to emulate a heroic guy whose heartache had caused him to retreat behind an impenetrable shield of calm politesse. Historically, the only acceptable escape for heroic leaders from intolerable emotions was either drink, or work, or a hideous combination of the two.

I said, "I wish I'd been able to see Gran's first step back on Dobreni soil."

"It was very low key. In fact, you could say she's effectively invisible. She didn't want anyone to know. She said she preferred to enter as quietly as she had stolen away all those years ago. They arrived just a few hours ago, and Kilber took them straight to Ysvorod House. When I left she was resting in the guest room, the plan being to recruit themselves for an evening of mending fences over a picnic dinner."

"Winter picnic?" I asked.

"Since my firing squad's on holiday," Alec said dryly. "Last thing Tony did before you two left for the mountains was to send a letter to Baron Ridotski formally rescinding the demand for indictment, stating poor Marzio's bones as immediate cause."

"He didn't tell me that."

"He didn't tell anyone that, including his family. I found out when the Prime Minister sent the letter to me, saying it had arrived by messenger. Robert von Mecklundburg is furious. Everyone is out of sorts, because no one knows what's true and what isn't."

"We've been trying to figure that out," I said. "And I have news, but finish, first. While we get going," I added, as everything else began crashing the gates of my happiness.

"Not much more to say. Milo sent Emilio around with the spoken invitation to the picnic dinner to at least get them talking to one another again."

"What is a picnic dinner in the winter like?" I asked as we climbed into the vehicle.

"Winter custom. Impromptu dinner."

"What's the picnic part? You're not eating outside, I hope."

"Everyone brings enough of something to share. It also enables the Ridotskis to actually get to eat when the meal isn't arranged through Hanging Gardens or one of the kosher kitchens."

"We call that pot luck." My heart began banging my ribs again. "Who will be there?"

"Heads of families. Milo and your grandmother; Dmitros Trasyemova and his sister; your Aunt Sisi, who insisted on Jerzy accompanying her since Tony hadn't returned—"

"Jerzy?" I squeaked.

His smile faded. "Kim?"

"Now for my news. Pedal to the metal. I'll tell you as we go."

We weren't that far from the outskirts of Riev. The sun was going down, texturing the undersides of the departing clouds with ruddy gold. The city lay like a lake of golden, twinkling lights on the slope as Alec roared up Prinz Karl-Rafael Street, then jinked upwards in right-angle jumps, using seldom traveled streets and alleys.

We zoomed over the bridge, Alec grimly dodging the little traffic remaining. The city, he explained over the roar of the engine, was still under sunset curfew.

We were half an hour past the start of the picnic. I was trying not to envision a dining room full of poison victims when we pulled up at Ysvorod House on its quiet street. No signs of anything terrible. As we leaped out, Emilio's grandson appeared to take charge, grinning at me when I waved.

Alec and I started on the long walk to the back of the house.

"I hope we're not too late," I muttered, cherishing every sign of normalcy.

"If he's a game player, then he's going to choose his moment."

"So you believe Jerzy's the one?"

"I don't know. The stories about his youth were sordid, but that was forty years ago. Petty, most of it. We did have him watched the first couple of days after he showed up with Tante Sisi, but he seemed content to stay put at Mecklundburg House. Christmas Day we shifted some of our watchers to Tony, who was much harder to keep track of." Alec paused on the icy walkway.

"What's wrong?"

"Nothing. Something?" He looked upward, then grimaced. "Milo had always been suspicious about the disappearance of Honoré's and Gilles's parents. And the accidental deaths of the Danilovs' parents. But there was no proof of anything. Everything happened somewhere else, and Robert seemed the likeliest candidate, as that generation cordially hated one another—though he always turned up with an alibi. Anyway, the von Mecklundburgs never saw fit to further investigate these accidental deaths, once the disputed inheritances were subsumed into the family fortunes." Alec looked grim as he started walking again. "Milo said that the older generation grew up accustomed to relatives' meeting violent ends, thanks to the war years, which might explain their lack of pursuit."

"Okay, now you are really creeping me out. Are you saying that Uncle Jerzy could be a serial killer? Why? What could he possibly get, unless it's just jollies? If he's mad that he won't inherit anything, offing his family isn't going to fix that—won't the money just go to the younger generation? And why do that when you're like seventy years old?"

"There has to be a bigger goal. Like, if he's behind Marzio's death, why the mystery around Ruli? More to the point, why wasn't I killed as well?"

"Maybe you were supposed to freeze to death on that ledge?" I said doubtfully. "And Tony did say that someone tried to poison you."

"No, someone tried to poison my household. And they put your scarf in the garden."

"So it was supposed to look like you and I did it? That's just crazy!"

"I wonder if it was desperate," he said.

"Here's what creeps me out about that accident," I said. "If you had frozen to death on that ledge, you were meant to die with your reputation ruined. Because you had Ruli's purse, but she wasn't in that car. You really were set up."

"Either way, with me dead or convicted of murder, Milo would be devastated." Alec wiped his hair back. "Somehow this is worse than vampires. Let's get inside."

Though I'd stayed in Ysvorod House for a couple of weeks, I'd never been in the lower portions where the servants lived and worked. The house was bigger than I'd guessed from its relatively modest front—most of the mansions along that street had more impressive facades.

Alec led me past an efficient service porch, along whose walls we found the ubiquitous coat pegs and neat rows of boots. A huge washer and dryer kept the room warm—both were going—and the next room was an airy sort of pantry, much like the one up at the Eyrie, with garlic hung up, and other herbs that had to stay dry.

Through that, and we reached the main kitchen, where gray-haired, comfortably square Madam Emilio looked up, laying her hand on her broad bosom in relief as a red-haired woman took her coat off.

The red-haired woman turned our way.

"*Mom?*"

"Darling!" Mom bustled forward, arms out.

"*Here* he is," Madam Emilio said in relief.

She indicated Alec as Mom and I hugged. Instead of her patchouli, familiar from childhood, Mom smelled like something sophisticated and French.

"You look so different with your hair that color," I exclaimed, and then introduced Alec as I shrugged out of my coat.

At least I'd been able to tell him that the Von M.s' red-haired chef was Mom.

Mom was scarcely recognizable even to me—she wore bright red lipstick to match her hair, which brought a startling change to her face. Her green glasses were up on the top of her head, not on her nose, but even without their masking effect I could see instantly that no one would be looking for resemblances, in spite of that lopsided grin with a single dimple. She was wearing a very chic apron over a black dress completely unlike anything I'd ever seen her wear—almost a parody of the French maid.

Mom and Alec exchanged a fast hello-nice-to-meet-you as she fluffed her stop-sign-red frizz off her forehead. "I walked over from the von M. House of Horrors. I didn't want them to know I'm here, but in case they found out, these tartlets are my excuse. In case the dessert I sent over with the family earlier isn't enough."

Mom nodded at the huge covered basket that Madam Emilio was just carrying through an open door into another room of the kitchen.

Mom said to Alec in a low voice, "With Tony gone, I thought I'd better find either you or Milo." She pulled from her apron pocket a small ceramic jar, and pressed it into Alec's hand. "You can have that tested, but my guess is, it's bad. Freaky, how someone thinks even the most wigged-out cook wouldn't notice ingredients behaving funky."

"Is poison in the dish you sent over?"

"Nope. But it's supposed to be! Substituted my precious pear sauce for the sweetener. He's going to know what I did as soon as they take a bite and nothing happens."

"'He.' So you know who did it?" Alec asked.

Mom crossed her arms and sighed, leaning against a prep table. "I didn't *see* Jerzy do it. But I'm fairly sure. Tony insisted the danger was from outside, but I've heard enough about that family." She grinned at me. "I 've been watching them like a hawk. Then this afternoon—this was just after Emilio cruised by with the invite to the picnic—I had to hit the can, but first I scoped 'em all out, like always."

Mom tapped her fingers one by one on the prep table as she recited, "Sisi was asleep, Robert and Percy had been called to the opera house on some emergency. Luc was smoking outside, and Paul had driven Cerisette and the monster-mother to ear-bend some poor schmuck. The housemaids were upstairs, and Jerzy was in the servants' room watching a DVD, twenty feet away from the kitchen. When I came back, my sauce was still boiling, whiffing of badly burnt almonds. I had not even poached my almonds yet." She made a face. "So I tossed it all, and sub-stituted my pear sauce without saying anything to anyone. Jerzy's been the nicest to me. Total bummer."

My stomach churned.

"You didn't tell anyone?" Alec asked.

"No. I'd promised Tony I'd wait until I had evidence, but he split two days ago. You knew that, right?" She grinned at me. "Of course. Weren't you going with him? What did you find, Kimli?"

"Mom, it's too long to tell. We better crash that picnic," I said to Alec.

Alec held out a hand. "I've got to pull together some of the outer perimeter—everyone is deployed to watch for danger from without. We had no idea it was right here with us." He turned to Mom. "What do the von Mecklundburgs know about Tony's mission?"

Mom said, "Before he left, I heard him tell them that he had to find some portal. Ever since he left, Sisi's been tripping out about 'Esplumoir,' whatever that is."

"That's what I was afraid of." Alec's mouth tightened. "What time is dessert?"

"They're almost ready for it," Madam Emilio said, coming back inside.

"Can you stall them?" Alec asked.

We all looked at each other, then Mom grinned. "What could be simpler? Serve the tartlets I just brought. Say that's the prelude dessert. We'd better get them into the oven to warm—they are prebaked. They'll be ready in three minutes."

"Thanks, Marie. Kim, I'm going to get a fast look inside to see where Jerzy is in reference to everyone else. Then I'll get a team put together. We had better assume that he's armed."

Alec walked out of the kitchen, ducking around Madam Emilio who was just re-entering. She gave Alec an absent smile, then said to Mom and me, "Emilio told me he can use up time serving coffee and tea. I've got to supervise that. The oven is ready, if want to put your tartlets in to warm."

Mom kissed my cheek. "Lend me a hand, Kimli?"

"Sure. Though I better wash up—I haven't had a bath in two days."

"You're just going to be on mitt duty. Talk to me instead. Tony told me he was taking you along, so I insisted he take some of my pears for dessert. I thought you might like that."

"Oh yes." I had to laugh. "Though I nearly murdered him. I thought he'd kidnapped you."

"Not me! Everybody knows, don't mess with the cook, or you will pay." Her grin vanished. "That joke was funnier before I heard about that poor dog. Geez, it really creeps me out. Jerzy's my half-brother, and a poisoner? Can't get my head around it." She led the way into the bake room. "So what have you been doing?"

"Oh, Mom, it'll take hours. Tell me about your gig. Is it weird, them not knowing who you are?"

She chuckled as she carefully lifted covered pie tins out of an enormous basket. "Until today, it's been a blast. I thought it was going to be roughest around Sisi, because I knew she'd tried to shellac my daughter. But she's been so stoned until the last day or two, she's like a zombie. The worst is Cerisette. Even her own mother told her to mellow out yesterday—that's right, put the tray in as soon as I get the tartlets on it—and Robert shouted all over my *Cotriade Bretonne* that if she brought up your name one more time he would change his will and leave everything to you. What did you *do* to that girl?"

"Nothing. At all. Whatever happened is entirely in her head."

Mom waited until I'd slid the last tray in, then dusted her hands. "Three minutes." She cranked the timer, and set it down. "That's what I figured. So I said . . ." Mom switched abruptly from her L.A. Americanese to her elegant French, "'My dear girl, you are young and thin and rich, so why are you not enjoying life?' Her mother tried to lay a heavy, '*Voilà tout, Madame Tullée,*' on me, like the Queen Bee, and so I gave her a dose of, 'Nobody is ever rich enough, and beauty doesn't guarantee happiness, but you know what? You've got a head start on someone sixty-five who can't get up from their bug-filled sleeping bag in order to dumpster dive for breakfast.'"

"Wow, Mom! And they didn't kick you to the curb?"

"And go without my *pâte feuilletée* and *brioche* every morning? Robert said to her, 'Why *don't* you stop whining and go do something?' The Twiggy twins slammed off in different directions, leaving us some peace and—"

The door opened, and Alec poked his head in. "I got a glance past Emilio's shoulder, as I'm supposed to be lying down upstairs, sick with the flu."

"Jerzy's in there, right?" I asked.

"Next to the duchess. If he has a weapon he's got both doors effectively covered, and he's definitely on the watch. I think if I try to get Dmitros's attention he's going to know something is up. I don't want him suspicious until I can get people in place." He pinched the skin between his brows. "Milo didn't want Vigilzhi guards in sight—looks bad—so this will take a few minutes. Please stall the pears so he won't get suspicious." He ran out.

"I wish I had my sword," I fretted.

Mom grinned. "Wouldn't a sword fight in a dining room be more danger to everybody else?"

"But Gran is in there!"

"No, she's not. She's upstairs—in the guest room you used last summer. Madam Emilio told me right before you arrived that it's the nicest one. Milo was going to scope out the vibe before springing Gran on them. Right now nobody except Kilber and the Emilios know who she is, or that she's here. That's the way she wanted it."

A minute later the timer went off. Mom and I looked at each other.

Madam Emilio bustled in. "Those ready?" she asked, as I fetched out the trays, the hot air buffing my face. "Good. It's positively wintry in there, Emilio says. Not the air, the atmosphere! Br-r-r-r! I think they need something sweet."

Mom was swiftly setting the tartlets on a beautiful tray in Royal Doulton's blue-and-gold rimmed Harlow pattern. I watched her fingers, so skillful as she carefully removed curling sprigs of orange zest from a napkin and sprinkled pinches of cinnamon over the tartlets, which completed the presentation.

"There," she said, and made a face. "Do you think this is my last Madame Tullée dish? I don't know about this spy gig. It's weird, pretending to be somebody you're not. Like reality TV that never turns off. I get it, how tough this was for you last summer." She leaned over to give me a cinnamon-scented kiss. "Okay, over to Jeeves. I'm going to ready the *Pièce de résistance* myself, since I'm here."

I picked up a couple of the fine porcelain trays, and headed toward the servants' door to the dining room so I could hand them off to Emilio in his butler outfit.

These tartlets should buy us time, I was just thinking, when I heard a familiar voice coming from the other entrance to the dining room.

Tony's voice.

THIRTY-NINE

TONY AND PHAEDRA HAD GONE straight to Mecklundburg House, where they discovered that everyone had come to Ysvorod House for the winter picnic. They came armed to the teeth but hadn't counted on Kilber, who wouldn't let them in unless they surrendered rifle and sword at the door. So they entered the dining room unarmed.

The second Tony walked in, Jerzy stood up and pulled a pistol out of his pocket. He pointed it at Milo.

Everybody froze for a nanosecond, then the duchess screamed.

From my stance just outside the servants' door, I heard Tony's greeting cut off, and then the duchess's scream.

I shoved my trays at Mom, who was right behind me with the third tray. I banged open the door in time to see Commander Trasyemova lunge out of his seat—across from Jerzy, whose head turned.

He grinned.

Tony leaped in front of Milo, and I swear Jerzy's grin widened as the muzzle of the pistol shifted. He pulled the trigger.

Tony's hands went up as blood flowered in obscene crimson in his chest. He spun around and fell across the table, smashing face down into the dishes. Milo threw his arms across Tony, shouting, "Kilber!"

Beka recoiled, head back in such anguish she might have been shot as well. *She has,* my hindbrain gibbered. *She has, straight through the heart.*

That's when everybody went berserk, shouting and screaming and getting in each other's way. Kilber arrived at a run through the dining room doors as Jerzy shoved the Prime Minister violently into Beka, causing the two to crash into Shimon. Two steps, three. I braced myself in the door—*you were wrong about the sword, Mom*—Jerzy's distorted grin loomed.

I brought my hands up, but I didn't have a sword. He grabbed my necklace and used it to sling me face first into the door frame. I staggered back just in time for the commander to smash into me, and we both fell to the floor.

My head buzzed. I was barely aware of the commander's brief "Sorry, Kim," as he helped me sit up so I wouldn't block the doorway, then he dashed after Jerzy.

There was a confusion of stamping feet around me as I gradually regained my senses. I discovered I was sitting in a moat of tartlets. My head and neck throbbed. Mom lay groaning a yard away, her face covered with pastry where Jerzy had smashed one of the platters over her head.

"Mom?"

"I'm okay," she whispered. "No. I'm alive. Ow."

My necklace was broken. It lay a few feet away, the crystal glittering wildly with color. I scooped it up then got to my feet, my head doing that whirl-stop, whirl-stop of dizziness as it throbbed where I'd hit the doorjamb.

Through the open door came shouts, "Where is he?" "Must be in the garden!" and "What happened? What happened?"

I bent down to help Mom to her feet but staggered, too dizzy to steady either of us.

"Busted!" she muttered. "Got to sit down."

"I'll help," Madam Emilio said, one hand pressed to her hip. "Oh. Our sitting room is through here."

She and Mom helped each other out. I started after them on autopilot as rainbow lights twinkled up the wall and across a framed photo in sepia tones of some Victorian-era woman. I blinked down at the crystal necklace in my palm.

My prism!

I can find him, I thought, and ran painfully through the main kitchen to the service porch, where our coats lay. Cold air flowed in through the back door, which had been left wide open. My hands shook as I dug my prism out of my coat pocket and held it up to my face. If I could just see what direction Jerzy had run in, I could find Alec, Dmitros, someone, and tell them where to look.

I gazed into the crystal with Jerzy's face vividly in mind. Iridescence flared all over the ceiling, drawing, no, *forcing* my eyes upward.

Upward? Like, in the house? I peered at the back door, which was still open. Distant voices were sharp in the chilly night air, the search being organized.

It made perfect sense—open the back door, then run back inside and hide until the search had spread beyond the house.

Hide . . . right where Gran is.

If my head hadn't been swimming, if I hadn't been so full of anguish and rage about Tony, I probably would have thought about why I was seeing lights instead of Jerzy's face. And I probably wouldn't have done something as stupid as trying to chase an armed maniac all alone.

But I didn't, and I did.

I replaced the prism and stashed my broken necklace in a coffee mug on a shelf to keep it safe and to keep my hands free. I knew where to go.

Weapon . . . weapon? I grabbed up one of the kitchen knives, then whirled around and pounded up the back stairs toward the upper part of the house. The only clear thought in my head was a voice loop, *He can't get my Gran, he can't get my Gran.*

Except for the glittering chandelier hanging over the front stairwell, the upstairs wasn't lit. Rainbow sparkles splashed the stairs, and the walls, as I ran up, my head throbbing in time to my steps.

I reached the darkened hallway, and slowed, knife at the ready.

I remembered the layout: the big rooms at the front belonged to Milo and Alec. As I started down the main hallway toward the guest rooms, I caught the murmur of voices almost smothered by the louder noises echoing up from below.

The door to my old room was open—empty, except for a trace of Gran's familiar scent, Shalimar. She'd been here and recently, too.

She wasn't downstairs, and she wasn't in the room . . . that meant she'd been grabbed by Jerzy. To use as a hostage?

Oh no you don't, I muttered as I tiptoed down the hall, then paused at the corner to listen. The adjacent hallway led to the wing called the Children's Suite, unused by any actual kids since the early thirties, when Milo was a boy. It had been closed off, unheated, so it was deep-freeze cold.

From the far end came noises. Voices. I ran soundlessly, closing the gap.

". . . but your father was not a villain," Gran was saying to someone. "One might say his heart was perhaps too generous."

Jerzy laughed softly. When you didn't see his handsome, friendly face, the sound was creepy.

"Might one?" Jerzy asked, mocking her elegant diction. "Or might one say he could not keep his trousers buttoned? He was certainly unable to resist my mother, who was an evil witch, I was often told as I was growing up. Who knows? It might even be true."

I slowed, staying back about fifteen yards. I had two weapons: the knife, and surprise. I had only one chance, and I had to get between him and Gran.

"Do you believe she was evil?" Gran asked, calm and conversational, as they turned the far corner.

I tiptoed behind, wildly making and discarding plans.

"Do you really want to know, Princess Lily?" Jerzy asked. "Or are you just speaking to postpone what awaits you here?"

"I wish to know," she said, still calm, still conversational. *Everyone is king or queen of their own demesne.* "And if what you say is true, that you will live forever, and that my life is ending, well, I would like to enjoy what remains by gaining understanding."

"They all said she was the devil. I never met her. She sold me to Sisi's family when I was a baby—of which they never failed to remind me. How poetic, this justice! And how fitting, that my first meal will be the purity of Dsaret blood."

Now. I hefted my knife, poised to close the distance—

And froze when a third voice spoke, a female voice, low with laughter, said, "Are you not a little ahead of yourself, dear boy?"

Jerzy said, "I have someone much better than Alec Ysvorod. Who can wait his turn. Discovered her quite by accident. Or is this what you call synchronicity? Why are you here? Where is Elena?"

"Elena is not here," the female cooed. "She and her followers seem to be caught outside the city. But Augustus is present. You may complete your covenant with him."

"Augustus," Jerzy stated with satisfaction. "Better than Elena." Then, with a kind of ritual cadence, "I offer my blood in covenant."

I popped around the corner just in time to see Jerzy and Gran, outlined by silvery moonlight, passing inside a room.

"We will accept of your blood in covenant," repeated the female. She sounded young. "Chérie, will you do the honors?"

How many people were *in* that room?

"—*you?*" Jerzy exclaimed. "But I thought—"

"Your covenant is about to be kept. Or shall you wait another year?"

"No, no," Jerzy said in haste. "It does not matter. Merely surprise. By all means—it should be a pleasure of an agreeably twisted sort."

We will accept? It was time to run for help. But first I had to spot Gran, make sure she wasn't in imminent danger.

"Chérie?" the female said.

I pressed myself flat against the wall and sidled to the door, then carefully peered in. The moonlight streamed in through two tall windows. It was enough to reveal a confusion of figures. Which was Gran?

Jerzy's ruddy hair glinted like dying embers. He seemed to be sitting in a chair, with a female in a long pale blue gown half-leaning, half sitting on him in a parody of passion. That's when the noises started. He gave a groan and a hissing indrawn breath as the female made kissing, sucking sounds—again, a horrible parody of passion.

"Not all. Not all," whispered the female from the shadowy corner of the room. "We must keep our covenant."

Reality hit me then, knocking my wits askew as I realized, *These people are vampires.* For the first time I could actually see them. *No crystal.*

Gran's pale face was outlined by moonlight. She'd been shoved into a carved wooden chair, from which she gazed into the face of a young woman who was also silhouetted against the window.

For a heartbeat I stared in astonishment at the two profiles, one young and one old. It was as if the same woman faced herself at her coming of age and at the other end of life: They were the same size, the same build. The only difference, besides the aging in Gran's face, was the silver of Gran's hair in its coronet, unsteady after a long journey and being shoved around by Jerzy. The other's pale hair was perfectly coifed, marcelled around her face, and twisted up into an elegant chignon in back.

Gran seemed utterly dazed. *"Rose?"* she whispered. "Rose, is that you?"

"It is, Lily. *Quelle surprise*, eh?" Rose turned her head. "Neatly done, chérie," she cooed in that distinctive old-fashioned French that Gran had been taught, and that Gran in turn had taught to my mother and me. "Not a drop spilled. *Chic alors!*"

At that moment, one of the shadows in the corner *moved*. Like ink, or lightless fog, it flowed across the room between me and Jerzy, and as every hair on my body stood up, Jerzy let out a long sigh, almost a groan, as a phosphorescent glow glimmered around him and the slim woman in ice blue, like moonlight on water.

She backed away, her head bowed as Stygian dark covered Jerzy, utterly blocking the light. Terror froze me—I could not have moved as I stared into that blackness.

Then it swept away from Jerzy's chair. I caught a brief ruby gleam of red along the inside of a pale, moonlit wrist, then the shadow blended into the darkness of the corner once again. *What was that?*

In the chair Jerzy lay, eyes open and reflecting moonlight, breath laboring. His mouth was a rictus, black-smeared in the faint light. "Oh, it's good! It's good! I feel . . ." He struggled up. "Oh yes, I feel *young*." He flexed his hands. "If I'd had this strength a week ago, that *abruti* Honoré wouldn't be running around the city now. Maybe it's better he's alive. He'll taste good." He laughed. "You first, though, Aurelia Dsaret, you first."

He lunged up out of the chair, and reached for Gran. Instinct unlocked my muscles. I hefted my knife, poised on my toes to spring—

But the slim woman in blue was faster. She stepped between Jerzy and Gran. She brought up her hands. The faint light from the window gleamed along something long and sharp in each fist as, with superhuman strength, she buried one in Jerzy's chest, and when his body jolted in shock, his hands going to the stake, she drove the other one up under his chin into his head.

He fell with a crash on the floor as I stuttered to a stop in the middle of the room, knife poised.

Jerzy wheezed, "What are you doing?" The thing in his throat bobbled obscenely.

"Keeping *my* covenant," the female in blue whispered.

Jerzy twitched and jerked and writhed, his body bucking like a beached fish as *things* curled out of his body, like ivy tendrils, only they glistened slick and red-streaked in the moonlight. From his chest, the stake sprouted twig buds. A lump forced up between his ribs, tore through his vest, and curled wetly over his stomach. He began to scream voicelessly, a high, thin, barely audible squeal as another tendril burst out of one eye, waving around slickly. From other parts of his body, tendrils emerged, budding tiny leaves, and seeking light.

Jerzy gave a long, agonized gasp, and then collapsed, lifeless.

Gran's whisper broke the terrible silence as she began saying her rosary.

I stood there, frozen again, as I tried to gather my wits.

Good thing? Jerzy was dead. Bad things? I'd blown my surprise, and here we were, Gran and I, surrounded by vampires.

I turned to the one in blue, still brandishing the chopping knife, and it was my turn to freeze, for I knew that face. It was my own.

It was *Ruli*.

She had become a vampire.

FORTY

"**WELL DONE, CHÉRIE.**" A rustle of silk, and Rose stepped into the soft light. She couldn't have been over nineteen at most, the soft contours of her face chillingly familiar. Her white satin gown draped in a thirties line.

She turned back to Gran, and patted her lined cheek. "Oh, how I hated you before you left," she said. "Why did Mandros choose you over me? Even after you ran away, when he came back, all he talked about was you. The night I *married* him, he talked about you."

"Rose," Gran murmured. "I am so sorry."

Rose laughed softly. "For years I thought about this moment, and how fun it would be to exclaim about how you had aged. So old! But it is not fun, now that I see you."

"I am old," Gran said, hands clasped together. "You are not. Rose, what happened?"

Rose pointed with a satin-slipper covered toe at Jerzy, whose tendrils' growth had begun slowing, now that his life force was gone. "His mother. She knew some of the mountain *inimasang*, cornered me at a Christmas party, and offered my life in trade for certain secrets of Vrajhus."

Rose gestured toward the corner where the fulgent shadow—really, the only word for that guy—*loomed*. "Antonius Augustus said I was too beautiful to be dead, and so I woke up and found myself in this form." She ran a slim hand from her youthful neck down to her hip. "In my turn, I had no wish to see Ruli dead. Jerzy's covenant was not made with me, but with Elena, a vampire who had been cut off from her followers when Mandro's plane closed the portal. Jerzy's mistake was accepting my offer to complete it, in his hurry to make the Ysvorods his first kills."

Gran whispered, "I do not understand."

Rose swooped on her. I have to hand it to Gran—she didn't jump or shriek or recoil as I firmly believe I would have done. She stilled, and I could see her gnarled hands tighten, but Rose just brushed her lips over Gran's forehead, laughing softly in her throat, then drifted my way. "Neither of us had Mandros very long, did we, Lily? My one comfort is that the *salope* had him even less. Though it was long enough to produce *this*." She nudged Jerzy with the toe of her silken shoe.

Rose lifted her hand toward the doorway. "We must depart at once. There must be no evidence in this house. As well he insisted that the covenant be completed here, *hein*? He was so dramatic, wishing the last desecration to be completed in Milo's home. We shall see that Jerzy takes root in an appropriate garden. *Mon ange?*"

The silhouette Rose called Antonius Augustus emerged, light shifting around him in a disturbing way so that all I could see, even though he passed within a yard of me, was a starlit masculine line of shoulder, bending inward to lean hip.

"You may regard Jerzy as your first kill," Rose said to Ruli. Then she and Antonius Augustus stooped, and without apparent effort picked up Jerzy's body, from which the horrible tendrils dangled around his lifeless limbs. "My sister and her granddaughter seem uncomprehending still. Please explain, Granddaughter," Rose murmured sweetly over her smooth bare shoulder. The moonlight was full on her face as she smiled. "Then join us. Lily, darling, I promise that you and I will have a chat later. Watch for me."

They bore their burden out of the room with no more noise than the whisper of silk, and the soft sough as the tall vampire's tenebrous cloak brushed the doorway.

The air stirred, bringing a coldness and a musty scent, as of ancient tombs, and the faintest tang of blood, not quite covered by the drift of expensive perfume.

Then they were gone.

Leaving Gran and me with Ruli, who sat in the chair that Gran had vacated, her long fingers spread on her thighs. The skirt of her gorgeous dress surrounded her like a rilling stream, glacier pale.

Gran sank onto the bed, her hands pressed to her heart.

"Oh, that was . . . wonderful," Ruli breathed.

"You're, um, breathing," I pointed out brilliantly.

"Oh yes. The blood does need oxygen. That much is still the same." She got to her feet and ran her hands down her gown again. The bodice was marred by droplets of black. "Ugh. I did spill. But at least not on the floor. I'll have to change."

"Ruli, what happened to you?"

She lifted her face. It was my face, heartbreakingly, eerily, my face, but thinner. "Jerzy opened a new portal to the Nasdrafus by offering me as a sacrifice on the twenty-first, on which coincided the solstice and the eclipse. Only *inimasang* know of this portal as yet. Many will not use it, Rose says, because of the way it was made."

"On your death?" I asked, and on her nod, "Rose mentioned a covenant."

"Yes, that is what they call it: a treaty, a pact, a covenant. There were two things he wanted." Ruli's voice was whispery, slightly eerie in a way I can't articulate. Maybe it was the way she consciously took breaths before speaking. "I heard all about it when I woke up on that mountainside, tied up with curtain sashes." She held up her hand, two fingers separate from the others. "He wanted to be a king, and he wanted to live forever. The vampires would make him one of them. He could make a portal with a human sacrifice on the day of the solstice. If he let them come over the border from the Nasdrafus, he could do what he wanted with the living—call himself king or emperor—as long as he didn't interfere with the hunt. That meant interfering with the Treaty."

"He made this pact with my sister?" Gran asked.

"No. With another *inimasang* named Elena. But all are subordinate to Augustus. When I was dying, Rose begged him to turn me rather than let the others drain me to death."

"So you were never in the Daimler."

"No. The last thing I remember was Alec and me toasting our agreement. Magda had brought in the drinks. I woke up with *him* patting my cheeks, and telling me that I must be awake for my sacrifice." Ruli's voice went whispery with venom. "I can't tell you how much I hated him for that, and for what he did to Marzio. Because he bragged about that, too."

"So the vampires were supposed to make Jerzy a king by killing the government leaders?" I asked.

"Yes."

"And he, in turn, was making a new portal to the Nasdrafus with a human sacrifice?"

"No. Yes. It is difficult to explain because I am still learning. Blood sacrifice can make a portal for the *inimasang*. Others will not use such, for there are certain bindings for anyone who crosses over a portal made that way. But Elena was willing to accept those to regain her followers, who had been closed beyond when our grandfather crashed his plane, so the Russians would not find the portal. Tell me, is that new portal closed?"

"Tony and I closed it," I said, sorrow crowding my chest and throat at the memory of him recoiling from Jerzy's bullet, and falling across the table. I took a deep breath.

Ruli became a little more animated. "I was glad when Jerzy's scheme at the Council building failed. I was with you when you ran down the hillside to the council building. I kept you safe from the others."

I remembered that—the vampire shape nearby, the squeals and hisses of vampire conversation distorted by my crystal protection.

Ruli gave another angry laugh, a soft, breathy huff. "I certainly had no covenant with Jerzy, and I hoped you would ruin his plan. Why couldn't he let Marzio and me be together?" She tightened her hand into a fist. "Marzio did love me. I don't care what anybody says. He did. And now he's dead." And another laugh, this one high and eerie. "So is Jerzy."

My neck prickled as I said cautiously, "Did he kill Magda Stos and Dr. Kandras, too?"

"Rose said he poisoned Magda. A fine thing to do to his lover!

Though I always hated her. She snitched on me to my mother. But yes, she executed his orders—he told her that you were talking to Alec on the phone, hoping to come here and replace me in a scheme. They had to act first."

Wow. So that explained one rumor, anyway.

"And the doctor?" I began moving slowly between Ruli's chair and where Gran sat, just in case.

"I saw Jerzy kill Dr. Kandras. They were at our house. It was very late, the day after Christmas. I was new-made. Mother and Uncle Robert and the rest were at a dinner. Rose was showing me how to use the shadows when we go in and out."

Gran was quiet, her head slightly tilted, the moonlight highlighting the tension in her face as she listened.

I said to Ruli, "So the charms *don't* keep vampires out?"

"Not if it's your own house. Or if the door is opened to you. Like here!" She flung her hands wide. "Alec brought me here, so I had entrance, and Rose had entrance from her young days. I don't know how Augustus gained entrance. It was probably centuries ago. It is an old house, under its Georgian façade."

"What happened to the doctor?"

"Poison in coffee. I was packing up some of my clothes—"

"Where do you live? I mean, as a vampire?"

"I can't tell you," she said, and then paused, her eyes wide, the pupils huge in her pale face. "I *can't* tell you. A compulsion. How strange!" She flicked her hand dismissively, a gesture that reminded me of Tony. That hurt.

She went on, "I heard them in the parlor. Jerzy bragged about it as the poison took hold. He said that a man who takes bribes too easily turns to blackmail. He'd done it too many times himself. When Dr. Kandras's heart ceased beating, Jerzy put him on the tea cart and pushed him out to where the doctor had parked his car. Jerzy drove away. I'm sure the car, and Dr. Kandras, are at the bottom of a cliff somewhere. They were to think he slipped on ice. Just like Phaedra's parents." Ruli's voice was low, almost dreamy. "He bragged about that, killing the twins' mother, for she had been a Seer, and then he said I wouldn't live long enough to hear about them *all*. How he laughed. Then the vampires came to get me."

Gran began to whisper. But it wasn't a prayer.

"As our blood labours to beget
Spirits, as like souls as it can,
Because such fingers need to knit
That subtle knot, which makes us man . . ."

Ruli took a step toward me. "Jerzy liked seeing people suffer. He laughed about what he did to Alec, too—he said that father and son were so alike, the same setup must destroy them both. He called that elegant. But Uncle Jerzy is dead now," Ruli said with morose satisfaction, then turned to me. "And all I feel is strong. It's just like they say."

"So you kill people by drinking their blood?"

Ruli backed away, gazing out the window. "No! You take enough." When I swallowed down my revulsion, she turned quickly. "Rose said, before my first time, how is it so different from slaughtering animals to eat their flesh? Our victims shake themselves and go their way. If they are human, they wake up with a headache or think they are ill. Or drunk. But Jerzy was afraid, a little." She sucked in her breath through her teeth. "His fear made it . . . sweet."

"He shot Tony!"

Ruli's hand came up sharply. "Tony's heart is still beating." She breathed out the words on a sigh. "But the blood is filling in his lung. I can hear it. Beka and Shimon are taking him away." Ruli hugged herself tightly, twisting back and forth. "Rose said it's good to be forever young, and thin, and beautiful. I never wanted to have children anyway." Her voice sank lower and lower, almost a whisper.

She seemed to flicker, and then she was next to me, a shadow wraith in the weak light. "Kim," she breathed. Her breath smelled like blood, zinging the primal urge to flee. "Rose said I will come to love existence as *inimasang*, and that we are not monsters. But I enjoyed killing him."

"I saw you in a vision," I said. "You asked for my help. That's why I came. Was that you?"

Her eyes closed. "It was a little like a vision for me, too. It was when Elena first buried her teeth in my neck to give me the kiss of death, and I was so afraid as my life began to fade. I thought you were coming to be with Alec, and I wanted you to come, to help me get away. I was thinking of you, and then I saw you, and I thought, if I could just take your hand, you would save me . . . and then the next thing I knew, Rose was waking me up, and the world was sharp and clear though it was night. And I had to remember to breathe."

Ruli gripped both my wrists. "Promise me, Kim. Promise me." She gazed into my face, her pupils so black there was no sign of the honey brown iris that we shared. "At my funeral. I was there, hiding, and I saw you, and the priest talked about the peace that passeth all understanding. I never listened before. I want that, the peace that passeth all understanding."

She was talking so fast I almost couldn't understand her. "Ruli, what is it you want me to do?"

"Rose said this was my first kill. I don't want to love to kill people. Then I'd be a monster. I won't be a monster like Jerzy. If that desire comes over me, I want to have the strength to walk into the sun. But not to be dragged, or stabbed with yew, so a tree grows through my flesh. Kim, promise, if I do turn into a monster, and they come after me, you will help me walk into the sun, and you will put me in a garden in Paris. Where I can see the sun again, every day, forever and ever. Promise!"

Gran whispered, *"So must pure lovers' souls descend. . . ."*

"I promise, Ruli," I said. "I promise."

She released me. "I hope they save Tony." She sounded fretful, an echo of her old self. Then she sighed, passed through the door, and was gone.

I turned to Gran, my mind so tangled with enormous subjects, as usual all I could grasp was the most trivial. "That was John Donne you quoted," I said as I helped her up. "Later I want to know why, but right now I think we'd better get out of here."

Her thin hand clung to mine. "I know what to do, but you must help me. No one will listen to an old woman."

"An old woman who is a princess," I reminded her. But she didn't need reminding.

She gave me a look midway between tenderness and severity. "A princess who once threw away all responsibility when she was needed most. I hope the people of Dobrenica will have enough charity in their hearts to see me as an old woman, and not as a traitor." She made a gesture as though pushing that aside. "I know who can help, but we must be fast."

"What do you need, Gran?"

"Sleighs. For a journey."

I had a sudden memory of Nat. Here was a wounded dog situation! I didn't ask Gran why she needed the sleigh, or where she was going. It was enough to know that here, at last, there was something I could do.

As soon as I got Gran safely to the stairway, where there was light and the noise and warmth of humanity, I leaped down four steps at a time and raced into the dining room, where I found everyone swarming around. Tony and the von Mecklundburgs were gone. So was Beka.

"Search," I said to myself. "Be organized. Start in a small circle. Spiral out. Ask everyone you meet where Alec is, because he can give orders, and you can't."

So that's what I did. The first two people I talked to stared at me as if I'd just landed from Mars, so I pushed on. Madam Emilio hailed me gratefully, and started asking me something about dessert, but I ran on. A Vigilzhi ("I heard him in the garden not twenty minutes ago") and Emilio's grandson ("He's in the street, and how many people did they shoot?"). Later, I found— "Dad?"

"Rapunzel!" My father emerged from the archway in the hedgerow dividing the garden from the garage area. Every light in the downstairs floor seemed to be on, flooding the area with bleachy electrical glow. Dad's grin contracted to concern. "Honey, are you okay?"

"Cold." I jumped up and down, shivering. "I have to find Alec."

"Nothing easier. I'll take you myself. They've set up a command post right here in the garage." He paced beside me. "I've been sitting with the chauffeurs, trading war stories about driving, trying to top each other with our worst—you know they actually use Santa-style sleighs here? In all weather, even when it's snowing! I thought everything stopped when it snows. It sure would in L.A. Then the door blew open and all hell busted loose."

"Horror stories about traffic," I said, trying to laugh, because otherwise I was going to scream and cry and shout. "Who won?"

"L.A. rush hour, hands down. What happened, sweetie?"

"Dad, I can't talk right now—oh, Alec!" I cried thankfully, as we reached the garage, which was lit up, men crowded around a work table that had been forcibly cleared, from the looks of things.

Alec looked up, blue eyes distracted, then instantly alert. "Kim?" He slid off his jacket and dropped it around my shoulders.

His warmth, his scent, made me go weak at the knees. I clutched his jacket gratefully as I said, "Gran needs transport. Right now. Is there any way to get her some help?"

Alec turned his head, and lifted his voice to the volume I heard the day of the ball, when Jerzy tried to stir up a riot. Because I was sure by now that he'd been behind that, too. "Princess Aurelia Dsaret requests transport," Alec said. "Any volunteers?"

"Princess Aurelia?" "Dsaret?" "She's back?"

The shocked words seemed to come from every direction, then a roar of voices as everyone, from the teenagers to grizzled Vigilzhi vets, crowded forward asking questions. I crunched my toes tight in my shoes, afraid for Gran.

But most of those who thrust forward seemed surprised, even eager.

Alec waved toward the house. "All of you go—give her an honor guard." He waited for the stampede to die down and said, "There's something more."

"Oh yes." I looked around. Kilber, loaded shotgun in hand, stood on guard over Milo, who was in head-bent discussion with Baron Ridotski and a couple of the other oldsters. "I think I better go with Gran, but they'll have to get the sleighs ready, right? Can we talk alone?" I whispered.

Alec laid down the child's chalk board on which he had been scribbling. "We can go up here."

Dad gave us the Mick Jagger point-and-shoot. "How about I scout out some comestibles? Drinkables? From the look of you, it's been a while, eh, Rapunzel?"

"Ate at dawn. Seems like three weeks ago."

Dad grinned, clearly glad to have something he could do. Alec led the way upstairs to a tiny parlor with a card table-sized dining set. Every surface was covered with mugs of half-drunk coffee and little plates. From the (few) crumbs, I figured that Mom's tartlets hadn't gone to waste after all.

It was warm there, so I handed him back his jacket and sank down onto a three-legged stool. "Alec, Jerzy is dead. And I spoke to Ruli." I told him what had happened.

Alec listened, as always, without interruption. And as always, once I got it out—once I'd shared it with him, and we were matching rhythms again—a lot of my stress eased. "That second blackout of mine," he said. "That has to have been Magda Stos, practicing."

"I think so, too. Jerzy had been planning this for a while. Maybe since summer."

Alec shook his head. "Magda. Was her motive loyalty? Or to please Jerzy? She had her reasons. What if I begin having reasons that seem convenient?"

There he was, thinking out the ethical and moral consequences of power again. "You won't," I said, "as long as you keep questioning. Right? Anyway, about Jerzy. I guess you can call off the search, huh?"

Alec looked out the window, then down at his hands, then at me. "I'll fill Milo in while you go on your errand. My guess is, he'll say to let them search, since the danger is effectively over. The von Mecklundburgs have enough to worry about right now."

FORTY-ONE

THE LEAD ARTICLE in the newspaper the following week described how Princess Aurelia Dsaret and her granddaughter swooped in like Angels of Mercy in a train of sleighs whose torches and lanterns looked like a river of fire coming down the mountain at dawn.

Other than us being angels, it's all pretty much true.

I ran inside to retrieve my coat, prism, and necklace. Dad and Madam Emilio met me, she bearing thermoses, and Dad handed off a sandwich packed with cheese and smoked meat, which I began wolfing down. We found Gran being tucked up in one of those open racing sleighs. Madam Emilio passed baskets of goodies to us and to the drivers as Dmitros Trasyemova himself fitted a wooly cap gently onto Gran's head.

I jumped in next to her, to find about ten blankets that had been raided from Alec's house.

"Thank you, my dear," Gran said, taking the basket. "What is in here?"

I unscrewed a thermos. Steam rose up, smelling of coffee laced with zhoumnyar.

"Oh," Gran exclaimed. "How that scent takes me back."

Little as I like coffee, I was glad of the warmth and took a good swig in celebration of trust. Then I replaced the cap to keep it hot. Gran took two or three sips before she capped hers. She had to be hurting, the way Jerzy had shoved her around.

As the crowd stepped away and the sleighs jolted into motion, I said, "So where are we headed?"

"Can you not guess?" Her profile was sad in the street light glow. "The Dominican monastery on Mt. Corbesc."

When Gran was sixteen, she ran away with Armandros only because she thought she was married. Armandros had hired an actor to pretend to be a priest. This man later joined the monastery on Mt. Corbesc and took a vow of silence.

I finished my sandwich as we turned up St. Katarina Street, the sleighs picking up speed as we headed for the St. Mihal Bridge. I polished off the last bite as Gran looked around, her eyes so wide and the pupils so dark I could see the city lights reflecting in them. Her expression was closed as she looked around the city that had once been her home.

"John Donne?" I asked Gran.

She sent a pensive look at the Vigilzhi drivers on the box, then said in French, "All my life I have been struggling to understand the divine plan. At first, after I ran away, I ceased to believe there was one. But as the years went by, the faith I'd declaimed by rote so thoughtlessly as a child gained meaning, a word or phrase at a time. It has taken all my life, and I might say that I wish I had done many things differently now."

She paused, and I said, "Go on."

"It is clear that my sister has now been a vampire far longer than she was human. She could have killed us both but did not. When I was young, there were two things you heard together." She held up her forefinger and second finger. "Vampires and evil. Evil, and vampires. I had never seen one, so vampires became synonymous with the devil. There was evil done in that room tonight, yet not as much evil as could have been done. And Jerzy? He did more evil as a living man than any of the undead."

The Vigilzhi swept up to the left toward the palace instead of turning right into the city. Gran turned as we glided by the front of the palace in the emerging starlight.

"'Blood spirits.' The phrase is in the poem." Gran studied her childhood home, then said, "Where are vampires in the divine plan? I wonder if John Donne knew about such things."

"Maybe. They definitely had a different view of the universe in those days. For many of them, magic was a part of rational science. How does the palace look to you, Gran? Has it changed?"

"Oh, so much is different. Not the palace. But here." She dipped her head toward Sobieski Square, where the gigantic hammer and sickle faintly reflected the ethereal light, and on its other side, the burned hulk of the Council Hall.

We were quiet as the sleighs approached the northeast edge of the city, and began the climb toward the main road up to Mt. Corbesc. Darkness closed in around us. In the flickering torch and lantern light, the world was draped in white. I fished my prism from my pocket and checked, but it stayed cold and dark in my hand.

Wherever those vampires lurked, it wasn't around here.

Gran took my hand. Hers was warm through her gloves. "Tell me everything that happened since you left London, Aurelia Kim."

"Didn't Mom and Dad tell you?" I hesitated, then said, "Or Milo?"

"I want to hear it the way you saw it."

So I did, as we climbed up and up. The journey had been about an hour the summer before, when Josip drove me in the ancient VW that their entire block shared. I wasn't sure how long it was going to take by sleigh, but I knew I had plenty of time.

When I got to Jerzy's first attempt on Honoré, and the burning house, she pressed her free hand to her chest, but said, "Go on, dear. Go on."

So I gave her the rest, up until Tony and I closed off the vampire portal above the Esplumoir. And thought, how did Jerzy know about making *that*, if the rest of the von Mecklundburgs didn't?

Oh wow, more questions, I thought. *Just* what I wanted.

After a protracted silence during which the only sound was the crunchy hiss of the rails, the muffled thud of hooves, and the quiet-voiced conversations of some of our escorts, I said, "Is it hard to be back in Dobrenica?"

Gran stretched out her hand and laid it over mine as she looked over her shoulder at the winking lights of Riev far below, and beyond it, the valley stretching away toward the eastern mountains, lost in darkness. "It is painful," Gran said finally. "But the pain is . . . just."

"By whose standard?" I whispered.

"Mine."

There was no answer to that.

"Armandros was so very impatient with questions of Nasdrafus and of faith. The modern world in his view was hard as steel, grim as death, the divine gone as if it never was. And with the war . . . it seemed he was right. I was so young." She sighed. "I'd heard all my life how smart I was, and I thought myself so wise."

"How are things with Milo? You don't have to answer if you don't want," I added quickly. Gran and I had been good buddies all my life, but though we'd talked about music, history, literature, and the minutiae of the day, we'd never talked about relationship stuff. Ever. I was just beginning to understand why.

She was quiet for so long I thought that that was going to be my answer, and I began searching for an easier subject, when she said, "Milo and I both want to reclaim our friendship, and we do have that. I am grateful for that gift."

Friendship. That pretty much fit what Alec had said.

She sighed. "Milo understands that Armandros was not wicked, he was . . . he was who he was. He never lied to me, Aurelia Kim, you must understand. But he didn't tell me everything, either. For example, this woman whose son caused so much grief. The last time I saw Armandros, he told me he'd been wounded, and was nursed back to health by a village stonemason's daughter. He just did not tell me anything more. But I'd begun to piece together the silences."

"Oh, Gran."

"I think he knew this baby was to come when I saw him last, and when I think back over his words, I believe that Jerzy's mother had threatened to make trouble. But at the time all I could think about was my own hurt. I confronted him about Rose, and he admitted that our marriage was a sham, and that he'd married her because she was so persistent—because of the settlement—but I think because he loved her

in his way, too. It was then that I understood why he had been so resis-
tant to my getting Marie baptized—he would have to admit the false
marriage to me. He'd never meant to be unkind, he meant for me to go
on believing I was a wife, since in his mind it hurt no one, and didn't
matter. But it did matter. With his brother dead, he was now the duke,
and with the country overrun, he had woken to responsibility—in his
own way."

"By joining the German air force."

"Yes. He could not bear the idea of Stalin finding the Nasdrafus.
Nasdrafus! He had always said such things were mere stories, and so I
called him a liar. . . . Well, the past is past. And now, to discover that he
crashed his plane at the very gate of Esplumoir . . . it seems that even
in death he did his best to protect Dobrenica, does it not? That was a
heroic act."

He'd tried to take responsibility in his own way, just like Tony had,
with his annoying secrets and his outrageous coup that was supposed to
force the truth about his sister's death. And, like his grandfather, there
was a very good chance he was going to die as a result of his trying.

I glared up at the stars, angry with the universe. Gran took her rosary out of her pocket. For a while we were quiet, and when she put it
away again, the rest of our talk was about the inn, Dobreni food, and
easy things until we rounded a last moonlit cliff, and there was the Augustinian monastery.

One of the Vigilzhi banged on the wooden door, calling loudly,
"Wake up! Open the door for Her Highness, Princess Aurelia Dsaret!"

The door opened, and a monk carrying a lantern looked out.

We were soon inside, and the guy in charge met us in the same quiet
room I'd sat in to recover when I first discovered the truth about Gran's
fake marriage.

Gran said, "I would like to speak with Brother Ildephonsas. I understand that he has made and kept his vows, but I have a boon to ask."

A few minutes later, there was the tall, grizzled old monk, who in his
many decades here had become a Salfpatra.

Gran said to him, "I was told that you possess the art of healing. A young relation of mine lies close to death, having thrown himself in the way of a bullet intended for another. Your thoughtless action harmed me once. Will you amend that wrong by coming to heal him?"

The other monks betrayed surprise, misgivings, and a couple of them turned to their leader, who just waited.

Brother Ildephonsas stared down at Gran, his eyes closed as he rocked gently back and forth on his feet. Then he worked his mouth, and in a rusty whisper, said, "I will."

We reached the hospital to discover all the von Mecklundburgs in the lobby, Alec with them. Nat and Beka were inside Tony's room. Nat was in the Dobreni version of scrubs, which is kind of like doctors' outfits of eighty years ago.

When we got to the door, Nat made shooing motions at me. "You look like a walking germ pit," she warned.

"Nat, I won't breathe on anyone. But I want to see this through."

"You and half the city," she muttered, but it was clear that she wasn't going to be able to stop the von M's from crowding in behind Gran and Brother Ildephonsas, who walked up to Tony and looked him over carefully. He crossed himself, his lips moved in silent prayer, and then he stretched out his long gnarled hands, crisscrossed with old scars from animal claws and bites, and held them just above Tony's chest where the bandages were wrapped.

That skin-prickle of magic, like static electricity except without the painful snap, ran all over my body. The others reacted, some shaking themselves, or blinking. Only the duchess stood absolutely still, tears running down her face from under swollen lids.

My chest hurt. I discovered I was unconsciously trying to breathe for Tony. The air stirred, bringing the scent of pine forest and running water, of forest and of spring. I sensed light, even if I didn't see it. No, what I sensed was warmth.

Tony gave a gasp, his eyes opening. Color flooded his face.

Brother Ildephonsas stepped back. He signed a blessing over Tony and then withdrew, a step at a time, so quietly that no except me really noticed. Their attention was on Tony and on Nat who began doing doctorish things while elbowing Tony's high and mighty relatives out of the way with decidedly un-doctorish mutterings in English like "Butt out, gang" and "Shift it."

Nat said to those of us crowded at the back, "I'm reasonably certain that the internal bleeding has stopped." She wiped her eyes fiercely on her sleeve. "If he makes it through today and tomorrow, we can say he's out of danger."

The duchess put her face in her hands and sank into a chair on the other side of the room from where Gran sat, pale and worn out.

I sank down next to Alec. "Hold your nose. I haven't had a shower in two, no, three days."

His smile was the rare, real one. He put an arm around my shoulder and pulled me up against him, then pressed a kiss on my grungy hair. Warmth flooded through me as I took a quick look around. The others were so busy yapping at each other, I used the cover of their conversations to whisper, "Do they know about Ruli?"

"Milo told them late last night."

"What's the etiquette when somebody in the family goes vamp?"

"No etiquette that I know of. It hasn't happened to anyone for a very long time. That we know of," he added as an afterthought. "What will probably happen is that we'll all finish out the half-year of mourning, as Ruli is legally deceased. If the von Mecklundburgs want to release the truth that's their prerogative, but I doubt very much that they will."

"Grandma Rose." I shook my head. "It was so weird—she looks like a high school kid. One dressed up in thirties styles. In fact . . ." I had a sudden thought. "I think I saw her before. At the gala, when I went chasing after Jerzy and his crossbow. I think she was backstage. I am very sure she was leading me to safety."

Alec's brows shot up. "That's interesting. Did Ruli say where the vampires live?"

"No. What's going to happen to Ruli's grave?"

"Gilles's agent promised to discreetly remove Marzio di Peretti's remains and escort them to his family. Milo said he'll leave it up to the von

Mecklundburgs to decide what to do about Ruli's monument. Oh. Here's a bit of news too late to do any good: The palace service vehicle was found abandoned at a private air field. A man fitting Jerzy's description paid in cash for a ticket from there to Paris on the twenty-first."

"So he could get back in time to receive Magda's phone call, and establish his alibi," I said. "So he must have been in another car, following behind the Daimler. Beka did try to get me to see if there was someone following, but I didn't know what to look for."

Nat spoke up from the door to Tony's room. "All right, here's the deal. If you people don't get your germs out of this room and let this man sleep, I can pretty much guarantee he's not going to make it until tomorrow. He's still not out of the woods."

The von M's began trooping out. Their tired faces and rumpled clothes made it clear that they, too, had been up all night.

The duchess paused when she neared Gran, then she walked on. Gran turned to watch her go but didn't speak. She looked unbearably sad.

Alec got to his feet and moved to Gran's side. "How about a meal and some rest, Princess Aurelia?"

Gran's fingers fluttered, then she shook her head.

I have a feeling that hearing *Princess Aurelia* again was part of what she'd called the "pain of justice." The responsibility she had thrown away all those years ago had closed around her once more.

FORTY-TWO

B ACK AT THE INN, I ate a huge meal, took a long bath, and then fell into bed.

The next morning, I sat down to breakfast with Tania. There were no customers. The rest of the family was busy with their usual tasks and, outside, a bunch of kids had taken advantage of a fresh fall of snow to set up forts and commence battle.

Tania leaned toward me. "Miriam has a report. She will come later, if you wish, but she has nearly found out who was doing the shouting, the day of the ball. It was not very hard, actually, with Katrin's help." She paused then said, "They began at the tavern where Katrin's father likes to go. Meet his friends. They, ah, talk politics."

"I see where this is going. They complain about politics."

Tania gave me her quick smile. "Yes. So a few days before the ball, somebody came in and offered money to anyone who would shout *Murderer*, and other things, and there would be extra money if they threw rocks inside of snow, or offal, at you and the Statthalter, for you would be there at the same moment. This was to start an uproar."

"A riot," I said, remembering how Jerzy had insisted I sit all alone at the back. The cold *grues* ran down my insides. I had to remind myself that he was dead, and his plans with him, but I knew what creeped me out the most, out of all his horrible deeds: It was the deliberate cruelty in setting Alec up to take the blame for a murder that Jerzy arranged.

I looked up, and Tania said, "Katrin's father despised such trickery. He says, You look them in the face and demand justice."

"I see that. He's an honest guy, and I can't see him sneaking around in a crowd unless . . ." I thought about the desperate people of history, and how precious and rare has been the opportunity to stand up and speak what one thinks without goons coming out with the truncheons. "Here's what I do know. Miriam and her friends saved me from getting my nice dress pegged with horse poo, so I figure I owe them."

Tania shook her head. "No one would have listened to the girls if everyone in the city did not already know you were a hero." Her gaze dropped. "So Miriam wants to know, does she find out exactly who the man was who accepted the bribe? Is she to be a spy?"

"A spy?" I grinned, the image in mind stuff from movies—except that was so wrong, here. "No, she found out what I wanted to know: that someone had hired a claque. It was clearly Jerzy. Miriam can be a researcher, which is *not* a spy, because she can say to anyone who speaks with her, 'I'm going to share this with the Statthalter.' Or with me. Even if it's criticism. Everything up front."

Tania's brow cleared, and I understood why Miriam, usually so eager, wasn't there—she'd been afraid she might be asked to be a covert snitch.

"I'll pay her to be a researcher, but we'll have to figure out how to make it work, because—"

Madam banged out of the kitchen, saying, "We shall see it all in the paper on Monday. King Milo, I never thought we'd see him again! My, exciting days!"

Grandfather Kezh chuckled. "Told you they would solve things behind closed doors. That's their way." He chuckled again, then shook his head. "Better than a war, it is. Better than a war."

As they passed through to another room, Madam's boom echoed back, "You would imagine Mam'zelle Dsaret would consider bringing her family here. What it would do for custom! But that's the way with young people, always thinking of themselves."

Tania blushed. "I beg your pardon on Mother's behalf."

"It's okay, Tania. It's probably time for me to move, anyway. Once I find out where. And for how long. I really have no idea what's going to happen, though I suspect I'm going to be calling my college in Oklahoma to quit, first. Which will be a good thing for somebody back in the States. There are far too many teachers looking for work."

Tania sat back, hands tightly clasped, dark eyes wide. "That means you will stay in Dobrenica?"

"I think so. I'm trying to get used to the luxury of thinking about next week instead of the next hour. For now, let's carry on with the experiments. I really need to talk to Beka about some of the stuff I've noticed." I paused, remembering her anguished face. And Nat's words about Tony, *he's not out of the woods yet.*

I pushed grimly past. "I don't know if it's me, or Nasdrafus rules, or whatever, that sometimes I can only see ghosts in reflection, and sometimes the past I see in person."

"Then we will not stop," Tania said, and I could see how much that pleased her. I wondered if she thought I'd whiz off again and leave her jobless.

"Right. I hope soon to introduce you to my parents. I think you'll like them. Don't be scared off by Dad's beard. He only looks like Rasputin."

Tania choked on a laugh, and I said, "Speaking of weird old guys, I haven't seen Armandros's ghost. Is he still hanging around me?"

Her brows lifted, and she shook her head. "Not since your return—" She broke off when the front door opened, and Alec entered, glancing around with quick appraisal, then his expression shuttered when he saw the two of us.

Tania got to her feet like a startled faun.

"Alec? What's wrong?"

"Tony. Fever's shot sky high. Nat changed her mind about no visitors—he keeps asking for you. Natalie thinks that whatever is troubling him is preventing him from resting, and he's . . ." Alec made a gesture that could have meant anything, but his expression was sober. "He's asking for you."

"Me?" I looked around wildly, as if there was another me ready to step out of the shadows. "Why?"

"I suspect you will know when you see him."

Intense emotions chased through me: embarrassment, wariness, worry. "I thought we were overdue for a dose of happily-ever-after," I muttered. "See you later, Tania."

I grabbed my coat and followed Alec outside. I expected another Vigilzhi car, or one of the sporty models, but what I discovered waiting was a full-on long, silver luxury roadster with a smooth art deco running board that swooped up to a curved hood over the front tires. The grill had to be fifteen feet from the dashboard. "What is that?"

"It was the king's car."

"I'm about to sit in an honest-to-Hollywood kingmobile?"

Alec's smile was preoccupied, but there. "It's a Mercedes Benz 500K Special Roadster, built in 1936. Laugh at it later," he added with grim humor. "I thought this would be the fastest way to get you across the city."

He lifted his hand, and that's when I noticed the waiting parade—six guys on motorcycles, each with a bright pennon in green and gold, trimmed with scarlet. These flags were bolted to the back wheel. In the distance I heard a klaxon: someone was already clearing the streets ahead, and I remembered Jerzy's mildly disparaging comment about Milo passing a law against this very thing.

Alec was breaking that law. On Tony's behalf.

In the roadster's driver's seat sat tough, grizzled Kilber. He wore an old-fashioned chauffeur's uniform, complete to billed hat and black gloves.

A Vigilzhi cadet opened the passenger doors. He gave me a tentative smile, and I wondered if we'd met. Black hair—green eyes the color of spring—the cadet I'd seen when I first visited the palace. I grinned at him in recognition, and he grinned back, then carefully shut the door.

We sank into plush leather seats, and the cadet jumped into the seat next to Kilber. There was a sliding glass window between the front and back seat, giving us privacy from being heard, but not from being seen, as there were windows all around us.

Feeling like I was in a fish bowl, I resisted the urge to kiss Alex, and grabbed his hand. His fingers slid around mine and gripped.

The outriders took off in front of us, pennons snapping. They circled around one another, clearing not only the street before it, but blocking side streets. People lined either side of the street to watch us zoom by.

A minute or so later we reached the fountain, and there were the dancing animal ghosts, including Shurisko, tongue lolling, eyes glowing briefly when they seemed to meet mine.

"I see Honoré's dog," I said, pointing. "He looks happier—his tail is waving. Whoa! I wonder if he was trying to warn me about Jerzy."

Alec looked—and then shrugged. "As usual, I don't see anything. I'm going to have to get used to the fact that you do."

Kilber roared around a corner. I caught a flashing glimpse of a bunch of kids around fourteen who darted out to peer inside the car, then waved violently at us, shouting *"Urra! Urra! Urra!"*

Alec turned to me. "I don't know when we're going to get more than stolen minutes like this. Have you decided what you want to do?"

"No. Yes. Where's my family?"

"Your mother went back to Mecklundburg House as Madam Tullée for a while longer. She feels sorry for them, and she forbade Milo to tell them who she is. Said she'll do it herself, when the time is right."

"Dad?"

Alec's smile was preoccupied, but there. "Your father asked, over breakfast this morning, if there was a Royal Clock Fixer position in Dobrenica's court. In case Marie and your grandmother decided to stay on. He said he doesn't want any titles, because they might expect him to wear shoes instead of socks with sandals. I'm not sure who 'they' is."

I couldn't help a laugh, but then said, "What do you want us to do?"

"Kim, you know what I want—" He cursed softly. "Here we are."

It was like we were doomed never to get time to talk like any normal couple. "Okay."

He hesitated, then said, "Do you want to visit Tony alone?"

"Why? There can't be anything he can say . . . um, I take that back. I have no idea what wild ideas are in his head, but as far as I'm concerned, there's nothing he can say that you can't also hear."

Alec's lips parted, but before he could speak, the cadet opened the door. We got out of the car and slushed through the snow to the hospital side entrance. The building was an enormous neo-Gothic pile on Ysroel ben Elizier Street, just down from the opera house.

Through an arched doorway with winged bats and cat-footed beings carved over it shot Emilio, looking relieved. "He sent me with this, *Durchlaucht.*" The old German title for "your highness."

And "he" could only be Milo, the king now come home.

Emilio held something out, and Alec opened his hand. His expression changed when he looked down at the object. His fingers closed over it before I could see what it was, and he started walking fast.

Outside the room where two Vigilzhi were on guard, Phaedra paced restlessly back and forth. When she saw me, she wiped at her eyes with a fierce gesture, as Nat appeared in the doorway.

I said to Nat, "I thought Brother Ildephonsas healed him."

"Body," Nat said, tapping her chest. "But not here." She tapped her forehead. "He won't rest, he wants some kind of assurance that apparently only you can give."

Phaedra said in a low voice, "I told him, we all told him, that Jerzy is dead. But he keeps asking if we were there, and saying he won't believe it. We thought it better not to tell him about Ruli."

Enlightenment hit me. After a lifetime of lies and half-truths, Tony couldn't trust anything third-hand. We walked quietly into the room. Tony lay in the bed, his hair tousled with sweat. I didn't know if that sweat was a good or a bad sign. His eyes seemed too bright, his face wan as he squinted up at Beka, who was in the same clothes she'd been wearing the day before, blood splashes and all.

". . . long stay for a sociopath," he was whispering.

"So it is," she replied, smiling tenderly.

"Bek." He tried to speak, then twitched restlessly.

"I know," she whispered, though we could hear every word. "I know. Tony, I'm not going to wrap my life around yours until I can trust that you will wrap yours around mine. There must be two of us trying."

"Bek," he whispered.

She leaned down and kissed him softly on the lips, then turned her head. Her expression smoothed. "Kim is here."

Tony's head turned, and he tried to lift it, his feverish face anxious. "Kim. Jerzy?"

"He's dead, Tony," I said. "I saw it. I was there."

The pain in his forehead eased, and his head dropped back to the pillow. "What. How?" One restless hand moved over the bedclothes.

No more half-truths.

"Your family secret? About Grandmother Rose? Well, that now includes Ruli. And she kept her own covenant with Uncle Jerzy, I guess you could say." I made a gesture like driving a stake into my own heart, and watched his comprehension, followed by a slight grimace.

"World knows . . . my sister is one?"

"Not the world." I shook my head. "Your family and mine know. Alec and Milo. Beka and Nat, now."

The relief was back.

Alec stepped to my side. He reached down and took Tony's hand. "Milo sent this over," he said as he slid something up over Tony's knuckle. He lifted his fingers away, revealing a very old-looking signet ring. "Suitable for harness."

The flush spread across Tony's face as his cracked lips twitched in a smile, and I remembered what Tony had said so disparagingly after his attack on me with a sword. It seemed that this ring, and what it symbolized, meant something to him after all.

"That's it." Nat elbowed her way in, but at least she was smiling. "I think he's got what he needed, so I'm kicking all of you out. Right now his job is sleep." She turned her head. "You too, Beka. Go home and catch some Z's. I don't want you in here next. Bad for my rep."

We retreated in good order. Phaedra lifted her hand in salute, saying, "Honoré and Gilles are at our place, waiting for a report."

Alec said, "Tell them I'll be over as soon as I can."

Phaedra dipped her head and strode out.

Beka faced Alec and me. "Thank you. Thank you for everything. Both of you."

"Go catch those Z's, Beka," I said. "Or we'll have Nat cracking the whip over us all. We can talk later."

Alec and I walked out more slowly. Experimentally, I said, "*Love's mysteries in souls do grow/But yet the body is his book.*"

"Donne," Alec said promptly. "'The Ecstasy.' What made you think of that?"

"Gran and I were talking about it on the way to Mt. Corbesc. Blood spirits—Ruli. Vampires and the numinous. No. Wrong word for vampires. Liminal, I guess that's the word Beka used. Four languages, and I can't come up with the right word for the liminality of time and of reality here in Dobrenica. Oh, Alec, I hope Ruli can be happy, wherever she is—whatever she's doing, but I also hope I never see her again."

As we started across the street, Beka, a few paces ahead, collapsed into an inkri to be taken the eight or so blocks up and around the river to her house.

I shook my head. "I hope those two work it out, but phew, I do not envy her."

"So what he wanted seems to have been a debriefing," Alec observed. "That would imply that the two of you found some kind of balance."

"Balance—in the tightrope sense? Dealing with him is like . . . it's like driving that team of eight reindeer when the vampires were attacking, and the animals were on the verge of panic in eight separate directions."

"I don't think Tony himself knows which direction he's going. But then, neither do I." Alec took my hand as we walked up the street toward the Sofia Circle, afternoon traffic bustling around us. "Where I left off, Kim. What I want. I know what I'm offering—an endless train of problems."

Here it was at last. Every nerve was singing. I said quickly, before another crisis could interrupt us yet again. "I love you, Marius Alexander Ysvorod. If it means I have to be hitched up to half a million people along with you, well, I think I sort of started doing that anyway."

"I think you have, too," he said. "And I love you, Aurelia Kim Murray. Deeply. Desperately, because I was honor-bound not to. But I gave you my heart up there on the mountainside last summer."

"I know." My voice was unsteady. Though I'd imagined it—over and over—I'd never let myself believe this moment would happen. "You got mine in its place."

Except the moment was wrong, too, in that we were not alone. We were standing on the crowded street, with half a dozen outriders waiting for orders, and Kilber waiting next to Emilio as they chatted.

But Alec ignored them all. There was just the faintest quirk to his eyes, a suspicious curve to the corner of his mouth as he murmured, "In six months' time, I would like to formally request, in marriage, your—"

I stopped right there on the cobblestoned sidewalk, and put my hand on his chest. "No! *No* proposals in the middle of a street. This is not a proper, romantic setting." Then I saw that the lurking humor had flared into a grin, and I said suspiciously, "What exactly were you about to request of mine in marriage?"

He whispered in my ear, "Bra-a-a-ins."

I laughed, then in broad daylight, in view of the busiest street in Dobrenica, I took my revenge with a kiss.